I0663770

THE CLOCKWORK EMPEROR

VENNESSA ROBERTSON

GREEN GRIFFIN
PRESS

BY THE AUTHOR

§§§

Arcane Adventuress Book 1: Canithrope
Arcane Adventuress Book 2: The Clockwork Emperor
Arcane Adventuress Book 3: The Rail Specter (Coming Soon)

THE CLOCKWORK EMPEROR

A Green Griffin Press release.
www.greengriffinpress.com

ISBN: 978-0-9995724-1-2

CONTENTS

*For my wonderful, supportive husband and my two amazing children.
I could not have done this without you.*

SOS

CHAPTER ONE

THE EXPLORER'S SOCIETY guild house on Church Road was a brick faced building, rising three tall, proud stories like most of the brownstone buildings on Church road. The clean front stairs and yard were guarded by a pair of matching stone lions. They had been carefully scrubbed clean of the soot and lichen that dotted the rest of the buildings in the row.

Nathaniel took my hand and assisted me up the stairs. I gathered up my skirts, a beautiful blue silk and black velvet number fashionably cut just off the shoulder in the latest London style. I was wearing one of the necklaces we found in the Lamia's lair—an antique gold collar set with alternating pearls and sapphires. It was cunningly weighted, so it always hung to look like an unbroken gold collar. My hair was made up in complicated waves that had taken my maid, Jane, nearly an hour to do and was held in place by so many pins that I felt more like a hedgehog than a newly-landed woman.

There is an invisible mark left by the magic in my blood that links me to the tarot—fourteen swords mark my left arm, and fourteen coins mark my right. I know they are there, right below the flesh, but unlike a tattoo it is hidden from the light. Like blood, they flow through me. They are a part of me. But for now, they are beneath my flesh.

Nathaniel was dressed in a simple, black suit with a bright red waistcoat so he resembled a well-dressed robin. But Queen Victoria and her beloved Albert and their keen interest in culture had not made fashion easier on women. A man could look quite well-dressed in a proper fitting suit while a

1

woman needed much more care to appear proper. The irony of the animal kingdom and ages past was not lost on me. Within the natural world it was the male's job to impress—now the role among civilized humanity had fallen to the lady.

The cobbler had made him shoes almost three months ago, but they were still new as a copper penny, as he refused to wear them unless it was necessary, so they were quite stiff. He preferred his hard-soled riding boots and leather long-coat, a relic from his old life in a crew of lightning harvesters where thick leather kept the cold away. But where he was still unfamiliar with this new style of dress, the smile plastered upon his face was friendly enough.

He greeted an acquaintance who arrived at the same time we did.

"This must be the lovely Miss Harper." The gentleman bowed at the waist rather than the more formal nod of the head. "Colin Norbert. Your servant, Madame."

I curtsied back. Strangely, he treated me like there was no difference between our worlds, new money or old. No matter, I raised my chin slightly, meeting his eyes, and smiled. I belonged here now. He met my smile warmly. Yes, we belonged.

The footman waiting at the door nodded in greeting to us and opened the door. Inside, crimsons and purples dominated the paintings and wall hangings, as did the warm yellow of parchment and vellum. I could smell something spicy and earthy in the air, like clove and cinnamon and something else that lent an air of mystery and wealth. The room recalled the mystery of old books and slow-burning candles. As my eyes adjusted I could see a huge stuffed bear standing erect, and to the other side, a huge, burly, black-haired man wearing a fine suit and scowling from his place behind a large desk.

"Marcus." Nate nodded in greeting to the bear.

"Very funny." The man growled.

Nate smiled. "I overlooked you. I dare say, I think that bear might be dusted more often than you."

Marcus guffawed and offered Nate a hand. They jerked each other into a rough, manly embrace. As far as I could tell, the purpose was to pound the spine of the other through his chest.

He introduced me when they finally separated. "Vivian Harper, my fiancée."

"Miss Harper." Marcus took my hand with surprising gentleness for his huge paws. "London owes you a debt. Only those who are blind do not know it."

"Thank you, sir," I said extricating my hand. "Though I would assume most of London is quite blind."

I was sure our exploits into the underground waterways that crossed beneath London and covered a long hidden leywell of magical energy had gone mostly unnoticed by the public. It was hardly our fault the madman attempting to harness the magic from the leywell caused a fire that burned Lord Sterling's Emporium of Uncommon Goods for the Common Man and the factory attached to it to ashes days before its grand opening. It was also hardly our fault the man responsible for the plot, Mr. Newton Geiger, escaped in the resulting chaos.

A voice carried across the small hall. "Not as blind as you'd think." Mr. Langston, dressed in fine, green velvet made his way to us, a glass of port in his hand. "As I am sure Mr. Valentine has informed you I am the head of the Explorer's Society, and he has sponsored you for membership."

I nodded. There was no preamble, just his offer to join a secretive society—well, perhaps it was not so secret. Everyone seemed to know it existed, though it was generally accepted that it was merely a group of mostly men who were affected with wanderlust and general irresponsibility.

Mr. Langston continued, "I would like to meet with you and Mr. Valentine before dinner, if that is acceptable."

"Of course," I said, swallowing the butterflies swarming my stomach.

He nodded to Marcus the Bear, a subtle indication to his door guard there was something different about tonight. This was clearly more than some mere dinner party. "Excellent, right this way."

He led us to an office on the second floor. It had several wide desks like you might expect to belong to the law office of a wealthy solicitor. A cozy fire was burning in the fireplace, but not coal, it was wood, a real wood fire, a luxury in the city. The floor was a fine tile covered by a colorful oriental carpet. Red, green, and blue chased themselves in brilliant waves across the plush carpet terminating at a spinning golden orb in the center. The rug maker must have used fine, gold thread, for the carpet glimmered as the firelight hit it. Everywhere I turned maps were hanging on the walls, all hand-drawn and illuminated with beautifully rendered compass roses and details like mountain ranges and forests.

I have a love affair with literature, the older the book the better. Our library at home was full of wonderful books and watercolors. It was one decorating choice the previous mistress of the manor, Lady Rothechild, and I shared. To our great surprise, we had been gifted the estate a few short months ago for services rendered, and she had left her mostly unused English country manor beautifully furnished and stylishly appointed with only a few holes in the general décor. The study was the best room by far. She left us hundreds of books. I had a goal of reading them over the coming winter and perhaps, if the farms attached to the property had bountiful harvests, I could purchase a few new tomes for myself as well.

I admired the room as Mr. Langston poured glasses of wine. "I am glad you appreciate my collection."

"Very much!" I said, taking the offered glass. "It looks as though a dozen scholars could work here, all on separate projects and never have to share materials."

"Yes." He smiled and took a swallow. "This is my workroom." He paused, a sly smile upon his lips as he glanced at me over his wine glass. "Miss Harper, do you know why the Explorer's Society exists?"

I took a deep breath, I supposed my general assessment about providing for socially acceptable wanderlust was incorrect. I told him my suppositions anyway.

He gave a kindly laugh. "Yes, I suppose we do provide for that, but that is merely our public face. Really, we are committed to protecting the treasures of man." He paused for effect. "Humanity is much older than the common man can appreciate. Today, we are in the end of the nineteenth century. That is nineteen hundred years of progress, of experimentation, of lore and legend. And that is all just in the time since Christ left this world. We can conservatively guess that there was at least a thousand years of humanity before God sent his son to earth to care for, protect, and save man. God must have been watching us for quite some time before he realized we were not capable of saving ourselves."

I had read histories before. Egyptians and Indians had lived for centuries before Christ, they had entire dynasties devoted to ruling families. But having read that dry fact and having it presented in this way were quite different. I swallowed hard. Nate touched my hand. His touch reminded me that, of course there was more, there were the Vikings and Scandinavian peoples that had inspired Father Henri Poullain's research, there was the druids who experimented with pagan magic.

Nate was a living, breathing example of that mystical history of man. He suffered under a frightful curse binding him and his beloved dog; a man by day, his dog by night. Only recently did he learn to control his form between man and dog and turn into something that was an amazing mixture of both, a Canithrope. He was more than man, more than dog— larger and more powerful, with claws and teeth and covered in a dense pelt, an intelligent predator both cursed and freed by ancient magic.

It should frighten the wits out of anyone. Strange that it didn't seem to have that effect on me. But then again, I am a strange girl, everyone knew that.

It was easy to pass it all off under the murky veil of history, but to reflect upon what that might mean was a bit overwhelming. I stood to take a deep breath, the room suddenly felt too warm and my corset too tight.

"My dear?" Mr. Langston said.

"I am fine, Mr. Langston," I said straightening. "I had never considered the actual ramifications of society existing for so long. It took me aback."

"Your reaction is actually quite heartening," he said, patting my hand. "Nathaniel had asked that we consider you for membership in the society because of the wonderful way you handled yourself in sealing the leywell beneath London last year. He also said you displayed courage and quite the level temperament when encountering a Lamia."

I turned to Nate, and he snuck a look at me while staring into the fire. He gave a ghost of a smile.

I walked to where Nate stood and linked my arm with his. "Yes, we had quite the adventure on the Molten Cay."

"He regaled us with quite the tale." Mr. Langston said. "We were all in agreement that your relationship with Nathaniel would make you two ideal for a quest I have in mind. But to send you with the society's approval you must be a member of the society."

"A quest?" I asked.

"Yes, but I am ahead of myself," Mr. Langston said, smiling. "First of all, I need to explain the true purpose of the Explorer's Society." He pulled out a roll of parchment and set it out on the largest desk, weighting the corners with two empty wine glasses, a candlestick, and a revolver pulled casually from his belt.

"Man has always had treasures, but the most important of those display how man exists within his world. They reflect how he sees his world and his place within it. People make art of their deities, write down their cures, protect their inventions. They even record their weapons and their battles." He motioned to the parchment, a map of the world with a huge compass rose embossed in gold across the continents. It was covered with marks and notations, the meanings of which I could not even begin to guess. "We protect the treasures of man. We preserve them for future generations to observe and to learn from."

"That makes sense," I said. "Papa tells me that during the crusades the Arabs had medicine and surgery that were far beyond anything our ancestors were doing. But rather than bring the knowledge back to better man, it was destroyed, mocked, and ignored. People died needlessly of diseases and illnesses that the Arabs learned to cure long ago."

Mr. Langston nodded sagely. "Yes, arrogance is often man's greatest enemy."

Nate sat on the edge of the desk, tracing the trade routes from the east to the west. "But rather than trade for secrets, some explorers were murdering others for their knowledge, then keeping it for themselves. Or worse, they were hoarding artifacts to keep in their own homes or selling them to whomever could pay the most."

"That's awful," I said, aghast. I was thinking of the other apothecaries, men, unlike my papa, who sold false hope and false cures to the desperate. Our family is, sadly, a rarity. There was nothing to be gained from selling powdered horse dung, dead woodlice, or mouse ears to people desperate for cures to their woes.

"It is," Mr. Langston agreed. "And, even worse, some treasure hunters have false duplicates made so they can profit from the same items several times."

"So, you strive to keep artifacts safe?" I clarified.

Mr. Langston refilled everyone's wineglass. "Yes."

"Forgive me," I said. "If you have been searching out treasures, you are either new at it or you are not successful. Though I spy some fine items in your home, I cannot imagine your home is large enough to keep valuables adequately displayed and protected."

Nate was at my shoulder with his glass of wine. "Marcus," he whispered unnecessarily.

"Yes, you are a sharp one." Mr. Langston laughed. "Mr. Marcus is security for my private home. He protects my home and possessions. But as I said, the artifacts of man do not belong to any one man. They are the heirlooms of peoples long past. There are many secret vaults all over the world where items of importance to human history are stored and studied. I myself only know of a couple. Their locations are a heavily guarded secret." He leaned in and gave me a conspiratorial wink. "You'll forgive that I am not forthcoming with that information."

"Of course." I was really starting to like Mr. Langston.

Mr. Langston was suddenly quite serious. "We need more members, especially now. The nineteenth century is ending, but technology is suddenly exploding. This is the time of industry, of revolution, of advancement." He stood and put away the revolver. "And with it, the old world and many of its treasures are at risk of being destroyed, or worse, falling into the wrong hands."

"I can see how that would be catastrophic for humanity." I agreed.

Mr. Langston continued, "Now, we hire explorers. We have had to expel several members in the past for treasure hunting without license."

"Treasure poaching." I laughed. Nate chuckled and put his arm around me.

Mr. Langston busied himself in a drawer, searching for something. "Yes, poaching." By his tone he didn't find this as amusing as we did. "If you are interested in joining us we require a contract."

"A contract?" It seemed a silly thing to protect such valuable property. I told him so.

"Yes, my dear, a contract. If you are caught poaching artifacts of significant value or artifacts you are quested with returning, then your properties are taken as forfeit by the collected Explorer's Society."

He was correct, this wasn't funny. I looked over the paper he thrust before me. "Certainly that is not much incentive for poorer members of society," I jested to cover my nerves.

He explained. "We require dues to be paid quarterly by all members, in coin or in trade. Generally high priority quests are only undertaken by members whom we have vetted."

"And have reasonable fortunes to risk to prevent thievery," I finished.

"Nathaniel warned me you had a knack for saying exactly what is on your mind," Mr. Langston chuckled. "Miss Harper, there is a very public face of the Explorer's Society, and then there is the other side."

I realized exactly what he meant. "You hide your actions in plain sight." There was also something he wasn't saying, it hung in the air between us. The common man risked little and gained little other than to provide a distraction for the public to focus on, a brotherhood of wanderlust. But society, high society, protected itself. If a member stole, then they could lose more than mere wealth, they risked the full wrath of upper society, including loss of assets and perhaps even transportation from London to the Americas or even Australia. It was a clever arrangement, and if more than London society was involved it was probably governed by its own system of checks and balances.

Mr. Langston watched me as I worked it out. It would all be stated in the contract if not explicitly worded. He nodded. "Members are encouraged to collect minor items for their own personal homes."

I nodded, that, at least, made sense. "Because it maintains the illusion of a wanderlust 'secret' society."

He handed me a pen. "You would be amazed to learn what man has learned. And what man has forgotten."

I made no move to sign.

"I will give you a few moments," Mr. Langston said.

He left us alone in the room. Nathaniel squatted down before me as I read the contract. I smiled at him before returning my attention to the document in my hands. I had just recently gained the wealth needed to provide for my parents as they aged, and I had done it quite by circumstance. Being on Molten Cay at the same time as the Rothechild family when they were being attacked by the Lamia's undead army put me in a wonderful position to help them mount a defense. It wasn't anything cunning or skilled done by my own hand, just an earnest desire to not die. At night I still woke shaking and sweating as I fight the dead men again and again in my own mind, but I hadn't done it out of desire for a reward. I'd felt honor-bound to help them. Lady Rothechild's gift of Albion Manor allowed me to remain myself rather than property of a man. I was able to follow my heart now. I was free to marry Nate, not for wealth, but for love. It was the only thing I had ever wanted, I just didn't realize I wanted it so much until I met him.

"Darling?" Nathaniel cut though my thoughts. "I know you're worried. They are an honorable society. They won't take your property."

"Our property," I corrected absently.

"Your property; it is still yours," he insisted. I was too preoccupied to fight with him about this again.

"It will be your property before long, what do you think?"

"I would accept membership," he said seriously. "I have never heard of them ousting anyone who didn't deserve it. It would put us on another grand adventure."

"I have developed a taste for adventure."

There was a knock against the door jam. Mr. Langston stood there, ready to summon us to dinner. "We will discuss the particulars after dinner, but I assure you both, this is an adventure unlike any other, and one unfit for any of our other members."

SŞS

The Langstons were canny dinner hosts and intelligent conversationalists. Politics and social events were the topics of the evening, safe and natural conversation for a large dinner party. I counted at least thirty guests, all finely dressed and all members of our new social circle. They were individuals we would have to get to know, sooner or later.

My attempts to enter this world last year when I thought I was going to wed Byron Goodwin was an asset here, but poor Nate just did his best to be quiet and agreeable. He probably would have been more comfortable if he were still suffering under the transfiguring curse that made him wear the form of his dog whenever the sun went down. Nate was a very agreeable dog. It was easier than being an esquire.

"Have you ever been to China?" Mr. Langston's wife, Marianne, asked me over coffee, once we were alone. Her violet gown was the modern style, with a narrower train and lace trim. Her curls were coming unpinned, but she was still a handsome woman who remained on the cutting ·edge of fashion—for being nearly my mother's age.

"I have not." I set down my spoon on the side of the saucer.

Mr. Langston and Nate were off in another room enjoying cigars and brandy. Most of the other members and dinner guests had already departed for the evening. The servants outnumbered us now, and they moved just beyond the lit rooms in the shadowed corridors like silent ghosts, setting the Langston house back in order for the coming day. All except for Marcus. *The Bear*, as Nate aptly dubbed him, was a silent sentinel across from the great mounted bear in the entryway. I pitied anyone who came uninvited to the Langston home.

"It is a wonderful place." Marianne stirred her own coffee. "Augustus and I traveled there to study their birds. We brought back an entire selection of tableware." She leaned in and gave a conspiratorial wink. "Of course we may or may not have been there looking into the fabled peaches of immorality."

The milk from the delicate creamer continued its faint swirl in my coffee like a watercolor painting. "Why do you ask?" It never hurt to get right to the point. Either she'd admire my directness or she'd be put off by it, but, either way, we wouldn't dance around the topic anymore.

"Why? Because China is where we desperately need an agent willing and able to serve the greater good of mankind," she said, giving me a small smile.

"I mean, why us?" If there was actually some urgent matter in China, surely they would send an agent they had other business dealings with; someone they trusted implicitly. China was so far away it would be nearly impossible to monitor an agent for the Explorer's Society there.

"That is a matter for the four of us to discuss," Marianne said deftly. "Vivian, I may call you Vivian, yes?" I nodded so she continued. "Vivian, many of our agents are nobles or wealthy gentry, but most of them come from a name that is known and respected in the four corners of the world. At least in our specific circles."

"You need an unknown?" I asked. I was expecting this trip to China to be a ruse, a wild-goose chase where we would be sent after some object that either didn't exist or was common and easy to obtain. A mission to measure our worth and something we would all laugh over with crumb cakes and tea in the years to come.

"We need an unknown." A voice behind me affirmed. It was Mr. Langston.

Mr. Langston and Nate returned to the sitting room with brandy still in hand. Mr. Langston carried the sweet smell of Straigh Tobacco, but it only lingered upon him like a caress, he must have protected his clothes with a proper smoking jacket. Yet another upper-class luxury I would have to acquaint Nate with.

My fiancé followed him, looking as though he had over indulged in smoke or brandy or both, but not in an ill way, he looked simply delighted, almost giddy. He mouthed *China*.

I tried not to stare but I found my mouth forming a grin. Here was the man I loved, the boyish zest that had been almost lost—trampled by the responsibilities of being an esquire suddenly thrust upon his shoulders. It was hard to remember he wasn't born to the life he was dealing with so well.

"We need an unknown because we have several known agents going to other locations. And we are rushing to send members to recover treasures before they are lost to us. With the expansion of the of the steam engine, the invention of the airship and the automobile, the world is becoming ever smaller, and if the treasures of man are not set aside they may never be recovered."

I set my cup and saucer down. "Then why China? Why us? I'm afraid I still don't understand."

Augustus and Nate sat in chairs opposite Marianne and myself so we made a cozy foursome. "I will do my best to explain." He paused to pour himself and Nate another brandy.

"First: why China? China has been a trade partner with England for quite some time, but trade is only profitable while the country is stable. Their queen, their Empress Dowager, recently lost her only son and heir, Prince Qixiang. He died of small pox or some such thing. She is in the process of naming a new heir, but no one believes her next in line will rule alone. Her son attempted a massive reform to pull China away from the old ways. He wished to make his country strong and modern, and he would have made a fine ally, but he was faced with fierce opposition."

"What opposition?" I understood the basic history, China lost the Opium Wars and was subjected to a treaty which was, at least on paper, blatantly unfair, including being stripped of the ability to have fair trade with other countries. They had no less than four trade ports they had no control over that caused Chinese goods, including tea and opium, to flood into the civilized world.

But opium was a double-edged sword, a horribly addictive drug that brought relief to those in need as well as misery to those looking to relieve the pain of pedestrian life. There were other amazing trade goods brought to the world though merchants; China still made the very best silks and the Chinese people jealously guarded their secrets to growing the most wonderful teas.

Augustus continued, "There are rumors, Vivian, rumors I already discussed with Nate here; China, under the rule of the Empress Dowager will cling to the old ways like ticks on a dog. But the old ways are dying. If the Chinese do not evolve they will be crushed under the wheels of modern industry."

"Medicine itself was set back hundreds of years, if not thousands of years, by language and cultural barriers in the middle ages," I said. "I suppose it is the responsibility of learned people to protect the knowledge and the artifacts of cultures for the good of everyone everywhere."

"I'm glad you share our noble aims." Mrs. Langston patted my hand.

"These treasures belong to all mankind. We are only holding them until mankind is ready for them again," Mr. Langston explained.

"Actually, Vivian brings up a good point, why China? Why now?" Nate asked, "If China is imploding and being carved up, why doesn't England just go in and take the artifacts as we want before another country beats us to them?"

"China has become unstable," Mr. Langston said again. "It is cracking under the strain, fracturing from the inside out. We need someone who can travel within China while keeping a low profile. They may yet recover. The Empress Dowager is a cunning and shrewd ruler. We need to appear to be her ally unless we are certain she will not rally."

"A low profile." I wasn't sure I heard him correctly. "Mr. Langston, with all due respect, I would argue that we are not suited to low profile."

"Ah, yes, Nate, your"—he struggled for the right word—"malady. I trust you have yourself under control?"

"Completely," Nate assured him.

While Nate could control his form now, last year this had not been the case. He had been exploring underground rivers that traversed London when he and his dog managed to disrupt some old magic. His dog, Ranger, sacrificed himself to protect his master, but in doing so they were bound together. For a time, Nate had been unable to control the transfiguration, turning into his canine every night and turning back with the light of the sun. We had journeyed together to cure it only to learn that magic cannot be purged, merely altered. We found another leywell of old magic that allowed him more control over his form, man, canine, or some fearsome blend of the two—a monster of jaws and claws that was neither man nor beast yet both at the same time.

He had been exploring the rivers under the orders of this very man, in fact, when he was stricken. I hoped that fact had escaped neither of them.

"A low profile politically," Augustus clarified. "Right now the Empress Dowager requires all foreign lords and ladies to be properly introduced at court. To travel in her lands without showing the proper respect is an insult. It is not wise to insult the Empress Dowager. Cixi is a force to be reckoned with, and she and her court cling to the old ways."

"But someone who is new money, an esquire, is not of noble bearing and would escape her notice," I surmised.

Marianne smiled. "Exactly our thinking."

One of their servants came from the shadows and brought us a fresh pot of coffee and pitcher of cream. Though silent, well-mannered, and impeccably trained, her presence ground things to a halt. Augustus seemed to struggle with how to renew our discussion while I digested the scene we would be walking into.

"What exactly are we looking for?" Nate asked finally, for it seemed no one else was going to restart the conversation.

"Yes." Augustus clapped Nate's shoulder. I wondered how much brandy they shared before rejoining us, I was beginning to suspect it was even more than I first believed.

"Actually, it is the strangest thing," Mr. Langston began slyly. "We were approached by a man who said he could acquire for the Explorer's Society the most amazing artifact. Something worthy of full, unrestricted membership into the Society."

Nate leaned forward in his chair.

"Oh?" I was careful not to point out that we were not members yet. Perhaps that was a moot point, after our adventure into the bowels of London to stop a madman. Never mind that we nearly burned London down in the process.

Mrs. Langston gave a dismissive wave, "This sort of thing happens from time to time. They believe they have stumbled upon an extraordinary story or an amazing discovery and it turns out to be hokum. But this man was most adamant that he could prove it. *If* we allowed him access to the vaults of the Explorer's Society."

"Naturally, we refused." Mr. Langston said.

I nodded, "Naturally." Of course they would refuse someone who wasn't a member. Why would they allow just anyone access to their vaults? Their security, Marcus, was meant to protect the treasures just held here in the house. The treasures in their vault must be impressive indeed.

"Though, he did tell quite the tale," Mrs. Langston continued. "He spoke of a legendary hunter who killed a beast and buried its corpse in a grave no mortal man could find without his help."

"What was he offering? The pelt? This sounds like the plot to Jason and the Golden Fleece." Nate laughed. "Though, it may make the crown richer, so there's that."

Mr. Langston leaned forward, mirroring Nate. "He promised a weapon that could end any threat to the realm. Can you imagine? An end to expensive wars?"

Nate was suddenly listening intently; the man was positively fascinated by interesting weapons. Yellow wool and the cost of war was suddenly forgotten.

I raised an eyebrow. "Not to mention preventing the needless loss of life."

"That goes without saying, my dear. Your father was an apothecary, if I am not mistaken?" Mr. Langston said kindly.

"That is correct.," I said.

"He passed those skills on to you?" Mrs. Langston said. "How fascinating. We must discuss that some time."

"He did. I am fortunate to have learned much from him. It is a skill that has served us well in the field; one that I hope will be useful to the guild in the future, too. And I would be happy to discuss it with you." I added, eager to get back to the tale.

Mr. Langston continued. "He promised us an arrow."

Nate set his drink down on the table. He was no longer interested. "An arrow. That is hardly a weapon of the ages."

I knew him well, he would have preferred some sort of impressive cannon to be carried by hand, or a gun that shot bolts of lightning, or even a version of Excalibur that would allow England to expand her influence across the entire globe.

"Ahh, but he promised a magic arrow that felled a dragon." Mr. Langston wagged a teasing finger at us.

"A dragon." Nate snatched up his glass again. "There's no such thing." Then he paused, the brandy at his mouth, considering the possibility.

Mrs. Langston laughed. "And so we thought. But our records listed an artifact in our vaults matching the description of one of the items he mentioned. Suddenly, the possibility of a dragon having existed became more real."

Mr. Langston was looking positively pleased with himself. "This scale was recovered from the royal family of the Qing Dynasty, a princess, I believe it was. She found herself stranded in London and sold it to the Explorer's Society for a pittance."

I looked around the room where the servants were moving around like well-trained ghosts. They must have been accustomed to this sort of discussion, they did not stop working; they cleared the coffee and plates of cake.

"And that is the reason for China." Mr. Langston sat back, a satisfied smirk on his face.

Nate, on the other hand, looked as though he had been thrown from a horse, staggered and stunned. I wondered how much was the news of dragons roaming the earth and how much was the brandy.

Mr. Langston and his wife shared a small smile. "The Explorer's Society wishes you to recover that arrow." He said with a flourish.

I couldn't believe my ears. "That arrow?"

"Yes, Vivian, the very arrow that was shot from a bow, centuries ago, to slay a dragon." Augustus dared me to laugh.

"A dragon?" I repeated slowly. Dragons were a symbol in mythology. When Saint George had slain the dragon, it wasn't a literal dragon, but the serpent that represented ignorance and resistance to Christianity. Some scholars believed they didn't exist at all, but were in fact a symbolic form of the Devil. Still, dragons had to come from somewhere, we had books at home with stories from all over the world. Dragons were hardly a Christian invention. "I suppose China is a land of mystery, and it is said to be home to old world monsters." I immediately wished I chose another phrase. The Lamia had been an old-world monster and she still haunted my nightmares with her bone flute that brought dead men back to walk the land.

"The arrow was fired by Master Hou Yi, using his cinnabar-red bow to slay a dragon demon named Xihuan-Lung, or so the stories say," Marianne Langston said.

"There are many tales to suggest the dragon existed. It had become a plague upon man." Augustus motioned beyond where I was sitting, and Marcus the Bear brought in a wooden box heavily banded with iron. "I had this brought from one of our vaults for this occasion."

Markus's shirtsleeves were rolled up to the elbow. I watched his densely muscled and heavily scarred forearms flex. The guardian of the Explorer's Society's treasures was clearly a man who had been challenged countless times and won. Something Augustus believed needed this level of protection must be valuable indeed.

The box sat before me, daring me to open it. Nate stood behind me in mute support and, I suspected, to get a better look once I opened it.

The wood was warm and pulsed beneath my fingers. It set off a tingling, which started in my arm, just below the elbow. I was instantly glad I was wearing long sleeves. *The Five of Swords*, on my left arm, would be rising to the surface like a drawing on my skin, first charcoal on vellum, then it would darken like a tattoo on a sailor if I spent too much time reflecting upon it. It was the result of my own brush with the wild magic that had awakened my mother's gift for reading the tarot, and had somehow magnified it a thousand-fold.

The tarot mark—, *The Five of Swords,* a man standing triumphant watching his opponents retreat as he held five captured swords—grew warmer. If I rolled up my sleeve the Langstons would be able to see it clear as day. There was something of great conflict in this box, a trophy. Someone had risked everything to win it, and though the battle had ended, the conflict was far from over. I absently rubbed the spot on my arm.

Nate placed his hand on my shoulder, well-aware something was stirring within me. I pulled the pin back from the hasp and opened the box. Violet silk, the color of a fine orchid, lay in an untidy heap as though some creature had used it to make a nest. I carefully peeled back the silk wrapping.

It was a scale, not unlike the scale from a fish though larger than any I had ever seen, nearly the size of the palm of my hand. It gleamed, possessed of its own beautiful light. It reflected a purple pearl luster so beautiful I felt a piercing pain below my breastbone. A pain so sharp it brought tears to my eyes.

Behind me, Nate cleared his throat. I was feeling the husky pressure there myself. I knew what it must be, yet I needed him to confirm.

"Is this a dragon scale?"

"One of her Yin scales," Augustus said reverently.

I couldn't care less what a Yin scale was. All I knew is I would do anything to shelter this treasure. It had to be protected at all costs.

"How could something so beautiful come from a creature that was the plague of ancient China?" Nate said.

"Legend claims that when the dragon was slain her scales were given as gifts to the royal family and other important nobles," Mrs. Langston said.

I couldn't tear my eyes away. The scale's luminous glow penetrated my eyes no matter how I turned; no, it poured itself beyond my eyes. Its light touched my soul. I forced myself to look elsewhere and felt an immediate, palpable sense of loss.

"Some orders search for holy relics, others search for the relics of man," Mr. Langston said.

I felt a stab of irritation but squashed it. I didn't want to hear him speak, I wanted to gaze uninterrupted upon the scale.

"Suffice to say, mankind has spent many years searching for proof such a creature existed," Mr. Langston said.

"I dare say this is proof enough," Nate said.

I was staring at the scale again. I hadn't meant to, but it was irresistible. I couldn't tell if it was glowing on its own or reflecting light from the Langston's fancy electric lighting in the sitting room. Nothing else reflected, neither shapes, nor shadows, nor my own flesh as I passed my hand close.

Nate's hand rested heavily on my shoulder. "If this is a scale of the mighty Xihuan-Lung, then logically—"

"The arrow that slayed the dragon may be as well," I said.

Mr. Langston nodded and closed the box. The room was darker for it.

A long, quiet moment passed.

Nate sighed noisily. "So our assignment is to travel to China to follow a legend of a long-dead dragon, to find an arrow that may or may not have existed, and may or may not still exist?"

Augustus smiled. "And you are to return the arrow to us."

"Why is this arrow so important?" I asked. Nate did have a point, why all the trouble if this arrow might not even exist? Proof of a dragon we might have, but to believe such a mighty beast could be killed by something so mundane as an arrow was laughable. Arrows had wooden shafts and it would have turned to dust by now.

Augustus helped himself to the coffee. "It killed a mighty dragon with a single shot. The arrow of Xihuan-Lung can kill any target with a single blow."

The thought sent a chill up my spine. Such a weapon couldn't exist, could it? It certainly *shouldn't* exist.

"So, the person who wields the arrow of that dragon can kill anyone, anytime?" Nate looked a little green himself. "I suppose that would be like returning Excalibur to the crown."

Augustus laughed. "Though I agree such power would be tempting to wield, we seek the arrow to keep it out of the hands of those who would wish harm."

Nate cocked an eyebrow. "And place it into the hands of the Queen of England?"

Augustus had the decency to give a shocked look. "You do not suggest that our Queen would be heartless and cruel to anyone who angers her, do you?"

"No, of course not," Nate said quickly. "It just seems that if such a weapon exists it would be under heavy guard and their Empress Dowager—this Cixi—would be using it against her enemies. I'm sure I don't know all the affairs of China, but I believe they lost the Opium Wars."

"They did, they did," Marianne said. "The arrow has been lost. But if they were to ever start searching legends for powerful weapons, now is the time. There is talk of open rebellion in China. If they had a mind to start another war, it could happen soon. China is slowly being carved into pieces between England, France, Japan, and Germany."

"And Russia, dear," Augustus added.

"Ah yes, of course, and Russia." Marianne clapped her hands and gave a little laugh. "One must never forget Russia."

"We are to search for an ancient lost weapon," I said slowly. "And we are to get to it before the Empress Dowager Cixi or her agents, English agents, German agents, Japanese agents, or French agents?"

"Or Russian agents," Augustus added helpfully.

"Or Russian agents," I added gloomily.

"Or treasure hunters," Nate added.

"Treasure hunters?" I turned in my chair.

"Yes." Marianne smiled. "When war is on the horizon, treasure hunters seek to pilfer the treasures of a nation before they are lost forever, either by destruction or pilferage by treasure hunters who got there first. Terribly exciting, huh?"

"Terribly," I said quickly. "And we are to do this posing as travelers?" It was a wonderfully exciting opportunity to be sure and the idea of another grand adventure with Nate made me giddy. But traveling to a land where I did not speak the language that was about to descend into open war gave me pause. This would not be a trek through jungles and ruins where the most dastardly thing we could find was merely a dragon. From my experience, mankind had the capacity to be much more brutal in their dealings.

Augustus took his seat again and fixed me with a look. To my credit I do not believe I flinched, even for a moment. "Nate has told us a great deal about you. After the unpleasantness with Sterling's factory and Nate's accident last fall, he has told us countless tales of your bravery, your valor, and your sense of honor."

"I was forced upon adventure by Mr. Valentine's old crew." I answered honestly. "I hardly entered into adventure with a willingly stout heart and a battle cry."

Marianne waved it off. "Don't be modest, my dear. Nate told us of your exploits. You are a regular adventuress. We would be honored to have you among our members. But as you are thus far an unknown in the world of treasure hunters, and Nate is nearly as new as yourself. Combine your assets and we have every confidence you will be successful."

Our assets? I seemed able to spiritually read tarot meanings without use of the cards and Nate could transfigure into a half-man, half-canine monster at will. "Ah," I said, trying to sound agreeable. I was not pleased to see I appeared to have fooled my fiancé as well. He was practically giddy.

I was not so sure. "Mr. Langston. The man who brought you this fantastical offer in his bid for membership, was he a Chinaman?"

"No, he was an Englishman," Mr. Langston said. "We were skeptical, of course. Especially since one does not generally find the highest levels of education among his sort."

"His sort?" I raised my eyebrows.

"One might have mistaken him for a dockman who read stories in his spare time," Mrs. Langston said airily.

"Tell me about him." I could only picture a man of high ambition, trying to raise himself above his birth, looking for the unknown and the obscure, seeking knowledge and examining problems in a different, sinister way.

"Oh, the common sort, I suppose," Mr. Langston said. "He struck me as a man seeking desperately to improve his own fortunes and rise above his misery."

"Misery?" Nate was suddenly interested, the dog in him finally caught whatever scent I had, and if I thought there may be something to it, Nate now confirmed it.

"Poor fellow had some sort of accident. He had the most unfortunate burns; I would think an industrial accident."

Mrs. Langston nodded. "Quite ghastly, an explosion I would guess. Being an official Explorer would lend mystique to him and allow him to become a man of history and not a man of misfortune."

Nate and I exchanged a look. A dockman covered in burns with an interest in the fantastical. If he had lost an arm, the man could be none other than Newton Geiger, the mad inventor whose plans we foiled beneath Sterling's factory. The factory had burned and Nate and I assisted his hireling, Columbus Baxter, out of the factory as the fire brigade descended, determined to keep the flames from consuming the block. The factory and the emporium were a total loss and with it, Lord Sterling's fortunes. But a body was never recovered. Geiger's inventions and his clockwork men were lost along with the machinery designed to make Lord Sterling a very rich man.

"I'll inquire," Nate assured me in a whisper.

"I would think applications to the Explorer's Society are quite numerous," I said.

"That is the fun of an exclusive guild," Mr. Langston winked, "the more secretive we appear, the more desirable we are to all."

"And the more choosey we can be in regards to members," Mrs. Langston finished.

"Surely, that is only the public face." Nate said somberly into his cup

"Quite right", Mr. Langston was suddenly serious, "That is why we need to be choosy. We are so much more than a social club. The sacred secrets of mankind are our true aims and that man knew that."

Their last exchange reminded us all of the looming business ahead that waited in China. This was no mere holiday but a mission and a sudden shadow was cast over the evening. I barely heard the Langstons bid us good evening and was only partially aware that I was led to a small, but clean and smartly furnished, room where I was to spend the evening. The room was cold, except for the warming pan placed in the bed by a caring maid. I would have loved a maid to speak with.

It was one of those evenings where I wished Nate would transfigure into Ranger so I could whistle for him to come sleep on my feet. I would have given a lot to be able to caress Ranger's silky, pricked ears until I fell asleep.

The lack of someone else to talk to for distraction left my brain worrying against the thoughts long into the evening. The Explorer's Society had set us an impossible task. At least, I was sure it was impossible. Travel to China to recover an arrow that was, if legends were to be believed, shot from a bow centuries ago to kill a dragon by a legendary archer.

The Five of Swords, in most decks, is represented by a contemptuous young man holding the swords he took as spoils of battle from his dejected enemies. The sky is cloudy and tumultuous, indicating that not all is well despite the battle being seemingly over.

Could we achieve this goal no matter what it could cost us? With war looming in China, as well as in the cards, would we win the sword,—or in this case, the arrow—but ultimately lose when a weapon this powerful was brought back into the hands of men? Wouldn't such a powerful weapon be best left lost?

CHAPTER TWO

NATE WAS RESTLESS and needed adventure. He paced the manor with the rolling gait of a working dog desperate to ensure all his flock was still present and accounted for as a storm loomed. I could sympathize. Despite my misgivings, I found that I needed adventure as well, the small taste of it we had shared was far from enough. I longed to see things I had only read of in books and seen in paintings. I was quite excited about our coming trip to China.

I finished laying out what I was taking. A few changes of clothes and a pile of medical supplies, along with my leather long coat and, of course, my mother's old tarot cards. I was more concerned about being prepared with the bandages and tinctures than with fashion, unlike other women might be. After a moment, I added an additional dress. It never hurt to be prepared, and one never knew what China might hold.

Now that the adventure was nearing, I found my own excitement growing. It was one thing to worry about not speaking the language, and the politics of a nation that had been crippled by a recent trade war, but all that had melted away. We were about to embark on another grand adventure into the great unknown.

There was a knock at my door. If it was my maid, Jane, again trying to persuade me to pack as a lady might to avoid scandal, I would have to be more forceful in my insistence that she go sweep the hall rugs again.

It was Nate. A much preferred visitor. He looked at my bed where my clothes were laid out and made a stern face, which he then softened. Just because he could travel the world with little more than a spare shirt didn't mean a woman could. He wisely recognized this and left it alone. He set my seax in its leather scabbard down on my pile. He had been sharpening the long, single-edged knife for me. The more adventurous members of the Explorer's Society found the weapon's style to be without comparison, so they were nearly synonymous with the society now. Also, on the belt was my revolver.

Nate picked up the book on top of my satchel. "*Concerning Myth and Legend in China: A Scholar's Guide*. A bit of light reading?"

"You are a riot." I said replacing the book on my pile. "Mr. Simon Carrington of the Explorer's Society brought the tome back from a visit to China and Mr. Langston insisted we take it with us on our journey. He thought it might be useful. There is a whole section on dragons and all sorts of fascinating creatures. Did you know there is a creature that is something between a lion and a dog that is the champion of the household?"

"Like the stone lions outside manor houses in London?" Nate looked quite pleased, "It's a small world."

I wasn't entirely sure he wasn't on to something. I had had the same thought earlier, dragon myths existed all over the world, though the European and the Eastern variety looked different, but they also looked strikingly similar to the paintings of sea monsters. Dragons also had a resemblance to the dinosaurs the naturalists of the day were obsessed with. Dragons, lions, creatures with single horns that could be related to unicorns or narwhals; creatures worlds apart were similar. The world was very small indeed.

I chose boots, a shirt, corset, and trousers from my piles to wear the next day. Nate sat in the chair in my bedroom watching me with an amused smile on his face.

"What?"

"Nothing," he said. "I was merely reflecting upon what a lucky man I am. There you are, the future Mrs. Vivian Valentine, setting out a wardrobe for an adventure."

"Mrs. Vivian Valentine." I sauntered over to him. "I like that."

"I'm sorry," He said suddenly.

"Whatever for?"

"I know you had hoped for a May wedding." He stared at his hands, wringing his fingers until the knuckles cracked.

We *had* been planning a May wedding. We had even sent out the invitations. Earlier, Hiram and our footman, Aaron, ventured out to all the invitees and delivered notes expressing our regrets that a business venture had interrupted our plans and the wedding had been delayed.

For a moment, we had considered moving the wedding up, holding it before we left, but a rushed wedding would leave the impression that we were expecting a child and would make us and our loose morals the talk of the season. At least until another scandal found its way into the lives of those with nothing better to do than follow gossip. One thing I did not miss from London society was the gossip and judgment. Those women really should read more, perhaps it would keep their brains occupied with more important matters.

"I understand, really I do," I assured him. "So long as you are still planning on marrying me when we return home."

"You couldn't prevent it if you tried," he said, gathering me up in his embrace. "I find that country life suits me."

I threw back my head and laughed. "Now you are acting like a man of the nineteenth century, more concerned with the property I bring with me than the charms I possess."

"Your charms won you the property you possess," he reminded me. "If it were not for your valor I would still be sleeping on the floor of your father's apothecary shop waiting for our wedding so I could move into a proper bed with my wife, rather than waiting for our wedding so I can join my wife in our bed."

"And we would be saving our pennies for a house of our own with a small garden," I added.

"Whilst I remained vigilant for your father's apprentice to make attempts upon my person so he could have you all to himself," he finished ominously.

We both laughed. My father's apprentice, Calvin, had made no secret of his desire to wed me. He was quite conflicted when I returned from my first grand adventure with the dashing Nathaniel Valentine. On one hand, he had lost any opportunity to marry me, but on the other hand, Nate was an adventurer. He had returned with stories of adventure, magic, and treasure, and Calvin couldn't get enough. They stayed up long hours into the night drinking small beer and discussing everything from airships to foreign politics to the best way to adventure into far off places.

I did feel a pang of regret for crushing Calvin so. He was not a bad match, but the affection I felt for him was more brotherly, rather than the passion I had for the man standing before me.

"And we wouldn't have Hiram or Aaron or Jane and Helen or Mrs. Simms to take such good care of us," I returned.

"None the less, it is my intention to make an honest, if somewhat eccentric, woman"—he motioned to my assembled wardrobe—"out of you, Miss Harper."

"Duly noted." I replied, and we kissed.

"I suppose you are already packed."

"Not yet, I figure I can do that tomorrow morning," he said.

"We are leaving at two o'clock," I chided gently. "Does that give you enough time?"

"Of course." He gave a dismissive wave. "But first I'll have to make sure Hiram has all the keys and accounts he needs to keep this place running while we are gone."

It was good to have a butler we could trust so completely. It eliminated the need to hire an agent to look after things while we were gone.

"Then I'll have to visit Mr. Crossdale so he knows he has to manage our part of the spring planting." He rubbed a hand over his face. Although the land surrounding our manor house was a relatively small twelve hundred acres, they were prosperous and well-tended by our tenants. Nate rubbed the bridge of his nose with his eyes closed, a habit of his when there was quite a bit on his mind he was trying to take care of. He felt me watching him and froze. "What?"

"You are becoming quite the landlord, Mr. Valentine. Or should I call you 'Mr. Valentine, Esquire'?"

"Har, har, har," he said, the sound muffled slightly by his hand. "Though, I do see why landed gentlemen become heavy drinkers and gamblers."

"You handle the managing of estate governance well, my love," I said, dropping my hands on his shoulders and starting to massage the tension from him.

He reluctantly got out of the chair and bid me good night. I could see Hiram following him to his quarters in the west wing to attend to his duties as valet. Hiram was truly a wonderful butler. I was even sure he would have looked the other way were Nate to close the door so we could spend the night together without the protection of a wedding ring between us.

My May wedding was just going to have to wait. Mama would handle changing all the arrangements to September. Five months was more than enough time for us to journey to China, locate the arrow of Hou Yi, and return … I hoped. But waiting to reschedule until we returned would ensure it took even longer to be married. Knowing Nate realized it too made it easier to bear.

With him gone I turned my attention to the book I brought with me from our meeting with the Langstons.

> *Concerning dragons. There are few things in China of more interest than the dragon. To the Eastern mind they closely resemble long serpents with four legs, but they are also capable of several additional forms, including those of turtles and fish and powerful human beings. They have control of waters, including storms, typhoons, and floods. They are creatures of the mist. They are the symbol of the emperor and his line.*
>
> *While European dragons are creatures of violence and fire, Chinese dragons are creatures of harmony, prosperity, and balance. But like all creatures, even dragons can fall from balance.*

A dragon that could control the storms, typhoons, floodwaters, and was a symbol of prosperity and balance, but was capable of falling out of balance? What did that mean? Floods, typhoons, and endless rains upon the people of China? Surely that would be devastating. Since it was the symbol of the emperor would it be an emperor falling out of balance? That would bring true ruin to the people. England had had its own mad rulers in the past. If the people could be saved with a single magical arrow to set things right then maybe Hou Yi would be justified, not right and certainly not legal, but just.

And we were supposed to retrieve a weapon capable of slaying a beast that wielded this power? It *would* be the second coming of Excalibur. In the hands of Queen Victoria, England would become the most powerful nation in the world. But if it existed within the bounds of China then shouldn't it remain there? Surely there would be consequences to appropriating such a powerful artifact.

But then, China had gone to war with the rest of the world over trade goods and was now on the edge of chaos as its ability to double-cross all its trade partners came back to harm her. At least, that is what I had been taught. Opium was the main trade good in question, and when something as highly addictive as opium is involved, the truth is generally far more complicated.

I was interrupted when Jane came in and helped me neatly fold all the clothes on my bed and place them into the chest Nate and I would be sharing. Good manners kept her from mentioning Nate's late visit to my quarters, that consequently kept her up late to help me deal with my wardrobe. I let her unlace my corset, and I changed into my nightgown. I insisted on brushing out my long brown hair myself while she finished tidying my room. Then she, too, bid me goodnight and left me to the smoored fire and its comforting orange glow as I lay down trying to get some sleep on the eve of my second grand adventure.

CHAPTER THREE

MR. LANGSTON ARRANGED for us to meet unofficially with a captain under the employ of the Society. His name was Captain Remington, and he was to oversee our transportation to China personally aboard his own vessel, the *Nomad*.

Captain Remington was a smartly dressed man with an upper class British accent. He was handsome and blond, with bright blue eyes and a thin pencil mustache that looked striking on him. Though both Nate and the captain were tall and lean, that was where their similarity ended. Where Nate had light skin and dark brown hair with caramel eyes that ladies would commit murder for, Captain Remington was blond and tan with blue eyes. It was obvious he spent a life outdoors.

Captain Remington wore a French gray coat of broadcloth with pink trim and a turned cuff, similar in style to the uniform coat of a naval officer, but that is where the similarity ended. His blue eyes were merry in the reflecting light from the sea and his easy smile left me sure there was nothing to fear. I was sure our adventure would be a smooth and happy one, and I was ecstatic to be off on this grand adventure.

The captain extended his hand for mine gallantly, "Shall we?"

We piled our luggage and ourselves into a longboat with four rowers. How strange the ship was not docking at the wharf waiting for us to cross the gangplank like proper guests. I supposed there could be many reasons for a ship to be absent from the busy wharf, and pushed it from my mind. I had never traveled by sea before.

The men leaned hard into the oars as they fought the waves boat rowing past the breakers. Beads of perspiration stood out against their foreheads as their forearms strained against the exertion. I held tightly onto the edge of my seat as we were tossed about, the sea spray drenching my face and hair. Now this was exciting!

Certainly he didn't mean to row us across the Chinese Sea to get us to Beijing.

Nate, on the other hand, was less than pleased. He sat fiddling with the silver buttons on his new waistcoat. He tapped his boots, fidgeting as we rode the waves, seeking an outlet for a sudden burst of energy. I leaned over and took his hand. He must not have liked being on the water. How strange for him to feel this way—he was fine in the sky with nothing but a balloon and steel cables keeping us from crashing.

I loved it, this was how travel to a new destination should be. True, the airship was smoother and there was a distinct lack of choppy waves in the sky unless you counted sailing into a storm, but here there was nothing but a bit of wood lifting me off the waves. And far below the soft waves, was the land, reduced to sand and mud. Were I to fall out, there would be no messy end, merely sodden trousers. It was not like traveling far above the land in the sky where I was as safe as an egg being juggled on the roof.

I let my fingers trail in the water; I could just reach it if I leaned over the side. The salty spray hit my face, drenching the wisps of hair that had fallen from my pinned-up hair and plastered them to my face. I licked my lips, enjoying the salt. Suddenly, a hand grasped the back of my belt and hauled me back.

Nate was scowling at me. He clearly did not appreciate the sea as I did. Perhaps, I mused, his dog-self didn't enjoy getting wet.

The men stopped their rowing. For a moment I feared it was me—women were supposed to be bad luck for superstitious sailors. But no, they sat patiently with the oars up.

"Mr. Valentine," Captain Remington said, "I do hope that you were informed as to the method of travel by Mr. Langston."

"By sea is all he assured us, Captain," Nate returned.

Captain Remington chuckled. "Well, then, you are in for a treat." He turned to me. "Hold tight, milady. I do hope you don't faint."

"I assure you, Captain Remington, Vivian is not the type that faints," Nate said dryly.

I just grinned at him.

Captain Remington's rowers pulled the oars from the eye bolts and secured them with ropes to grooves in the bottom of the longboat. The eye bolts were worn shiny within the rings themselves, and not from the way the wood of the oars had rubbed upon them. Clearly they were not used for oars exclusively. I suddenly had a sinking feeling in my stomach.

The captain pulled a hooded lantern from the locker in the bow of the boat and lit the oil wick. The scent of burning kerosene mixed with the salty air. He flashed his hand over the light disrupting the beam of, signaling. This repeated for quarter of an hour or so. I sat on the bench of the longboat fighting boredom, my back resting against Nate's shoulder.

A light blinked from high above us and I groaned. Another airship. Nate squeezed my shoulders and gave me a thin smile. He either knew or suspected we would be traveling by airship.

I suppose it made sense, and I tried not to be too disappointed. I had consulted a map before setting off on this adventure. China is eight thousand kilometers away as the crow flies, but as a boat travels, because one has to sail around the horn of Africa, the trip is more than twenty-five thousand kilometers. Even if a ship could travel twice as fast as an airship it would still take much, much longer. And Mr. Langston had asked us to make haste.

Though I had managed to overcome my morbid terror of heights and transform it into a mere belly-deep fear of heights, I wasn't eager to get into another airship so soon. Even if it was taking us to the mysterious Orient. I steeled my nerves and resolved that this trip would be more enjoyable. The trip would fly by, so to speak.

My leather pack, that had been a parting gift from the crew of the airship the *Lightning Aura*, sat next to Nate's matching pack on the shared chest containing our clothes and other belongings.

Over the creaking of the wooden longboat on the waves and the heavy breathing of the men I could hear the *clink-squeak* of ropes being lowered on winches. The sailors heard it too and they all looked up. I bit my lip, trying to pull my stomach back up from the depths of the ocean below our little boat. I did not believe I was going to be able to remind my nerves who was the master in this situation.

Having rowed out past the moored ships under the cover of darkness to be hauled out of the water like a fresh catch to the airship, as well as waiting in the cover of darkness, it was like we were spies. Except our mission was not one of subterfuge. Or if it was, we had been misled.

I took a deep breath so my voice would not shake. "What's with all the secrecy, Captain?"

The first mate was now reaching above his head and guiding a coil of ropes and hooks and securing them into the eye bolts around the boat.

Captain Remington didn't even turn my way, "The harbor master has informed us of where we may and may not dock."

"That and our mission relies on stealth and speed?" I said while reminding my nerves that shaking here would do no one any good. "We are to beat treasure hunters to China."

The hooks had been put in place and all the ropes were tied. It was a matter of moments until we were hoisted into the air and off on a new adventure. *I like adventure,* I reminded myself. I knew I was being argumentative due to my nerves, but even knowing why I was cranky did little to help me control it.

"I am sorry, Miss Harper, Mr. Langston and I agree that time is of the essence. By sea it is six weeks to travel to China. By air, it is three days," Captain Remington reminded me.

I nodded, though I was sure he couldn't see that in the dark. I was fine with him believing he had convinced me.

Captain Remington flashed the hooded lantern to the sky. The ropes and the wood creaked as we were slowly reeled in like a marlin on a hook. I did hope our outcome would be much more favorable than that of a marlin, though.

There was nothing for me to do but sit as we were reeled into the sky. I recalled that during our last adventure Nate and I were hauled up from the square in a giant net designed to catch lightning. At least this was an improvement, I was being winched into the airship seated in a longboat rather than hauled up like a great catch of mackerel and my limbs were not thrust out all akimbo through the netting. When we had reached the airship, two sailors had taken hold of me, one at each arm, to gently guide me out of the longboat as though I was an invalid, but I shook them off. I would not be handled in this way. I was no shrinking violet.

Captain Remington calmly asked for his first-mate to get us moving. So different was this from the *Lightning Aura*. There, Captain Morgan had barked his orders and the men ran to obey. The decks on board the *Aura* had been clean but displayed signs of wear. Here, the *Nomad* had a small docking area where the longboat was slid up to the airship and set into the side like they were a key and a lock. The longboat locked in place and a fine wooden door set with a circular window opened. Beyond the door I could see a well-lit parlor with soft music and a plush purple carpet.

A friendly woman with a wide smile curtsied and took my leather bag. "Greetings, Miss Harper. Welcome to the *Nomad*. I will show you to your room."

"Thank you," I said. If the *Aura* had been utilitarian, then the *Nomad* was comfort, and I resolved to at least compose myself for travel. The book on Chinese creatures was in my satchel as was all the information the Explorer's Society had on the arrow. I had three days to educate myself.

Nate rested his hand on the butt of his revolver, for want of a better place to put it, and gave a low whistle through his teeth.

If I could whistle as he did, I might well have added mine. The parlor was set with fine electric lights. I longed to take off my boots and walk barefooted across the plush purple carpet with a bright yellow border. The curtains that hung on the walls were blue velvet.

The floors were clearly the same fine wood as the paneling, for it bordered the carpeting evenly all along the walls. All that interrupted the wide room was a single column rising from floor to ceiling through the center of the room. There were benches set into the walls, each with cushions and the occasional half-circle table set into the wall to hold vases of gardenias.

Captain Remington puffed out his chest. "Here aboard the *Nomad* we aim to make travel a luxury. Often the most tedious portion of holiday is the travel. We have made travel itself part of the holiday, not a delay of it. If you need anything, anything at all, Beth will assist you." He motioned to the friendly woman who had greeted us.

"We do not currently have a personal valet for your use," he said to Nate. "But my own man, Stephen, will assist you if you need anything."

Nate nodded. "Captain Remington, just how many people are going to be traveling to China?"

"You and Miss Harper," He returned. "There is another couple that are headed to India, so we will have to make a brief stop there, but we only have three occupied cabins for this journey."

"Out of how many?" Nate asked.

"Fourteen." He smiled. "Since air travel is still in its infancy, there is less demand. Be sure you tell your friends." He made a tight bow then exited.

SஜS

We were shown to a state room decorated in the same style as the rest of the ship. It must have cost a small fortune to outfit. It had the same plush carpet, the same velvet window coverings, the same beautiful, warm, chestnut-colored wood. There were two doors leading off on opposite sides. Bedrooms, with narrow but fully furnished beds set into the walls and narrow wardrobes ready for our garments stood ready for our pleasure. If this was the future of air travel, I just might manage to get used to it.

Then Nate opened the curtains that covered the round porthole windows. I felt a quiver cut through me and I must have exhaled nosily because he wheeled around in alarm. Nope, I probably would never get used to it.

There was a knock at the door and Beth, the maid, entered the room with a tray of brandy and cakes. "Begging your pardon. You two lovebirds can get right to your canoodling, but I thought you might fancy some refreshment. Your chest will be brought up in short order."

Nate nodded and motioned for her to set the tray on the table beside us. At least I was reasonably sure that is what happened, it was hard to observe anything with my blood rushing through my ears.

"Darling, if you hold those armrests any tighter Captain Remington will accuse us of smuggling a hawk on board."

I breathed deeply and forced myself to relax. Really now, this was getting to be too much. After a few days I adjusted to life aboard the *Lightning Aura*, I would adjust to the *Nomad* as well.

He cocked his head to look at me, that chronically untidy hair falling into his eyes—beautiful amber eyes they were, the color of whiskey. I could get drunk just staring into his eyes.

And like a fortifying shot of whiskey, soon I felt strong enough to move. "Just avoid opening the window, please."

"Of course." He stood and cranked up the phonograph on the stand in the corner. A lovely waltz poured from the thin metal cylinder and flower painted bell. He offered he his hand. "Miss Harper? If you would do me the pleasure of this dance?"

"You don't dance well." I protested, giggling.

"Ah yes, but perhaps fear of preserving your feet will take your mind off the very great height from which we travel." Nate took my cold and clammy fingers within his. "It is a fact, one can only be afraid of one thing at a time. It is simply all you have time for."

"Where did you hear that?" I laughed.

He shrugged and spun me around. We narrowly missed a table. "It sounded quite learned to me."

For a moment, air travel aboard the *Nomad* seemed a reasonable mode of travel.

SOS

The next morning, we set off to find breakfast. The dining hall was a marvel, with vaulted ceilings painted bright yellow, featuring a cut-glass chandelier and beautiful wallpaper with white lily of the valley flowers and thin vertical green stripes. The wooden floor, decorated in a beautiful herringbone pattern, was covered by a lovely red and gold oriental rug. The aroma of fresh wood lacquer remained in the air. The windows slanted outward, catching the sunlight, turning the room into a wonderful glass conservatory. Wonderful, that is, if I ignored the terrifying drop just beyond the stunning view.

Though magnificent, it was also deserted, giving it an air of loneliness and neglect. A fine table was set for us including poached eggs, mushrooms on toast, kippers, strawberries, butter and jam, seared tomatoes, and cold ham. It was far more than we could eat.

At the other side of the room, an elderly couple raised a cup of tea acknowledging our presence. She wore a beautiful violet gown with lace cuffs decorated with many little yellow flowers. A parasol decorated with matching ribbons was propped against the table. Beside the butter dish sat a hardback book and what looked to be a box of watercolors. Her companion was a gentleman in dressed a fine linen suit with distinguished, salt and pepper hair. They could only be the couple traveling to India, Kenneth and Carolyn DeBurgh.

Once breakfast concluded, Nate set off to explore the ship. His love for airships knew no bounds. I suspected he was off to find the crew and climb the rigging with wild abandon like some sort of air-born monkey. I left him to it, I had much more pressing matters: the *Nomad* had a library.

Past the atrium and up a curved staircase, glass doors in wooden frames welcomed travelers to an opulent library. The library was full of wonderful leather-bound tomes. It was most agreeable to study among all these beautiful books.

Sir Kenneth was in the library nursing a glass of scotch by himself when I arrived.

"I hope I am not disturbing you," I said.

"Of course not," he answered. Even if I had, I doubted he would admit it. He closed the book before him gently and set down his glass. "I find that as I age I cannot resist the call of a good book. You are looking for my wife, Carolyn, I trust?"

"No, I'm afraid I have something more productive in mind." I pulled out a chair at one of the library tables. The woodwork was so new I could still smell the stain made of walnut crystals, which gave it a harsh woody, nutty scent; I supposed fresh flowers were not practical for an airship, though they would have helped cover the scent of the new furniture.

I pulled *Concerning Myth and Legend in China* and the folder of papers from my satchel.

The people of China are quite concerned with securing good fortune for themselves and their lives. It is their sincere belief that their fate and personal attributes are determined, in part, by where their birth lies in a great chart of annual cycles ruled by animals. There are twelve of these such animals, and each is further classified by an element. This is further complicated by an adherence to a non-standard year that may alter one's ruling animal. The belief in this is so strong that it even determines compatibility to another person.

I skipped over this part, while interesting as a cultural study, I needed information we could use.

These are also divided further into trines.

Trines. I had read that before. I moved over to the papers. Research had been done on this by the Explorer's Society before. I quickly scanned through the information. Trine temples.

Many of the monks had made mention of specific temples erected to the trines of the great lunisolar cycle. It was a rural calendar for farmers. There was a crude sketch, a circle with four dots making a square, with points all connected, creating an "x" in the middle. Dragons were sacred creatures, tied to all matters of belief. If the sacred grave of a dragon existed then it would be logical to start where the lunar cycle temples would meet.

The pages of notes had a sketch of an arch.

The Dragon, Xihuan-Lung, did not fall in a valley easily accessible by the average man. Like many legends, the dragon fell in a hidden valley called the Dragon Gate. Like all sacred places, this one is only accessible by a key or keys and it is my belief that the key and the trine temples are connected. Each trine temple will have to be carefully searched for the key. Perhaps the key is moved from location to location to prevent it from falling into unfriendly hands.

I made my own small note in the margin like I was conversing with the original researcher. *Why did no one seek the treasure before us?*

CHAPTER FOUR

CHINA WAS EVERYTHING I dreamed it to be. Large wooden ships resembling Marlins with their long, spear-shaped noses and their thin jagged sails dancing upon the waves, fighting their moorings. Nate informed me that the term was "battened sail." He said they were common on the ships the Chinese called junks, and they were cheaper to build and maintain than the ships we were more familiar with from England. They bowed and bounced on the waves of the harbor of the Tanggu Wharf like dolphins at play. If someone cut them loose they would dance and bound as they disappeared over the horizon.

We followed the railway from Tanggu wharf, where the British and the Chinese set up a trade station east of a truly impressive sandbar that spanned most of the mouth of the *Haihe*.

It was a short matter to dock at a huge tower made of new timbers that still bled sap, bound with rope so fresh they were still being stretched by the spacers placed in the joints every few meters. A rope bridge secured us to the tower, if one used the term "secured" loosely. I was sure one strong breeze would tear us free. Once the bridge was secured we were reeled in as though the *Nomad* was a huge fish on a line. The dockmen grabbed at ropes and worked to secure an air and sea ships in a similar manner. If an airship was out of the ordinary, it didn't show.

Several more ropes were secured with belaying pins and heavy capstans and we were slowly winched into place. I released the breath I was holding and gulped down another one. They looked to be planning some sort of slow collision. I gripped the rail for all I was worth, stubbornly reminding my breakfast to remain where I put it earlier. Oh, how I hated heights!

As soon as the ship was deemed secured by the port master, the *Nomad* was swarmed by Chinamen. They wasted no time adding more lines, and began offloading our cargo or consulting with the captain as they poured over books and barked orders at crew members in both English and Chinese.

The absurdity of securing an airship to a tower several stories off the ground with mere ropes seemed akin to attempting to tie down a stallion with embroidery thread. I was no longer sure if we were safer in the air or on the ground. I was only terrifyingly sure that being tied to this new, frighteningly fragile, wooden structure was the worst idea so far. That is, until they wanted me to cross the wood-slat rope bridge to the wooden tower.

I must have turned some awful color because a short, stocky Chinese man wearing a braided band around his bald head set down a barrel and eyed me appraisingly. He used the white headband to wipe the sweat away before he asked Captain Remington a question with his hands firmly planted on his hips.

"Miss Harper, Zhen wishes me to tell you that if you cannot walk off the ship he's sure you are a good deal lighter than the wine barrel and it would be his pleasure to carry you himself."

I gasped. Nate was careful to keep his face blank. I was sure I was being mocked. "You can tell him that I will walk myself, thank you very much!"

Zhen shrugged and set the large barrel back upon his shoulder, eased himself around me with a deceptive amount of grace, and went about his duties unloading the ship.

I tucked my satchel beneath my arm and followed. If it could hold both Zhen and his barrel, it could hold me.

My bravado lasted only until both feet left the airship. The rope bit through my calfskin gloves. The ocean below me was so close and yet so far, and the hated airship was now the place I longed to return to. I had to force myself to breathe. *In. Out.* If I bit the inside of my own cheek any harder I would bite straight through it. *In. Out.*

Nate appeared beside me and linked my arm with his, and stiffly pulled me along. The wooden tower was only marginally more solid beneath my feet, I could feel it sway and creak with the wind. The sap leaking from the new wood made the soles of my boots sticky.

We rounded landing after landing, descending twelve tight, steep steps between each platform, until at last we were on solid ground. The airship danced above us, looming like some giant monster playfully waving and saying her goodbyes. For just a moment, I could understand how Nate must have felt about leaving the crew and his old ship. Ships did seem to have a life of their own.

Captain Remington's man was waiting for us with a sheaf of papers. "Do not worry for your belongings, I will have them taken to the harbormaster's office, and from there sent to wherever you wish them to go. The harbormaster needs to sign off on these forms, and since air travel is still a new phenomenon, he wishes to check the passenger manifest."

We followed the purser into the office where we were greeted and processed by a smartly dressed man in modern clothing, like what would be worn back home. His suit was a few seasons out of fashion, but respectable and clean and far from the robes or tunics and trousers that seemed to be worn by most Chinese. He asked us to sign our names in a book so new the leather on the spine of his register had not yet been trained to lay open. Nate had to prop it open with his forearm then hand it over to be sanded and blown upon before the ink smeared.

Paperwork in order and stamps still glistening, the harbormaster directed us to the Viridian, a fine hotel frequented by travelers from Europe and the Americas. Most of the residents spoke English, French, or German so we would be comfortable there.

Our luggage was sent ahead, so all we had to manage was Nate's battered and faded backpack and my satchel full of the medicines and tinctures I feared we might need during our stay.

Our previous adventure had been rather violent and dangerous, so I had crammed clean bandages and simples into my satchel until my shoulder ached under the weight of it.

Nate took up his pack and offered me his arm as though we were going for a garden stroll. High above the docks where the ships that traveled the seas were moored, the *Nomad* pulled playfully at the ropes that bound her to the land.

Nate was watching her, too. Adventure called to him but in a different way. He was made for tearing lightning from the clouds and bottling it into tiny batteries; he was made for riding on the winds of those air monsters. We shared a smile. We were on adventure and we were on land. Happiness for all.

We walked across the planks of the dock, threading our way in and out of the general hubbub and clatter of a busy marina, shouldering our way through the press of people. I could not understand the language; it was a horribly isolating experience.

But I could still connect with them.

I reached out in a sort of dream state, receptive and open to everyone around me. They were a flood of images: tarot cards, wands and coins, swords and cups and arcana all around me, humming like a live wire, and I was suddenly adrift in a sea of hands and unfamiliar touches. I held my satchel tightly, mindful of robbers, but as the press of people closed in around us I was bombarded by the readings and representations of the people we passed.

At times, the snippets I got were very literal; coins for the working men and women, the tradesmen and the moneylenders and those who worked in physical goods; swords for those who were not only warriors but who had strong personalities and made laws, those who relied on their great force of character to make their way. Cups swirled around those connected with others through their emotions, the artists, the gentle and the creative; the staves and wands for the priests and philosophers who pondered life and the meaning of all around them; the thinkers. It was all horribly disorienting. I closed my eyes and tried to shake it away.

That was a mistake. There were too many people. I was disoriented. Then I received a touch, a strong read like a punch to the face, enough to snap me out of the drone of arcane energy all around me. *The High Priestess* inverse , distorting and clouding over all other images, including the real world that lay before me. Her cloak was spread out between the pillars of knowledge, keeping those without the ability to understand from accessing the sacred knowledge. The High Priestess maintained balance between knowledge and ignorance, she upheld a sense of duty, she was nobility and grace, and she sat between the darkness and the light. It is the High Priestess who maintains us when we walk the fine line between intuition and learning as she keeps the moon at her feet and learning in her hands.

But she was inverse. I have been not listening, or not learning; or I would be soon. We were seeking a dragon, I was learning all I could—what if that would not be enough to complete our task? Or was it something more literal? The High Priestess championed knowledge. Knowledge could be hidden or distorted. I blinked hard, but my vision was dull and cloudy.

The High Priestess was not the only card blocking my vision. Round and bright, the sun was not the only light I saw. *The Moon* was bright and cool and shining down upon us, lengthening shadows and playing tricks, deceiving and teasing. Illusion—

"Mr. Valentine?" A musical voice speaking halting English made us both turn. I was startled from my vision. A beautiful woman bowed to us. I couldn't help but notice her beautiful almond-shaped eyes, skillfully painted with lilac shadow, and her straight, shining black hair adorned with a jade comb.

"I am MeiLin. Welcome to Beijing. I have been hired as your interpreter."

Nate looked skeptical. "The Explorer's Society sent us a translator? It has always been the responsibility of the agent to hire any help we might need."

"Well, time is of the essence. Maybe they anticipated that we would need assistance," I said.

"Maybe." He looked doubtful. "What would it cost us to maintain your employ?"

"As I have stated," she said. "I have been already hired as your interpreter."

We exchanged a glance.

"Forgive me, I have never heard of the Society hiring interpreters for their agents," he said finally.

"As your companion said, time is of the essence," MeiLin said. "Several other agents from your guild have already met up with their translators and have headed to their destinations."

Nate's eyes narrowed, but whatever he was thinking he was not sharing.

"I am Vivian Harper." I introduced myself.

She didn't take my hand. She gave me a small bow from the waist, her palms touching before her breast.

"Vivian is my fiancée," He explained with a boyish grin.

"What does that mean?" MeiLin asked Nate.

"It means we are engaged to be married," I said, linking my arm with his. Such a simple action still gave me a small, warm rush of pleasure.

MeiLin met my eyes for the briefest moment. "In China, ladies do not speak in front of men unless they are asked. They are only asked if the man believes they have something valuable to add."

I was stung. "Excuse me?" I suddenly got the feeling that she knew very well what fiancée meant, she was asking him something else entirely.

MeiLin glanced at me again before casting her eyes back to the ground. "What I meant: no one asked you," she replied in that beautiful, musical tone.

"No one ever does, that is why I speak up," I said crossly.

MeiLin fluttered her eyes at Nate. "Perhaps if you respected your intended you would remain quiet in his presence," MeiLin said.

"Vivian is quite valuable to me," Nate said quickly. "Things are done differently in the West."

"How sad Western men must be," MeiLin said softly as though no one could hear her, "to not be shown proper respect by their women."

I forced down my irritation. Not long ago I would have been content to be a meek, quiet woman. But not anymore. Nate smiled at me, that foolish, boyish, charming grin, and my irritation melted away.

"Surely women are respected for their voices here." I said doing my best to remain cheerful. "You are ruled by a Queen."

"China is ruled by the Empress Dowager Cixi." MeiLin corrected. "She holds the throne since the death of her son. There has only been a single woman Emperor before. China has had a few Empress Dowagers who held the throne in trust until the proper ruler came of age. The mandate of heaven must be upheld."

"The mandate of heaven?" Nate cocked an eyebrow.

"The Emperor of China's divine right to rule. It keeps this land safe for all who live here." MeiLin said.

It was a beautiful land, I did have to admit. I turned to look out at the city that spread past the dock. When I turned back, MeiLin had her hand on Nate's arm. She was staring into his eyes, an odd intimate look. He returned the stare, like a man bewitched.

"I would be honored to show you true Chinese cuisine," MeiLin offered. "A fine dinner where you can enjoy China and all she has to offer. Then I will take you to the market where we can arrange for supplies."

"Of course," Nate replied. He didn't look away. His voice was soft, gentle, charming. His head was tilted slightly to the side.

I was annoyed to realize the tone he used was not exclusively for me.

CHAPTER FIVE

THERE WAS NO SPACE for me to walk alongside them, so I was forced to walk behind Nate and MeiLin as she told him about the buildings, and the beautiful trees and small gardens of flowers that decorated the fronts of the buildings. Many of them had small planters. Where in London the buildings were right on the cobblestone streets, nearly upon the gutters or the cobbles themselves, these buildings were set back from the streets, leaving spaces for a bit of greenery and fine, carved, wooden barriers or statues depicting various animals or shapes delicately carved and colorfully painted in mostly reds and golds and black.

The city spread out further than I could see, yet the sky above was clear and blue. It was so different than London. There was no hint of dreary gray or a sky burned by constant coal fires.

A woman in grass-green robes and a blue sash was driving an ox and cart full of cages with large white ducks, quacking and flapping. In the back of the cart, an aged man with a white mustache was smoking a pipe and sitting by a girl who cuddled a piglet. A young boy trotted along behind with a monster on a rope; it may have been some sort of pig but it was black and covered in dark spiky hair and had deep wrinkles like a boarhound. The pig-monster snuffled and snorted as it ambled along, its round nose *huffing* the ground.

Nate missed all of this.

"The world in the West calls Beijing 'Peking.'" MeiLin said leading us to a small building off the main road. "It is an unfortunate circumstance of not sharing a written language." She pushed open a door revealing a room, but it was a room unlike anything I had ever seen before.

The pillars were bright red, a scarlet that even the richest dyes would be hard pressed to match. Behind the carved wooden door sat a woman on a bench dressed in violet and green silks. She bowed to MeiLin and they rapidly exchanged something in Mandarin. MeiLin motioned to us, then turned and bowed, more to Nate than to me. I already disliked the way she stared at him just a little too long, her beautiful long eyelashes fluttering just for him, smiling and blushing prettily when she caught his eye and regaling him with tales of the language and architecture.

"The one benefit is we have created local dishes that are pleasing to the Western palate, but which also maintain the mystery of China. I thought you would like to try our Peking duck."

"Peeking duck?" Nate gave a wide grin. "What does it peek from?"

I smiled. "The bushes. No doubt I would be in hiding if people were eating me." Nate and I shared a laugh.

MeiLin gave me a look, clearly she didn't appreciate my humor. "Not peeking, Peking. China has many things that do not translate properly for the West. It is a famous dish here, we serve it to scholars and nobles alike." Then she turned away from me to speak to Nate. "I thought you might enjoy a taste of China. A sample of the riches China has to offer." She gazed at him through heavy-lidded eyes.

I couldn't draw a breath deep enough, she was clearly presenting Nate with more than what just *China* had to offer.

"China is beautiful. But if it is all the same, our home is England and when we are finished here, Vivian and I are to be married." He opened the door for MeiLin and myself.

My annoyance instantly melted away. I had never seen a place like this. The wooden panels, with their intricate carvings, were merely acting like the inner wall for the hallway we were in. Though the building itself seemed a box—it was slightly wider in the top with beautiful sloping slate roofs that curved upwards at the edges, all the buildings shared the same look. I expected for them to be dark and boxy inside, as well, but nothing could be further from the truth. Beyond MeiLin stood large, carved wooden panels that let in more light than the room behind them should have possessed.

We stood on a walkway made of silky, polished wood, but the center of the building stood open to the air, letting in the bright sunlight to illuminate the fine garden, throwing tendrils of light across everything, like fingers yearning to touch every corner. In the center, a pond had been formed with fine ceramic tiles, like the paintings of an ancient Roman bath, in beautiful aqua, cream, and peach. Huge orange and black and white fish danced beneath waters so clear I doubted the water was there at all. I looked up, realizing belatedly that my mouth was open. The clever use of silver mirrors made it as bright as our open garden back home, even though the high wooden walls should have blocked most of the light unless it was high noon. Beautiful, bright embroidered panels covered the walls, and were done in a style that utilized minimal detail to present sophisticated beauty. I could think of several London who that could take a lesson from minimalist approach.

One wall was adorned with a mountain covered in cherry trees in bloom and a beautiful red pagoda. The panel on the opposite wall had a dragon—not the style from storybooks I saw as a child—but a dragon without wings shaped like a giant serpent with four clawed feet, a long sweeping mustache, and a crest flowing from its forehead down its neck and shoulders. It was the type of dragon we had been sent to find. And what a noble beast it was. This dragon lay guarding a stack of books, handing a man dressed in robes holding a scroll, a quill pen and a scale shaped like a shield.

We sat at a low table without chairs, just thin embroidered cushions that padded the wooden floor. MeiLin spoke swiftly. All the words ran together in a restless tangle of foreign syllables. The air smelled rich and spicy, and even the company couldn't turn my stomach.

A man dressed in beautiful dark blue robes and a red apron brought us a roast duck, skinnier than a turkey but nearly as long as the serving dish. He made a great show of slicing the crispy, fried skin and dipping it into sugar and a fragrant garlic sauce. I had never had anything so delicious in my life—slightly smoky and spicy sweet. If all dinners were served this way in China I would have to hire a tailor to alter my wardrobe before long.

Unlike fine meals back home, here conversation was discouraged. We were expected to quietly enjoy the show as after the skin was served, the chef carefully carved the meat and served it rolled in little flat cakes with vegetables and a fragrant sauce made of sweet plums with a delightful sour pickle bite. MeiLin carefully served Nate from a flat dish, maintaining his tumbler of tea and generally making sure he wanted for nothing. A woman in pink and green silks assisted the man in the apron with the plating, dishing out steamed vegetables in bright colors and rolls of formed fish loaves with swirls of color floating in broth.

It was then I noticed the plates that we were served from were different. MeiLin was serving him from one dish, carefully dishing up pieces with the utmost care and presentation. The other woman served me from another dish.

"You must try this." I offered Nate a piece from my plate.

MeiLin interrupted me. "No. That is rude here. Just as one does not shovel food into their mouth with a fork, one does not offer food off plates. It is an insult to our gracious hosts."

I nodded, feeling foolish. I was being silly, there was nothing nefarious going on here. China was merely a society like most others, where men were more valued. Women were ornamental. But as I looked around I noticed there were more and more ornamental creatures around and less important ones. Where were all the men?

The courtyard was almost empty now, and from the bright light of the central square I had trouble seeing into the covered walkway bordering where we were eating. I turned on my cushion, where *were* all the men?

My breath grew short. When we entered there had been several tables of men, all native oriental men, playing a board game with black and white ceramic disks and enjoying dinner. There had been tables of men enjoying dinners much like ours and sipping tea served out of beautiful but frighteningly hot cast iron pots. People ate and left, the rational side of my mind argued, but something else made me feel like someone had painted a target on my back, right between my shoulder blades. I swallowed back a harsh feeling rising from my stomach.

"Nate." I turned to him. We should return to the Viridian for the night.

MeiLin had her hand on Nate's arm.

My eyes ached. There was something wrong with them. I raised my hand but it felt weak and shaky. Maybe it was from reading too many people at the marina. But then the light caught MeiLin's eyes. They had been hazel, but in this light they were some green-gold, her face pale, her hair brighter, almost ruddy, her nose and chin dainty and pointed.

"Hmm?" He was attentively listening to MeiLin as she spoke to him in a low voice.

"Nate!" I said, this time sharper, more insistent.

He turned to face me, the look on his face turning from enjoyment to worry.

MeiLin gave me a look that could curdle milk. "Excuse me, please. I must attend to the accommodations."

Harm, she meant us harm, I could see a tarot card just beyond my natural sight as though it was glowing in the air before us, existing both beyond and alongside everything else. *The Devil* glowered at me. *The Devil*, the master of deceit. I generally hate drawing this card in a reading because people tend to only picture lovers enslaved by the Prince of All Evil. I always caution them to look at the image beyond the shock at seeing the Devil leering up at them from the cards; to see more than what they first see. The chains binding both the man and woman hang loosely on their necks, they are enslaved by themselves only. Learning to read Tarot from Mama also taught me to read first with my heart, then with my head. My heart suddenly froze in my chest and the image before my eyes changed, the Devil laughed and pulled the chains tightly, dragging the man and woman to their knees.

We were enslaved by ourselves—we allowed ourselves to be misled. MeiLin passed quickly into the shadowed overhang.

My breath felt cold. "Nate, something is wrong here," I whispered.

Nate patted my hand. "I know you feel that way but everything is fine. MeiLin is setting us up with accommodations that will be much more affordable. She told me the English hotels cheat the English tourists."

"Nate, listen to me. Where is everyone?" I turned. Aside from the woman serving us we were alone in the courtyard. She must not understand English. She finished the little rolled up morsel of food she was preparing for me and sat back with her head bowed.

There were women milling about, moving around on tiny slippered feet in dresses and robes. Nate seemed to notice this for the first time. He tipped his head back slightly and sniffed the air. I was grateful he seemed to retain some of Ranger's senses when he was wearing his Nate-skin. He brought my plate to his nose and carefully picked the roll apart.

"Why do they smell different?" He demanded of the woman.

"She doesn't speak English," I admonished.

A woman's voice said from the shadows. "You should not be here." I couldn't tell if she was addressing him or me or both. She did speak English. It was a slow, stupid thought.

I blinked hard. The light reflected from the mirrors were too bright. All I wanted to do was retire to bed. My head was so heavy; all I wanted to do was sleep.

"You are not welcome here," she said again.

"What did you give her?" Nate demanded, grabbing ahold of the woman who sat before us. She hadn't spoken, she merely sat limp in his fist. Was she the one who had addressed us?

Nate shook the woman violently, her long black hair whipping back and forth. "MeiLin!" Nate screamed.

"You leave now." The chef pulled the serving woman from Nate's hands and stood between them. The chef had been butchering meat. His blue tunic was dark with blood. Was it blood? I was having a hard time focusing.

It dripped from the his knife and hands and pooled on the floor, larger and larger, flowing into the pillows around him and darkening Nate's boots, then slowly climbing up his legs like a sentient wave intent on strangling him.

"Nate," I whispered. I could barely lift my head. "I think something is wrong."

I felt him seize my wrist. He wrenched my arm, dragging me to my feet, leaning me against a reassuring bulk. I stumbled. "Where is MeiLin?" My voice sounded funny, as if it were not my own.

Cards, which card was appropriate now? *The Fool?* New Beginnings, naïvety; no *the Fool* had a staff but wasn't bound to one and he had a hound at his heels, this fool did not. No dog. Where was my dog? I mean my Ranger. I mean my Nate. Was he my dog or my man? Did it matter now? He was both and more.

The Fool, or whoever's card was hovering before me, the one in this picture, his hair stood out on end. I tried to turn my head, maybe I was seeing it wrong.

"What are you doing?" Nate said. His skin had gone slick and clammy under my hands. "Why are you turning upside down?"

"I'm trying to see." Why was he asking at a time like this?

The card, it might be *The Hanged Man.* But if so he was upside down.

Why in the world would I be sent a card upside down? "Nate? Why would I be presented with a card that is upside down?"

"What?" He was panting now, we shifted to one side and I slipped off his shoulder onto the dirt. We were on cushions a moment ago and *if* Nate knocked me over he had some explaining to do. I waved my hands in front of my face, trying to dismiss the card like a swarm of bothersome gnats. At least I hadn't fallen far.

I heard scratching and scrabbling, like people scuffling in the sand, and the horrible echoey sound of flesh connecting with flesh. Was someone fighting? Why was it so hard to tell?

Something important was happening but I couldn't seem to grasp it. It was worse than being drunk, it was deeper and more painful, but I felt somewhat insulated from it, like I had been wrapped in cotton then battered with a rug paddle. Wait! Not upside down, the card was in reverse.

The Hanged Man!

"Nate, it's *The Hanged Man!*" I cried triumphantly.

Properly positioned, *The Hanged Man* represents choosing to let go. Sacrificing to the greater self for knowledge, suspending disbelief to learn.

"You foreigners are under arrest!" A man shouted. I couldn't see him, that would involve being able to see past t*he Hanged Man*.

I heard Nate snarl, more the snarl of Ranger than his own manly warrior sounds. He was transfiguring. And I heard a lot of scuffling. Well, at least we wouldn't be taken without a fight.

I heard grunts of pain, snarls, and under it all, rapid Chinese flowing from the mouths of our attackers, or the observers, or maybe law enforcement; heck, probably all three. Nate and his transfiguring condition must be an oddity, even here in China, a land that decorates with monsters trapped somewhere between creatures and men. I wondered if they had canithropes of their own here. Well, maybe not men bound to their own dogs, but men who could transfigure into other beasts. A man who could turn into a dog is a canithrope. A man who can turn into an animal is a therionthrope, a wolf would be a lycanthrope. What would a bird be? A man with wings and a bird beak? I laughed—now that would be a sight.

A dark shape stood over me, protecting me, guarding me. Weapons flashed from all sides and then everything faded into a white haze.

CHAPTER SIX

A DRIP HIT my head. I flinched and tried to wipe away the water. My arm flopped over my head disjointedly, like it wasn't connected to my body, more like a limp fish thrown at me. I wiped my forehead. The water smelled metallic and oily at the same time. Where was I?

I rolled over, which was a mistake. My stomach seized horribly and I vomited up all the wonderful roast duck.

"Vivian?"

I couldn't see Nate but I could hear him. I managed to get both arms under me and pushed myself up. My gut rumbled alarmingly. I had eaten a dragon. It felt like a twisting, writhing worm was clawing its way through my body, desperate to get free.

"Vivian!" Nate shouted at me. I wished he would be quiet for a moment; the dragon was taking all my concentration.

Then I vomited again. I lay wearily in my pile of sick, unable to move. I felt hot tears of shame welling up within me and I was unable to help myself. To add insult to injury, I soiled myself as well.

"Vivian!" He was being kept from me. For the moment, I was glad. I was dizzy, just so dizzy. All I wanted to do was close my eyes and sleep.

My hand moved of its own volition and reached out for him. Directly beside me was a set of bars, large enough that I could barely close my hand around them. They were slimy and slick under my hand, and I found it comforting that I could discern beneath the slime that the metal was rough and pitted. The texture gave me something concrete to cling to.

I would sleep, I told myself. After a rest I could figure out exactly where I was and what could be done.

A bone-rattling shudder came from the floor I was resting on.

I caught a glimpse of *Strength* as I faded away; a man holding the jaws of a fearsome beast; calming it and making it feel peace. But the beast under the man's careful hand transformed from a lion to a large caramel-colored dog with prick ears that crouched on hind legs, like something caught between man and dog. Not a man or a dog. It was my canithrope.

The floor I was lying on shuddered again and again.

$$SOS$$

A voice cut through the haze "… not friendly to Westerners."

"… tourists…"

"Did you see…"

The voices cut through me again and again. I was being moved and then stripped of my clothing. If it had been food poisoning I should be running a fever now and I would have chills. When the air touched my naked body it was a lover's caress with gentle fingers. I pretended it was Nate, it was his strong hands I had seen skillfully holding the lion at bay.

But no, the touch had gone cold. I called out to him but he didn't answer me. I was in purgatory, and I was alone with nothing but the wracking pain to comfort me.

$$SOS$$

I was unsure how to count time as passing, I heard voices but it seemed I had lost the ability to understand any language now. Somewhere in the back of my mind I could see a card, *The Star*. Have hope. It burned into my vision. I suppose it made sense, when the pictorials of the tarot appeared on my flesh, *The Star* was always over my eye. Hope. The thought burned brightly, and I prayed it was my guide to lead me out of the desert of despair and back to the earth where Nate waited for me.

"You were most likely poisoned with white arsenic," a voice said. "You need to swallow this."

A vile and gritty potion was forced between my lips. I tried to fight back, but the hands were too strong. I could either drink or I could drown. The mixture was smoky, though I couldn't tell if I was associating smoky with the taste or the smell. After it went down into my stomach it quickly came back up, ripping me raw as it did so.

Someone gently patted my back and handed me a tumbler. I had no presence of mind to object, so I drank. This was chalky but soothing to my throat, and at least sat comfortably in my stomach like I had been swaddled in soft woolen batting. It was slowly dragging me into a drugged fog. So long as I was not vomiting or consumed with horrific cramps, tremors, or chills and I could find some form of repose, I was willing to accept my fate. I was too tired to fight it anymore.

"Rest now."

§§§

Time passed for me in a swirl of color. A strange man kept kneeling over me, pressing warm cups against my lips, sometimes honey-water, often foul peppery liquids. The first time I woke well enough to take in my surroundings, I was lying on a thick padded mat on the floor, covered with a blanket. There was a lean, blue mass sitting to one side smelling of medicine and black pepper. When my vision cleared, I realized it was a man, bald—but too young to be naturally bald—with a long, braided black queue of hair, lean and tall, and who was paying me no attention as he sat with his eyes closed, deep in thought.

He wore sapphire robes embroidered with silver cranes, and silver collar and cuffs. His hands were folded into his bell sleeves. The room was warm, kept so with a brazier. A long wall had large windows covered with thin parchment paper that let a golden glow into the room. It allowed enough light to illuminate ink diagrams of human beings sporting enough needles in their skins to resemble hedgehogs. Each site was carefully annotated with several words in the beautiful flowery Chinese writing.

The wall opposite from where I lay was decorated with several beautiful paintings, men and woman richly depicted who could only be royals or nobles. One painting was twelve different animals dressed as people; dragons, roosters, pigs, oxen and dogs and cats and rats and a few animals I could not identify from this angle. But the most interesting painting by far was of an archer shooting a red bow into one of those Chinese dragons, the type with a body like a snake with four legs and no wings. This serpent dragon had four horns and four eyes and a beard and mustache rearing up on its rear legs, eyes narrowed with hatred, snarling and spitting flame. The side of the dragon was patchy and mottled, and painted so on purpose. There was no mistake it—this dragon was a beast driven mad.

The rest of his walls were covered with shelves of jars and racks of herbs, either bundled or in various stages of being dried. I knew the den of a healer when I saw one. Perhaps that instant recognition of something familiar kept me from being frightened.

I tried to sit up and realized how weak I was. I also realized I was naked under my blanket.

"If you insist upon rising, I will call my servant to attend you," he said.

Before I could speak, a young woman appeared at my side, gracefully kneeling with her feet tucked beneath her. She carefully helped raise me to a sitting position. From seemingly out of nowhere she produced a clear broth in a shallow bowl, slightly salty, with an onion flavor. A bit of mushroom cut so thin I could see through it floated with a curl of green onion. I carefully sipped it, thankful for its delicate flavor that seemed more an aroma than an actual taste. I was even more grateful to not be vomiting it up all over my host and his clean white blankets.

The woman kept her eyes low, refusing to look directly at me. Her hair was artfully styled into two small bobs at the top of her head then gathered at the nape of her neck into one queue that had been brushed to a blue-black sheen. She wore no makeup or jewelry, only a gray, long-sleeved gown and what looked to be a short-sleeved gown belted over the top, with the most amazing high collar, offset, and fastened with covered buttons. If merely his servant, she was a house servant and treated well. Her hands were red and dry from repeated washings and she looked strong, at least in contrast to my weakened state. She had the same slight build as most women here, and she did not look starved nor did she carry the look of one who was often beaten by a cruel master.

I forced myself to address my host. "Where is my Nate?"

He did not turn, "You should rest."

"I have no desire to rest." I said, "I am quite well, thank you. I have to find my fiancé as soon as possible." I realized my lack of clothing would hinder that, but I would crawl naked out upon the street if it came to that. "However, I must beg your indulgence, I seem to have misplaced my clothes and I need to send for my things. I am staying at the Viridian. I will be sure to pay you for your most thorough doctoring."

"Pay?" My savior looked up at that with a slight grin. "Forgive me. We have not been properly introduced." He motioned to his servant.

"You are in the presence of Master Healer, Wei Huan. He serves the people of the Middle Kingdom, the Mandate of Heaven and the Empress Dowager." She took the empty bowl from me with both hands.

"Ah, yes, Master Wei Huan, thank you so much for treating me. I shall make sure you are—"

"You do not understand." She tried again, "You do not pay him. Master Huan serves those in need. If he wished payment he would have had you taken to another Master and payment would have been negotiated before services were rendered."

"Then, you have my humblest thanks," I said, dipping my head. "My father often does the same, there are too many poor souls who need good care and simply cannot afford it. I dare say it is the duty of those who can help those in need to assist those in need. It is called Christian charity, but I rather think it is kindness. Of course, it nearly put us in the workhouses more times than I care to think on—" I realized I was prattling on and flushed bright red. Master Huan was staring at me much as a cat watches a mouse-hole. I closed my mouth with a snap.

"Please continue," he said with a small wave of his arm. "Your father treats the sick and wounded?"

"My father is an accomplished apothecary. He trained me. Some," I added modestly. "Herbalism and wound care and such, much like here. Well, I mean he stitches wounds and mixes medicines and sets broken bones and my mother is a midwife. Well, she doesn't do much of that anymore. In London, England, across the sea, well, across many seas." What was wrong with me? I was sounding like a young girl fresh at lessons rather than an adventuress or a lady of means, but apparently that wasn't going to stop me today. "I have never seen anything like this, though." I motioned to his figures of men sprouting needles. "This is fascinating."

"I am pleased to find you so intrigued." He smiled.

"You are the royal healer?" I asked

"I am." He gave the briefest of bows.

"I am sorry to hear of the Prince's passing."

"The prince's passing?"

"Forgive me, Master Huan." I said softly, "In London. We were told that Prince Qixiang contracted small pox and he passed and it was the great duty and sorrow of The Empress to regain the throne." I immediately felt like I was going to be sick again. "I only mentioned it because Queen Victoria lost her beloved Albert. She rules though deep in mourning. It is a horrible burden but one great rulers must bear."

"Yes, Prince Qixiang was lost. It was a great sorrow to us all." Master Huan did not smile. "I shall have Chen Xia bring your effects."

I immediately hated myself, Papa always took it as a personal failing when a patient died in his care. I was still not myself that I could be so callous. Master Huan turned and left me in the room. I realized I was completely alone. Chen Xia had also left me to my own devices, at least for now. However, I did not have long to enjoy the art. Chen Xia soon returned with my gown held over her arm and my boots in hand.

My dress had been expertly cleaned and pressed with hot irons so perfectly that for a moment I thought I might have imagined being sick all over my gown. Chen Xia helped me dress, and if she was at all confounded by my English dress, she did not show it.

"Now that you are strong enough, you are to be brought to the Empress Dowager. Your presence has been demanded. She planned to expel you from China, but someone interceded on your behalf and begged an audience so you could explain your presence in China. I have arranged for you to meet with your companion first," Wei Huan said.

"As for where he is," the healer continued, "he has been imprisoned. Fighting in the streets in illegal, no matter the cause. I am fairly confidant no serious harm has befallen him. Since I am one of her royal physicians I am sure that though they are aware of his peculiarity, they have not attempted to separate him from the demons that plague his soul without my guidance."

I took that to mean they had not tried to damage him because of his transfiguration powers, they were merely keeping him under lock and key. It was a cold comfort. He would hate it with every part of him, and I could sympathize. The idea of him being trapped in a jail cell in a land where he couldn't speak the language surrounded by people unsympathetic to Englishmen, and not knowing my fate must be driving him mad. And they knew he was a canithrope. My heart ached for him.

I needed to see Nate right away. I struggled to stand. Huan's assistant aided me.

"We shall leave as soon as we finish our meal." Wei Huan said evenly.

I opened my mouth to protest, but I realized that events moved at their own pace within Master Huan's home. I sat down on a cushion and did my best not to look like I was about to leap out of my skin while, inside, my mind paced miles in my haste to get to him.

§§§

The prison was a squat stone building with small, metal-framed windows, and a metal-framed door. At first, I worried that I had been brought to the wrong place, it was nothing like any jail I had seen before. The tight-fitting bricks were stacked so the mortar was almost invisible. The brick was kept in impeccable shape, carefully scrubbed and maintained, the walkway was swept and clean. There was no sign that labeled the building, no lion-dogs that crouched by the door.

Every other place, no matter how humble, was decorated with their beautiful writing of pictures and lines. Many homes had carefully carved wooden emblems or painted signs. Paper lanterns adorned doorways, flowers welcomed people to homes or shops; many of the buildings of this size had stone carvings of the exotic lion-dogs, frogs, birds, and other animals, real and imagined.

What would have been a building of class and simplicity in London was void of all that made a building a place of joy and humanity here in Beijing. In China, this was a place of misery, a place without humanity, a place where lost men would be kept. Chen Xai brought me to the prison where she and Master Huan swore Nate was held. She opened the door of Master Huan's private carriage and bid me good day.

The warden was expecting me. He stood when I entered the front room of the prison. He wore a black and red robe and had been kneeling at a small table over a book. "You must be Vivian Harper." It was not a question.

"I am." I raised my chin. "I am here for Nathaniel Valentine."

"Yes." He turned slightly toward the large, ironbound door behind him. It was made of heavy wood covered with a rich, dark stain. The door itself was set in a stout metal frame. "He caused quite a disruption."

I thought I had imagined the floor and the walls rumbling all around me. "I suppose he did."

The warden stared at me for a long moment. "I am pleased to see you have made a recovery. Master Huan took a particular interest in your care, and that of Mr. Valentine."

"Yes, I have been informed that we are to speak to the Empress Dowager personally." I said. My head was throbbing again.

"I will have him brought up immediately." The warden turned to the door and rapped twice. "Interestingly, he made no move to fight us any longer when I assured him your care would be provided for by the finest healer in Beijing. He asked about you every moment he could." He turned to the window looking out at the street.

I didn't know what to say to the warden. I couldn't tell if he was offering me a kindness or baiting me. Four coins—the wonderful Chinese coins with holes drilled through the middle. *The Four of Pentacles*, he was a man, safe and stable. He was conservative. He would give nothing up. He was probably not baiting me. His position in life was too important to him. He would not lie to me, but he would not betray anything either. He would be honest and hard working.

"What will happen when we meet with her?" I asked quietly.

"The Empress Dowager Cixi expressed a deep interest in a man able to change his form. She was less interested in any battles that may have occurred. Despite our deep concern and interest, we have been forbidden to explore this further until she has a chance to speak with him. I suspect that if she continues to have an interest in him, Master Huan will be employed to further discuss his condition."

The ironbound door opened. My Nate came in, followed by two men in red tabards and dark trousers and sleeves. They wore swords. Nate was unarmed, but I knew that did not mean he was not deadly.

His clothes were dirty and worn. He had not changed. He had not slept well. He wore deep hollows beneath his eyes, his warm caramel hair was darker as a beard and he seemed somewhat paler and leaner. He was a man in desperate need of a few good meals and rest in the sun. I longed to rush to him and press my forehead to his, to feel him next to me, but I was afraid that if I moved too quickly it would galvanize his guards into violent and sudden motion. We had spent somewhere between ten days and two weeks separated. Though I was quite weak from our ordeal, I was clearly not the only one who suffered from our time apart.

The warden turned to his table and pulled Nate's Gladstone bag from beneath it. "Your servant brought over your affects." He handed it to Nate.

We immediately exchanged a glance. Who had been impersonating our servant? For a moment, I thought he might mean Chen Xia. "I was informed you are to be delivered directly to the Imperial Palace. You may use my personal office to change, and I will have what you are wearing delivered directly to your hotel in the foreign quarter by messenger."

"Thank you, very much," Nate said stiffly. His eyes had not left mine.

"Until such time as you are properly washed and dressed, I will happily entertain Miss Harper."

I had no desire to be separated from him even for a moment, but I stood as stoically as I could manage and watched as Nate tucked the bag neatly under his arm and allowed a guardsman to lead him into the next room. It was like I was being torn in two and a piece of me was slowly being taken away again. But, I reasoned, if they were not intending to let us leave, they would not have given Nate supplies with which to make himself presentable.

Another man in red came in carrying a tray. The warden poured me a cup of tea from one of those beautiful cast iron pots into the painted tumblers. I clung to the tumbler. It was something hot to hang on to, and even though it lacked the refinement of a proper afternoon tea with cakes and biscuits and cream and lemon it was comforting nonetheless. I enjoyed the fragrant, slightly tangy green tea.

I closed my eyes and let my mind drift to our manor with its lush gardens and our library; to the seldom used great room and the study, the solar and the conservatory and the beautiful indoor greenhouse full of the lush green plants that could be turned into simples and cures to heal hurts.

The door opened.

And suddenly all was right in the world. This was the only thing I actually needed from back home.

Nathaniel wore a heavy burgundy serge waistcoat over a striped tick shirt, rough clothing, hardly fit to meet an Empress Dowager, but it was clean and pressed.

He had washed with heavy lye soap, lightly scented with manly pine and sandalwood but enough to burn away the stink of the prison. The soap and the razor had done a number on his face, scraping his cheeks and chin raw and red so he looked windburned.

The warden spared us a glance. "I will see your effects returned to the Viridian. My rickshaw will take you to the Imperial Palace."

And with that, we were dismissed. Since Nate was no longer being held as a criminal, the warden had no other interest in us.

Except Nate had other ideas.

"What about the people who poisoned Vivian?" Nate said. "Surely you will be pursuing a criminal investigation against them."

The warden paused but did not turn.

"I said, surely you will be pursuing a case against the people that tried to poison my fiancée and a citizen of the British Empire?" Nate demanded, louder this time.

The warden turned. "As far as we are concerned, Mr. Valentine, no crime has been committed. Your fiancée is still alive and well. If she happened to eat something that disagreed with her in a dining establishment after she was warned to remain in areas that are friendly to foreigners, then perhaps her misfortune does not lie with the people of China, but in the carelessness of her intended husband. If you cared for her wellbeing you should exercise more caution in where you take her to dine." The warden went to leave again. "You are no longer in the British Empire, Mr.

Valentine. You would do well to remember that, particularly when you meet the Empress Dowager. Now, your property will be waiting for you at the Viridian."

For a moment I feared Nate would strike him, but instead he nodded. He appeared to be agreeing but I knew him well enough to know the matter was far from over. I let him wrap his arm around me and lead me out to the front of the prison.

There was a queer carriage waiting for us. For a moment, I was sure the horse had run off, but then a man with a cone hat sprinted up and set himself between the posts where a horse would go, and offered us a hand in getting into the carriage. He then started off at a trot as if he were a pony, the driver, and footman, all rolled into one.

Just when I thought this country could not be any more peculiar, it presented me with another surprise.

CHAPTER SEVEN

THE PALACE WAS nothing like I would expect a royal palace to be. Though a beauty of marble wood and stone, gold and pottery, crystal and gleaming metal, the molding had been either cast from gold or gilded later in shapes of the serpent-shaped dragons, clouds, and phoenixes. The woodwork and pillars were painted in red with blue accents and the tops of the columns were guarded with sculptures of dragons, each reaching out with five-toed claws to touch the one across from it. It was a marvel.

Everywhere I turned, the walls were covered in silk screens painted with mountains and animals, trees that hung low with peaches or bright flowers, and beneath the trees, maids frolicked in colorful robes. We had traveled to the other side of the world and the grandeur of this place touched my heart. It was nothing like the grace and elegance of home. The dragons and phoenix that made their homes in the walls, the lion-dogs, the tigers, the cranes, the frogs, they would all be vulgar at home, but they were so enchanting here. They would all have a tale to tell. I immediately wanted the book from my satchel. England may be the home of the Barbary Lion and the Tudor rose, but China was the land of the dragon. I reached out and took Nate's hand.

Music filled the air. It was a haunting melody. Never had I heard something so beautiful, so foreign. Incense filled the room, overloading my senses with drunken calm that had nothing to do with being drugged. It was the magnificence of China. This was the China I had seen from the *Nomad*, the China I expected. We were led by guards and servants all dressed in silk and finery that whispered as people moved.

We crossed a grand entry chamber, passed through several sets of doors to the throne room. Behind the throne was a painted silk scene of a dragon dancing in and out of a cloud above a mountain that was dotted with little sprouts of green. Along the painted frame, small golden fish darted in and out of a crane's beak. Pale peaches were stacked high in black lacquered bowls resting in delicate stands on either side of the huge stone dais, giving off a fragrant bouquet, heady and sweet.

The Empress sat straight backed upon a wide, wooden throne, large enough for three men to sit. Though she was surrounded by servants and nobles and council, she was alone, regal and without equal.

Her round, stern face was painted pale with a single stripe of color upon her lower lip. She wore a soft, dark hat on her shiny black hair. Her gown was of the finest silk I had ever seen, black, embroidered with golden Chinese writing in circles, each as large as my palm, and butterflies in a rainbow of shimmering colors. The lining of her robe was yellow silk, I could see it in every carefully placed fold, every turnback. There was no careless positioning here. She sat like a statue, like a goddess on a throne, ready to be obeyed and worshiped. The black rippled every time she moved. I saw that it was textured with patterns of snakes and vines dancing around her in folds. Her hands were flat on her thighs, the last three fingers of each hand were adorned with long golden claws fitted over her fingers like the dragon sculptures on the tops of the columns; she would not be able to pick anything up on her own. A fan of coral silk sat next to her, decorated with painted white peacocks. I could not imagine she would fan herself so it must have a ceremonial purpose. Her ears were pierced and adorned with ear bobs that were made of some coral. I had seen something like it years before in a museum of oddities with a collection of shells. She watched us the way a well-fed tiger watches deer bound around on a country estate. She had to only will it, and we'd be executed. She had no master. Here was the Empress of China.

I curtsied as deeply as I was able. I waited for her to acknowledge me and let me rise. No such order came. When I finally rose of my own accord, she was still staring at us. Nate rose stiffly from his bow. The graceful acknowledgment of a social better was still foreign to him, being born to a station where he hadn't come into contact much with nobles. He always looked like one of the wind-up tin soldiers that marched and bowed. I hoped the time he spent in the warden's care didn't leave him too stiff.

"Welcome to the Imperial City," a man at her feet said in a voice that shouldn't have been so booming coming from someone of his size.

It was a cold welcome. I didn't know what to say.

"The Current Divine Mother Empress Dowager of the Great Qing Empire would like to know why you are in China." The Voice said.

"We were arrested and brought here." I said unable to stop myself. "We were simply in the wrong place at the wrong time."

Nate stared at me.

"That is not the reason you were detained." The Voice said pointedly. He turned to Nate. "You were fighting in public with several members of the *Yihequan*. They seek to purge China from outside influence. The Empress Dowager does not agree with their methods."

"The who?" Nate narrowed his eyes at The Voice

"*Yihequan*, your people call them boxers. They call themselves the most righteous and harmonious fists and the sons of China. They see themselves as protectors of the very soul of China. They seek to protect their home from foreigners. Their loyalty to this most sacred and noble of dynasties is admirable." The Voice motioned with an open hand to the room addressing the empress dowager, her court, her throne. She gave the briefest of nods. "It is an unfortunate their methods are so violent."

"We were just seeking dinner while our interpreter arranged for supplies." I said.

Empress Dowager Cixi raised her hand. It was a little motion but the bells sewn into her garments tinkled and everyone froze.

"Supplies for what purpose?" Her Voice asked.

"We are traveling," Nate said before I could answer. "My wife wishes to take a grand adventure and see the great stone warriors of China and visit Beijing and Hong Kong. She wishes to see the Great Wall."

I did not correct Nate. We were on a mission to recover an item they might not want removed from China. If I were China, I would not want a weapon of legend, able to eliminate a foe with a single blow, removed and turned over to an invader either. As awful as it was to lie to the Empress

Dowager, it was better to lie than to admit we were there to ~~steal~~ recover an artifact.

"As you were told, the Empress Dowager does not agree with the methods of *Yihequan*. It is a dangerous time to travel within our borders. We cannot be held responsible for any misfortune that befalls you. China is currently overrun with foreigners from many lands. The people are suspicious and anxious. It is not a friendly, peaceful time for the Middle Kingdom. Especially when one considers something so unnatural occurring in their presence. The less educated might assume he was a demon from across the sea sent to harm our people when less effective means have failed," the Voice said.

"But you do not disagree with their reasoning," I said. The Empress Dowager gave me a look. It was the look a pawnbroker would give a piece of jewelry to assess its worth. "You said you do not approve of their methods."

There was a small smile on the Empress Dowager's lips but she would not yet lower herself to speak to us. She left that to Her Voice. "China is overrun with Germans, Japanese, French, English, Russians—and each wishes to carve out a piece of the Middle Kingdom. When they see what China offers they are overcome, and sensibilities clouded. We find foreigners bring trouble."

"We are not here to make trouble," I said as calmly as I could manage.

The Empress gave an almost unperceivable shake of her head. The Voice stood, careful not to obstruct her view, and pulled a scroll from his wide sleeves. Her attendants were ghosts in patterned silk. No one spoke. Her guards, in their beautiful livery, were painted statues of deadly armor and steel.

"Why are you here?" Empress Cixi spoke. Her voice was quiet, and I could tell it had once possessed a musical quality but was now somewhat flat.

The stillness of the room was unnerving. I took a deep breath. "To see the Wall—"

"Do not lie," the Voice warned. "China is currently plagued by traders, mercenaries, missionaries, industrialists, and business men. But it is also a place where a person could secure a powerful contact in the Court of the Empress were he or she daring."

"What do you mean 'daring'?" Nate asked. He had caught the scent of a challenge and was unable to release it, like a hound after foxes, a trait he shared with most males. I was just hoping to get out of there in a way that did not include being returned to a jail cell. Since we were not officially members of the Explorer's Society I doubted they would intercede on our behalf.

The Empress Dowager shifted in her seat, rising slightly higher on her cushioned throne.

"Why are you here?" the Voice demanded impatiently. "The Current Divine Mother Empress Dowager of the Great Qing Empire is aware you are no mere man. Are you here to be of service or for adventure?"

"For adventure," Nate said, proudly squaring his shoulders and raising his chin.

There was a moment where I could taste my pounding heart. Something very dangerous had happened or was about to happen. I could not breathe. Then, just as suddenly, whatever challenge the Empress Dowager had subtly issued, Nate had inadvertently, and thankfully, left it unanswered. If he knew, I'm sure he would have been crushed.

I could not be happier.

The Voice considered the matter closed. "The Empress Dowager hopes you find China to your liking but we urge you to use care. This is an unfortunate time for"—he paused searching for a word—"a holiday." He made a note in his scroll. "The Empress Dowager would like to remind you that while you are in China you would be wise to remain in areas sympathetic to foreigners. If you are unsure, please hire a suitable guide. The Imperial Court is not responsible for your safety."

Nate glanced at me, glad we were not to be returned to a cell. I wasn't fooled for a moment. Someone who spoke English as well as the Voice of the Empress Dowager Cixi did, would not have had to search for "holiday." He was baiting us. The Current Divine Mother Empress Dowager of the Great Qing Empire wished to use Nate and me, and I had no desire to know what for. We needed to get out of there and turn our attention to the relative safety of retrieving an arrow from the long dead corpse of a dragon rather than tangle with a live one that sat on a golden throne beside dishes of peaches and issued veiled challenges.

§§§

The livery of the guards were banners leading us back to the relative safety of the courtyard outside of Empress Dowager Cixi's presence. I breathed much easier when her heavy doors were closed behind us, and with them her unspoken offer.

MeiLin was waiting for us outside of the palace. There was our guide, now if only we could find a suitable one as we had been advised. Our escort handed Nate back his seax blade and his revolver.

"Did you know they were going to poison her?" Nate demanded, stowing his weaponry in tight, angry motions.

"I thought it possible," she said smoothly. "You clearly are the stronger of the two, if they wished one of us harm I am glad you were protected from the poison. We can move your companion. She and I would not be able to move you as easily."

"She will be my wife!" Nate snapped. "You cannot just use her as bait to see what cafés are poisoning westerners and which are not!"

"I am sorry to have angered you," she whispered, her eyes averted. "I have acted as a poor guide. Since it is all I have, I offer myself to you to do with as you see fit." MeiLin knelt before him, collapsing into a neat bow on the busy street.

Nate's anger melted away as he tried to make sense of this. The rest of the people on the street didn't take a second glance, just moved around us as though this was commonplace. He blushed furiously. "Get up."

"No, I have brought dishonor to my name and my trade." She limply resisted his attempts to haul her to her feet. Then suddenly, she accepted his help and her hand was on his forearm.

I caught a warning flash, too quick to tell which card, but my attention was focused. Her hand was wrapped around his wrist and, from my angle, her fingers were impossibly long. I was too far away to push her hands from him. They locked eyes, and for a brief second the light caught hers and they became amber-gold, the color of dark honey. She blinked and looked away, a coquettish look on her face. Nate blinked too and steadied himself, his chest expanding with a deep breath. She turned. I pretended not to have seen it. She was doing something to him. Whatever it was, it was subtle, something Nate didn't realize was happening. It was no accident that I was poisoned in Beijing. MeiLin wanted Nate, or some aspect of him, for herself. And I was going to find out what.

"Please, get up," Nate implored, completely at a loss.

"And to you, I offer my humblest apologies," MeiLin said, raising her eyes to me.

Caught off guard, I stared at her. I longed to slap her face and fire her on the spot, but the fact remained I did not speak Chinese and we needed a guide. I was sure she was sorry, sorry her plan to kill me hadn't succeeded. Then she would have had Nate all to herself.

She spoke quietly. "You were arrested for disturbing the peace. I arranged for you to be able to plead your case directly to the Empress. That, at least ensured you would be treated well within the prison. I arranged for your possessions to be returned to your hotel. The hotel is managing your credit."

"How?" I demanded, my eyes narrowing. Servants were rarely that dedicated without reason. I was sure I knew her reason all too well.

Nate was delighted. "Never mind how. That is something that we are truly grateful for. Right, Vivian?"

"What?" Never mind how? Yes, I minded very much how! Just how did an interpreter arrange for two foreigners to speak before an Empress? I took a deep breath. I knew how, she made sure the right people either saw Nate transfigure or reported to the Empress Dowager that he could transfigure. Cixi had issued a challenge to Nate. If he was willing to be of service he could have made a powerful friend of the Chinese Royal house. Cixi wanted the arrow, or something else that was beyond her reach.

I thought of the crude diagram of the four trine temples where the key or pieces of the key were supposedly hidden. If the Explorer's Society knew about them, then surely the Chinese people knew about them, too. I wanted to return to the hotel to rest, and time to look over the book and notes.

MeiLin may have fooled Nate with her humble act of offering her own life to him, but I was not fooled in the slightest. I opened my mouth to protest, but Nate's tight hold on my hand stopped me.

"If MeiLin had not intervened you may have died. I thought you were going to die. I was about to tear the bars from the cells to get to you. Then that healer came and took you away—" He stopped, stumbling on the words. He put his arms around me and squeezed me tight. "I thought I was going to lose you." He whispered to me.

It made sense now, the only way he would have been able to get to me was to break down the bars. He had transfigured, his massive strength in the hybrid form is what shook the floor. He showed everyone our secret to try to protect me. They could have killed him for that. I imagined them drawing and quartering him in the square, seeing him not as a man but as a monster. I set my head against his shoulder to quiet the little moths in my brain. It was only now that I realized how badly I needed him near me.

"How was it to speak to the Empress Dowager?" MeiLin's voice was midge flies spoiling my lemon squash in a fine garden party. I wished she would just go away so I could have one moment alone with my Nate.

"Why is she the Empress Dowager?" Moving through class circles taught me that royalty and nobility was nothing if not specific with titles.

"Her son was the Tongzhi Emperor. When he died, last year she reluctantly resumed her rule as she had done before he came of age. His unborn child will be the next Emperor, and until her grandson comes of age, she will rule in his place."

"Why would his mother, the Tongzhi Emperor's wife, not rule for her son?" I asked out loud without really thinking.

"Why would any woman willing surrender a position of power?" MeiLin asked me in the slow deliberate tone one used with simpletons.

I immediately felt foolish. Queen Victoria was Queen, and after her King died there was no talk of her abdicating the throne, she was still a competent ruler, just as capable as any man. Her heart ached for her lost love but she was a beloved queen. Why, that was one of the benefits to living in such a modern age. I could not fault an Empress Dowager for not wanting to give up her throne just because her son died.

"The Empress had a man speaking for her," I said, returning hastily to the matter at hand. "We did not have to plead our case only explain our business in China."

"Of course she did; Empress Dowager Cixi would never lower herself to speak directly to someone so low born."

"Actually, she did speak to us," I said, enjoying the surprised look on MeiLin's face.

"What did she say?" she demanded.

This time, even Nate caught her dramatic shift in tone and glanced at her peculiarly as he answered, "She asked us directly why we were in China."

"What did you tell her?" MeiLin asked, "Certainly not the truth?"

"That we were looking for a long dead dragon and the arrow that shot it? No." Nate scoffed.

"At first, we told her we were on holiday," I explained.

"At first?" MeiLin pressed.

"She kept asking if we were here to be of service to someone or for adventure," Nate said.

MeiLin turned. "She asked if you were here to be of service?"

"Yes, after she said that a man or woman willing to be daring could make a powerful friend."

"The Empress Dowager is looking to hire a foreign agent then," MeiLin concluded.

"Whatever for?" I said. "Surely she could have anything she wishes." I really didn't want Nate starting to wonder what sort of exciting trouble he could have gotten himself into.

"If she is asking foreigners is must be something she doesn't wish to be connected to," MeiLin said patiently.

"A crime probably," Nate concluded. "If a foreigner commits a crime she can use it to fuel the rebellion that Mr. Langston was worried about."

"And we all know rebellion is a breeding ground for wars," I said, happy he was speaking to me alone this time.

"A rebellion is a wonderful way to hide all sorts of things in plain sight," MeiLin said evenly. "If you two wish to complete your task then I suggest you obtain your supplies. If you wish my help, I humbly request you inform me of your intent in China."

There was nothing humble about MeiLin. If she could manipulate, then I could, too. I had practiced on the best London had to offer, upper-class ladies trying to secure wealthy husbands. She had me poisoned and was manipulating Nate with what I suspected was magic. I was quite keen on regaining the upper hand.

"Well then, MeiLin, you will first have to lead us to the Viridian where our belongings have been waiting. We will not be transferring our accommodation no matter your recommendation. I have had my fill of the local color and I find that I must change my clothes. I will only discuss our future need for guide services over a proper *English* tea."

CHAPTER EIGHT

THE VIRIDIAN WAS an island of comfort in a sea of unfamiliar waters. Here a woman was treated properly: a man stood when she entered a room, she was seated at a table with chairs to eat, and could enjoy pastries and teas. The phonograph in the corner of the lobby played the beautiful compositions of Balfe and Braham and Field.

More importantly, if MeiLin truly believed I was a meek lady and unable to fend for myself, then here was a place where I could regroup and look over my research without her interference. I opened *Concerning Myth and Legend in China* and spread the papers out on the table. The four trines of the lunisolar calendar were twelve symbols divided equally in a circle. Each trine was four symbols. Each symbol was an animal. I squinted at the book where there was a list of animals: rat, ox, tiger, snake, rooster, rabbit, horse, goat, monkey, pig, dog, and dragon. Each trine temple was watched over by monks.

The circle was divided into four little quarters, a square inside a circle and each connected to the others; an X inside a square inside a circle. The dragon's grave could be at one of these temples, or maybe between them all at the X. Five sites to check. Though, someone else might have gotten to it first. A handwritten note had been added:

The key to accessing the final resting place of the dragon may yet be found in China. Further investigation is required. Royal family needs to be consulted. Tread lightly.

Unless someone else beat us to the dragon.

The Empress Dowager wanted powerful friends willing to serve her and to bring her what she desired. And what more could an Empress desire than a weapon that would rid her of foes intent on carving her nation up into pieces like a great tart. She needed someone to do what her own people couldn't do. Or wouldn't do. Either way, I suspected she would not be willing to assist us in this matter now.

Dragons are creatures of great nobility and power. They are creatures of balance and are immortal to the touch of all but a God. Though several dragons have fallen in the times of man, their gravesites are considered sacred and never shared with naturalists or scholars. They are a part of the land, they are a part of the people. Their very bones belong to the land. They are a part of the water and the sky. For as long as the people raise their eyes to the heavens and give praise to all that has come before, the sacred dragons will look after them.

My tea had gone cold. I sat back and sipped it anyway. The Empress Dowager knew where the trine temples would be. She would know they pointed to the grave of a dragon. The thought kept moving through my mind. We needed to get the arrow out of China before someone else did. Dragons were creatures of balance, and the idea of a lunisolar calendar where the sun and moon moved together to create a cycle of birth and death, and for farming and charting all the people of this land followed so closely that they believed their personal fortunes were tied to it was a very druidic, earth-centered idea. It was much like the Celtic druid ideas that were tied to the site Nate accidentally disturbed that linked him with his dog, Ranger. These sites were not to be taken lightly.

I glanced out the window at the crowded streets of men and women in their silk robes and shuddered. Out there someone tried to kill me. They would have succeeded if not for Wei Huan and Nate.

At the next table, Nate sat staring at a book of maps, pouring over them, lips moving as he muttered to himself trying to memorize every fact in case we needed the information in the future.

On our estate, he would spend long hours pouring lovingly over our own maps, learning the land on paper before learning the physical land, until he was sure he could place every rock and tree and blade of grass. I half suspected he could help a wayward stone find its proper positioning by now if one of the horses kicked it awry.

He paused to scrub a hand through his hair, not merely an action to smooth it back, a fierce irritated, scratching motion that made his hair stand up. He must have been an adorable, precocious child, and given his mother fits.

What would our own children be like?

He felt me watching him and finally looked up, mouth half-open as though he were a boy caught sneaking tarts. He promptly closed his mouth and smiled. "Tomorrow morning MeiLin will meet us to go secure supplies. Unless you're not feeling strong enough, then we can leave you here."

"I'll be fine." I assured him. There was her influence again. I was not about leave her alone with him if I could help it.

He looked relieved. "We will need to rent horses." He started to make a list so I grabbed a piece of paper and a fountain pen to make one of my own. Our last adventure without proper curatives had been a disaster.

Bandages and salves, tinctures for pain, I had brought some of my favorites along, distilled from the willows on the property in my satchel. As Nate scribbled out his own list, that grin was back.

SOS

The next morning, MeiLin was waiting for us with a pair of rickshaw carts. She protested, but Nate set her in a cab by herself and settled himself beside me in the second one.

The rickshaw took us down the streets and into a marketplace. Nate pointed out the sloping curved roofs and informed me it was so the rain would not seep into the homes during particularly bad storms called monsoons. He informed me over breakfast that one of the Englishmen he met over brandy in the study of the hotel believed it was so the evil spirits would slip on the tiles and be shot right back into the sky.

Bad spirits indeed! I giggled and rested my head upon his shoulder. With just the two of us, and him free of MeiLin's influence, I was free to enjoy the market as we passed, its rich aromas of street food mingled with bright pink and white flower blossoms on the twisty-branched trees. Painters worked and musicians played between the shops and booths in the square.

It was late in the afternoon before we were outfitted for adventure. We each sat alongside one of the fat Mongol horses, their strong, stubby legs stamping the ground as they trotted along. MeiLin had a horrible time with hers, which kept tossing its head, snorting, and rolling its eyes like it could bolt at any moment. Her willowy grace was lost on the back of a pony that seemed to have its own mind as to how we should travel. She would be sore, and both she and the horse would be exhausted by the time we rested.

We stopped for afternoon tea at a street vendor near the market. Thankfully, people of all nationalities milled between the native Chinese, adding their own languages to the general din of unfamiliar linguistic noise. They served us steamed dumplings stuffed with spicy, roast pork and paper cones of rice fried with oils and sauces and bits of scrambled egg. We sat at low tables watching our horses wander hobbled around a picketed paddock while we sipped green tea from the cast iron tumblers. I simply had to remember to bring some of them home with us to London. They would fare better with Nate's general banging than fine tea sets.

"Well Blimey! Four in the afternoon, sipping tea, couldn't be anything more British!" A heavily cockney accent squawked as only a cockney accent could squawk.

I turned and found two men and a woman watching us. The man in the forefront was a gentleman dressed entirely in black, head to toe, gray hair, almost white, peeked out in wisps from the wide brim of his black hat. Even his boots had been dyed black and were shiny new leather, as was the belt circling his hips keeping a revolver slung at a low angle. His thumbs were hooked in his belt in a lazy, bored stance.

The woman who had addressed us was standing at his side. Her hair was dark and done up in curls and a purple ribbon. Her dress was purple with tiny red flowers, and though it was well-made it was cut just a bit too low for decency's sake. It would have been okay if she wore a chemise underneath, but she did not, and she didn't seem bothered by the looks she was receiving from the men. In fact, she was clearly proud of the attention. Her lips were a bit too red, her eyes painted too dark. She did all she could to look seductive.

The second man wore a pith helmet over dark hair that was beginning to shift to the soft gray of the old driftwood. He had a tan linen suit and tall riding boots, and kind, intelligent eyes that were in stark contrast to his companions.

MeiLin was entirely unimpressed by the new guests standing by our table. Like anyone who was not Nate, they were simply beneath her. She sat silently serving him from our communal platter and refilling his tea and acting as though as though I did not exist.

Nate stood to greet them.

"Good Afternoon, sir," I said.

The one in linen swept the pith helmet off and bent his head over my knuckles. "I am Daniel Quinn. At your service."

"A fellow countryman," Nate said, with a welcoming smile. "Please, sir, join us."

"Oh, Quinn here is no sir." The man in black laughed and offered a hearty handshake, though from my vantage point it seemed as though it was more an exercise to attempt to subtly crush each other's hands. "For tea? No, thank you. I'm sure Miss Ratham may like some, but for an American man there's nothing like coffee. Tea just won't get the job done. No offense meant there, ma'am."

"I'm not offended," I said smoothly. I took pity on MeiLin and pulled a twist of willow in a bit of paper for her to chew, and set it beside her tumbler. She ignored it, like I knew she would.

"And how do you find coffee here?" Nate inquired, unrattled by the American's boorish manners.

"Rare and expensive." The American in black laughed, unaware he was being mocked, or perhaps he merely didn't care.

"Well the Dutch East India Company does make quite a fortune in the trade of coffee, but not in the land of tea," Nate said, smoothly taking an exaggerated sip from his tumbler.

The man's eyes narrowed. "I have never developed a taste for the stuff since we had the good sense to dump it all in the harbor a century ago with the rest of all that limey, British nonsense."

"Now, now, Mr. Barrett," Mr. Quinn admonished, wagging his finger playfully as one teases a naughty schoolboy. "I dare say, you are out of your element here. What with being surrounded by all us Limey Brits."

A glimmer of something dangerous flashed in Mr. Barrett's eyes but it passed so quickly I could have imagined it. In fact, had I blinked at the wrong moment, I never would have caught it. If I were a betting woman, I would not have wagered on Mr. Barrett was a man of even humor.

I glanced at Nate. Had he caught it as well? Months of moving in the social circles of the other land owners back home in London had made him quite good at hiding his thoughts. Only one slight movement betrayed him; the index finger of his right hand traced the pattern of his tumbler deliberately as though absently searching for the trigger on a pistol. Mr. Barrett made him anxious as well. I was not fooled in the slightest.

"Horses are boarded in Fen Wu Stables, boss," his servant said, a man large enough to crowd the sun from my vision.

"Very good, Lum," Mr. Barrett replied.

Over Nate's shoulder I spied a large man I recognized. He had absolutely no business in China. The last time I saw him he was unconscious, shot and bleeding and being dragged from a burning factory in London. I blinked hard. Surely I was seeing a ghost. The only consolation to my plight was that my presence clearly had the same effect upon him.

Nate noticed the change in my attitude and turned.

His sense of social decorum was less refined. His right hand twitched, aching to reach for his pistol. There was no hiding the motion now, after all, it was Nate who had shot him. Not without cause, of course, but the last we saw of him was when we dragged the senseless Mr. Baxter out of Mr. Sterling's factory and left him to the care of the waiting constables.

Obviously Mr. Baxter had found other employment.

I desperately wished we had been able to get a clear answer from Mr. Langston as to whether the man he had been approached by for membership in the Explorer's Society had indeed been Newton Geiger or not. I was still betting it was. Fantastical weapons, legends, and now Columbus Baxter. I hoped we did not run into Geiger here, the Empress

Dowager would not allow us clemency for fighting a second time, even if it was British invaders tearing each other apart.

"Mr. Baxter," Nate said. If his voice was any cooler my tea would have frozen solid.

"Miss Harper." Mr. Baxter doffed his cap at me and bowed his head. "And, you have me at a disadvantage yet again, sir."

"Nathaniel Valentine," Nate said stiffly.

"Esquire," I added impulsively.

Mr. Barrett was unwilling to let the uneasy silence sit. "In any case, it is wonderful to meet another treasure hunter."

"Treasure hunter?" I was aghast. It was that very crime for which members had been removed from the Explorer's Society in the past.

"Perhaps our colleagues favor the term 'antiquities acquirer' to 'treasure hunter,'" Mr. Quinn said gently. "Members of the British branch of the Explorer's Society are generally more refined than all that, Mr. Barrett. There are very strict regulations against treasure hunting for personal gain."

Mr. Barrett nodded. "Oh, of course. Though, treasure is treasure, the only difference is who ends up with it I guess—scholars call it knowledge."

"I suppose that is one way to put it," I conceded. "Won't you join us," I said, motioning to our luncheon. I had only meant Mr. Barrett, Mr. Quinn, and Ms. Charlotte Ratham, but Columbus Baxter sat down with a heavy, bone-rattling thump as well. I could not very well ask him to get up and leave. Our luncheon was mostly picked over so we would not have to suffer their company long.

"Well, since we are all friends," Barrett said jovially. "Let us discuss our little venture, shall we?"

"It is not 'our' venture," Nate said tersely. "I—We are on a mission from the Explorer's Society of London."

"As are we. Really now, Nate, we have the same goal. There is no reason we cannot work together." Nate glared but Mr. Barrett continued. "Treasures of China for the guild and all. Of course, then, you know about all the keys to raise the gateway."

"Gateway?" Nate repeated through clenched teeth.

"Keys?" I said at the same time.

"Oh dear, did you not research the site before you left London?" Mr. Barrett asked, smirking.

Charlotte giggled. I noticed she was missing several teeth.

"I assure you, we have the site thoroughly researched," I said with my most enigmatic smile. My brain raced through everything I had read. The mysterious researcher that had provided the notes the Explorer's Society armed us with had been correct, the Dragon Gate required a key or keys. Mr. Barrett and his men were one step ahead already.

"We have a guide who will lead us there," Nate countered.

"You don't need a guide," Barrett scoffed. "All you need is a map. You can learn the rest as you go. Isn't that right, darling?" He turned to address Charlotte.

She nodded. "That's right, life is just as much luck as learning, and a person has to make her own luck. When that fails, then use the learning. Why, our own Mr. Quinn studied here with a medicine man. He knew nothing of the land before coming here as a missionary and now he's practically fluent in the language."

"And of course, I gather you already know Mr. Baxter." Mr. Quinn waved a casual hand over his shoulder at Lum who was propping the long gun that had been slung over his shoulder against a carving in the wood.

Lum nodded to me, looking for a moment he as though he wanted to say something. His eyes narrowed at Nate. Nate glared back.

"Yes, Mr. Baxter and I have met," I said, as formally as I could.

Try as I might, I could not focus on the luncheon turned meeting now that it included Mr. Barrett and Mr. Baxter. I was not sure which man bothered me more. Fortunately, Nate seemed unimpressed by either of them and refused to discuss the specifics of our business in China. He let them drive the conversation and only responded with non-committal noises, a phenomenal skill he had that made people believe he was actually participating in the conversation that exposed neither his political leanings nor his true feelings on a variety of topics—a handy skill for an esquire.

Another group of adventurers in China seeking treasures. Surely there were treasures and adventure enough for all. But then, Mr. Barrett called it knowledge. He said scholars seek knowledge. He also spoke of the Explorer's Society, and Mr. Quinn was their interpreter.

Fortunately for my nerves, Nate's hospitality lasted only as long as the tea and luncheon did, and then he rose to his feet and bid them good afternoon. No matter what information, Mr. Barrett may or may not have, Nate was not in the mood to even entertain working with them.

I traded ponies with MeiLin for the return to the Viridian, sure I could handle the flighty fat Mongolian pony. A gentle tug at the bit and a press of my thighs and she obediently moved forward. I pulled her to a halt and turned to assure myself that I had, in fact switched mounts with MeiLin.

The ponies were different but the problem remained, my earlier mount, a lazy, piggy-eyed, but sweet-natured darling danced to one side, snorting in indecision, weighing the effort of tossing MeiLin to the mud or submitting to the new mistress on her back. Had I not saddled her myself I would had suspected a bad girth or a rough bit. Under MeiLin she was an entirely new animal.

Nate looked over in gentlemanly concern.

I kicked my new mount into action and trotted to where MeiLin was fighting her pony back onto the side of the path. Both were visibly panting and sweating. "Try giving her a bit more slack in the reign," I offered.

MeiLin gave me a sharp look, scowling with her bright white teeth displayed in a snarl. For just a moment she was not beautiful or foreign— but inhuman, hateful and ugly. I gasped. I resolved immediately to try to be nicer to her, perhaps in time I would win her over and she wouldn't hate me so.

CHAPTER NINE

WE WERE HEADING off to the first trine temple. The notes I had gathered only referred to it as the Temple of Yi, a temple of seasonal meditation. I only hoped that MeiLin could help us find the correct place. The maps we were able to locate were infuriatingly incomplete. It was almost as though the maps had been wiped clean of any mention of these places. It bothered me to no end that Mr. Barrett seemed to have maps of his own.

Keys, Mr. Barrett mentioned keys. And they had a map. I only hoped that more would become clear when we reached the temple. If the key wasn't there then at least we would have a direction.

Nate should be able to figure out where we were from the map we had and the diagram from the scholar notes from the Explorer's Society. Then we would at least have a direction. All MeiLin needed to do was get us that far. I would worry about keys when we reached the Temple of Yi.

I never imagined such a place existed. As we plodded down the road leading out of the busy city that was Beijing and past small farms, we soon came to areas too boggy to pass merely by land. Bridges were made of timber and stone, carefully crafted to allow carts and carriages and horses to pass at least two abreast, or crowds of people on foot. The land was covered by a fine mist that rose from the ground, swallowing the feet of the farmers who wore conical hats designed to shed the rain carried by the mist as they worked their farms.

Many of them wore pants, slops like sailors, rolled to the knees, and stood in the soft earth, bending and stooping as they pulled small green plants from their baskets and set them in the earth.

I would have loved to stop and watch them but MeiLin drove us ever onward down the road that was often stone slick with moss so I had to pay attention to my mount and where she stepped.

We turned off the main road as it wound around a large hill and off into a looming forest. At least for a moment it was looming, then peaceful, and then suddenly foreboding again. Its beauty was both alluring and intimidating. It filled me with a beautiful dread I could feel beneath my breastbone and, despite the misty air, I could scarcely breathe for the sudden dryness in my mouth.

I had never seen such a place. White stone like the Cliffs of Dover and steely-gray like old London steel rose above as great mountains whose proud peaks disappeared into the clouds that settled into the valley, blocking out the beautiful blue sky. But the gray mist made the pines greener and more beautiful in their shades of artichoke and thistle, and the green of the leaves of my beloved English Oak by our home.

Over the *clip-clop* of the horses' hooves on the stone, MeiLin was talking to Nate. Again. "The arrow you seek was used by Hou Yi to slay an evil dragon. She fell into darkness when she was removed from balance after the taking of her sacred scales. To locate her bones, we will have to make a charm."

I tore my eyes from the forest. "A charm? Well, that doesn't sound so hard." I said sensibly. I had assisted my mama in making charms before.

"Why exactly do we need a charm?" Nate asked suspiciously.

I stared at him, how could he not respect the mystical nature of something magical when he was so intimately familiar with several types of magic? Maybe it was only unfamiliar magic that made him anxious.

"Xihuan-Lung fell in the Tianmenshan Forest. There, a heavy mist has fallen and remains forevermore. It is home to many creatures that are unnatural to you and your western way of thinking," MeiLin said, her voice sweet and soft. "Many of those creatures will consume you. To wander through the endless mists unprotected is to invite death."

"It would be best to avoid that." Nate agreed reasonably.

"Wax and *hum nyee*—that's a dragon's favorite fish—but the most important of items is one of her scales."

"Pardon?" he asked, "We need a scale of a long-dead dragon to find the aforementioned dragon?"

Convenient that we knew just where to find one: London.

"The dragon's scales are a powerful magic item." MeiLin said. "They do not fall away and rot."

"Then where do we find one of these scales?" Since we were not going to be able to go back for the one in London, we needed a lead on another one.

"Several of them were presented as gifts to the royal family." By the annoyed look on MeiLin's face, I should have known this.

"Then what are the odds that we will be able to get one?" Nate said doubtfully.

"I'd assume dragons are quite large, there can't be many places one could hide, and if its long dead I can't imagine it travels very quickly." I offered.

Nate smiled.

"Surely *you* understand. You have seen so much more of the world than your lady friend," MeiLin said soothingly.

Nate turned back to her, "Hmm?" He opened his mouth like he was going to defend me. Atta boy Nate!

Then MeiLin leaned over and put her hand on his. "*You* know there is much magic in the world; many things exist that you cannot possibly comprehend."

An odd look crossed his face. He shook his head hard.

"Oh, of course," Nate said agreeably. "Vivian and I have seen enough magic to know that to be true. Right?"

"Right," I said smiling.

MeiLin's pony side-stepped and she fought with it for a moment as it danced and shied. Finally, the pony relented and MeiLin was able to continue. "We need a Yin scale from Xihuan-Lung. That will be the hardest piece to obtain. When the great Xihuan-Lung was slain her Yin scales were given as gifts to the royal family and their important retainers."

"If that's what we need, then we shall have to get one." I said. "Can you guide us to one or broker a deal? I would think that is right up the alley of a skilled guide."

MeiLin grunted with the effort of not being scraped off her horse by a low-hanging branch. "Some are buried in the tombs of the high-ranking retainers."

"I had hoped my trip to China might be complete without grave robbing," I said shaking my head. China was, at least, interesting.

"Isn't there some other way to get a Yin scale?" Nate asked softly.

"Some are still in the possession of the royal family," MeiLin said to him.

"So, our choices are grave robbery or robbing the royal family." I couldn't help but smile. I did enjoy adventure, and so far China was not disappointing.

"You wish to find the arrow that slain Xihuan-Lung, shot from the cinnabar bow of Hou Yi? Then this is the only way." MeiLin said.

"Oh, darling, can you please give me a hand with this?" I feigned not being able to lift my saddle bags.

He got a strange look on his face but excused himself from MeiLin and came to my side. I threw open the saddle bag and chose to ignore the look on his face, "I don't trust her." I whispered furiously.

"Come on, Vivian." Nate was cross. "How else are we going to find the arrow?"

"Oh, I don't know, ask Barrett's privateers?" I set my hands on my hips. "They have a map."

"We have a map. And a guide. And I told you", he whispered furiously, "we can't trust them! If they were sent by Langston he would have told us!"

"We were all sent out in small groups to not attract treasure hunters", I said in my most placating tone. "Doesn't it at least make sense that he would send more than just the pair of us? You have to admit, I was just initiated into the society and you're not the most accomplished member."

He made a face. That wasn't exactly what I meant, but now that I had his attention again I wasn't about to stop to apologize and give MeiLin another chance to secure his attention. "Don't we have to assume that if the arrow is as wonderful as it's claimed to be the Explorer's Society would send more than just the pair of us to retrieve it? Or don't they believe it really is the weapon that we think it to be?"

The little muscle in his jaw twitched. We stared at each other for a long moment. Whatever was wrong with him, whatever she was doing, she had done it again. This was not my Nate. In the background, I could hear

MeiLin make a small pitiful noise. Nate heard it too and he glanced up at her. "Are you done pretending to need my help? If you don't trust her then read her. That should tell you all you need to know." He dropped my hand and returned to where she sat looking demurely into the distance the way cats stare into the sun.

"I've tried," I whispered after him. "But I *can't* read her."

§§§

The road quickly faded from the fine brick and cobblestones of Beijing to dirt and stones flanked by tall grasses. It resembled the landscape back home, but whereas we had the beautiful hawthorn and English Oak, these trees were thin spindly things that looked bedraggled and wind-blown. MeiLin and her pony struggled for dominance behind us, cursing and snorting. I wasn't sure for whom I felt sorrier.

We came to a halt before a pair of stone lions guarding the road. Nothing like African Lions, they were a cross between lions and dogs, crouched and resting one massive paw on a ball marking the road leading back to the Imperial City of Beijing. Each was taller than a man on horseback, but was partially obscured by the grasses. The beauty and majesty of China was being reclaimed by the land. That which was not being picked apart by the vultures of Germany, Russia, France, and even England. China may have lost the Opium Wars, but they had lost themselves as well. Progress indeed.

"We will need to visit the Palace hidden within the Tianmenshan Forest." MeiLin interrupted my melancholy reflection of the lion-dogs. Both horse and woman were panting. Her pony tried to scrape her off again, this time on the paw of the lion-dog and she hissed at it and slapped it hard across one ear.

It was nearly evening when the Tianmenshan Forest loomed before us, the path winding out of sight and disappearing into a fog that rose from the forest like a silent gray ghost, nothing like the nasty, yellow, pea-soup fogs of London. This fog was cool and beautiful as though a cloud had settled upon the land, bathing it like the steam that comes off a glorious hot bath.

Nate insisted we dismount and lead the horses lest one stumble and break a leg before we could set up camp. Unfortunately, we never got that far.

The jangle of harnesses and buckles, the clatter of rocks underfoot, all the unfamiliar sounds and the war of wills between MeiLin and her mount made me ignore everything but my drive to put one foot in front of the other. Nate was looking for the best place to set up a picket line for the horses and our tents for the night.

The fog muffled and distorted the sounds; they were all around us. My left arm ached deeply, bone deep, near the elbow. I had been gashed there six months or so ago when Nate and I were attacked by gargoyles upon his old ship, the *Lightning Aura*. It was where the *Seven of Swords* would be on my arm. I cannot access that card anymore since the deep slash had nearly led to me losing my arm to injury and infection. The *Seven of Swords* represented stealth and deception; in the tarot card a man is escaping a military camp with stolen swords. Were we stealing away from something or toward something? Were we sneaking? I nearly stumbled into my pony. What were we doing? I could only guess without direct access to the symbol itself.

The mist made sound disorienting. There was commotion everywhere and nowhere at once. I spun around trying to locate the source, but it was nearly dark and the tall trees cast shadows. My heart set a fearsome tattoo in my chest. The shadows were looming and every one of them was a monster ready to snatch us up, possibly ready to feed us to a dragon.

Several men armed with spears and swords stepped from the mists yelling commands. I didn't need to speak the language to know we were being called to surrender. The card wasn't congratulating me on our stealthy enterprise; it was informing me of our failure.

Nate froze for a moment, and I could see indecision dart across his features. He was ready to fight. as a man or as a canithrope, but then reconsidered. He pulled his pistol from his holster only to have a spear shoved inches from his face.

I was stunned at how quickly it happened. Nate was mortified. They plucked his pistol from his hand and two men gave glared at him, their spears at the ready. I willed him to be patient. If they wanted to murder us, we would already be dead. It was unlikely they just happened upon us and took us prisoner that quickly. It was much more likely that they had been stalking us for a time and planned their attack.

He glared, his jaw clenching so hard I thought he might crack his teeth. His eyes swept over me before flicking to MeiLin, then moving back to me. He huffed loudly through his nose and bared his teeth in irritation. There was no way of knowing how many of them there were out in the fog and he was not willing to risk us. One man firmly took the reins out of my hand and I was too startled to resist.

In the tarot, the *Temperance* card is a beautiful angel with one foot on land and one foot in a stream, balanced in both the material and the subconscious. She teaches calm and peace in times of great stress and anxiety. I focused on where the angelic mark, serenely passing water from one chalice to another, rested on my skin until it became warm and soothing as though I was being wrapped in a blanket and soothed with mulled wine. It was peace and warm fires, it was a clear morning in our solar, enjoying tea and watching rabbits play in the yard. I gathered the feeling in my hands. Temperance, Temperance, Temperance.

I pushed past my guard and pretended to stumble into Nate, my hands latching onto his arm. I felt the heat radiating from me and into Nate. He turned back causing his guards to stop short or else ram into him.

Wait, I mouthed, hoping he could still see me in the dim light.

He nodded.

The armed men jerked us apart, but as they did I noticed he looked less furious though his brow was still furrowed in concern. He scanned the trees and the guards with a careful practiced eye. He would plan our escape.

I leaned heavily against the man pushing me along. Calming Nate had left me cold and trembling. I could barely put one foot in front of the other. I had been so warm and happy a second ago. Now I was filled with shame and rage and a rapid sense of dread that was creeping up my body and wrapping its tendrils around my throat.

"Failure! Failure!" A voice in my head screamed. I stumbled and shut my eyes tightly trying to force it back. I hadn't failed, I had kept Nate from doing something stupid which might have resulted in him getting killed. I shook my hands trying to return feeling to them, but the anxious, angry feeling was annoyingly slow to recede and stayed with me until we finally reached a large stone castle with curved roofs that came to a point that

curved upwards. Gilded seals decorated the walls, reflecting the torchlight, and banners flittered in the near-darkness like massive bats. We must have stumbled very close in the darkness. Strange that MeiLin didn't know this castle was here.

I tried to get a good look at her. She did not seem concerned with our capture in the slightest.

We were marched across a stone courtyard lit by torches and guarded by men with spears wearing similar livery, up some stairs, and through a wooden door into a startlingly well-lit chamber, lit by oil lamps made brighter by mirrors. It was nearly as bright as our own home though not nearly as welcoming. Instead of party guests we were welcomed by guards.

Though many of the Chinese people looked the same to me and my culture blindness, I was starting to be able to pick out some of the subtle differences in their faces. This man was tall, nearly as tall as Nate, huge compared to the other men I had seen in China. He was dressed in fine, supple brown leather and silver silk that rippled as he moved, like the skin of some powerful animal, barely restrained and authoritative. A master without equal within his own palace, and he would have been a man of rare charisma even in London.

He had a beautiful face, though pock-marked by some long-conquered illness, he had fine, chiseled features and the beautiful olive-skin and almond shaped eyes that blessed many Chinese. His hair was long and black, nearly blue, as fine and shiny as lacquered armor and tied in a club queue. His violet sash, embordered with green symbols, fluttered across his thighs. His cape was violet and gold silk trailing out behind him.

"I am sorry my men arrested you."

"I find myself becoming accustomed to being arrested in China," I said, not bothering to hide my contempt.

"My men are suspicious of outsiders." He sat with casual grace upon the carved throne beside a woman with whom he shared the same high cheekbones and fine porcelain features. He looked casual, relaxed, on the dark wood throne but I was not fooled. This was a man whose body was rarely, if ever, at rest.

The longer I looked at him, the more familiar he seemed. It was more than the look all the Chinese people seemed to share. These two shared a regal similarity and, unless I was mistaken, I had seen it before.

The woman was a younger version of the Empress Dowager Cixi, and she could only be the twin of the man who appeared to recline upon the carved throne before me. This must be her son, a young man exiled to death. We had been told he was dead, of small pox. He bore small, dipped scars on his cheeks, faint marks of having beaten the disease, but he had not been welcomed back to the royal family.

No, Wei Huan never said he died. The prince had been "lost." The legislation he tried to put into place therefore failed and the Empress Dowager had resumed the seat of China. Now I wished I had thought to inquire who had reversed his decrees and who had sent him off to the Tianmenshan Forest to be treated for small pox.

He watched us with a small smile on his face, his eyes watching us in that cold way one watches those beneath him. Had he been any less handsome it would be a sneer. It was the look of a man watching prey, sizing us up, waiting for us to play false. Prince Qixiang fooled no one, though he gave the appearance to be resting comfortably in his throne, he could, at a moment's notice leap into action like a panther.

"Did the Empress Dowager send you?"

There was nothing in his handsome eyes, no hate nor love. Perhaps I was wrong and he was no relation to the Chinese Queen.

The woman at his side hiccupped into her elegant fan. The prince was strangely silent. Snakes behave like this, hypnotically silent before they strike.

Nate shifted on his feet, in case he had to leap to protect us from the prince.

"She did not," I said as respectfully as I could manage. "We are merely touring China." If Nate's lie was good enough for the Empress, it was good enough for the prince, "We are on an adventure; we wished to see the Wall and the famous stone warriors."

The prince gave a very un-princely snort. "The stone warriors. They are relics of a China that will never be again." He looked over my shoulder to where two of the stone men stood in their ancient armor, at attention in silent vigil, guarding the door to the chamber. "They were in dire need of improvement."

"Still, they are quite beautiful," I offered, unable to keep from staring at them. Their beautiful, blank almond eyes stared off into nothing as they stood in molded armor, adorned with a thin, well-kept mustache and carefully sculpted terracotta hair. Their armor was carved in the likeness of lacquered plate and topped with scarves and ties, all sculpted to perfection. A real metal sword hung at his side, the handle clenched in a clay fist.

"Now that you have seen them, what else do you wish to see in China?"

"Many things," I offered offhandedly. "I love the art I have seen so far."

"She wishes to see the tombs of the consorts that have come before," MeiLin said quickly bowing. "Silly English girl wishes to see such things they do not have in England. They do not understand the role a royal consort has in China. A royal consort is so much more than a mere woman. She is the second most important woman in all of China," she pointedly explained as though I were a simpleton.

MeiLin kept her eyes forward and refused to look directly at me. This *Silly English Girl* did all she could to not huff in annoyance, but I was not about to fight with her in front of Prince Qixiang.

The prince nodded, and one of his servants rang a gong, which summoned several more retainers, all scraping and bowing and nearly tripping over themselves in a comical manner as they lined up before the dais where Prince Qixiang and his sister sat on their thrones.

"Help the Princess YaMing escort these two down to the regal tombs of the Royal Madams. You will find their tombs a beautiful sight—all the Madams are buried behind beautifully painted scenes depicting their beauty and grace. Several of the Madams buried beneath this palace were Lady of Bright Deportment, Beautiful Lady or Virtuous Lady. They have the most beautiful chambers for the Emperors of old could not stand to be without them."

"I'm afraid I don't understand." I said.

YaMing stood with great difficulty and bowed deeply to her brother. Her arms, weak and painful, were bound carefully to her body in slings. I had seen such wounds in soldiers treated from the war. It was telltale of nerve-dead limbs, but the bearer could not accept being separated from them. She shuffled along ahead of me and every few steps I would catch a view of tiny, beautiful silk slippers on wooden platforms that kept her from treading on her long delicate golden robes. The wide blue belt around her waist, a shining silk, reflected the light as though it was made of shimmering scales. Only the russet fox fur draped along her shoulders seemed out of place, breaking up the shining, painted silk dress she wore.

Every so often the deep green jade bracelets and ornaments she wore clinked musically. Her pale, painted face reminded me of a beautiful porcelain doll my mother gave me when I was a child, but the paint stopped at the nape of her neck, artfully angled where her raven black hair was pulled up and mostly hidden beneath a red cap dotted with irregular tear-shaped pearls and fresh orchids.

The servants, more of the men dressed in Prince Qixiang's livery, walked before her pushing open doors and waiting in pairs as we descended a long corridor that sloped down toward a beautiful golden door flanked by more of the clay men, standing by sconces of oil lamps and incense whose perfumed scent almost covered the acrid stink of the oil the lamps burned.

"Men are forbidden here." YaMing said, her voice merely a whisper in the quiet hall. "This is where the beloved Madams of Emperors past find eternal rest. Those that are not resting in the Imperial burial grounds, that is."

"Are you wounded?" I asked impulsively.

"I am," she said. "It will pass."

"May I help? My father is a healer of some renown in London. I might be able to help you." Well, that was stretching things, but I cringed to see her move as though every gliding step was causing her jarring agony.

Pausing before a huge antechamber she said, "You are kind to offer." Then she pointed. "The tombs are through here. Each is behind a *bìhuà* depicting the grace and beauty of the Madame behind it."

"You are not joining us?" I asked.

"It is not proper for me to be in the tombs of the Madams," she said simply. "I have shown you the way, I will return to wait upon Prince Qixiang. When you are finished, follow the lit torches; they will lead you back to the servants."

I curtsied to YaMing. When I turned around, MeiLin was already within the antechamber where the Madams of Emperors long-dead and buried their Bright Ladies, Virtuous Ladies and Ladies of Bright Deportment.

"Were all these concubines of Emperors?" I asked peering from one small inner chamber to the next seeking MeiLin. I was relieved there were no tombs in sight. Off the antechamber were a large grouping of small rooms, each maybe the size of our maid's room in my childhood home back in London, holding a small table lit with incense and small oil lamps standing before large murals, or *bìhuà,* depicting beautiful women in flowing silken robes. Some of the women were feeding animals fruit, others were playing instruments or sewing or holding flowers. One was holding a bird. Their remains must be safely out of sight behind the painted walls.

"You see, the scale you seek is there. It is out of your reach." MeiLin set her hands to her hips and smiled. She stared up at an iridescent scale set in the arch above the alcove in the wall where the corpse of a royal concubine lay in eternal rest behind a mural.

Whether she led us here on purpose or by accident I honestly wasn't sure, but I intended to take full advantage of it.

"Is this truly what we need to find the dragon?" I asked.

"Yes," she smiled.

"And the arrow?" I clarified.

"Yes." There was that smirk again. The smile that mocked me for my defeat.

But MeiLin didn't know who she was dealing with. The altar held a small oil lamp burning fragrant oil that burned so floral and sweet that it was cloying. I moved it and a bowl of sand and incense ash aside and hopped up on the altar. Balancing on my toes, I could just reach the scale and the mortar it was set in.

"What are you doing?" MeiLin gasped. "Someone will see you!"

"The guards will not be down here. They are all men." I said reasonably. "Off-hand, do you know the penalty for damaging these tombs?"

"Execution, I suppose!" MeiLin snapped.

I paused for a second, hearing my knife scrape at the plaster. Would it feel the same when Prince Qixiang's executioner sawed through our necks? I shuddered. Whether it was the same scrape, scrape, scrape or not, one thing was for certain, Prince Qixiang would do it himself. But if it was what we needed for our mission, then it was what we needed.

I finished my defacing and grave robbing in what I hoped was record time. I shoved the scale down my blouse and leapt off the altar, turning to casually scrape the incense back into the painted pot and plunk the oil lamp back into its rightful place. MeiLin stared at me, her mouth hanging open in a most unladylike fashion. The plaster in my hair and clothes stood out like snow showing off our crime like a bloody red hand print of guilt.

"You have to put that back!" she whispered feverishly.

"We need it." I said. "You said we needed to make a charm to find the dragon's grave, and I do not wish to return to return to London empty handed."

"Yes, your Mister Langston would be so disappointed with *your* failure," she said.

"*My* failure? Nate and I are a team—" I froze. "Hang on, did you just say Langston?"

MeiLin ignored me and pushed open the door with a creak, but then I heard another sound. A cracking sound, low at first, then louder like the sound ice makes in the winter during the first real thaw.

"Did you hear that?"

She turned to me scowling, clearly I had annoyed her with my *silly English girl* concerns again. Then the scowl fell away and her eyes widened as she shoved past me as though I was not even there.

Every corner of the palace was decorated with beautiful stone statues of warriors in a different style of dress and livery than Prince Qixiang's personal guard, but they held real weapons in their stone hands. They were beautiful sculptures, but now as I followed her to one of the two that stood guard of the tomb of the Madams I swallowed hard—one was cracked.

"What did you do?" MeiLin demanded.

"What do you mean, 'what did I do'?" I demanded.

MeiLin scowled at me. "First you deface royal tombs, now you break the sculptures. These are the famed terracotta warriors, they are marvels of the ancient world. They are the Royal Army of Qin Shi Huang, the first Emperor of China, his legacy to dynasties to come. They have survived two thousand years of guarding and serving the emperors in the afterlife but they cannot survive you!"

"Shhhh!" I snapped. *Could she not hear it?*

I grabbed MeiLin's hand and she went white with fury. I pointed, the cracks were spreading, a fine clay dust falling to the marble floors. In this silent tomb the cracking echoed and the dust was horribly out of place. The scale in the tomb was one thing, if men were not allowed in the tombs, our theft was likely to go unnoticed for quite some time. But guards patrolled these hallways, these damaged statues would be noticed. We needed to get out of here before anyone discovered the statue shattered.

I backed up, but the cracking grew louder and more ominous. A sword shuddered in a clay fist. I prayed it would not make too much noise when it clattered to the ground. Then something grabbed my shoulder and I nearly leapt out of my skin.

A metal hand, skeletal and bony latched onto my shoulder, digging its metal fingers into my flesh. I wheeled just in time to see it raise its very real single-edged sword above its head. I wrenched myself away and ducked, jerking out of its grasp. The second one broke out of its shell like some horrible metal butterfly in a clay cocoon. The cracks spread like ripples across the red-brown surface, falling apart and shattering onto the floor, where the heavy metal feet stomped over them crushing them underfoot to dust. Metal feet that had more in common with a skeletal frame than a fully-formed human body, let alone the sculpture of a man. The clay face cracked, bleeding green light through the breaks and revealing glowing green eyes.

They were nothing like the guardian Mr. Geiger built to protect the leywell Nate and I had battled under London last season. Geiger's mechanical man had been a behemoth of design—nearly twice as tall as a man and strong, with a single eye that could send forth a bolt of fire and light to burn anything in its path. Nate had transfigured into his canithrope form to battle it, and together they nearly collapsed the chamber, threatening to drown us as the Thames leaked in. No, these were more elegant, faster and more skeletal in design. There was not a wasted ounce in these creations. These were clockwork men working like an elegant machine as living men in flesh bodies did. I could see no batteries or power canisters controlling their locomotion.

But I had little time to marvel at these wondrous machines. Both were armed with swords and they turned their large, metal heads toward us as they began to advance. I whipped around feeling my mouth go dry as panic set in. There were two. Were there more? How many did we pass?

MeiLin looked pale, her composure finally breaking under the strain. I took a step to the side. With luck they were not interested in me alone. Maybe we could divide their attention by giving them two targets. No such luck; both turned toward me.

My shoulder throbbed and my arm trembled from the brief crushing grip. I tried one slow, careful step to the side, one of the clockwork men followed me, sword lowered, watching me with glowing green eyes, waiting, waiting, trying to figure out my movement. MeiLin moved opposite me. She glanced in my direction, biting her lip. I swear for a moment she was considering bolting and leaving me to them. The clockwork men saw it, too, and they took one step to block the door.

Only I was not without weapons myself. I snatched my seax from the small of my back and dashed to the side. For a moment, I thought I might get past them unscathed, but the one furthest from me saw me move and swung its blade. By sheer dumb luck I twisted away and brought my seax up, hitting its forearm and sending a shock up my arm. I nearly dropped my knife.

As a statue, the one closer to me had been a handsome Chinese lad with a large bun and no mustache, but a bit of a beard just below his lower lip. It reached out, sweeping blindly, and slammed into the back of my already bruised shoulder. I rolled with the blow, but too far and dizzily crashed into the wall.

I staggered to my feet. Both clockwork men turned to me. MeiLin bolted past the distracted clockwork men, presumably leaving me at their mercy. I tried to stagger to my feet. My vision swam. I shook my head hard and nearly stabbed myself in the eye; my seax was still clenched in my fist. Something snatched my wrist hard and jerked me forward. I sucked in a breath to fight.

"Let's go!" MeiLin snapped, dragging me forward.

The gust of breath I was preparing to fight with was lost in a huff as we pounded up the stairs and into the hall, passing another pair of terracotta statues wearing armor cunningly sculpted out of clay but also holding very real swords in their clay fists. I did not stop to see if they were cracking or glowing. I didn't want to see.

Clearly the terracotta warriors were more than mere statues. How many of them had we seen as we traveled? How many of them were mere clay statues and how many held clockwork men ready to spring to life, shattering their clay skin. I would never sleep again with one in the same house. In fact, the moment we returned to our manor home outside of London I was removing the Greek statue of Hercules battling lions, just to be safe.

There was no way to fight them, my chipped and blunted seax blade was proof against that. They did not bleed, they did not stop. Our only advantage would be in numbers. And, of course, we would have to evade Qixiang and YaMing and any of their human guards as well. Being chased by their metal clockwork guards was bound to alert them that something was amiss.

One problem at a time. We bolted for where we had left Nate and Prince Qixiang. It occurred to me again, as MeiLin and I ran from these mechanical constructs with deadly weapons raised and at the ready, nothing good ever came from graverobbing.

CHAPTER TEN

WE BURST THROUGH the heavy wooden door, followed closely by the clockwork guards.

There was no way we could quietly slip out. Nate saw us, and them, and immediately pulled me to him, jerking my injured shoulder. I gasped. It wasn't that I didn't appreciate the protective, manly gesture, but I could do without being shoved and pulled aside.

Nate immediately turned from Prince Qixiang to the clockwork men. "What is the meaning of this?"

Prince Qixiang gave a small smile watching the scene unfold. Did he know what I had done or was he just amused that these clockwork creations were distressing us so?

"Tell your creatures to lower their weapons," Nate commanded. His eyes had gone dark and wild.

"You do not command the Emperor of China." Prince Qixiang's smile vanished into a sneer.

"No man threatens Vivian," Nate snapped, his voice held a rough, feral quality as his words slurred from between a sudden set of fangs. His eyes grew dark and his mouth could no longer fully close.

"Darling, we could use a little help here," I panted. I appreciated his protective side but I needed him to keep his head.

Prince Qixiang glared. "I am Emperor, I do what I like!" he snarled at Nate. To his clockwork soldiers he commanded, "Bring the women to me!"

As much as the warriors terrified me in all their wanton inhumanity, I could not allow Nate to battle them alone. He spun and shoved MeiLin and me away from him, toward the empty wall.

His leather long-coat fanned out around him and he flung it free. His belt clattered to the floor, the only other leather he really cared about. He didn't bothering to waste the time to fully strip off his remaining clothing.

His shoulders spread and his shirt tore, revealing flesh darkening past tan to the deep color of his dark caramel hair. His jaw and nose extended and stretched, and he hissed with the pain of it. His head lengthened and widened, ears rising, shoulders shifting. His nails turned into deadly claws; haunches became more muscled, hips widened and moved forward; his feet shifted to very canine hind paws and hocks. The expanding flesh split the skin, and the shaggy pelt broke forth, as though the savage beast was shattering bonds that kept him clothed in man-skin.

Nate, now in his canithrope form, stepped away from the tattered remains his human clothing. Now towering above the clockwork warriors, he snarled a challenge: *If you want them, come and take them.*

Not to be outdone, I grabbed a metal stand that held a burning brazier of charcoal and incense and threw it down so at least Prince Qixiang's human guards could only attack us from a single side. If we were very fortunate, the clay and metal guardians might grant us a respite as well. The metal stand was longer than I was tall. Though heavy, I swung it hard, forcing the human guards back a step to avoid being battered in the face with hot metal.

But they no longer had any interest in getting involved in this fray. Between Nate's canithrope form, the barrier of flaming coals releasing a smoky backdrop for our furious battle, and the clay covered metal figures, the human guards remained well out of the way, instead forming a last line of defense between the dais holding Prince Qixiang and the Princess YaMing and our battle.

I slammed the pole into the coals sending sparks at our remaining attackers, but they lacked human eyes and flesh to burn. They lacked human fear to exploit. The pole was much more effective when I managed to spear one through the torso. The metal pole jammed in its back and hip, bringing the wide-toothed gears to a halt with a grinding screech. The speared metal soldier turned, jerking the pole from my hands and battering his fellows before collapsing to his knees from the added weight.

Prince Qixiang stared, first stunned then delighted, as a slow smile crossed his face.

MeiLin had not seen Nate like this before. She sat crouched before me. I could not see her face but I did not care. MeiLin might be content to cower, but I was not about to let Nate fight without some sort of support.

My canithrope husband-to-be was an imposing figure but the clockwork men had swords and I had the sick certainty that no one would escape unscathed.

There were more of them now, I was not sure where they had come from, but I assumed they were the terracotta statues we passed in the hall. Nate snarled and shifted his weight, careful to keep himself between MeiLin and myself. Nate was not usually this patient. I had seen him reduced to fisticuffs in a bar; this must be Ranger. His dog was always more level-headed. His dog, which he had become bonded with in the druid leywell when we met, must be more reserved when battle loomed.

The clockwork men raised their blades, ready to strike as one. Nate backed up, then suddenly lunged forward. He snatched up the closest one and slammed it into its fellows, the shriek of rending metal echoed through the chamber. The second clockwork soldier dodged the airborne construct, turned its weapon, and slashed with its sword sending a splash of blood through the air. Nate grunted in pain and back-handed the clockwork soldier into a column. He was a blur of dark fur surrounded by bronze metal and green light, flinging metal bits across the audience room. He tore through them, never satisfied until the gleaming green eyes went dark and the metal limbs moved no more. The broken clockwork soldiers became a tangle of metal and wire, gears and pistons, all the bits and bobs required to create movement in steel.

More of them kept coming, what started with the two we managed to bring in pursuit of our grave robbing, had quickly turned to seven, then nine. And they seemed to replenish themselves as quickly as Nate could dispatch them.

I spied movement from the dais where Prince Qixiang and his sister sat on their stone thrones. The prince slowly stood to get a better look at the fighting. At least I hoped he was fascinated by the spectacle and not calling for more of his monsters to overwhelm my fiancé.

Though I was not the fighter my husband-to-be was, I could do something to keep more clockwork men from entering the battle and shifting the odds. I was not dumb enough to get in Nate's way as he raged.

I ducked around the other side of the column where there was more than enough open space. From their cracked clay forms, two more of the metal men stepped forward, intent upon joining the fray. I needed a plan. Quickly.

I took a deep breath and examined in my options. My knife was woefully too short, it would let them get too close. But they carried weapons of their own. The ground was littered with their shattered metal limbs, discarded weapons, and red-black fluid that leaked from their machine bodies like blood, that foul fluid that kept them running. I shoved a broken limb out of the way and found an arm holding a sword. Just like my knife, but longer. I jumped forward with it and stabbed at the nearest clockwork man. The blade passed through his clay body, knocking off large pieces that shattered on the floor.

It fell free too easily and I stumbled forward. "Damn!"

The clay dust made the marble floor slick. I stepped back and slashed at the warrior. This time the sword connected hard, jarring my arm. I nearly dropped it.

A sword was not the way to go. Not for slashing at any rate. I could pierce the monster. I raised it over my head and launched myself forward, stabbing hard, catching the clockwork soldier between a set of gears.

The sword was jerked out of my hand. There was a grinding screech of metal against metal, sending up a shower of sparks. The metal man stopped in its tracks and tried to turn to jerk free the blade that bound its movement. There was a shriek, something greater than metal, something both human and inhuman and a great flood of a foul red-black fluid gushed forth, splashing over my boots.

I slipped and flailed my arms, trying to keep my balance. His fellow wheeled upon me, slashing out with his own blade. The air whistled as it went past.

Swords were not the way to go at all.

I dodged backward, slipping again in the mechanical man's blood, and closed my hand on something cylindrical and heavy. I swung it with all my might.

My Nate is not an elegant fighter, neither as a man nor as a canithrope, but one cannot deny that he is an effective one. He shredded the mechanical men with ruthless efficiency. What I hoped was a weapon was an arm, freshly torn from one of the mechanical men, still sparking from dangling wires and leaking more of the foul fluid.

I gave it a glance before I swung it as hard as I could into the face of the nearest warrior. My foe, an archaic swordsman without flesh, clay or otherwise, raised his weapon and battered the arm away easily. He advanced.

I stepped back again as the arm rolled in my grip and bent at the elbow. What had been a sturdy club a moment ago was now a flaccid, dead limb. The hand turned toward me, palm up, a beggar asking for my favor.

I dropped the limb. And slipped to the side, remembering just in time that it was the only thing protecting me from the metal warrior intent on my life.

My breath caught in my throat. Think. Think. Think. I needed a weapon. A real weapon.

I saw that of the metal men had been armed with an axe, a war axe, with a metal shaft and a curved face, the entire length of which was less than a meter.

I dove for it, slipping around the edge of the pillar in more of the red-black liquid and came up with the axe. It had a rounded, heavy back-end, like a hammer. I turned it in my hand and came up swinging. The hammer end caught a knee joint, cracking the casing and bending the gears. More red fluid, inky and irony, spilled down its leg.

It didn't cry out, but did kneel over the wounded limb. Its temple was at the perfect height. I reversed the axe, spun and turned my hip into the swing. The axe buried into the side of the head so deeply that as he fell he took the ax with him, the blade buried in his metal head.

I shuddered at the sickening crunch that vibrated up my arms and the dark lake spreading on the floor. Whatever powered these monsters was inhuman.

Prince Qixiang snatched up a spear from one of his human guards and slammed the butt sharply against the floor. Nate wheeled around to face his new foe. "Very impressive."

For a moment—only a moment—I hoped Nate would just kill Prince Qixiang, then maybe the nightmare would end. The guards were still in a state of shock. We could probably make a break for it.

"Would it pain you to know what you destroyed?" Prince Qixiang taunted. "The lifetimes of work that went into these soldiers? The lives that paid for them?" He playfully lunged at Nate with his spear, but Nate batted it away as one swats away a gnat.

"Can you understand me when you are like this?" Prince Qixiang continued, "Do you hear me or do you hear noise?" He playfully slashed at Nate, which he easily batted away again. "Are you a demon, a *mó*? Or are you from *Tian* to help me reclaim what is mine?"

Nate snarled and snapped his powerful jaws and spat out a large chunk of one of the clockwork arms in Prince Qixiang's direction.

"You are impressive, I give you that," Prince Qixiang said. Then he lunged forward, feinting with the spear.

Nate bought into the feint and batted to the left. Qixiang spun and stabbed, grazing Nate's right ear with the spear before spinning back again and ending up in a crouch with the spear at the ready like an extension of his own arm.

Nate snarled and snapped, shaking his head and spraying the floor with blood. I gasped. Qixiang stabbed again, this time lower. Nate leapt back, following and mirroring Qixiang's movements. In any skin he was a natural fighter and learned quickly.

Qixiang slashed with the spear. Nate stepped in, caught it at the haft, wrapped his arm around it, and closed the space between them. He punched Qixiang hard in the chest then swiped at him with an open claw, but missed. He did not miss the alabaster pillar leaving deep gouges in the soft stone.

Qixiang jerked his spear free and came at him again, this time twirling it over his head, the point nearing Nate's eyes. Nate ducked and threw up his hand. Qixiang threw a hard punch into his side, but Nate, being taller, ignored it and slammed the point of the spear down and seized the haft in his massive jaws. The wood gave way with a *crack*.

Nate twisted, jerking the spear out of Qixiang's grasp and one strong arm reached out and slammed into the back of Qixiang's shoulder, knocking him across the floor. The prince winced and YaMing shrieked.

Nate, with the prince's spear between his teeth, crouched menacingly , waiting for Qixiang to make his move. Qixiang was a better fighter and may be faster, but Nate was stronger, and with Qixiang now unarmed, the battle was all but over. Nate growled.

From the corner of my eye I saw him lunge, using the spear to launch himself forward and slam into Qixiang, planting both feet into his chest and knocking the prince backward, his lacquered armor clattering noisily.

YaMing gave a strangled gasp and doubled over, struggling for breath.

"Nate, stop!" I rushed to YaMing's side to offer her aid. The clockwork men paid me no mind. They seemed to have no interest in anything but the cares of Prince Qixiang. YaMing's bandaged arms struggled to wrap around her chest and she gasped, blood staining her lips.

Nate's hulking form, tall and shaggy, sagged. With great effort he restrained himself from landing the killing blow. Nate dropped the prince, who dexterously rolled backward out of Nate's grasp. As soon as Qixiang was clear he flipped up to his feet. In one smooth motion, the prince swept one booted foot under the shaft of his spear and kicked it up into his hand. He spun it into position, pointing it at Nate waiting for him to charge again.

But Nate was not going to attack; he fell forward and began to transfigure back into himself. He stopped his attack for my sake.

He seemed to shrink and curl like a snail into a shell. The dense dark caramel pelt fell away to the marble floor, leaving him bare and shaking, crouched on the floor by his ruined clothing. He clasped his hand over his damaged ear. Blood leaked down the side of his head where the prince had dealt him the glancing blow with the spear. His other hand wrapped around his ribs, covering a scratch that seemed mostly superficial.

Prince Qixiang's noble mask of composure fell away for a moment. He wiped his mouth on the back of his hand and spat blood on the floor. "You dare strike me, peasant!" he snarled.

MeiLin stared at the scene, torn between the men fighting and the princess gasping through what I believed was cracked ribs.

"What are those things?" Nate breathed, motioning to the broken clockwork warriors.

"Those are my soldiers." Prince Qixiang wiped his mouth and laughed, a high deranged, thin sound. It was the sound of a boy pretending to be a man. The sound of a boy stretched to his breaking point. I had heard it before when poor families lost their fathers too soon, and young men were suddenly the head of households with mothers and sisters to support. They drank and laughed in this manner when the world threatened to suffocate them.

Prince Qixiang thumped the butt of his spear against the marble floor again. He crouched by the puddle his blood and drew with it on the tiles with one finger. The moment was gone and he was a prince again. "It is a crime to spill the royal blood of the Emperor."

He did not look at me, but he lowered the tip of his spear in my direction in a casual threat. His clockwork soldiers moved into a fighting stance and drew their weapons. I forgot how to breathe, but my instincts remembered the seax in my grip.

The clockwork soldiers crept toward the dais, but I was sure they were not coming to harm YaMing.

"But this!" Prince Qixiang crowed. "This is an interesting opportunity! My ancestors send me a precious gift, a man and a monster dressed as an unassuming Western traveler and his wife." He faced me, stepping down like a panther stalking in a cage, and I felt my blood run cold.

"Tell me, darling flower, what secrets do you hold?"

"N-none," I stammered, taking a step back.

"You will tell me everything you can do, both of you, and then we will devise a plan to rid China of the Empress Dowager and restore China's rightful ruler."

"We are not here to fight your war," Nate panted, eyeing the remaining clockwork soldiers that had resumed their places along the walls.

"My war?" Prince Qixiang said slowly. "This is not my war. The Empress Dowager brought this upon herself when she exiled me here. She brought on this war when she imprisoned my wife, the Empress Alute, to ensure I remained in my exile with nothing but my dear sweet sister for company. No, she began the war, and you, my friend, will help me finish it."

"I will not fight the Empress," Nate said.

"I am the Emperor!" Qixiang screamed. "You are here in *my* land, the glorious empire of the Middle Kingdom. Your duty is to serve." He gestured with the spear. "She says I died!" he snapped. For a moment, I thought he might have forgotten that we were even there. He was gripped by madness. "She holds my wife and my unborn son so that I maintain my exile here in this place."

He rounded upon Nate. To his credit, my fiancé didn't flinch. They stood, nearly touching. "She wishes to rule in her own right. So she names the child Emperor so she can remain Regent until he is of age. Not an Emperor—a puppet—against our ancestor's will. Soon we shall lose the mandate of heaven." Qixiang sagged for a moment, then he straightened and carefully slicked his hair back. The gold ring on his finger quivered as he did so.

"Dress yourself. There are noble women present. I do not know how things are done in London, my new friend, but it is not fitting for my sister and your interpreter to see you nude. Then I have something to show you." Prince Qixiang turned to me. His eyes were little pieces of flint, cold and menacing, sharp in their sockets. It was hard to believe he and YaMing were twins, they could not be more different. "You will accompany us," he said to me, motioning carelessly to his sister. "She does not need your care."

Nate had become adept at dropping some of his clothing as he transfigured. It was actually a small matter to step out of his trousers. Shirts and vests did not fare as well and were nearly always shredded but because canine hips were so different than man flanks, his trousers didn't take as much damage and fell away when be transformed. He warily padded over to his pile of clothes and separated his trousers from the rest of his garments. His eyes did not leave Prince Qixiang.

He secured his trousers with his belt and shook out the rest of his clothes and draped them over his arm with as much dignity as he could manage.

I had the scale in my shirt. Prince Qixiang was unstable. Not doing as I was told was not wise. But more than fear, more than anything else, I was not willing to let Nate go where I could not follow. If he was going to be taking Nate somewhere, I would go, too. There was danger with that man and I would not let Nate face any danger without me. But refusing would make me look weak. Though if Qixiang planned to kill me, I would at least meet it on my feet, supporting Nate with my last breath. He might command me but he didn't own me.

Nate and I followed him down another hall lined with his clay soldiers.

His guards—the human guards—opened heavy wooden doors that led to stairways that took us lower and lower until we were far beneath the palace, beyond where the sun could reach. Oil braziers and torches lit the walls and we passed workers dressed in white linen robes stained with streaks of red-brown, carefully crafting clay bodies on the clockwork forms.

Workers with white cloths wrapped around their heads built wooden crates around the clay warriors.

"They are reborn, and I am their father. They answer my call." Beyond the clay warriors came hammering and other sounds, cries and whimpers. Rising beyond the scent of rich clay and wet earth was the scent of blood.

If birth was messy, then rebirth was more so.

One look into the room burned the image into my soul forever. The men—Prince Qixiang's own beloved *Yihequan*—, his own beloved boxer warriors were no longer men. They were being transformed into clockwork versions of themselves. He was torturing them.

I gasped and turned, burying my face into Nate's chest. I felt his heart pounding away in his chest, his breath caught at the horror before him.

Here there were workers dressed in red. Whether they began white and were red from blood and gore I did not wish to contemplate. One man, a bald portly fellow with a thin sweeping mustache, was sawing the arm off one soldier tied down to a stone table. His screams echoed through the stone chamber.

"You will be reborn through glorious transformation," Prince Qixiang whispered. Oddly his voice cut through the screaming, the man's whimpering cries. "Shh, shh, shh; your arm will cease to pain you soon."

Another man already had clockwork limbs tied firmly to the table and was arcing away from the stone altar as another man was busy with his hands buried in the soldier's torso. I could not help but glance over. The workman was busy with wrenches, inserting a large gear into the man's writhing body. I felt as though I had swallowed a nest of snakes. The scent of burnt flesh and spilt bowel was overwhelming. Beneath it all I could smell the sick sweet scent of opium. The men were being kept sedated and senseless with high doses of opium, so much that my head swam just being in the room. I heard Nate's stomach give a disconcerting gurgle and he looked pale.

"These are your soldiers?" Nate breathed.

"They are. Unfortunately, not all survive the process." Prince Qixiang smiled like a proud father staring at his newborn offspring. "But those that do are stronger, faster, and ageless. They can withstand sword strikes, gunfire, cannon fire. In their terracotta shells they are nearly invisible to their enemies and they can withstand nearly anything. Except you, of course."

Nate shifted uncomfortably.

"I wish they all had a twin," Prince Qixiang said. He slowly unclipped his lacquered armor and handed it to a guard. The beautiful leather beneath his armor that I knew would be buttery soft to the touch, looked deadly as a viper's belly. I knew what he was going to show us. I feared it. I did not want to see. I could not look away.

He unbuckled the leather waistcoat and handed it to the guard. The silk shirt was all that remained, hiding what he would show us. I gritted my teeth. It was not possible. And yet…

Prince Qixiang opened his shirt revealing a muscular chest, strong and lean. I breathed a sigh of relief, it was human flesh.

But then…both arms had been removed at the shoulder and replaced with clockwork versions, pistons and gears in tight housings, clean mechanicals that were a parody of human muscle in bronze, right down to the hands.

"I would never ask my men to undertake what I would not do myself." Prince Qixiang said, beaming. He set his metal hands on our shoulders. "I have not lost the Mandate of Heaven. It is the wish of *tiān* that I rule. My sister and the bond we share anchors me, so my transformation is perfect. My *Yihequan* undergo incomplete transformation, they serve me as fearsome warriors but retain so little of who they were. I retain all the power and strength of my transformation. I have lost nothing."

Nate pulled me into his arms, away from Prince Qixiang. It was a protective gesture and gallant of him, but I was not a fragile lady in need of his protection.

I stared at all the blood, all the death, all the pain. It was a crime against humanity, against the very nature of man to harm them, to carve them up like cattle. I closed my eyes, a simple prayer for those suffering and lost in this ghastly place. No prince, no emperor, no man should abuse people so, no matter his aims.

Prince Qixiang did not seem to notice. He wheeled around and grasped a spear from a guard and stood like a conqueror.

He stamped the butt of the spear, the sound piercing and sharp on the bloody stone floored chamber. "Our dynasties rise and fall as the ancestors will it, like waves on the sand. Once we were mighty, now we are unworthy. All because of my damnable mother."

"You are not like them," he said softly touching Nate's shoulder. "You are something different. You can aid me."

I wanted to slap his hand away from Nate. His very touch was poison.

"We are seeking the Arrow—"

"Yes, yes, the Arrow of Hou Yi." He waved our mission away as though it was a bothersome fly. "Your Empress—this Queen Victoria—she knows strong allies are valuable. She would reward you greatly to see the rightful Emperor restored. More importantly, so would I."

"I cannot," Nate said. "We do not have the authority to speak for Queen Victoria." The tendons in his neck tightened. "We are merely researching the fable."

"Do you believe I am a fool?" Qixiang's spear slammed on the ground. I nearly leapt out of my skin. He was poison; he was unhinged, the very soul of madness. He carelessly twirled the spear in his hand as he moved from one of his whimpering soldiers to another. "You research nothing." His voice was dangerously soft again. "You seek a weapon. An ancient weapon from a fairytale, but a weapon nonetheless."

"Yes, the Arrow of Hou Yi," I said.

"The Arrow of Hou Yi, shot from his cinnabar bow to slay the mighty and terrible Xihuan-Lung?" He turned his attention to me. The kindly smile did not reach his eyes, twisting his handsome face into a grotesque mask. "You, Vivian Harper, are a sensible woman. Surely you see that a powerful ally in the East is worth more than a slave."

I nodded slowly, how very much like Geiger he was, and insane. The center of this man's attention was a very bad place to be. It suddenly dawned on me, if Geiger had been able to make an alliance with this man, they would have gladly watched the world burn.

"Empress Dowager Cixi would make a slave of the Middle Kingdom. Without strong rulers the world descends into chaos. But I can assist you. You will tell your queen that Cixi is no Empress—she is a pretender. Tell your Queen Victoria that she could support the true Emperor and gain a powerful friend in the East. Together, an Anglo-Sino alliance will bring the world to its knees. Imagine our resources, our science, our advancement; together we will usher in a golden age, a new world order."

"And how would you accomplish this? If you care for China unite for one strong rule, forge treaties, protect your people. Stop this," I motioned to the suffering bodies. "Good kings, good emperors, they care for their people! This is not love! You are a tyrant!"

He gave a bark of laughter, "There will be no unification! Before my mother saw fit to exile me, I set forth a great bill of reformation." He twisted the spear in his hands idly, but no one was fooled, there was violence just under his words. "When the Opium Wars crippled China and made her the servant of all the world we needed to look within ourselves to become strong again. I healed our land, quelled rebellions, restored our coffers, distributed seeds and tools to my people so the common man would not starve. Still, my mother, that great pretender, painted me a child, uninterested, unfit to rule. I demanded we build factories to restore our military strength, she demanded we modernize! When my people looked to me for strength she demanded we scrape and bow to the westerners and become their puppets!" He took a deep breath to calming himself and dragged a bronze hand through his hair, smoothing it back into royal semblance. "But there is great strength in not denying what you are."

He motioned us toward the door where we entered with his spear. His smile did not reach his cold, sharp eyes.

Nate's hand was steel on my bicep. He was willing me to be silent with this madman. I glanced at him. He didn't disagree, just begged me to not incur any more wrath.

Once we returned to the beautiful throne room with its marble floors and high ceilings I released the breath I wasn't aware I had been holding. His servants had cleaned it so there was no evidence of the battle aside from the gouged pillar. YaMing sat, a silent pawn awaiting his pleasure.

The prince was a shard of ice in my chest, driving out all breath and, with it, all reason. Clearly, I was not the only one. I swallowed hard and glanced around as unobtrusively as I could. No one would look at him, from his guards to his sister. MeiLin's attention was diverted as well, though it was not fear with her; she was staring with unabashed lust at the russet fox fur wrap the woman on the dais wore wrapped around her frail shoulders as though she longed to tear it from the woman and run.

Prince Qixiang walked the length of his throne room in slow measured steps as though he had a full court watching his every move instead of just the four of us. Eventually he sat upon his beautiful carved throne, settling himself, straight and tall, bare chested, bronze arms gleaming, hands flexing and crushing the carvings on this throne. A man in his power. "As I said, there is strength in not denying what you are."

"Then you would be a valuable ally indeed," Nate said.

"Consider my words. My thanks would be limitless. My patience is not. I will rise again. I will depose Cixi and become Emperor again. I will remember those who aided, or hindered, me."

"That sounds like a threat, Prince Qixiang," I said evenly. I couldn't help it.

"It is not a threat. It is a promise," he said turning to me. "I will rule China again."

"My brother is a man of great passion," YaMing said to me softly. It was a warning, and more. Before me I saw clearly *The Two of Pentacles*—a man juggling two pentacles within a lemniscate, the symbol for infinity—it floated before my vision. Pentacles were mainly concerned with the physical world or our connection, our bonding and grounding, to the physical. There were very serious consequences with whatever we were about to get involved with in the palace of Prince Qixiang. But there was something else going on, something much more literal. She clearly read physical, while he read as more the vulnerable, emotional, and intense suit of Cups. It was rare for siblings to be so different, but as I allowed myself to fall more and more into the reading them, their cards were transparent, resting on top of each other as though one was a part of the other. She was as much his prisoner as anyone.

What had started in me as fear now became something akin to cold rage.

"Then, by your leave, Prince Qixiang." I raised my chin as defiantly as I could. "We will take your offer to Queen Victoria when we return to London."

"I wish it were that simple," Prince Qixiang said softly. "But I must insist you stay in my palace as my personal guest so we may discuss your man's amazing abilities."

Nate's eyes narrowed suspiciously.

"You and your friends will join me for dinner and we can discuss our new friendship." Prince Qixiang motioned and two of his men stepped forward. "My men will show you to your room where you can rest and refresh yourselves until dinner."

His servants approached us, real people in robes, not the clockwork men from his clay statues, and motioned for us to follow. I could have believed they were merely servants were they not armed with swords, daggers, and spears. Qixiang turned back to his throne and his sister. We were obviously dismissed.

CHAPTER ELEVEN

I THOUGHT WE WOULD be led to the palace entrance, but instead we were guided further into the castle and up several flights of stairs.

We moved beyond the beautiful tapestries and the marble to where the walls were plain stone and the servants dressed in robes of linen rather than painted silk. We climbed until my calves ached with exertion. "Where are we headed, please?"

If the guards spoke English they felt no great desire to let me know. MeiLin tried in Mandarin.

"The Emperor wishes for you to have a restful evening. He looks forward to speaking with you soon," MeiLin translated.

I bit the inside of my cheeks. Restful evening indeed.

We were ushered into a large room with two beds and a fireplace that crackled merrily. A long wooden table was set for three, with some of those lovely dumplings called *bao*, steaming, squat cast iron teapots, and small baskets of lightly cooked vegetables. Several sauces sat in porcelain dishes.

One of our companions said something, turned, and left, leaving the three of us alone in the room.

Then we heard the door lock. "Why do I get the feeling that we're not going to like the conversation we're going to have with the Emperor?" Nate asked to no one in particular. He tried the door, setting his shoulder on it but the door was stout and the lock too sturdy to force. Then he stopped, head cocked to one side.

"What do you hear?" I asked.

"Guards. There's that little *click, click, click* from his clay soldiers moving."

I took the opportunity of his undamaged ear being mashed up against the door to give the gashed one a closer examination. The bleeding had stopped. I would have loved to stitch the wound closed and give it a greater chance to heal without leaving some permanent mark but I doubted he would sit still that long. Instead I wet a cloth napkin in one of the teapots and carefully set to work cleaning the bloody wound.

Finally distracted from the sounds on the other side of the door, he smiled and pulled me close. He gave me a gentle kiss, then started taking down my hair. This was hardly the time or place for such behavior. I told him so.

He laughed. MeiLin scowled. He pulled two of my hair pins from my hair and unbent them. He pulled a small pen knife from his pocket and flipped it open with careless, practiced ease and stabbed it into the bottom of the window between the frame and the sill.

"What do you think you're doing?" I asked. We had climbed several flights of stairs. I was quite sure we were in one of the towers, and that meant we were far from the ground.

"I'm opening the window," Nate said matter-of-factly.

"It's too far to climb down." I protested.

"Perhaps for you ladies," Nate said with a smirk. "I can think of a way down."

MeiLin was content to ignore us for the time being, and sat cross legged on the floor beside the low table and fed herself with long chopsticks held in her dainty hands.

For one ungracious moment, I wished Qixiang had left us forks. I could eat prettily with those, but with chopsticks I was embarrassingly clumsy. Every time I had attempted to eat rice I ended up finding it down my blouse.

Nate shifted from an awkward crouch, stretching one leg out and rocking his weight backwards. He jammed the knife further in the crack beneath the window to take the weight of the window off the lock. It was newer than the leaded frame, an addition to this tower prison.

There was a *click*. He cursed sharply and jerked the pins free of the window lock. One was now several inches shorter than the first.

MeiLin looked up as though she would scold him, but then her look softened and she made her way over to us with a porcelain plate of food. She set it at his knee, bowed, and then backed away.

I flushed. I had been so worried about being poisoned again I didn't think of making him a plate, even after I saw that MeiLin was eating. The Emperor wouldn't poison Nate, he wanted Nate to side with him. I suppose Qixiang might poison me or MeiLin to force him to cooperate for an antidote, but he wouldn't risk poisoning Nate.

He gave her a grateful look and scowled at the lock while absently eating. He was always hungry, more so after transfiguring, and was so used to being served back home I don't think it even occurred to him that he shouldn't be accepting food from MeiLin when he could be accepting food from me. If I had thought of the loving gesture first, that is.

"Where did you learn to pick locks?" MeiLin demanded.

"I grew up in a group home," he answered, his attention still focused on the window. "A bunch of older boys were hardened street urchins. They taught me a lot of shady skills."

"I suppose it was an education of sorts," I said loving him so much at that moment.

"I can't read flowers or speak French. I can't read Latin. I get confused if there's more than two forks at my place setting. But if you need petty crime, I'm your man."

I set my hand on his shoulder and we exchanged a smile. Yes, he was, and a more fitting adventuring companion I could not have imagined.

"That sounds fascinating," MeiLin said in her musical, flattering voice. "What an interesting upbringing. Truly you are fortune blessed."

His grin widened, displaying his teeth. Nate had such a beautiful smile.

"Your hands shake," she said, bringing him a tumbler of tea from one of the steaming pots.

"Becoming—well, what I became—it's hard on me." Nate took several sips before turning back to the lock.

"Then I am fortunate indeed you were willing to make that sacrifice to protect me," MeiLin said gently.

I really disliked MeiLin. I hated that I looked jealous and petty. Nate was mine, I knew that. But something was wrong here; she was doing something to him. MeiLin would touch him and a queer change went over to him. He would become distracted to the point that I could barely get his attention.

I took a deep breath, in the throne room he hadn't transfigured to protect her alone. I felt a stab of pity for her. She longed to escape something and felt Nate was the only way to do so. I tried again to read her but I was still coming up blank. It was as if she was somehow able to block my ability to read her.

"I would do it again to protect you both," Nate promised. He levered the knife between the glass panes and wiggled them back and forth.

"I have a plan," I said, finally making them turn. "But I'm not sure how well it will work. The glass is set in these ancient metal frames. The window frame itself is steel." I paused. Nate absently ran a hand through his hair, twisting the chronically untidy locks to lay more to the left than the right. It made me smile.

"The hinge is on the outside," I said. "Could you break out the panes and take the hinge apart?"

"How will we get down?" MeiLin asked.

"I will crawl down, one at a time with each of you on my back." Nate nodded to himself then turned to MeiLin. "Don't be afraid."

"I am not afraid," she said, gazing at him.

I cleared my throat loudly. They both glanced my way, MeiLin scowling for an instant before the mask of cool politeness slid back in place. Nate turned his back to us and stripped off his waistcoat and shirt and handed them to me. I made a neat bundle of them and smiled to myself. I was quite sure this new modesty was for MeiLin's benefit. I never objected when he removed his clothing.

Then I got a flash, and the familiar nettle-like prickle starting on my arm. *The Tower* warmed upon my flesh.

"The guards will hear," I said.

Nate heard something in my voice. He quirked an eyebrow at me, asking. I nodded. MeiLin glanced between the two of us, for a moment looking annoyed that she wasn't privy to our subtle language. We had to utilize care or, like the people in the pictorial of *The Tower* card, we just might be thrown to our deaths on the stones below.

"We're gonna need the table," Nate said, carefully removing our supper from the long table.

I nodded. If nothing else, he always was working on some sort of plan, and, often, fate seemed to bend to his will.

He carefully levered onto one short side, setting the long flat tabletop against the door. I grabbed his shirt and tossed it to him. He wrapped it around his fist and threw one neat punch at the glass.

It gave a loud *crack* but held firm. Nate stepped back, shaking the fist in pain. He shifted slightly, straightened and squared his shoulders. Muscle swelled, straining against his flesh, and he gave a slight gasp. Transfiguring always pained him, but when done only a bit at a time it was torturous.

He punched harder this time and the weakened glass shattered under the force of his blow. He pulled his hand back, his shoulders already returning to their usual size and strength. I leaned out to touch him and he winced.

Nate wasted no time jerking the broken bits of glass from the frame, which he passed to me. They were very old. Thick patterns traced the glass in waves and whorls. I wrapped several of them in a cloth napkin and tucked them away in my pocket, to be knives should the need arise.

He thrust his arm through the broken pane and reached up and behind himself. He set himself up on his toes like he was willing his arm to have a bit more length.

"Can you not reach it?" MeiLin demanded.

"I can," he grunted, his tongue returning to between his teeth. "But barely."

I left him to his work, grunting and scratching the remaining glass as he struggled to get a better angle on the elusive hinge pin.

Since neither MeiLin nor Nate had keeled over with colic or any other symptom of poisoning, I packed the vegetables and *bao* into neat packets with the remaining napkins. When Nate got us out of the palace we would need supplies.

"I need a damn hammer," Nate muttered.

I dumped the rest of the tea from the pot into a planter and brought him the heavy cast iron teapot. He smiled his thanks and hammered the pot against the hinge. I winced every time it struck. The sound echoed across the courtyard, calling Qixiang's guards to come and lock us up into a proper cell, or worse.

The Tower suddenly flashed in my mind again, burning through my stomach worse than any poison. The representation of *The Tower* was nearly always a tower crumbling, sending the people standing on top tumbling to their death. We were those people, we were at the top of the tower waiting to be thrown to our deaths.

He gave a shout and grabbed the six-inch metal pin. With a theatrical flourish he gave the window a gentle push. Free of its hinge, the entire left window fell free, caught on the lock and jerked, banging into the side of the tower with a crash. Then, no longer supported between the hinge pin and the lock, it fell off the lock side and into the courtyard below. It slammed into the flagstones, shattering every remaining bit of glass into thousands of shards.

Our guards jammed their key into the lock. I grabbed one of the chopsticks that was sitting with the dishes and dove toward the door. I jammed it into the lock, forcing the key out, and shattered the chopstick inside the lock.

One of the guards cursed. Apparently shock and bewilderment sounds the same in any language.

"MeiLin, we have to go," Nate said.

He closed his eyes and furrowed his brow. Nate fell forward onto all fours, his sides heaving. His flesh swelled then split along the tight lines of muscle beneath his skin. He twisted and hissed in pain, then transformed.

"Nate," I touched his shoulder.

He snarled at me and gnashed his teeth. MeiLin stared, somewhere between fascination and horror.

"Nate. We need to get out of here."

He stood and turned toward the window. For a moment, I wanted to leave MeiLin there. We could escape this horrible place alone.

Somewhere, the mind of Nate—the part that remembered he was a man and not his beloved dog when these transfigurations took place— remembered the plan to get us out. He shook his massive head, ears slapping on his head. He swung his upper half out the window and grabbed MeiLin's hand. She gave him a startled smile as he tucked her against his back and started to climb down the craggy tower.

I blinked hard. He took her first. Why did he take her first? The heavy thud against the door didn't even register. *He took her first.* He left me alone to deal with whatever was trying to get through that door.

The door shuddered again. They were going to break it down. I couldn't think, I stood blinking stupidly with the teapot and the heavy iron hinge-pin in my hand.

The table we set against the door was holding it closed for now, but that would hardly last. I spun around looking for something else. Anything else. Then I looked dumbly at my hands. I had the pot and the hinge pin and bits of glass, hardly fitting weapons against spears and swords.

Tapered at one side, it looked more like an angled spike than a smooth carriage bolt that one would expect in a modern window. I set the angled end under the edge of the door and hammered it in place with the teapot.

The door shuddered again. Then an entirely different sound came from the other side of the door. It was sharper somehow. Clearly, they were incensed. I had no desire to know what they were using to take down the door . All I needed to know was they would eventually succeed and whatever they were using would be deadly to me.

Heavy breathing made me turn. Nate stood half crouched at the window, sides heaving. Though strong and formed in a manner with the best features of man and beast, he was nearing the end of his stamina. The transfiguration was hard on him, staying too long in the hybrid form made him nearly senseless, and he hadn't fully recovered from his earlier transfiguration when we were threatened by Qixiang's clockwork soldiers.

He crouched in the window and reached out for me, his tall ears twitching towards the sound of the guards at the door. The damaged ear was bleeding again, the fur around the wound was shiny and matted. I quickly snatched up the rest of his clothes and the food bundles. He tucked me up against his belly and started the three-limbed climb back to the ground far below.

We were nearly halfway there when I felt his shoulders start to quiver. He was moving faster, less climbing, more slowing our decent while letting gravity drag us to the glass-covered cobbles below.

He was shrinking, compacting, returning to his normal size. He was shaking and doing his best to hang on to the side of the tower. Then we were falling.

We hit the ground hard. All the breath was crushed from my body. I lay there, gasping. My corset made it hard to sit up. I struggled like a tortoise to right myself. And beyond the red agony of our impact with the hard ground, I dimly heard hoofbeats.

MeiLin was riding one of our horses. The others were led by ropes hastily tied to their headstalls. "Get up!"

I forced myself to roll over as one would move a log. Nate lay groaning on the cobbles. I gave him a hand up. He would not be able to do much without food and rest. Whatever irritation I felt at being last to be rescued faded. I had Nate's boots and the rest of his clothes in a little bundle under my arm. I passed him his pants and he rushed to put them on then we mounted the horses.

We needed to be far from here before Qixiang and his men mounted a search. No doubt they realized we were no longer in the guest quarters.

We would not be fully provisioned, just have whatever was left in the saddlebags as our mounts had not been unloaded, merely stashed in stables for the time being until Prince Qixiang had decided what to do with us.

MeiLin kicked her horse into action. The horse squealed and reared, threatening to scrape her off on the stone wall, but she managed to retain her seat. Nate took off in hot pursuit, bouncing with the awkward trot. As I followed them both I could see blood running down his back, gashed from the glass and the cobbles.

We rode hard for an hour or more, putting as much distance between us and Qixiang as possible. The moon hid behind the trees and the mist started up around us, rising from the ground like silver smoke to swallow up all sound.

Nate was sagging in the saddle, swaying with the movement of the horse. His back had stopped bleeding but the lines of where the blood ran were dark as ink on his skin.

"We need to stop for a moment," I called.

MeiLin turned her horse with a jerk on the reins. The mare tossed her head in protest. "We cannot stop."

"We hired you, I say we are stopping now," I snapped. My patience was worn thin.

She jerked her horse's head back around and dismounted, muttering something under her breath. Even though I do not speak Mandarin, I am sure it wasn't complimentary. I dragged Nate off his horse.

"I'm sorry, Vivian," he muttered.

"Whatever for?" I made myself laugh. "We're away from Qixiang; mad as a hatter that one."

He hung his head, though I suspect fatigue was just as much as to blame as him feeling as though he should have done more.

"Now, let me check those cuts on your back," I said, soothingly taking a jar of salve from the saddlebag, thankfully, I still had my supplies. Nate bore the scars of our last adventure together and I remembered all the names I had been called when all I had at my disposal was cheap alcohol for disinfecting.

I wished I could wait for daylight; lighting a lamp would give only the illusion of light. Growing up in London, I knew that trying to use lanterns make the fogs worse as the haze reflects the dim light back to you. And, if Qixiang was still searching for us the light would give away our position.

Nate shifted some as I cleaned and treated the wounds the as best I could. I pulled out a flask of tincture made of willow bark which would help with the pain. I took a healthy dose for myself then passed it over to Nate. The fall and then the hard ride had left me stiff and sore. I didn't look forward to waking up tomorrow morning. As much as I hated to admit it, MeiLin was right. We still needed to put as much distance between us and them as possible.

I decided we needed another hour, then we would stop for the night. I gave Nate the rest of his clothing and checked our supplies to give him a few moments to dress. "MeiLin?" He called from the other side of his horse. "Can you lead us towards the older portion of the forest?"

"Older, why?" She rose, and both her and the pony eyed each other warily.

"Because we are searching for the bones of an ancient dragon killed in the valley by the Temple of Yi." He gave his collar a hard tug. "Ancient dragon bones would be in the older portion of the forest. I'm not as smart as Viv but my brains do work that well." He gave me a wink. "The maps I copied from the Viridian says the temple should be in the oldest portions of that forest. The trees are dense. This palace may have been on the way, but I think the flight put us off track."

I hoped we would be able to put a few more miles between us and the Mad Prince before we made camp. At first light I would use the pilfered dragon scale to concoct the charm and we could begin our search for a long dead dragon and the arrow in the morning.

CHAPTER TWELVE

WITH THE CANITHROPE now a permanent part of him, Nate seemed to retain a portion of his animal senses all the time. His vision, sense of hearing, and sense of smell were frightfully acute, so when it was time for us to finally stop for the night he set up a picket line for the horses and set our tents up in the dark of night, before ushering us in to snatch a few hours rest before moving on.

The night's fitful sleep did not improve my disposition. It did little to improve MeiLin's mood either. That morning when Nate brought her tea, she gave him a look that could have soured milk. Nate shrugged and set her tumbler against a rock, then tightened the ropes that secured the guy lines of our tent. He moved on to pull something out of our supplies for breakfast.

MeiLin and I ground the dragon's scale and dried fish to powder with my mortar and pestle and then mixed it with perfectly white bees wax until the entire thing gleamed like a violet pearl. Then she banished me from the task and worked the entire lump of heat softened wax into a long rope. She carefully crafted the wax into a beautiful knot that turned on itself again and again until it was a beautiful unbroken disc the size of my palm.

At least I still had the book and notes to occupy me. I rubbed the back of my neck to cast off the impending headache. I could consult them, though I wasn't sure there would be anything on the terracotta warriors that would be of value. Prince Qixiang's inhuman soldiers were are a marvel of modern engineering and ancient magic. They had once been men, twisted and tortured into clockwork forms and then disguised as the terracotta soldiers that I had seen all over China. They were so common I had grown accustomed to seeing them everywhere, from the archways to the crossroads. How many of them were the clockwork men of Prince Qixiang ready to spring to life at his command? How many would it take to overwhelm the Empress Dowager Cixi's soldiers? It would not only be a battle between the Empress Dowager and the Clockwork Emperor, all of China would bleed.

I trimmed my fingernail with my teeth. He wanted Nate on his side, and if he knew what I could do, he would want me, too. I don't know that we would be enough to turn the tide of battle but our presence would cost more lives. The great tragedy of it was that our absence would not prevent the loss of life. War would come to this beautiful land whether we took the arrow to London or not, and a great unified China, the aim of both rulers, was not in the cards. I did not have to be able to read them to know that.

The song of the birds changed slightly, not enough to make me sure that danger was looming, but something in the forest around us had shifted— for the better or worse. I sat on a rock to pin up my hair and brush out my skirts, looking around unobtrusively as I did so. The trees themselves were shifting. Something was watching us.

A creature appeared in front of me. His lion-tail waved lightly from one side to another in casual interest. I turned back to the rest of the party but no one else had noticed.

Nate was folding up our tent, carefully coiling the ropes in his hand.

"Do you see that?" I motioned.

"See what?"

"He does not see me," the creature said softly in a pleasant rumble. It motioned. I followed. Whatever it was, I just *knew* it meant me no harm.

The body was distinctly feline. It sat placidly like a trained hound. It had a large square head, a sweeping mustache and pointed beard, and a single curved horn jutting from the top of its head between the ears. I had seen a horn like this before in a picture of a rhinoceros, but instead of curving back it curved slightly forward amidst a mass of wavy mane that shifted as though tousled by a breeze.

It waited for me down by the river, sitting on its haunches. It raised a front paw and gently stroked the mustache and beard with black-tipped nails.

"I know what you are!" I said suddenly. I had seen them all over China, guarding buildings and sitting in parks. But those had been made of stone. "You're a Foo Dog. A *Shi*."

"No, Child of the West," it said placidly. "I am Xiezhi."

"Oh, I am sorry. Pleased to meet you, Xiezhi." I was unsure if a curtsy would be appropriate, but did anyway.

Xiezhi chuckled, a warm sound. "To your eyes, I am merely a monster. To my people I am so much more."

I felt *Themis,* also known by her other name, *Justice,* at my throat burning under my skin. It was more than the usual warmth of reading something, this time it got so hot I was afraid it would soon glow under my skin. I swallowed hard.

"You are in the presence of Justice. I maintain all that is right and good in the affairs of mortals and immortals alike."

"That explains much." I said, swallowing hard against the burn. "What do you want with me...?" I paused. "Perhaps the better question is, why can I see you?"

"I deal in truth, Child of the West. You travel with a being that hides its truth from the light. It is more than it appears."

"Mr. Valentine is no danger to you," I said quickly.

"Why are you here, Child of the West?" it said, its eyes narrowing.

"We seek the Arrow of Xihuan-Lung," I said. I was positive this creature of truth would be able to sense any lie I might tell trying to keep our mission a secret. I had no desire to see how a truth creature would deal with one it thought was lying.

"Why do you seek the arrow?"

I frowned, considering my options. If Xiezhi was a truth creature then he would value honesty above all things. "I am a member of a guild of explorers who seek out treasures to keep them safe from others who would sell them or hoard them."

"The arrow is more than just a mere arrow," it rumbled.

"Yes, I know that. It was shot from the bow of a great Chinese hero, Hou Yi, I believe, his name was. He killed the dragon, Xihuan-Lung."

"Would the world have been better if Xihuan-Lung had never been slain?" it asked me.

"I don't know," I said honestly. "I believe it was long ago—I'm sure Hou Yi did what he thought best."

"Xihuan-Lung had been damaged beyond all redemption. She gave of herself until she was out of balance and fell into darkness," it said. "Do you believe a creature like that deserves to be free among the world of men?"

"I don't know," I said hesitantly. Then I thought of Nate and the fearsome beast he could become. I considered the Empress and her lost son. "No one is beyond redemption. There is always hope. There's always more than we see. It is not for me to judge."

"Very clever, Child of the West." It stroked its beard again. "I wonder, do you use the same clever judgment within your own party?"

"Always," I said, thinking of Nate. He was so much more than he appeared, especially when transfigured. Then, for some reason, I thought of Lum. Ham-fisted and heavy-handed in everything he did, still, he seemed conflicted in his dealings. Nate had shot him, he had reason to hate us. But we also pulled him from the fire in the factory. I hated him. Or was I afraid of him? Why in the world did I think of him now of all things? Xiezhi was still staring at me, waiting for me to answer.

"There is good in all," I decided. Answering diplomatically was better than nothing. Too late, I thought about MeiLin, I wasn't sure there was very much good in her. But then I paused, no, there is good in all things. There was a strange sorrow to her.

"Still you seek Xihuan-Lung?"

"Yes," I said confidently. "That is why we are here. We wish to take the arrow back to London to protect it. The *Ye-Yihequan* threaten everything with their violence and there is war coming, even to this ancient woodland. You should consider staying out of the way," I said gently. "The world has changed much in the last hundred years. There are weapons more destructive than anything you have ever—"

Xiezhi laughed, a warm deep rumble. "You seek to warn me, Child of the West?" It laughed again, as a grandfather to a child. "The world has changed much in a *thousand* years. The weapons of man rise and fall like waves on the shore. The only constant is the ebb and flow. Nothing will harm me here." It finally ceased its chuckle and stroked it beard, winding it between black claws the way a snake moves through tall grass. "But your concern is to be admired.

"I will tell you, Hou Yi was right to slay Xihuan-Lung. Had he acted in poor judgment I would have stopped him. She was beyond redemption. Even for a creature as great as a dragon." It paused and released the beard and reached out a paw to me. "Nothing is beyond falling out of grace, Child of the West. Not you, not me, not even China."

It touched me, the large black claw warmer than I expected. It gently stroked my cheek. I should have been terrified. It was strange that I was not.

"You have come far, Child of the West," it said wistfully. "But I fear China has lost the Mandate of Heaven and we shall fade into the eastern sun. All falls in time."

"Perhaps you can reclaim it." I was sorry this creature should feel pain.

It smiled at me. "Beware your own fall."

I took a step back. "What do you mean?"

"When one acts rashly, even in the best interests of the moment, one risks a great failing." It said simply.

"We should not be here," I said slowly. I knew it, but saying it out loud had a finality to it. "What is good for Britain is bad for the world?"

"No, merely being here changes nothing."

"You believe we should leave the arrow in China," I concluded. *All mystical creatures seemed to talk in riddles.* I resolved to thank Nate next time he plainly just said what he meant. "Then it could be destroyed," I argued, "There is talk of war between China and the rest of the world."

"The Arrow of Hou Yi was created for one purpose and one purpose only: To slay the enemy of man. An item such as that cannot be destroyed without impacting the deed it was forged for."

I chewed my lip. Xiezhi turned to leave.

"Wait!" I said. I reached deeply within myself touching that calm where I could feel the cards that marked my being. The creature radiated Justice stronger than anything I had ever seen.

"You are a creature of justice. Or a truth creature. Can you answer a question for me?"

"I punish mortals for being untruthful or twisting justice to suit their own needs," Xiezhi said, chuckling. "I do not answer to the whim or mortals. Still, I will answer one question to the best of my ability."

"We are helping MeiLin make a charm to lead us to where the Arrow of Xihuan-Lung lays."

"The charm you make will help guide MeiLin," Xiezhi said softly. "But you do not need a charm to locate the bones of Xihuan-Lung. She is merely beyond the Dragon Gate. If you manage to locate the seals you will find the dragon's bones and the arrow. What you do with that knowledge, Child of the West, is entirely up to you. But removing the arrow may prove to be a fatal decision. The arrow was created to take a specific life. To move it will have far reaching consequences for China and for all the world, beginning with those who remove it."

"If we remove it from the corpse of the creature it was designed to kill, will the creature cease to be dead?" I wondered out loud.

Xiezhi did not answer, but stared at me with a deep, knowing gaze, suddenly standing before me as though it had charged like an angry bull. The horn atop its square head gleamed in the mist, rust-red like it was covered in blood. I stumbled back. I wanted to scream for help, but something in Xiezhi's eyes was oddly comforting. Then it lowered its blood-red horn and touched my forehead.

All twenty-two symbols of the Tarot's major arcana burst into light, taking with it what I assumed was my soul, filling me with an elation and a dread I had never felt before. I was thrown off my feet, shattered into a thousand pieces, and slammed into the ground. Images raced through my mind, twisting my body in an agony and an ecstasy unlike any other. I could only decipher a few of them as they raced past.

The Wheel raced through my mind, spinning rapidly through the different arcana. The Hermit with his lamp and robes warned me, the Lovers clung to one another in holy union, while the Devil and Death squared off, change or perish; cling to what you know or be destroyed. The Tower shook and fell, tossing kings and queens, knights and pages to their deaths below, and Strength gently muzzled her lion, begging me to hold out. And over it all, from his place, just above my head the Hanged Man winked at me and laughed and laughed...

CHAPTER THIRTEEN

I WAS KNEELING in the grass where I had followed Xiezhi but now I was alone. I struggled to my feet, then sagged against a boulder and closed my eyes. I rubbed the bridge of my nose where Xiezhi's horn touched my forehead. I expected blood, but there was no blood, no pain, just a sensation of heat. I felt electrified, tired but electrified.

I needed to see the notes. I needed to see the book. It was a great effort to place one foot in front of the other to return to the camp where Nate and MeiLin waited, but every step made me stronger.

Trines were parts of the whole. We would need a key to get to the dragon's gravesite. But then again, it had been Mr. Barrett who had mentioned the keys. Then we weren't looking for *a* key, we were looking for *keys*, or parts to make a larger key.

As I walked I reflected on *The Wheel of Fortune*. There are four suits of Minor Arcana: cups, wands, swords and pentacles. Then there are the major arcana. Five parts. Five parts to a whole, five parts to a greater picture. *The Wheel of Fortune* reminds us that you cannot stand still and accept all that life offers. The only constant is that everything is in a state of flux. But as I walked the Wheel in my mind became the image of the hand-drawn sketch on the notes—a circle with four marked points, each a temple, and each connected and finally crossing in the center. Four quadrants and a point in the center.

Four keys and a gateway. The notes on the artifact had something about this:

> *It is my sincere belief that you will not find anyone of Chinese origin willing to assist in the recovery of this artifact, such is their superstition of the great power their ancestors and other such spirits have over their lives. And this influence is, to a large extent, based on the power these beings had in life. In fact, due to this superstition, some powerful artifacts are even broken apart and hidden in separate locations to keep enemies from gathering them. See "The Legend of the Headless Samurai's Sword."*

So, of we wished to raise the gateway to access the bones then we needed to find the gateway. If we wanted to pass through it we needed a key. If the key had been broken then we needed the pieces; their locations were likely the points in the circle, the trine temples, trines being quite literally, parts of a whole.

And we would have to do it without help. The people of this land and their belief in their ancestors and how they controlled their fate would leave us without allies in this journey.

Four trines, four suits in the tarot, five if I counted the major arcana; four elements in the natural world, five if you counted the spirit. Four parts to a key? Maybe there were five parts? Four keys and the gateway made five.

"If we are going to access the bones of Xihuan-Lung we are going to have to gather the pieces of the key," I announced. "A trine is part of a whole. We are looking for parts to make a whole. The key, or keys, is what we need and they are being kept in four separate places."

Nate just stared at me. "Won't the charm you and MeiLin made lead us to the dragon?" he asked.

I watched MeiLin carefully. Xiezhi implied the charm had nothing to do with the dragon's bones itself but was for MeiLin's own goals. I just wished I knew what those were.

I pulled out the diagram. "The circle that is marked, those are the locations," I explained. "They contain the parts of the key or keys. We will need to recover them as soon as possible."

"The charm will not help us if the gateway is sealed," MeiLin said smoothly. Far too smooth to be true.

"Then where do we go first?" Nate asked as he finished loading MeiLin's pony.

"The closest trine temple is the Temple of Yi. It is the temple of truth and willful thought, and the home of an order of monks," I said folding my arms. "That is where we need to go."

"I can lead you there." MeiLin narrowed her eyes at me. "Everyone in China knows of sacred temples. The most sacred of places are most vulnerable to corruption when the monks abandon them."

"Why?" I asked

MeiLin scowled at me. "When people feel weak, they go places of great strength to be renewed. But echoes of their pain remains. When the monks are forced to abandon the places, the weakness can remain."

"So, we are in China chasing fairytales?" Nate clarified smiling at me. "Adventure eh?"

We finally knew where we were going. This was what I had been looking forward to. I smiled and turned to look at the notes again to verify the name of the temple. When I turned back MeiLin had laid her hand on Nate's arm. They were staring at one another, her heavily lidded eyes, now red-brown rather than green, boring into him. He had his face half-turned toward her.

"Your fiancée may be better off waiting in the hotel. I am only thinking of her health," MeiLin said sweetly. "Chasing fairytales can be so tedious."

What was all that about? I hoped her pony scraped her off at the nearest low branch.

§§§

The Temple of Yi had once been a beautiful stone building. It was made of several circular levels, getting smaller and smaller as they climbed, like tiers on a cake, and was decorated in stone carvings of leaves and flowers of the same flora that grew and wove around the temple, working their way up the side. But the stone wall and wooden gate surrounding the building had fallen into disrepair. The stones in the walkway had shifted unevenly, causing the ponies to scrape and stumble along. Nate set a loose picket line for the ponies while I picked a path around the knee-high grasses to the tall bronze entrance.

There were snakes on both doors, curling to each other like an S and then another inverse. I had no general dislike for snakes, but these were more than tolerable, in fact, they were beautiful.

"This was once a noble temple where the monks would come to pray and reflect upon the nature of life," MeiLin informed Nate. "It is abandoned now."

"Convenient, you forgot to mention that until now," I said evenly.

"As I said, it is an old story. Everyone who belongs here knows this story. I forget you do not belong here. Nate, on the other hand, you are such an old, well-traveled soul, I forget you are not a native of this country."

I heard voices. The mist made trying to locate and discern sounds tricky, but the voices were coming closer. They were speaking English.

Mr. Barrett and his crew tramped out of the tall grass.

"Fancy meeting you out here." Mr. Barrett smiled jovially, as if we had run into each other at a society luncheon.

Today he wore a loose, black shirt tucked into black trousers. The gun at his hip was tucked into a black leather holster, polished to a mirror shine. His usually messy gray hair was hidden by a black cowboy hat; I saw untidy ends of his hair tickling his collar. The look would have been rakish on Nate, but on Michael Barrett it looked sloppy. The black from head to toe was nearly laughable. He was trying too hard to be both stylish and intimidating. It was a gift one simply had or didn't have. Mr. Barrett just looked silly.

"Miss Ratham," Nate said tensely.

"Miss Harper!" Mike Barrett greeted me as though we both had been longing for a reunion. "So good to see you again, my dear." He bowed to me. I couldn't help but cringe. "You remember my men, Mr. Quinn, and Mr. Baxter." The men nodded in turn. Mr. Barrett gave a friendly laugh. "Seems we share a common goal after all."

"I don't know that I would assume that." I eyed his bodyguard, the hulking Columbus Baxter.

Nate was staring from a lowered brow at them, his stance wide, the very picture of ferocity. His palm absently rested against the butt of his revolver.

"Oh, come now," Quinn said. "Whatever history you have is in the past. Surely we can work together. There is more than enough for us all."

I bristled. "Enough of what, exactly?"

"Explain to me why we need you," Nate said dryly.

"We have a good map," Barrett said.

"We found this site all by ourselves," Nate said, eyes narrowing. "So again, explain to me why we need you."

Mr. Barrett gave us a cocky grin. "We have a piece of the key."

Nate blinked twice.

"Specifically, the center of the key." Barrett pulled a grimy cloth from his pocket and revealed an uncut, polished stone, round like a bird egg, the color of claret. "Now, as I tried to tell you in Beijing, we could chase one another all over China, racing one another to all the pieces of the key…but since I already hold this, you really would do better to work with us."

I glared at Columbus Baxter. The first time I had met him he had been working for Newt Geiger. On that particular meeting, Lum wrenched my arm behind my back and held me while Mr. Geiger punched me.

"Certainly there is more than enough adventure for all," Mr. Quinn said smoothly. "Gentlemen, surely we can come to some sort of agreement."

But there was only one arrow, I thought biting the inside of my cheek, and that could not be split between two parties.

"I don't see why not," Barrett said. "An even split of the take, two ways. We share the map and the key, you share your guide."

Nate shook his head and turned away.

I was in hot pursuit. "What is the matter with you?" I demanded when we were alone. "Is it Mr. Baxter? I hate him, too, but you have to admit, when Prince Qixiang comes—and he will—it is better to have allies."

"Lum?" Nate laughed and scrubbed his hair back with his hands. "No, I can easily handle Lum." He turned his attention to the trees trying to put words to his thoughts. "Something about this is all wrong."

I frowned. "The Explorer's Society did say they encourage light treasure hunting, maybe they mean whatever can be taken from the dragon. Dragons have treasure hoards."

"Not this time, something is very wrong here, Vivian," Nate said. He checked the pistol at my side. "Don't let any of them close, not even Charlotte."

I hated the look on his face. Something about this unnerved him more than the Mad Prince. "Nate, what is it?"

"I don't know yet," Nate said. "Something smells funny."

"You're basing all this on a smell? Is this a literal smell or a figurative one?"

He gave me an indulgent look. "Really? Why would the Explorer's Society send more than one agent to recover the arrow when there are many treasures that need protecting in the world? If we are really headed to war we need—"

I interrupted. "Tell me specifically what is wrong about them."

He took a deep breath then looked over to where Mr. Barrett and his little group were carefully staking their horses to trees. It was a lazy way to care for their mounts. MeiLin had joined them. At least she was paying attention to someone else for a change.

Nate sighed and absently scrubbed his fingers through his hair, his nervous gesture. "Look at Barrett, he has all new gear."

"So do we," I countered evenly.

"All new, *expensive* gear. He has the center of the key. They smell like...like..." he paused, searching for the words. "Spices. I've smelled it before, like the healer, but not quite."

"Like the marketplace?" I offered.

"Yes. No." He stared off at them moodily, words failing him. "I'm telling you something is wrong here. I know it"

"The other you knows it." I offered, thinking of Ranger and his canithrope form.

"Yes." Nate pounced at the words.

At least I could understand that. "Well, if they try anything, transfigure and rip them to pieces. Until then, they are very dangerous and we need to play nice until we can figure out how to outfox them."

Nate scowled at me. He was right, of course. We were in China with very few friends, but I feared that before long, the Mad Prince would be coming after us and we could not afford to be so greatly outnumbered. They were our countrymen, at least Charlotte, Mr. Quinn, and Mr. Baxter were, and we needed to side with one another. If Mr. Barrett was a treasure hunter, then maybe we could appeal to his love of adventure or the promise of treasure to ensure his help should Prince Qixiang attack us again.

I made sure the leather loop that slid over the back of my pistol was secure, and went to rejoin Barrett's men, leaving Nate to stand bewildered in the dusk. We could at least give the appearance of working together. We could build a communal fire and I could start something for our supper. Nate may have wanted to keep us separate, but I needed to know what they were up to, and if being friendly could get them to share information then it was all the better.

Nate was still cross with me the next morning. He lay with his back to me, curled like a snail in his shell pushed up against the wall of our tent. His clothes were going to be soaking wet from the dew and mist that gathered on the tent walls. He rose when he heard me stirring and moodily left to start some water for washing and tea, leaving me free to change into my pants and shirt for the day of adventuring in the temple.

As soon as I was out of the tent, he started striking the tent in tense, violent motions. I was sure he would snap one of the guy-lines. He would eventually work through his mood if given enough time, on the other hand, in his stubbornness, not changing out of his wet shirt and letting it chafe and rub against him all day would keep him cross and irritable. I handed him a dry shirt.

I walked around the site and noticed that the ceiling of the ante chamber of the temple had partially collapsed so it was no longer protected from the elements. The blowing leaves and sand had covered everything, but there were several brass braziers that, if lit, would banish the cold and damp that infected everything.

Clearly, Mr. Barrett had the same idea. He sent Mr. Quinn and Lum out to gather more wood for the fires and stacked it around the feet of the crouched stone oxen as if patiently waiting for someone to lay fires in the stone bowls that balanced against their horns, though there were eight in all, one was shattered nearly beyond recognition.

Soon the crackling fires made the room thoroughly toasty, then stuffy, as it burned off the fog and warmed the moist air in the early morning. I took the coiled ropes and our tent and carefully laid them out against the backs of the stone oxen so the heat of the fires would dry them. Mr. Quinn helped me lay various gear from his own party along the backs of the stone oxen. I figured if making Nate warm and dry improved his spirits then a little good will between the parties could not harm anything either.

Charlotte was busy applying far too much eye makeup in a brass mirror by the front door and giving Barrett the same look a Jenny would give her latest John. Where had Mr. Barrett gotten her?

This raised a more important question, she hung on Mr. Barrett even more than a couple in love, but her provocative, low-cut gowns were not appropriate in the slightest for adventuring. Why had she come? The way she hung on Mr. Barrett implied that they had some sort of arrangement of that he either owned her or that she was afraid to leave his side. I resolved to be kind to her despite Nate's warning. Perhaps if I was kind to her, she would be willing to tell me why Mr. Barrett and his men were here and what they knew.

MeiLin ignored us. She watched us all with cautious interest.

The Temple of Yi had been dedicated to seasonal meditation and was decorated with snakes, oxen and roosters. I pulled out the book again.

"What is that?" MeiLin demanded.

"A book on Chinese mythological creatures I got from London." I said flipping through the pages looking for the section on the zodiac.

The dim light from the braziers made it hard to read, but I was able to determine that we were in the second trine. The snake, ox and rooster were animals—uh, signs—associated with planning, the slow building of energy, and endurance. It was the very nature of cycles of the earth. I raised my head to digest what I had just read and found MeiLin staring at me.

I turned away to think and something glinting in the light caught my eye. If it was a key or a piece of a key then this would be easier than I thought. No such luck, it was just a bit of tile. I set to work scraping the leaves and debris from the temple floor. Before long, MeiLin knelt down to help me, and together we revealed a beautiful mosaic labyrinth set into the floor. It must have taken us nearly an hour. It was the most manual labor I had seen her do since meeting her.

"Something's bothering me," I said to Nate as we sat back to have our breakfast of hard-cooked eggs from our packs and watched Barrett and his hired men cook up their separate meals.

Nate grunted in response, watching them. MeiLin wandered off on her own to wash up so we were truly on our own for a precious short while. He sipped a bit of coffee from a tin cup wrapped in flannel.

I leaned closer. "They have a map. And the center of the key. Why do they need us?"

Nate stopped chewing and stared at me as if seeing me for the first time this morning. "What?"

"I don't think they're following us. They have a map so they would have found the temple on their own. It was just a matter of time. So do they need us just to take the piece of the key from us? If so, are there ancient guardians here? Do they just plan on taking it from off our dead bodies?" I added another stick to the fire.

Nate stared off into the fire. "Either the pieces are dangerous to get to or they know where they are but not how to lay hands on the keys themselves. And here I thought we could just follow the clues and go get the pieces, unlock the gate, and go get the arrow."

"Aren't you glad we are doing this together?" I laughed. "Just the adventure for a couple on the eve of their pending nuptials."

"Yes and no," Nate said earnestly. "If we need to puzzle it out I'll be glad to have you here, but not if getting the pieces is dangerous. And I'll not be happy to have you along when Barrett and his men decide it's time to take our pieces of the key."

I gave him an affectionate shove and graciously poured him the last of our tea. "Then I pity Mr. Barrett and his men when he decides it is time to take something under your protection."

Nate gave me a wolfish grin. "I hope when that time comes he has a bigger army than just Lum. I can take him easily."

MeiLin was suddenly back. "The piece of the key should be hidden in the center of the temple." She announced to everyone and no one. "That will be the most protected place."

"I suppose it is time to get to work," I said to Nate, rising and dusting off my trousers.

He rewarded me with a smile that warmed me to the core. I said a silent prayer of thanks that we weren't still fighting.

"How do you figure, lass?" Mr. Barrett inquired, his thumb hooked in his stiff black leather belt.

MeiLin glared, angry he would dare to question her; so it wasn't a look she reserved merely for me after all. "The mosaic in the floor."

She pointed to where we had cleared off the beautiful tiles in the center of the floor—it was a maze, cunningly placed in the stone floor, but in relief, so it made a slight track. I wished for a ball or a set of marbles so I could lay on the floor like a child and chase them along the paths.

The tiles were painted and fired ceramic resembling the seasons, terminating in a central pit that sat perhaps four inches deeper than the rest of the floor. I knelt. The center had been filled with glass, revealing a serpent, a rooster, and an ox beneath the lake of glass, all in meditative poses.

I leaned in to get a closer look. Near the back of my knee, the *Seven of Cups* burned, seven different cups to drink from, so many choices, so many paths. I stopped and shifted to sit on the stone floor.

It was going to be a maze. MeiLin had said so. But the incident with the dragon scale told me I should listen not only to what she said but to what she didn't say.

I ran through what I knew: the animals the temple was dedicated to were an ox, a snake, and a rooster; China had a dozen such holy animals, Wei Huan, the master healer, had a tapestry depicting them and they were also in my book; there were four trines so there should be four temples with three animals each.

I tried to envision seven golden cups before me, the mark I felt burn on my leg. It could be merely warning me of too many choices or it could be warning me of too many directions to go. There were three of us and four of them, that could also be the seven, but in my heart I knew that was mere coincidence. *The Seven of Cups* typically marked confusion, we needed to keep our wits about us to prevail.

"Why have the monks abandoned the temple?" I wondered.

"It's fascinating, actually." Mr. Quinn came to stand beside me. "You see, China is in great turmoil. Empress Cixi wishes to restore China to her formal glory but is beset by enemies from all sides. It has left the monks fearful for their safety."

"The prince wished to bring China into the modern age," Nate said with a note of exaggerated care.

"It is most unfortunate that he fell ill and perished before he was able to do that," Mr. Barrett added. I caught the careless tone of his comment and the speed with which he added it. It was tasteless, but more than that, something about it caught in my brain. It was off somehow.

"Yeah, there could have been some sort of civil war," Lum said with a snort.

"Mr. Baxter, I was under the impression that China was staring at a looming civil war," I replied, baiting him. The conversation around us had suddenly reached an odd level of ugliness and tension. I wasn't exactly sure what about, but I had my suspicions, and I was sure Nate did as well.

"No, Miss Harper," Mr. Quinn said diplomatically. "China is facing war over unlawful occupation. There are some, the Crown included, that believe that a peaceful resolution can be reached, but only if the sovereignty of China can be respected. If not, then open war will be the result. China is being carved up like a lamb by clumsy back-alley butchers. It is only natural for the lamb to object."

"Of course. Though, Mr. Quinn, I do hope you are not suggesting that China is as helpless as a lamb," I said, offering my hand.

"A poor analogy, I assure you," he said, giving me a hand in rising. Mr. Quinn did not offer a better one.

Nate finished packing his rucksack, his motions sharp and stiff.

Charlotte lit a torch from one of the Ox braziers. "Well then, we shall get to it!"

We followed her up a handful of stairs where she yielded the lead to Mr. Barrett and he proceeded to stamp along in his new black boots, making it sound as though we were accompanied by a pony. Rather than fine English riding pricks he wore spurs on his boots that rang and jingled, a sound that I was not aware of until we had gotten away from the fires and the leaf litter.

There had been eight oxen braziers, the paths of the sacred maze in the middle of the floor in the antechamber had eight rings, there were smaller and smaller circles connecting little paths to each other or doubling back to outer rings before meeting in the center where the snake, the ox, and the rooster sat under a solid lake of semi-transparent glass in positions of quiet reflection and meditation.

I followed the rest of the party up the stairs, counting as I went. I watched the torch reflect off the stone walls, dusts, and covered in cobwebs. "MeiLin, what is the significance of eight?"

MeiLin cocked her head, her eyes narrowed. Finally, she decided to answer. "Eight is a lucky number, it represents cosmic order and equilibrium."

I leapt over the final step. Like the eighth stone ox it was shattered. Though the rest of the temple shared an air of neglect, everything had been well-maintained before being abandoned by the monks. The step, like the ox, had been destroyed maliciously, though by what I could not venture a guess. It would take a man quite a long time with a chisel and hammer to reduce the ox to rubble, but the damage done to the stone step gave me pause, I wasn't even sure Nate could do that in his canithrope form. I pushed against a chunk of stone with my toe until I felt the weight of it clear up to my hip. It barely moved. If eight is the number of cosmic order and equilibrium then did this count as seven, or as something else entirely?

An icy chill ran up my spine, even though I had put on my own leather long coat when we left the warmth of the ox braziers.

Nate took over the lead of the party from Mr. Barrett and Charlotte after she singed her dress with the torch and was reduced to an indelicate shrieking, cursing mess. Nate took the torch while Barrett worked to get her under control for the better part of a half-hour, assuring her he would purchase her another dress just like it and other such nonsense.

"The monks called this the Temple of Truth and Willful Thought. It was also known as the Temple of Intention," Mr. Quinn said, offering me a hand over the broken bits of stone.

"You are a scholar of all things from China, are you not, Mr. Quinn?" I asked, gratefully taking his hand.

"I find the culture fascinating, my dear," Mr. Quinn said. "Never have I found a country so embroiled in the battle to hold on to the old ways as the new world evolves around them. I find it quaint."

"Quaint?" I blinked, not sure I heard him correctly. So far in China I had been poisoned, imprisoned, held without cause; we met an Empress and her not-dead-but-believed-to-be-dead son, our guide was actively trying to steal my fiancé from me, and we were traipsing about an abandoned temple for a key to the grave site of a long dead dragon. *Quaint* was hardly the way I would describe our adventure thus far.

Mr. Quinn smiled. "Ah yes, Mr. Valentine told me of your misadventures. China does take some getting used to."

The light ahead of us stopped as the aforementioned Mr. Valentine stood at a fork in the path, squinting in the semi-darkness. He nodded to himself and headed off the main curved path.

The chambers would have been dark were they not set with bits of polished metal mirrors set into the walls far above my head, crudely focused to reflect the barest bit of light, giving the entire place an eerie glow. I turned, trying to see where the light originated from but I was unable to find the source, there were too many twists and turns and the light disappeared around the curves ahead of us.

I was so busy seeking out the source of the light I didn't notice we had stopped and I ran right into Nate's back. He was staring down another set of corridors that curved ahead, behind, and off to the left in a gentle loop, into darkness.

The light from the torch reflected the indecision in his face.

"Why have we stopped?" Lum set the huge gun he carried down on the stone floor with a *thunk*.

Nate turned with an irritated sigh.

"I think it is obvious, we need a vote," Mr. Quinn said diplomatically. "Do we go down the side path or straight ahead?"

I took a torch from my pack and lit it off Nate's and started off down the side path. Before I had gone two steps, a hand clamped down on my forearm like iron, nearly jerking me off my feet. "Ouch!"

Nate spared me an apologetic glance. "What are you doing?"

"I'm just taking a quick peek."

"We are not splitting up!" Nate said quickly. "If anything, we're sending *them* down that path."

"I'm just looking," I assured him.

The look on his face brooked no argument.

"That's actually not a horrible idea," Mr. Barret said. "No offense meant, Mr. Valentine, but you tend to be a bit, well, overcautious."

"Overcautious?" Nate sputtered.

"Fortune favors the bold." Mr. Barrett took my torch firmly in hand. "So we'll take one path, you can take the other, and if we are destined to, we will meet up later."

"What happened to working together?" Nate snapped,

I placed my hand on his arm. "If they wish to go their own way, let them."

"Brilliant, it's all settled. Which way do you choose then?" Mr. Barrett said.

"We'll continue along ahead," I said.

"Allow me to offer my services to your team since you are traveling with two of the fairer sex," Mr. Quinn said formally. "Mr. Columbus is more than capable of helping Miss Charlotte with her torch."

"I am more than capable of carrying my own torch, thank you Mr. Quinn," I returned, though I was less sure of MeiLin's ability to do much more than make eyes at Nate. I was predictably ignored.

I watched as the trio of Mr. Barrett, Mr. Columbus, and Miss Charlotte and their torch light fade into the darkness. Mr. Quinn gallantly took my shoulder bag and we headed off down the path that curved ahead, occasionally catching the echoes of the other party as they floated eerily on the stale air to us.

Their torchlight faded and left us in the light from our own, along with the eerie glow from the mirrors. I stared at them again, wondering if the light was better at other times of the day or could be adjusted to give better light.

Nate stood with his back against the wall allowing me to balance on his broad shoulders so I could examine them more closely. The mirrors had been held in brackets that were carved to resemble serpents. A mangled silver mirror lay at our feet, the stone snake bracket shattered.

"Was it shot out?"

"Perhaps." Mr. Quinn said.

"No," Nate said at the same time.

There was a long silence while the men, both learned in their way, stared at one another.

"A gun would shatter the bracket and bend the mirror," Mr. Quinn said sensibly.

Nate squinted up at the broken serpent, "There's no divot where a bullet would have struck the wall and no mark on the mirror from a bullet and no powder burn. Something took the mirror down." He helped me off his shoulder with a grunt. "I'd wager it was whatever destroyed the ox in the antechamber and the stone step, but it was no bullet."

The explanation was a cold comfort. Something, the same something strong enough to destroy solid stone, also wished us to be blind and stumbling in the dark.

Being afraid did nothing useful, so I did my best to put it out of my mind. Instead, I tried to figure out the path before us. The passage curved gently but surely around. I was positive we would be coming full circle before long. I wished I had thought to mark where we had parted company with Mr. Barrett. Nate must have had the same thought. When we came across another gap in the wall, Nate didn't hesitate. He pulled his seax from the back of his belt and set a small scratch in one of the stones near the floor.

The light from the mirrors returned. As welcoming as larks after the rain ends, I found myself longing to turn down the path that contained the light no matter how small it was, it was something more than the darkness, which had grown oppressive.

This path was a relatively short but straight one, leading to another curved path, leading off into another opportunity to turn either left or right. We could not continue straight. It was immediately clear we were in concentric rings linked by small channels. If I was right there was probably no way of locating Mr. Barrett until we reached the center. Logically there was a center to reach but there could also be dead ends and false endings.

So far, everything in the temple had been built in sets of eight. Well, it started in groups of eight but the eighth item had been destroyed, so perhaps the eighth ring had been damaged as well leaving seven rings.

I had seen eight concentric rings linked by short channels, I could visualize it clearly in my mind; I just couldn't remember where.

I set my hands on my hips. Tea. Tea was the thing to help me think. Fortunately, Mr. Quinn and Nate agreed a break was in order. We pulled nearly stale scones and warm tea in metal flasks from my satchel. We sat in silence, sipping in the dim light from the mirrors above us.

Suddenly I knew where I had seen the concentric rings. I leapt to my feet, accidentally coughing crumbs at the men in a most unladylike fashion. I did not, however, spill the tea. After all, a girl has her priorities.

Nate looked startled.

"I should have sketched it!"

All three of them stared at me like I lost my mind.

"We're in the mosaic by the braziers." I carefully replaced the stopper in my tea bottle. I was fully restored by my own cleverness, I needed no more tea. "There was a serpent and a rooster and an ox under melted glass in the center. I'm sure that's where we're headed."

"To melted glass?" Nate looked up at me.

"I'm sure it's not still melted. It had cooled or dried or whatever it does, the glass had been poured over what looked to be metal, or maybe ceramic figures in the center. Of course, now I wonder if it was a medallion we'll need to unlock some sort of door."

"You are a singular woman." Mr. Quinn laughed. "I remember seeing something like that in the room but I dismissed it as a curiosity."

"She has a cunning and agile mind." Nate beamed. "That is one of Vivian's many strengths."

MeiLin alone looked unimpressed. "The maze in the floor is nothing more than a meditative tool designed to help the undisciplined mind focus on the patterns of nature. It was placed by the monks for those who are unable to focus their minds on their own."

Even her rudeness could not dampen my spirits. I paced back and forth trying to remember where the damaged tiles were. But then again, without the ability to tell where we actually started in relation to the small maze it was hopeless. I really, really wished I had made the connection earlier and thought to sketch, or better yet, trace the maze with charcoal and paper.

Now I had a satchel full of salves and bandages and tinctures and all I wanted was a sketchbook and a bit of charcoal. How in the world did one learn what to pack for stupid adventures anyway?

I kicked a bit of scone in irritation and watched the stale bits explode and scatter into the darkness beyond the torch.

"If that's the case, I suppose there's no reason we can't start mapping it now," Nate said. "Quinn, do you have a pen?"

Mr. Quinn went through his jacket and produced a nub of a pencil, and Nate handed me a folded map he copied from the *Nomad* Captain's personal collection.

I carefully drew eight concentric rings then randomly picked a place and drew in the stairs, if it were true circles then where the stairs were wouldn't matter. I added in the first short connecting tunnel where we separated from Mr. Barrett and then the second tunnel where we moved in to the next ring and added a small X where we marked the wall. Then I went ahead and added small S marks, approximating where the mirrors hung in their snake-shaped brackets on the walls, carefully marking the one that had been broken.

"We can't prove it unless we walk the entire outer circle," Mr. Quinn said over my shoulder, "but I'd be willing to bet there are eight brackets, evenly spaced—"

Nate interrupted Mr. Quinn. "Seven".

"Right, seven," Mr. Quinn conceded good-naturedly. "We have found everything to be in groups of eight, I mean, seven, so as the circles get smaller, if the rules of eight hold up, even if they are reduced to seven, the reduced space will mean there is less space between the mirrors and the circles will be brighter and brighter."

"Well that's a relief," I said with a smile. "We only have so many torches."

"I believe we can safely assume the reduction to seven is intentional," MeiLin said.

"I'm glad to see you're still with us." I couldn't help myself. I really should not antagonize her so. I was immediately sorry.

"I was merely thinking." She gave a heavy sigh. "Eight is order and harmony, perhaps the order and harmony of this place has been disrupted and therefore it was unwise to split the group."

"What kind of thing could do this?" I asked.

"There are demons," she said casually.

"What in the world are you talking about?" I demanded.

"Other worldly creatures exist in China, much, much older than any other demons man has battled before. The creatures of the underworld are attracted to the great cultures of man. They are jealous of all the Middle Kingdom has achieved."

"We have devils and demons in England, too, you know," I snapped. And here I thought she had actually decided to be helpful for a moment. Maybe she was pointing the finger at demons because she was one. That would explain a lot.

Mapping the circles turned out to be a wonderful idea. In mere hours we managed to enter what we assumed was the fifth circle of the maze. We kept hearing something just beyond my own range and I could tell by the way Nate kept cocking his head to the side that he was having trouble making it out as well, even with his wonderful dog-like hearing.

"Perhaps Barrett and Miss Charlotte got to the piece of the key first," Mr. Quinn said for the fourth time, laughing nervously.

Even MeiLin looked unnerved.

The sound seemed to come from behind us and before us, to the left and the right and even through the solid stone wall. I held a torch so closely that the heat reflecting back almost burned my hand, but I couldn't locate the sound.

We had found more dead-ends than I had pencil for and after a time I had to have Nate sharpen the nub again with his penknife. I scowled at my crude map. What started as a great idea had dissolved into a pile of untidy scribbles.

Finally, I could stand it no longer and swept off my long coat and spread it out on the floor before me. I pulled out my tattered pouch of worn Tarot cards from my satchel.

Nate carefully crouched nearby to give me the light. Finally, I seemed to be engaged in something that MeiLin found to be of great interest. She sat next to me, crowding my elbow and carefully examined the cards as though she was handling something precious and fragile.

I patiently took them back, then cleared my mind and dealt out several cards.

Contradictions, the lot of them.

I scowled, shuffled, and dealt again. I must have been staring at them for too long because I nearly leapt out of my skin when Nate set his hand against my back. "What do you see?"

I frowned at him. "What do you hear?" He shrugged. "Whatever it is, I suspect it is much the same as what I see—everything and nothing. I'd wager it's much the same for what you can smell. Everything and nothing all at once." I scooped the cards up and carefully packed them away, feeling much more discouraged than before.

We had packed a light meal, not hearty provisions, but by unspoken agreement it was time to stop for a fortifying rest. Bao dumplings filled with smoked pork and lemongrass and a hard cheese from the Viridian made a great light meal that mixed Chinese flavors with flavors from home. We even had some of the wonderful dried peaches that had been bathed in a ginger syrup.

I finished off my tea, now stone cold, and the gentlemen passed another bottle of water and a flask of something stronger back and forth. MeiLin finished the last bottle of tea, remarking that it would be preferable to have a small fire so fresh tea might be brewed. I never expected anything else.

"Where do you suppose Mr. Barrett got to?" I wondered out loud, more to make conversation than because I cared.

"Oh, I am sure he'll turn up," Mr. Quinn said with a small smile. "He has a knack for rising to his feet."

"Maybe it's them we hear." MeiLin offered as another echoing murmur came from before us and from the left at the same time.

"I hope so." Nate packed away the waxed paper that had held our meal.

"If it is not them, whatever could it be?" I laughed.

"I don't even want to speculate on what else it could be," Nate said evenly.

Something had destroyed the ox statue and the step and one serpent shaped mirror bracket in every ring and several of the pathways. Even MeiLin had to admit that perhaps the damage was intentional since the monks would have made the maze for meditation and contemplation and all paths should have led to the center.

Nate handed me the torch for a moment. There were only two more in my satchel. He had several more in his backpack but I was unsure of the number. I stared up at the light reflected up in the mirrors. Mr. Quinn had been right, as we got further and further into the maze, the circles had gotten smaller so the distance between the mirrors was less and the light was more concentrated. It made the rings feel brighter. If it were sunlight, though, we would eventually lose the it when night fell ,and then we would be plunged into darkness.

My stomach told me it was just past lunch so we had several hours, but then what? If there was something else here making that sound I had no desire to be trapped in the maze in the dark with it. To be honest I had no desire to be here in the dark with anyone besides Nate. Even in near darkness he would be able to lead us out, he was able to see perfectly in the dark. Being a canithrope had advantages that went beyond shapeshifting into a hulking half-man, half-canine, or into his beloved dog.

"There are many things that live in the ancient mists," MeiLin said casually.

"That is not helping." I suppressed a shiver. Leave it to her. She offers nothing of value all morning then believes it is her duty to scare the pants off me.

"So, say we are to be attacked by something," Nate said slowly. "How would that go?" He rolled his neck easing the tension.

"Chinese demons do not do anything so clumsy as attack people directly. They attack people's virtues. When they are helpless and when they have lost their nobility and their humanity is when they strike," MeiLin said with a sweet smile all for him. "That is why it is so important to live an honorable life. Our demons are confounded by most Western travelers and find them an easy meal. People without virtues are easy targets."

"Which is why they would attack places like this? Temples? Places of virtue? The demon corrupted it?" Nate clarified.

She gave him a graceful smile. "When people lose places of contemplation and worship, places to renew their spirit, they become easier to control."

SOS

The echoing scrape followed us.

No matter where Mr. Quinn held the torch or where Nate glanced in the shadows, neither of them was able to locate it. I was not inclined to look. I wasn't sure I wanted to see what might be stalking us in the shadows, but my hand never strayed far from either the seax knife at my back or the revolver at my hip. I am a far cry from the shot that Nate was, but it was a comfort to touch it, nonetheless.

I slipped my hand loosely in Nate's as we marched along in the dying torchlight.

"What did the cards say?" he whispered.

"It was very unclear," I whispered back. "I cannot be sure, everything was a contradiction."

He nodded absently. I wondered how much of an explanation he was expecting or if he was merely making conversation.

He suddenly froze and drew his revolver.

Someone or something screamed. And then just as quickly as it began it was over, leaving me to wonder if I had imagined it. My ears were ringing in the sudden silence.

I closed my dry mouth with a *snap* trying to forget the sound and replay it at the same time. Once when I was a little girl, Papa had set several bottles out in the garden with different amounts of water inside and blew across the tops. Blowing across them had produced warm tones, but when the harsh wind blew across the wet bottle tops that evening I remembered being awoken by a piercing scream. This sound had been similar but louder and more shrill.

Nate gave his head a sharp shake. He looked as though he expected his ears to start bleeding. It was the same annoyed, betrayed look all the dogs in the neighborhood gave when the bobbies came around with their police whistles.

He squinted into the darkness trying to discern shadows just past the light from the mirrors. "It's no use going this way anymore, the path ahead is blocked."

"What do you mean blocked?" MeiLin demanded. Clearly the maze was finally taking its toll on her as well.

"I mean its impassable," Nate returned evenly.

"Surely, you do not mean to shoot the obstruction," Mr. Quinn scoffed.

Nate brushed past him, and quickly moved back along the hallway.

I drew my own revolver, determined to back him up. The grip, fine rosewood, was slick and oily against my palm. Maybe I should not attempt to shoot from behind him. My aim was nowhere nearly as sure as his.

Then I heard it. A low thrum of sound, a growl, a whine—something that grumbled and scraped as it traveled. Claws strong as steel that could shatter stone. *Oh Jesus!* I crossed myself and whispered a prayer under my breath. Then I paused and almost laughed, would Chinese demons fear Jesus Christ? Maybe I should have asked Xiezhi for a prayer.

I hoped it was just our British minds going a bit batty with the fear of ghosts and goblins and things that went bump in the night, but even MeiLin looked peaked and frightened. Nate alone, my knight in leather and linen, seemed immune as he strode forward, cautious but never a wavering step. And in watching him I found my confidence grow once again. We were not weaklings waiting for death to come and claim us.

Deception. The Arcana spoke to me and I stumbled. I realized this was what the cards meant when I held them in my hands. *We were being deceived.* We were being deceived now; nothing was what we believed it to be. Well, technically the cards said we were surrounded by untruth, but Xiezhi warned me that I had to open my eyes if I wanted to see the path before me. Though there is a certain amount of subjectivity in reading the Tarot this was as good an interpretation as any.

Nate whipped around the corner with his gun drawn and a series of frantic cries jarred me out of my thoughts. There was a shot, then shouting.

And for a moment, the world was all chaos.

CHAPTER FOURTEEN

THE OTHER HALF of our party were coming down the hall.

Mr. Barrett, Charlotte, and Lum had run out of torches and were wandering by the light of one oil lantern and the mounted mirrors. Lum's giant shoulder cannon of a gun had scraped against the walls as they bumbled about in the dark. Charlotte was positively fed up with all notions of adventure, and swore that if it weren't for this one big job she would be done and done for good!

After much shouting and explaining, everyone calmed down. They informed us that after we separated they went the opposite way around and found that all tunnels leading to the next concentric ring had been blocked and destroyed.

"We can't go any further. I say we just report back that we did our best," Charlotte huffed.

Mr. Barrett gave her a sharp look. She folded her arms and flounced off to sit on a broken bit of stone.

I watched the mirrors overhead as they reflected their light into the circles of the maze. If the monks used these to contemplate the seasons and the cycles of life then logically there was a middle to the maze. And the middle of the maze was where the prize must sit. Its where the cast metal animals sat in their cast metal robes at their cast metal tea table under a bit of hardened glass.

"The guild will not be happy that we gave up after a week," Nate said moodily.

Lum set the butt of his cannon down on the stone floor with a sharp *chink*.

They were too quiet.

I knew Nate well enough to know that he was thinking. I also knew men, as a gender, well enough to know that they were not always, silent as they thought. Some paced, some talked, some drank, there was a tension in the air; more than merely the anxiety of going home empty handed. I was also fairly sure that if Mr. Langston sent one pair of inexperienced adventurers after an artifact in a land as exotic and foreign as China, he probably would not send *two* new groups.

"Nate, be a lamb and bring me my satchel," I called sweetly.

He looked up, startled. I rarely used the phrase "be a lamb." When I used it at home, it was always loaded with sarcasm. He quirked an eyebrow at me, but brought me the bag as I asked.

What's wrong? he mouthed.

I was considering how to mime my concerns when the mirror from the first broken bracket fell out of my bag. I had planned on leaving it in the entrance of the temple for the monks to find and fix.

Then everything clicked together in my head.

"I need a boost!" I said, trying to scramble up the stone wall in my earnestness.

Mr. Barrett pushed the black hat off his brow and scratched his graying hair. "What in the world is she going on about?"

Nate tried to position himself under me. In my excitement, I'm sure I was causing him more trouble than I was worth.

Finally, while standing on his shoulders I managed to haul myself up on the wall and then crouch over the side. I immediately remembered why someone else would have been a better choice at this than me. My stomach did some sort of flying leap into the stones while Nate stared up at me thousands of miles below. He saw me go green and a look of concern flooded his features. I could taste the tea in the back of my throat and I suddenly wished the scones from earlier were staler and the cheese less oily. Breathing like a grampus, I huffed noisily though my nose, willing myself not to vomit on my fiancé or fall onto the stones below and break a leg.

I managed to hold the mirror up and catch the light that would have hit from the previous ring were there a mirror in the bracket to catch it.

From this vantage point it was clear, I needed another pair of eyes to be sure but there was a pattern to the lights. They came from one source in the middle of the maze! If the next concentric ring had been destroyed, the final ring was intact and bright as day from all eight mirrors hanging and shining brightly with barely a dozen feet of wall space between them. Those mirrors would be large too, catching and reflecting an impressive amount of light.

There were eight rings. Well, seven intact rings, each had seven hanging mirrors, the eighth mirror bracket had been broken. The breaks must have been done on propose, there was a clear path of darkness that led to the center circle. If eight was the number of harmony then this site had been purposefully taken out of harmonious balance.

"Nate, you need to see this," I called.

Nate got Columbus Baxter to give him a boost and soon he could see what I could. We stared at a maze, made not of stone or light but of darkness. What creature in their right mind would follow a path of darkness into the darkness?

Well, clearly we would. We would have to. We left all the mirrors, except for the one in my hand, where they fell. There were seven of us, that would mean that each of us would have to somehow fix a bracket and rehang a mirror.

"Vivian's right." Nate called down to the rest of the party. "There's no doubt the damage was deliberate." He helped me down into Lum's waiting arms. I remembered him striking me last autumn and quickly moved away. "We have to get to the center—the middle is where the piece of the key will be. And, everyone is going to have to get the mirrors repositioned so we can get the light focused back into the center circle."

"What makes you the boss all of the sudden?" Charlotte said.

Mr. Barrett hushed her and nodded. "We saw the mirrors on the way in, we can get them reset."

"Well then, tally-ho!" Mr. Quinn smiled and took up his pith helmet.

Lum looked as though he wished to say something to me. Then he shouldered his long, heavy shoulder cannon and turned to leave. "Come, missus, I'll take you as far as you're going." He offered his arm to MeiLin.

"Oh, MeiLin," I called to stop her. "I have this, it may help." I pulled a rather large piece of pine resin from my satchel. It was one of the items I had selected from my larger kit of simples, tinctures, and bandages, thinking it would be helpful.

I watched the rest of them disappear into the maze to rehang the mirrors. "I'm not sorry to see him go."

"Who, Barrett?"

"No. Lum," I said with a little laugh. Had he forgotten that the man tried to cleave his skull in with a pipe half a year ago?

"Oh, he's not all that bad," Nate said as he absently checked his weapons.

"Not that bad?!" I wasn't sure I heard him correctly.

"He was working for Geiger and we were technically trespassing," Nate said sensibly.

"In the lair of a madman," I said evenly. "Honestly, Nate, whose side are you on?"

"I'm always on your side, Viv, but good work is hard to come by. He was working as a factory hand for Geiger and he lost his job when Sterling's Emporium went under because of Geiger turning out to be a madman. He got the raw end of that deal. The poor bugger was doing honest work then he got shot, nearly burned to death, and lost his job. It wasn't his fault he was working for a madman. You know, Viv, sometimes you forget—you may not have been born a lady but you were not born a pauper either. Your father runs a good, solid business. You may not have had everything growing up but you surely had more than most."

I stared at him. For a moment—just a moment—I was indignant. Then I really wanted to be angry. I hated when he was all noble and right like that. If Lum wanted to be a thug or a robber he could have turned to a life a crime quite easily. Could it be as simple as him merely being in the wrong place at the wrong time? But then I remembered how he had held my arm twisted behind my back as the mad Geiger struck me and I felt sick and hurt and angry all at the same time.

Nate was wrong in this, Lum was a cad. I turned away from my fiancé with a huff.

"I said, 'do you want me to carry you to the center circle so you are ready to locate the piece of the key?'" Nate repeated. Idiot man! He didn't even know I was irritated.

"I suppose so," I turned back around.

Nate gathered me in his arms and I draped my arms around his neck. I could feel his muscles bunch and swell slightly as he drew upon strength that was more than that of a mere man. He sprang up, powerful legs gracefully carrying us to the top of the wall we made such a show of reaching moments ago. The slack in his clothes disappeared as he gathered himself for a greater spring, one hand reaching down to touch the stone by his crouched legs for balance. His dark caramel- colored eyes had turned deep chocolate. Then, with one powerful spring, we were completely across the ruined ring of stone and to the inner circle—where all eight mirrors each hung on the walls—each one as large as the mirrors in a lady's dressing room.

The room was as bright as noon and comfortably warm.

He set me down and we both released the breath we were holding. He took a steadying breath, panting with the effort it took to keep the beast in check. I gasped for another reason, the danger, the power, my husband-to-be—it was all terribly exciting.

And then he was gone, springing back into the darkness, presumably to hang up the mirror to catch the light and direct me to where to find the piece of the key that would lead us to the Arrow of Hou Yi.

SOS

Slowly, very slowly, the rest of the party got into position and held their mirrors. The lights wavered and shined and came together and came apart, but after a time one clear pattern emerged.

I took my seax and set scratches in the dirt to mark the places that could be locations. I had narrowed it down to two possibilities. I suppose this was as good as I could expect considering I could not communicate with the other party members.

The floor in the center circle was dirt, a striking contrast to the stone in the outer circles. With nothing better to do I started to dig. Surely the piece of the key had to be here somewhere under one of these two wavering circles of light. They shined then shifted or went away entirely as someone's hands fatigued.

I was so intent on my task that I nearly leapt out of my skin when Nate jumped back across the collapsed ring and landed with a heavy *thud* beside me, throwing up a spray of dirt. He didn't bother to hide what he could do when it was just the two of us.

"I really ought to attach bells to your boots," I grumbled, not for the first time.

"Such a manly noise I would make," Nate mused, staring at the marks I had made in the dirt floor.

I stood with my hands on my hips and stretched my back. Another of the mirrors fell as another succumbed to fatigue. It didn't matter now. "The piece of the key is under one of these two marks." I motioned, sweeping my sweaty hair back with my forearm. Some wisps of hair had escaped my neat plait and were mingling untidily with sweat and dust.

Nate was staring at me with a slightly offset, handsome smile. I blushed and turned suddenly warm in a way that had nothing to do with the work. I hoped he would always look at me that way.

But there was little time for that now, the light would be failing us before long. I wished for a shovel or one of my little gardening trowels. Then took a deep breath, picked one of the spots and squatted over the hole as I had seen dogs do, and started tearing into the soft dirt, flinging it between my legs with reckless abandon.

The look on Nate's face—I burst into giggles, nearly falling over.

"I do not dig like that," he muttered crossly, thinking me mocking him.

"No, but maybe you should so we could get done with this faster."

He shot me a dark look then gave a heavy sigh and mimicked my position over the other marked possible location and started on his own hole.

I felt my nails tear as the sand dug beneath them and shredded them. My mother would not be pleased as my wedding was just weeks away and I had been doing my best to stop biting them in an attempt to make my hands more lady-like.

There was nothing but dirt here.

Maybe I was wrong. I worried my lip between my teeth. Barrett and his men would think I was an idiot. Nate would forever be defending me for being so wrong. Or worse, what if he didn't defend me at all? What if the mirrors were off? My mouth was dry from the exertion and all the sand we were kicking up. I was finding it harder and harder to swallow. I could see us digging in the fading light, trenches large enough to be buried in, looking for the key as we moved ourselves around the room.

Nate gave a grunt, he was throwing up sand at a furious pace. If we didn't find it, MeiLin would never let me hear the end of it. I felt as though I had swallowed a very hot bit of something that refused to cool off.

Then something sliced into my hand.

Blood, hot droplets, stained the sand, falling into large dark splotches on the ruddy sand. Nate turned, his nose twitching. He was at my side in an instant, reacting faster than I thought possible. He grasped my injured hand and turned it into the fading light.

"I'm fine," I said.

Nate wrapped me in his arms, ignoring the blood and sweat. "China has been hard on you."

"This had better be the piece of the damn key," I said.

Nate looked over my shoulder to the little pit I had dug. "I think you may have found something."

He released me and returned to my hole. He carefully used his seax to dig around and pried up something from the bottom of. It looked nothing like a key. Just a silver bit of jagged metal shaped a bit like a capital A and sharp as a razor along the outer edges. It was completely unremarkable. I would have tossed it away in the nearest rubbish heap.

Until he flipped it over.

It had a hollow portion near the center that was curved, but the back side had a bit of angular Chinese picture writing made up of the little lines that crossed each other, barely visible in the light that was slowly but surely fading from the chamber. If we didn't wish to venture from the maze in the dark a further examination of the key and my injured hand had to wait until we were safely back at the entrance chamber of the temple.

Nate was in agreement, but was not willing to move until I at least rinsed off my hand with the rest of my water bottle and bound it with a bandage from my satchel. I tried to protest but he fixed me with the same steely gaze I gave him when it was time to clean his wounds.

He tucked the bit of the key into his waistcoat and took me up in his arms as though I was made of glass. It was amazing what a bit of blood did to men—moments ago I was not nearly as fragile. Then it was back into the maze to collect our companions and decide how best to find the remaining pieces of the key so we could find the arrow and get out of China before it killed me, or worse, ruined my wedding.

CHAPTER FIFTEEN

NATE DID MY PART of packing the horses. He set me to looking after my hand and would not allow me to do anything else. Mr. Barrett was not inclined to leave the temple without discussing whether we were successful in recovering the piece of the key.

Finally, with the men displaying growing impatience with each other, a hasty camp was set in the shadows of the temple. We were surrounded in remains of the humble huts and gardens where the monks had resided. Nate set the horses to fresh pickets and, to my surprise, Lum brought all the mounts from both parties fresh water, completely unconcerned with the fate of the key and his own employer's growing frustration with Nate.

I heard Nate and Mr. Barrett arguing in the distance. Charlotte was back in her huff. I instantly wished she was more like MeiLin. At least she wasn't loud about her general dislike for adventure. While Charlotte Ratham was loud and shrieked like a parrot used to getting a cracker to shut it up. At least MeiLin kept her sulkiness to herself.

"I thought a fire might help you with your hand," Lum said, his voice a low growl in the twilight.

I must be getting used to him, I didn't leap out of my skin this time. "Yes, thank you."

"Yer pap, he runs that shop off Exeter in Limehouse," Lum asked. At least I think it was supposed to be a question, though he said it more matter-of-factly.

"He does." I carefully set some water in the cast iron teapot and set it near the fire to heat. I had some herbs in my medicine chest that would help clean the wound—garlic and goldenseal in a twist of paper to add to water. I set doses aside so it would be easier to instruct Nate in my care if I fell ill.

I cradled my right hand to my chest and awkwardly reached for my medicine chest to draw it close. I saw Nate busy building MeiLin a small fire of her own. She kept shooting him sly glances from under beautiful slanted almond eyes. I hissed in frustration.

"Don't you worry about that none, miss." Lum knelt as though my medicine box contained something positively volatile rather than lifesaving medicines and tinctures.

I bit the inside of my cheeks to keep from saying something I would regret. Of course, I was being ridiculous. I knew I had nothing to worry about with MeiLin. But she was so beautiful and she managed to get Nate to do anything for her with just a look. It didn't help that Mr. Barrett and Mr. Quinn seemed to stare at her every spare moment, too. I knew she was beautiful, they knew she was beautiful, even Nate *knew* she was beautiful, but he seemed not to notice for my sake. Only Lum seemed immune to her charms.

I froze, staring at him. He cocked his head and stared back.

"Columbus, why are you here? In China, I mean," I added hastily since he looked as though I had slapped him.

"Mr. Barrett hired me," Lum said, removing his bowler hat and smoothing a hand over his balding pate. "He was looking for a bit of muscle, a porter and such. A man my size ain't much good in mines or underground, and my paws are a bit too large for much delicate work. So I met Barrett when I finished up a contract on board the *Claudia Marie*."

"Is that another airship?"

"An airship?" Columbus laughed. "God's wounds, lass, no! I've seen them, that's for sure, every man with a bit of luck has seen one, but I've never had the good fortune to be on one."

"I assure you, luck has little to do with it," I said as dryly as I could manage.

"You don't fancy the airships?" Columbus settled himself with great effort. "You must be a lady of great means to travel by airship."

"No, just a lucky one I suppose." I said with a small smile.

"So lucky that you gashed your hand?" Columbus said with a gentleness that I would not have expected from a man his size.

I shrugged. I was not expecting kindness from him. I was not *ready* for kindness from him. Moreover, I was not ready for Nate to be right and for Columbus to be a good man. I could not forgive that not even a year past he held my arm behind my back while his employer hit me. He looked as though he wanted to say more, then closed his mouth and returned to his own camp, separated from ours by its own little fire.

Nate returned and watched me bathe my injured hand in garlic and goldenseal. "Are you all right?"

"I am," I said.

He fished the bit of metal from his waistcoat. He had wrapped in a handkerchief. In the gleaming firelight, the flames cast deep shadows across the piece we worked so hard to recover. One side was covered in the Chinese letters, some of them were partially missing. I couldn't read the words. That would be a job for MeiLin or Mr. Quinn once the key was fully assembled. The back side of the piece was rough. I carefully turned it over. It had some sort of markings that looked like rocks or plants.

I traced the symbols with my thumb. There was no tarnish. Dirt and sand, blood, nothing seemed to blemish the metal. It was a metal I had never seen before, light but I could not bend it, no matter how hard I tried. The partial ring in the center was a socket. It would hold the ruby Mr. Barrett so casually kept in his pocket.

"We're going to be forced to give this up," I said. The thought of parting with it was actually painful.

Nate scowled. "I know. For now at least. We'll get it back."

"They do outnumber us." I was trying to be sensible.

He had his arms folded across his chest looking anything but sensible. His look softened when he saw me struggling with the wrap for my hand. He bound the wound for me with more care than he needed to take, ghosting a touch that sent shivers up my skin. For a moment, only for a moment, there was only us in the whole world. And for that moment, it was enough.

SOS

The sun rose too early, bathing the valley in ethereal light. The fog rolled in with the morning. At first the mist had been beautiful. That was for the first few days, now it had become as tedious as an endless garden party. I would have loved a week of dry weather so I could properly dry out, lest I sprout mushrooms behind my ears.

The wood stored beneath the edge of the tent had remained dry enough for breakfast tea and pears, and those flat, hearty crackers with a bit of honey to start the day. But the fires were quite smoky, and while it drove away the biting insects, it created a ferocious stink that made my eyes burn.

MeiLin was standing with Nate again while he prepared to strike her tent. She touched him. He blinked hard. This time I was sure I hadn't imagined it. Something changed. MeiLin caught me watching her. The horses didn't like her. No, it was more than that, they didn't trust her. I didn't trust her. Nate was powerful. She was doing something to him, I was sure of it.

I closed my eyes and tried to empty my mind. She was hiding something. I couldn't bring a card to mind. I chewed my lip. I could always get some sort of a read on everyone. I hated feeling so blind, so normal. I needed more information.

I pulled out the book again. Maybe reading about the remaining trines would give us some sort of clue as to what could be hiding with the pieces of the key that remained. I opened it to the faint painting of the Chinese warrior instead. His single curved sword was point-down in the earth, his body covered in armor, and waves of cloth behind him that could be a cape. He didn't wear a helm like a warrior, but a headdress, something ceremonial like the Empress Dowager Cixi wore. It was like a crown, but not of the kind I was used to seeing on a king.

The image was printed upon paper that had been imprinted before. I held it up but it was too faint to read, and too blurry, in any case, it wasn't in English. I shook my head and closed the book.

"Perhaps we should get moving. We still have several more pieces of the key to retrieve," Nate remarked. "We'll head off to one, you head off to another. We can meet up when we have them."

Clearly, he didn't want anything to do with Mr. Barrett or his group of friends. It must have something to do with them "smelling off" again. I figured this wasn't the time to ask. Barrett's crew turned back to their camp, setting it to rights while Nate rushed to get our own possessions in order. He wished to be off before they could easily follow us.

Mr. Quinn spread a map out, smoothing out the creases. "Let's see what trine temples are left: The Library of Xiaoshuo, The Monastery of Yuè Liàng, and Shén Shèng de Shù Cóng; that is a massive sacred garden constructed in honor of the old Emperors. Interestingly, when you put them together, they will make a giant square."

I thought of the sketch on my own notes and smiled to myself. I already knew this. So did Nate.

Nate was interested. Weapons and maps, my Nate was a man of simple tastes. His attempt to get away from them as soon as possible was on a temporary hold.

MeiLin peeked over his shoulder. "The Dragon Gate to the grave of Xihuan-Lung should be where the lines connecting those four points intersect." Leave it to her to give away our information.

Nate looked over to me, our advantage was now lost so we may as well look like we were helping. He tapped the sites on the map. "Well then, that's one piece down, three pieces left to find."

I couldn't help myself. "If that is true, why wouldn't someone have beaten us to the gate and the grave of Xihuan-Lung long ago?"

Mr. Barrett fished a giant ruby from his pocket. "Because they didn't have this."

Nate's eyes lingered on the ruby just a moment too long. "And exactly where did you get that?"

Charlotte scowled at him, drawing herself up to her full height. "Just you never mind."

Nate held up his hands to ward her off. "The Explorer's Society believes war is looming in China. We are probably best served by getting this errand completed as soon as we can."

MeiLin touched Nate's arm. "Since there are three more pieces to recover perhaps you are correct, we should split up."

I didn't blame Nate. Though I couldn't *smell* whatever was wrong, something about Mr. Barrett was thoroughly unsettling, and it was nothing to do with his awful black wardrobe or even his hulking bodyguard. No, I was making peace with Lum. There was just something about Mr. Barrett, there was more going on there. I just wish I had better words for it. As Nate had said, something just *smelled* off.

Mr. Barrett tucked the ruby away. "I'll tell you what then, we will meet you at Shén Shèng de Shù Cóng in a few days' time. We'll take the monastery, you can take the library. And as a show of our generous good will, you can even hang on to that piece of the key you've got here."

Nate tucked the silvery piece of the key into his waistcoat. It didn't feel like good will. It felt like baiting. Truthfully, I would have preferred Mr. Barrett let us hold the ruby for safekeeping.

Once our supplies were repacked and we were settled in our saddles, Nate lead us away.

I turned in my saddle and watched Barrett and his companions fade. Columbus Baxter was watching me go, with no hint of malice. The queerest sensation came over me—I realized I had nothing to fear from Mr. Baxter. Mr. Geiger and Mr. Barrett were another matter entirely.

CHAPTER SIXTEEN

IT TOOK THREE DAYS of hard travel. Hard, wet travel across the open land of forests, misty hills, and a few meadows before we came upon small patches of land that had been painstakingly cleared for farms and small huts with thatched roofs. The rock walls of the farms had crumbled and toppled as nature reclaimed the land, overgrown by moss, obscuring the work the monks had done to make their home in this wild place.

And the green; everywhere the green—rich and vibrant—never had I seen so much green. The gray stone and sky, the rich brown earth, and black exposed soil made the green burst through as though it were the brightest color to ever exist. It was as though all the world was green and I lived within a world of emerald.

Only the tumbled-down buildings marred the perfect beauty of the land. It created a beautiful sorrow in the Chinese landscape.

MeiLin motioned to a crumbling building. "It is here. The Library of Xiaoshuo."

Nate carefully picked his way around MeiLin and the overgrown path that hardly counted as a path. The grass had broken any stone the monks had carefully laid by slowly working through the tiny cracks until they finally shattered the rock, and the mosses grew deeper than the plushest carpet I had ever seen.

The library itself was in a sorry state. At one time, it must have been a fine building of carefully cut timbers and a slate roof, but parts of the library roof had crumbled. Large patches of the interlocking clay tiles had either fallen or blown away, leaving it to look like a badly wounded creature crouching in the grass.

Like the first of the sites that held bits of the key, this one was also decorated with several statues of animals. Though I could not make out what animals they were, there were several huge squat beasts sitting by the slightly open doors.

"What do you suppose is in there?" I mused aloud.

"Books." Nate shrugged. "Dust, and moths."

"Your sense of humor knows no bounds," I said as dryly as I could manage.

"You mean what kind of monster is inside?" Nate said.

"Got that feeling too, did you?" I asked, slipping my arm into the crook of his elbow.

He gave me a knowing look and dropped my arm so he could check his gun. I was not the only one that likened the sight to something a creature might call home.

"There are many demons from the old world that are drawn to the ruins men build," MeiLin said, the chill in her voice made the little hairs on the back of my neck stand on end.

My bandaged hand reached around to my seax where it sat in its scabbard at the small of my back.

"There are many creatures that are just beyond the sight of man," MeiLin continued. "Demons and spirits, both vengeful and benign. Why, I could tell you a tale of a man, a spirit in disguise, that made a soldier eat the boiled head of his king."

I glared at her. If there was one thing I didn't need right now it was talk of spirits and demons that boiled heads and fed them to mortals. I could feel myself break into a cold sweat.

"What kind of demon?" Nate asked, his eyes narrowing. I could practically see him readying himself to transfigure into the hulking canithrope.

Werewolves! My God! Were there others like Nate? Canithropes of course, not lycanthropes, lycan being for wolves; okay maybe wolves—it was ancient druid magic that initially infected Nate and bound him and his loyal dog together to one body. What if every instance of werewolves or shapeshifters was another instance of the same malady Nate had found a way to live with?

"Did you hear me?" MeiLin looked thoroughly annoyed.

"Oh," I swallowed hard. Right, we were about to go into another ancient Chinese site to find part of a key to lead us to the grave of a dragon to recover a magical arrow. *One mystical creature at a time, Vivian.*

"The pieces of the key were separated and sent off to the four winds. We are being sent to four separate holy sites to recover them yet each has fallen to ruin."

"And you think there are demons guarding the pieces of the key?" Nate said slowly. "So what demon was guarding the last piece? Quite frankly, if this is the best China can throw at us, I'm not concerned about Chinese demons."

MeiLin gave a sharp smile showing her teeth, and for a moment she looked quite fierce. I thought she just might transfigure herself into something frightening and try to devour us both, then she softened. "Chinese demons are not as direct as Western demons. The Chinese people have both honor and poise, there is a way people are expected to behave. Demons do not have to directly harm you, they awaken sins and flaws deep within you and turn you into something dark and terrible. They consume you and torture you from within."

"You think people from the West are without honor," Nate said crisply.

"Some have honor," she said, looking into his eyes. "Most do not."

"I could say the same about some Eastern women," I added tartly.

"Well, if anyone feels the sudden urge to stab anyone else, please ignore it," Nate said, tugging his waistcoat into place and starting off again on the spongy moss growing from the stones at our feet.

MeiLin hurried after him, protesting under her breath in beautiful lilting Chinese, which I was sure was nasty curses calling every demon she could think of to corrupt me and turn me from Nate's mind.

The squatty figures turned out to be a pig in robes pouring over a book that at one time had several Chinese characters carved into the stone pages, but had been weathered to the point they were only barely recognizable as the angular Chinese writing. There was also a hare sitting in the grass with one long broken ear in the grass at his feet. The third animal was a goat, at least I supposed it was a goat—it wore a scowl so its teeth showed, but then again, it could have been grimacing or chewing. Goats seemed to be fond of both. The horns of this goat had also been long weathered by exposure to wind and rain. The air of neglect around the library filled me with sorrow—why would something so beautiful be abandoned? Unless MeiLin was right and a demon had taken up residence and driven the caretakers out.

"What was this library built for?" I asked.

"It was a repository of ancient knowledge gathered by the monks that served the ancient and royal houses of dynasties long past," MeiLin said. When she spoke of the past there was no malice or hatred in her voice. When she spoke like this I feared perhaps I had misjudged her. "The ancient world was quite advanced before the Western world invaded with their twisted morals and their ignorance."

Ahh, there was the MeiLin I had come to expect. I sighed. "Why are you here?"

MeiLin blinked. "Pardon me?"

"Why are you working for us ignorant, rude foreigners?" I snapped, folding my arms across my chest. "Aside from the obvious, I mean."

"The obvious?" She said evenly.

"I mean your interest in my fiancé," I demanded.

MeiLin's eyes narrowed and she glanced over to Nate, but he was too far away to have heard us. "You do not belong here. Either of you. But I will not deny there is a strength to him that I find intriguing. Whether I am pleased to accept it or not, my world is changing. I will assist you for as long as our goals align, that is all."

"So, you are going to help us find the arrow?" I doubted she was being truthful, but every time I tried to read her I was unable to come up with a clear reading, even when I physically pulled out tarot cards to focus my energies.

"Of course," she said. "I have just as much interest as you do in finding the resting place of Xihuan-Lung. She was a great dragon of immense power before she fell out of balance and fell into shadow."

It never occurred to me the dragon could have been good before she was slain. "She was not always an evil dragon?"

MeiLin laughed. "Of course not! You are ignorant in the ways of dragons. Xihuan-Lung was a great, shining dragon of power, the soul of generosity and great knowledge. But dragons are creatures of balance, and when they fall out of balance no good follows. Their scales are very valuable and focus magic and knowledge. Monks and nobles from all over China journeyed to Xihuan-Lung, bringing her offerings so she would bestow her gifts upon them. And she would bless them with gleaming silver scales of immense power and knowledge."

"Like the one we took from Qixiang's palace," I said.

MeiLin scowled at me but continued, "Some of a dragon's scales are full of Yin magic, others are full of Yang magic. A dragon is full of both, good and bad, light and dark, creation and destruction. A dragon is more Yin; more creation than destruction, but even a dragon can fall from balance if she gives too much of herself. And Xihuan-Lung gave and gave and gave to everyone who was worthy."

"Xihuan-Lung fell out of balance," I concluded.

"Xihuan-Lung gave all her creation, all her good, all her love, and she fell to darkness. She became a plague upon man. The monks tried to restore her. They gathered up some of her scales and tried to return them but they could not recover enough of them to heal the great dragon and restore her to balance. She became a force of destruction and the bane of all living things that crossed her path. And so the great archer god, Hou Yi, concluded he had to slay her with one of his magical arrows for the protection of mankind. She should have been restored, and maybe she could have been if her sacred scales had been returned. And so for that murder of a sacred being, he was cursed."

"Well, I suppose he meant it for a noble reason." I could not imagine killing dragons, but then all the dragons in the Western side of the world were killed by knights in shining armor before the civilized world began.

"There is no excuse for the slaying of such a noble beast," MeiLin said evenly. "No forgiveness. Hou Yi committed a mortal sin for the good of mankind. He will pay for all eternity; as will all who commit sins against immortal creatures. Immortal creatures are not subject to human laws!" She walked away before I could say anything else.

Nate was coming back from his scouting of the library. "Whatever was that about?"

"I suppose I struck a nerve," I said.

"Viv," he chided absently. "She is working hard to take us where we need to be, you should try to be nicer."

I stared at him. How could he not see what was going on? I wanted to scream! Ranger had such a nose for people, when I was about to be mugged, he smelled the danger and came to my rescue. How could he not see this? Was he just blind when women presented the danger? Or was he just not capable of believing a woman as beautiful as MeiLin could be so vile?

Stomping was exhausting and made no satisfying noise on the soft ground, so I squared my shoulders and followed them.

The great mosaic in the floor was broken. Like many of the walls, it had been cracked straight down the center. The goat, rabbit, and pig all sat together engaged in discourse around a pile of books. I leaned in to take a closer look and move the broken bits of stone off the mosaic. The crack that ran through the mosaic was filled with dust. I knelt down and blew it free.

For an instant the mosaic was cold and smooth beneath my hand, but the crack was sharp, like the air a second before a lightning strike.

I experienced the queerest sensation, then I was suddenly blown backward off a high platform and slammed to the ground. It was like I had had all the air crushed from my lungs, but I was not winded, just stunned. Something wrapped tightly around my chest, like a python. I blinked hard. The sensation was not uncomfortable, just ever present.

I was laying on something tucked under my lower back that made it clear I had not laid myself down intentionally.

The ground had been scraped and scratched in careful lines, I sat and traced them with my fingers. The lines intersected and crossed one another. There was a nagging suspicion that I was supposed to know that they meant.

I was laying on a man's arm. Tall, handsome, and muscular and blinking stupidly at the ceiling, clearly just as stunned as I was. He lay collapsed on the floor, his legs partially twined with another woman's, her face was covered with long, beautiful black hair, black as a raven's wing.

I sat up and scrambled away. When I went to stand I struck my head on a statue of a chubby pig with a round, jovial face wearing robes.

Thankfully, the man was preoccupied making sure his wife was okay.

"Are you okay, miss?"

I turned around holding my smarting head. "Yes, thank you." He was quite the handsome fellow, the kind that was not made less so by the fact that he had neglected his razor for several days and he had the appearance of someone who had been dragged through a hedge row by his heels. His claret waistcoat and riding boots were worn but well-made.

"Yes. Forgive me, sir," I said, trying not to look in his eyes. "I don't seem to know where I am." *Or who I am.* I finished silently to myself. I carefully patted my hair back into place, stealthily checking for bumps. I wasn't sure how I knew to do that, only that it was important.

The other woman was stirring. She made a soft hissing noise between her teeth like an angry cat and pushed herself up off the stone floor. Maybe we had all fallen. The floor was littered with tiny bits of stone, some were thin bits of shaped slate, others the same stone as the pig statue I hit my head on. The ceiling above us had fallen in. What in the world were we doing on the roof of—whatever type of building would have a statue of a stone pig on the inside?

The man assisted his companion to her feet, then he too looked up at the ceiling. Something scrambled in the shadows, making me jump. He pulled out a silver revolver and cautiously looked around. The sight of the gun should have made me anxious, but for some reason I could not quite name, I trusted this strange man.

"Don't worry." The man slid his gun into a worn leather holster. "We'll figure it out together."

He gave me a smile I could only assume was kindly meant and it set a little hot coal into my core, giving me strength and vigor. He would not abandon me here to my fate. What a gentleman he was.

I was wearing a satchel and a belt like his. Maybe I had a clue to my identity on my person. I carefully patted around my waist taking stock of my possessions. I, too, had a revolver but I was not confidant in its use so I did not draw it. There was also a long knife sheathed at my back. The man had one, as well. Maybe we both were servants of the woman with long black hair. We were dressed similarly enough that I could guess we were provisioned nearly the same so it stood to reason that we were part of the same party. I was probably her servant. The black-haired woman had neither a gun nor knife and carried no possessions. She wore a short silk gown of blue and violet, snug fawn colored trousers, and flat embroidered slippers on her feet. My own outfit of linen and leather was much more rustic and durable.

I kicked another chunk of stone out of my way, watching it skitter across the floor. There was another noise in the darkness, as though I had startled something that hastened out of my way. I hoped it was wasn't hungry.

"Where are we?" I wondered out loud, hoping not to be dismissed for my own stupidity.

"The Library of Xiaoshuo," she snapped crossly.

Immediately, I resolved to ask no further questions. My mistress must have an awful temper.

We wandered the temple aimlessly for the better part of the morning until I could see dark clouds gathering where the roof had fallen in. Such a lazy maid I was that I didn't even notice when my mistress wandered off. I should make sure she didn't need my assistance. I crept across the broken tiles.

She must have been horribly burned, though I was a poor servant, I could not remember when. She stood with her tunic removed, her back, bare and raw, looking as though she had been wearing a gown of stinging nettles. It was as though her flesh had been scorched and left an oozing, painful mess. I could not imagine anything more painful. Her thin arms were wrapped around her lithe body and she trembled and cried in the little isolating beam of light, whispering urgent prayers in Chinese.

My heart ached for her. She needed something, anything. I longed to help her, she was my mistress after all, it was my duty to aid her in all things. Surely this malady hurt her. She was weeping, she must be in desperate pain. Then I caught something that sounded familiar; *Xihuan-Lung* and then another word I swear I had heard somewhere before, *YaMing*. The names were a dagger in my brain, thrust by a single curved horn in a mass of wavy mane. Now that was a peculiarly disturbing image. Where in the world would I have come up with that?

My mistress's musical voice was furious as she spit curses into the darkness. She would not like me for spying on her, so I crept away, careful not to dislodge any rubble underfoot as I returned to where her other servant, the man, paced. He restlessly muttered under his breath. At least his ramblings were in English. It gave me comfort to be able to understand the language, if not the words.

We were getting nowhere quickly. I felt a great despair settling over me. All I wanted was a good cry. The woman had forbidden her companion to use the blank books as tinder, so we would spend the night in the freezing rain. I huddled down by the wall where the books were sheltered from the storm, where some of the tiles had fallen against the great fountain in the center of the room. The rain fell in musical *plinks*.

I sat, letting my eyes drift in and out of focus in a sleepy manner. There was a man in my mind…well, another man, the first of the men so thoroughly occupying my thoughts was pacing in a manner most unsettling. I longed to call out to him and ask him to sit down so he didn't tire himself out. But I didn't know how to address him. The other man on the fringes of my vision was like a dream forgotten, but specific, a watercolor of a great lord from the times when kings wore armor and sat on thrones made of stone. He sat neither scowling nor jovial, but stern and powerful, an orb in one hand, a staff in the other, and he wore the most impressive crown, a dome of gold and velvet topped with a cross, something Charlemagne might wear from tales of old. His long beard nearly reached his knees and he wore shining armor polished to a mirror sheen. There he sat, staring at me, daring me to understand. I blinked hard, willing him to speak. Certainly, this man, this king knew something I didn't know, something I desperately needed to know. My side burned like I had rubbed up against a hot pot. I could not pull aside my shirt, my corset and its linen cover were in the way.

Please, I willed him to speak, My lord, King, Prince, Emperor.

Emperor. Now that was right. He was *The Emperor*, lord of all his domain, possessing great wisdom and experience. He was aged, but it was his birthright and it was hard won. His stone throne was decorated with rams, their curling horns resting under his wrists, bowing in supplication. He had conquered all, he could offer me the blessing of his wisdom, all I needed to do was ask. And a man of such power, such wisdom could make order from this chaos. But how?

The Emperor was an aged man, he had battered his many enemies into submission when he was a younger man. I had no doubt that should he need to draw upon that strength it was still there, ready to call upon again. But there was something more, a knowledge, a patience hard won.

The answer was suddenly there: Listen.

Music, gentle and plinking, one note at a time, echoed through the chamber, through the back of my mind. I knew that rhythm. The plink of the rain on the slate roof tiles, the heavy drips into the fountain—it was something I could not ignore. It was in the three-quarter time and I could hum right along. I knew this time signature well. I could even dance to it. In fact, I had danced to it before. In a great metal and leather ship that floated in the heavens. While a handsome man spun me in his arms trying to make me forget that if something went wrong we would plummet to our deaths.

It was the same man who paced back and forth looking for a way to keep us warm, to find us in the sea of ignorance, in a time I had nearly forgotten had cranked up a phonograph and dragged me to my feet and we danced.

"Nate!"

He looked up, thoroughly startled as though I had shook him from a sound sleep. He blinked twice.

"The drips, it's music—a waltz! We danced in the *Nomad*," I said.

It took a moment longer to dawn upon him. The music pulled him from his daze as it had me. He crossed the wet, broken floor and scooped me up into his arms.

Like aboard the *Nomad* he spun me in his arms as though we had not seen one another in months. It was *The Emperor* from the Tarot emblazoned on my side I felt earlier. And the black-haired woman, MeiLin, our Chinese interpreter; scowled at us, clearly we were entirely too jubilant for a broken down library of blank books.

I suddenly broke free of Nate's embrace. I had to know right then— were the books still blank? I dashed to the nearest set of shelves and seized a sturdy book with a thin wooden cover bound heavily in a double-wrapped twine and riffled through it. It was blank, just like the others from before.

I set it back on the shelf, albeit a bit more hastily than I should have when handling such an old book and pulled a scroll from the shelf. It, too, was blank, both sides.

"Blank?" Nate clarified.

"Blank." Why would monks be dedicated to maintaining a library of books with nothing inside?

Except there was nothing inside, nothing at all—most old books had damage from moths and bookworms, small amounts of staining and water damage. These looked new. It was as though these books had been bound then set to the shelves to sit forever with nothing inside only moments ago. I had never seen so many blank books, even in the fancy stationary store that sold blank diaries in Kensington.

I grabbed several more books just to confirm what I already knew. The entire library was blank.

"MeiLin, you said Chinese demons don't prey on people directly, they prey on their virtues."

"That is correct. When the people fall from grace they can be consumed easily."

"Knowledge is a virtue, correct?" I didn't wait for her answer. Neither did Nate.

"So then ignorance, is that a sin? Something is making us stupid," Nate concluded peering suspiciously around the darkness as though he suspected a dastardly monster to leap at us from the shadows to devour us. "Well, stupider."

"A library is the seat of knowledge," I said glad we were thinking along the same lines again.

"We need to find a passage that has something to do with knowledge." Nate spun slowly, taking in the room.

"What would the pig say?" I turned in a wide circle expecting to see the answer written on the walls.

"Oink." Nate muttered under his breath and laughed at his own joke. I sighed.

"I meant on his book."

"How am I to know?" MeiLin asked. "I speak and read Chinese, I speak and read English, there are many things I can do but do you know how to know everything that has to do with England?"

I blinked hard. "No, I suppose I don't." Maybe it was unfair of me to assume she would know everything I needed to know. Maybe we should have hired a scholar as well.

Nate lowered himself to one knee. "The pig, then, is the key."

"How do you know?" MeiLin demanded crossly.

"Well," I said, "we don't. But in the first temple, eight was a number of order and harmony but whatever creature had taken up residence in the temple had destroyed one of everything so all the sets of eight became incomplete, representing discord. The pig is reading from a book. The books are blank. Therefore, whatever the pig's book says is whatever the creature wished to hide by destroying the book itself."

Nate gave an agreeable nod. "Sounds right to me." He knelt and started to gather the bits of the shattered stone that had been the pig's book.

We all scowled at the pieces of the shattered stone for hours, the rain continued its steady *drip, drip* beyond the ruined roof. Even MeiLin was intrigued by the puzzle and she joined us though she clicked her tongue in annoyance from time to time.

It took us the better part of the afternoon to assemble the pig's book. It didn't help matters that whatever was looming in the skittering darkness remained maddeningly just out of sight, but hardly out of mind. Nate's hand was never far from his pistol as we scowled at the bits of stone. Our own puzzles at home were made of more than one color and the only one with writing was in a language we could understand. By the time MeiLin assured us we had characters in Chinese that were ancient but something legible, I was nearly mad from whatever was stalking us from the shadows.

She cleared her throat. "Here, drink deeply from the well of knowledge."

Nate scowled at the bits of stone, willing them to say something different. "There's no way it's that easy." He dragged his hand through his hair. Bits of it stood on end from the damp. He slowly turned and faced the fountain in the center of the library, regarding it as though it contained a deadly vitriol.

He pulled up his belt and peered into the fountain. Here was where he hesitated?

My satchel was sitting against the fountain. The final shreds of daylight filtered through the broken slate tiles. I had no desire to be here after dark when whatever was hiding in the shadows might feel emboldened by the lack of daylight and came out to devour us, or just as likely, our intelligence, and left us stupidly wandering in the crumbling library until we succumbed to starvation or some other misfortune.

I could just slap myself when my thoughts headed that way. My imagination could be surprisingly vivid. Bleak but vivid.

Nate pulled the metal tea bottle from my satchel and slowly unscrewed the lid. Like a man awaiting execution he surveyed the waters again. I placed a supporting hand against his back.

He wheeled around like he had been burned, and yelped. "Christ, Vivian!" he snapped.

"I'm sorry!" I snapped back, shaking.

He stepped back, one hand clasped against his chest as though he was experiencing sudden heart trouble.

"Don't do that!" His voice echoed uncomfortably, drowning out the dripping rain against the slate tiles.

"Do what?" I demanded. "Don't touch you?"

"Yes. I mean no!" He combed his fingers through his hair. "Don't touch me when I'm about to—" he paused, motioning with my empty tea flask.

"Touch water in a fountain?" I smiled. He could be so silly sometimes.

"We don't even know it is water," he snapped.

"What else could it be, it has been raining all day long," I said.

"Acid…poison…really, Vivian, it could be any number of things."

MeiLin gave a very unladylike snort.

We both turned and gave her a look.

The setting sun temporarily broke through the clouds letting the light and shadow play across the water's surface. For just a moment, the library was moved beyond eerily quiet, it became peaceful and beautiful. If I could ignore the fact that I was certain there was something sinister stalking us from the shadows, shadows that were growing with every passing hour. Something more magical than the fact that something within the Library of Xiaoshuo made us completely ignorant of our situation and our own identities. More magical than the Tarot arcana and the power of the Emperor that guided us back to ourselves; the magic and majesty of nature.

But there was more than just the fire of the sun's reflection in the water of the fountain. There was also a beautiful silver gleam beneath the waters of the fountain, angular and sharp, like an arrowhead.

I thrust my hand into the fountain before Nate could stop me.

He hissed sharply under his breath. Were he wearing Ranger's skin I was sure he would have been snarling at me. Other than being cold, the water was nothing sinister. But it was not so cold I could not feel the raised lines of delicate Chinese picture writing against one side, the engraved lines of the picture on the reverse. I was sure that when I pulled it from the water it would add to the picture of a Chinese man with a bow, strong and regal, but in ancient dress, shooting an arrow into a dragon just like the tapestry in Wei Huan's chambers.

The piece of the key!

With a smirk I didn't even try to cover, I pulled it out with flourish and handed it to my fiancé. To my surprise, he was less than pleased. Maybe I should have been a bit more gracious.

He took it from me, wrapped it in his handkerchief, and set it carefully in his waistcoat.

I was not sorry to put the Library of Xiaoshuo behind us—and if the way the ponies trotted and stamped their hooves and swished their tails—they agreed wholeheartedly. Whatever stalked the halls and wiped the knowledge from the books would have to wait for easier prey without the memory of a waltz to return their memories of themselves to them.

Nonetheless, I would not let Nate stop to make camp until we were several miles back the way we had come, no matter the danger of riding in the dark. As when we were fleeing Qixiang's palace, we let the ponies pick their own path, only directing them to stay together. For once, MeiLin did not need to struggle to retain her seat, her own pony was less concerned with trying to scrape her off on low hanging branches than she was about putting as much distance between the Library of Xiaoshuo and themselves as possible.

CHAPTER SEVENTEEN

NATE WAS DRIVEN by a strange force only he understood as we traveled to the final site of keys. He spoke little to us until it was time to make camp at night. He just drove us relentlessly onward, only stopping from time to time to squint suspiciously at the sun or the mountain ranges as though it held some mystery he was trying to puzzle out.

But at night when we dismounted and made a small camp, my thoughts were consumed by all we had learned. It no longer seemed a journey to recover an arrow. China was a land complex and rich in history and culture. The people were abandoning their temples, they were going to be caught up in a civil war between two rulers desperate to save China in their own way. Neither would preserve this wonderful land. It was being consumed by science and industry and the great world powers were destroying everything that made this place unique. It filled me with sorrow.

Now that we were away from the library with its wealth of books that were frighteningly blank and its ability to remove knowledge from our minds, I took a moment to think. The library would be where knowledge was stored but all their knowledge was gone, consumed and lost.

The knowledge from the books in the library had been damaged.

I pulled out the book on Myth and Legend in China again. I wanted to enjoy the uniqueness of China. The part about the trines might be helpful. Maybe I missed something. The Chinese zodiac was divided into a cycle of twelve years, each represented by one of twelve different animals. And this was further complicated by months, days and hours. They further divided into four groups called trines. The concept made my head hurt no matter how many times I read it, it was just so complex.

On second thought, I wanted to look at the drawings of the dragons again. I opened the book. My tea bottle must have spilled in my satchel. Two of the pages were smeared. I leaned forward for a closer look.

Not exactly smeared, it was like the words were...wrong. The words were still there but I couldn't read them. I turned back a page. That was English. I turned forward. That was English. I blinked hard and twisted the page, willing it to make sense.

If I looked at it just so, I saw a picture. A man. A man standing in Chinese armor with a single sword pointed down into the earth. The blade curved slightly. It was faint like a watermark. There were other drawings in this book, it was not unreasonable that I missed one when looking over the book before, I guess.

I tucked the book away. I didn't want to look at it anymore. It was fading away, like much of China. I needed sleep if I was going to keep up with Nate's mad pace.

On the third day it finally dawned upon me exactly what he was going on about. His affinity for maps was proving to be an amazing asset. He had managed to memorize landmarks and was navigating by memory to our final location, drawing us against the places we had already been to the Garden of the Sacred Grove, where we would be meeting up with Mr. Barrett and his companions to locate the final resting place of Xihuan-Lung and the Arrow of Hou Yi. I was about to ask him why he wouldn't just pull out the map when suddenly the trees parted before us, and we came to a clearing that was both like the other sacred sites that held the trine temples and unlike anything I had ever seen before. It could only be Shén Shèng de Shù Cóng, or the Sacred Grove of Gardens.

The ponies nickered to one another gleefully celebrating that their long journey was at an end. Soon they would be done with this nonsense and be returned to their stables where they could be assured a much simpler life of regular meals of hay and rentals to sightseers whose aims were much less ambitious.

They started clipping the soft meadow grass, oblivious to my attempts to pull the reins. I gave up and slid off. They would not wonder off here. I set a quick hobble and set off to the garden and the wonders contained within.

Wild apples, thistles, and tall bamboo, flowers exploding in colors of purples and red, yellows with dark spots that looked like they were sticking teasing tongues out at us, and beautiful scents that tickled the nose. And everywhere, statues placed to look like they were cast by some magic spell rather than carefully carved from smooth, gray stone.

Of all the statues we had seen in China, my favorite by far were the beautiful, fat little ponies. Strong and short, back home they would be ugly, but they had a charm I found irresistible. They were always wearing beautiful barding with decoration that I think was supposed to be bells and tassels, and their hair and manes were always trimmed short, bobbed, or carefully combed and tied up in neat little tails like the terracotta soldier statues everywhere. The horses they were modeled after are just as beautiful, even the horses of the poor are well cared for with carefully bound manes and tails.

I was pleased to see the horses in the garden standing like stout sentinels guarding the beautiful garden before us. Aside from being in sore need of a gardener, there was little that identified the garden as a site to find an ancient key. There were five of the horses, all in beautiful clean stone facing some unseen point in the center.

There was a beautiful red wood pagoda impeccably kept. The lacquer was fresh and free of scratches and wear marks. The pagoda was guarded by stone statues of dogs, but not the foo dogs I had seen everywhere that were the guardians in China, these were dogs as I was familiar with—the four-legged companions. I noted with a warm feeling beneath my breast that their familiar appearance made Nate smile. A dog was a dog was a dog. Ranger would be at home here.

It was a comfort to finally see an animal that was so familiar to the animals I was used to. In China, every animal we encountered from the chickens to the horses were a stark reminder of how far we were from home. The oxen looked nothing like our bovines, being more robust and stout—they must be valued for meat over their milk. Their hogs looked nothing like our little pink piggies; their pigs were hairy, wrinkled black and gray monsters looking more like wild boars in paintings than the pigs I had seen on farms. Even Chinese chickens were far from the light-colored chickens that dotted the English countryside. All the live chickens I had seen were colorful creatures with a stunning amount of bright plumage. Truly, it would not take more than a dozen to fill a feather bed. The hounds, however, were pleasantly exactly what I expected. I was half-anticipating any dogs I saw to be the lion-dogs or foo dogs that guarded temples and important buildings with one paw resting on an embroidered ball.

"Is this where the map says the piece of the key is?" I asked.

"Mr. Barrett is supposed to meet us here when they are done searching for the other piece, yes," Nate assured me.

"So, do we just wait here?"

"We won't have to wait long," Nate said.

"Do you see them?" I looked around, expecting to see them riding up.

"No," Nate said. "But Barrett is like me, he's competitive. There's no way he's gonna let us wait for long. If he could beat us here, he would have."

"Maybe they're lost," MeiLin offered.

"They can't be, they have my map," Nate said simply.

I turned, the tea I was making forgotten in my hands. "What?"

"Barrett stole it." Nate grunted, pulling loose a saddle bag so he could set up our little tent for the evening.

"That little blighter!" I said, thinking of the most vile thing I could bring to mind. Nate was far from shocked, in fact he laughed. MeiLin was the one that appeared scandalized. "Oh I know, I know, ladies don't speak that way," I snapped.

"If that's you cursing, Viv, I'd hate to hear you really mad at me!" He snickered and set the tent poles down before he hurt himself.

I made a face at him. "Why are you not livid?" I demanded.

"Because I have the ruby." Nate reached into his pocket and pulled a handkerchief out of his waistcoat and tipped the egg-sized ruby into his palm.

"Where—?" I couldn't finish the thought as he dropped the ruby into my hand. It was heavier than I expected it to be, warm from his pocket, and it seemed to glow from within. Whatever I was going to say was lost. I swallowed hard, managing to tear my eyes away from the depths of the ruby. "How?"

"I have a handful of skills more suited for street curs than for respectable gentlemen," Nate reminded me, as delicately as he could.

"Oh, really?" I closed my fist around the ruby and smiled down at him. He gave me that charming crooked grin that showed off a glint of teeth, dark caramel-colored hair falling into his eyes.

"I told you, I can pick locks and pockets. You will never starve," Nate promised with the same grin before he turned his attention back to setting up the tents for the evening.

I didn't know what to make of that. But when in doubt a proper English woman takes tea, so I turned my attention to filling the metal bottles at the stream and did just that.

§§§

Now this was the adventure I had been longing for. The night was cool but clear. The North Star winked down over us as we sat around the small campfire after a supper of dried fish and root vegetables cooked into a light soup flavored with some *Tauco*, a paste made of a fermented bean. It was positively ghastly by itself, horribly salty and faintly fishy, but mixed with sufficient water it made a fine broth. It was in the bottom of our supply packs in a small metal tin that I avoided like it contained a foreign plague until MeiLin had made a special dinner for Nate with the last of our smoked pork.

I leaned on Nate while we sipped some green tea and nibbled little peaches, smaller than the variety back home but sweeter and a good finish to a fine meal. With full bellies and a fire, I sat back to brush out my hair in the open air, headless of the smoke. Everything smelled of campfires now, there was no use in protecting my hair from it.

We were free from Mr. Barrett and his obnoxious, loud companion and the hulking brute, Mr. Baxter, and even the charming and knowledgeable Mr. Quinn, and there were no monsters stalking us in the shadows ready to make us bumbling idiots or shattering stone statues to frighten the life out of me. But the true blessing of the evening was the absence of MeiLin. She had wandered away from the firelight and off into the darkness.

She was not moving among the ponies, they had no love for her. They stamped their feet and rolled their eyes when she was near, so I doubted she was taking the time to sabotage me or any of my possessions. For a moment, it was if we were truly alone and the world was peaceful and wonderful.

Except that we were not truly alone and everything was not right with the world.

I sighed bitterly, wishing my thoughts would just give me peace. Somewhere in this lovely garden there was a piece of a key that would make a full key when joined with the other pieces that would lead us to a door that would, in turn, lead us to the bones of a long dead dragon and the arrow that slayed it. And that was the true reason we were in China. We were not here on holiday.

"What's wrong, pet?" Nate added wood to our little fire.

"We are not on holiday," I said.

"True. We are here on business," Nate said. Thought I could not see his eyes, I knew they were warm like whiskey in a glass, glinting in the firelight, beautiful and magical in the darkness.

"We love adventure," I reminded him.

"Yes, but perhaps some time exploring the adventure of being a married man would suit me for a good long while." I could tell he was smiling though I could not see his face. His tone belied him.

"Dinner parties can be treacherous. Nearly as deadly as a fountain of acid."

"That's not funny, Viv." Nate suddenly turned to face me. "You had no idea what that actually was."

My papa taught me how bases and acids reacted with one another. "You're right, to be sure," I said demurely. "But I wasn't worried."

"You should have been," Nate chided gently. "You're the only one that can patch us up. If you got hurt I'm not sure how I could have helped you."

A snippy retort came to mind but I bit it back. "Perhaps we should just go to bed. We have a long day tomorrow looking for the key."

"You go, Viv," Nate said, poking a long stick at the fire's core. "I'm going to make sure MeiLin didn't get lost in the dark."

I froze, my blood running to ice in my veins. *MeiLin. Leave it to her to ruin our night and she's not even here!* I almost screamed. Instead I stamped my foot in the darkness startling one of the ponies who snorted and stamped right back. I forced myself to be calm. "Are you sure? I could wait up with you."

Nate stretched. "No, go on to bed. I'll be along shortly."

If he noticed the false sweetness in my voice, he said nothing. If he didn't, it somehow made it worse. I took my time getting ready for bed trying to give him time to meet me there; to hurry and find MeiLin and return to me. But it seemed like he made no special effort, so I eventually climbed into my own cold bedroll.

When he finally came in and crawled into his bedroll on the other side of the tent, he said nothing, just curled up and went to sleep. I know it was irrational but I stayed up for a long time hating them both.

§§§

Even the beauty of the garden could not fully restore my good mood when I awoke the next morning and set about the task of making breakfast. My mind was foggy from the lack of sleep. A good cup of tea would do me good.

"Blimey! Lookie who's here!" Charlotte cursed, her shrill voice echoing in the garden. If I had been one of the stone dogs I would have growled at her.

Our ponies whinnied their welcome to Mr. Barrett and his party's mounts. They welcomed the company of other horses no matter who rode them, and wanted us to know just how enthusiastic they were just in case we somehow missed the loud and boorish manors of Miss Charlotte Ratham.

"Ho!" Mr. Quinn raised his arm in greeting.

Mr. Barrett looked less than pleased to see we had beat him to the last location. He pushed his black hat back on his head and spat like a dockman. Seeing them so stunned was almost worth the staggeringly bad headache I had that morning. What sleep I had gotten was haunted with dreams of finding Nate and MeiLin together in a loving embrace beneath the soft, green brush that dotted our estate outside of London.

Nate brought me willow tonic with my tea and could not understand why I glared at him so. He served us gummy overcooked pancakes and tinned sweet plum sauce for breakfast, then went to take the ponies to the stream for water in turns, all the while ignoring the appearance of Mr. Barrett and his party, aside from bidding them a cursory "Good Morning."

Charlotte helped herself to the dregs of the tea and Mr. Baxter set up their own coffee to brew on the edges of our fire. They did not bother to ask first.

"It's nice to see you, Miss Harper," Mr. Baxter said gently. "I trust your hand is nearly healed."

"It is, thank you." I gave it a flex. "And how are you this morning?"

"Fine, thank you," he returned formally.

"Mr. Barrett, were you successful in locating the piece of the key?" I inquired as politely as I could as though we were meeting at a party.

And what a party we were, a giant of a man in patched workman's wear, Nate and myself, a Chinese interpreter that would not speak to anyone except to make eyes at my fiancé, a learned adventurer, a woman who I believed with all my being was a former lady of the streets but in a finer dress, and her companion, an American man whom I was not yet able to figure out beyond that I knew him to be entirely untrustworthy.

"Oh, I was," Mr. Barrett said slowly. Something passed between him and Miss Charlotte Ratham, and for the first time I saw her flush and pale at the same time as though she was mortified and scandalized. "But I also discovered that I lost something else. You wouldn't know anything about that would you, my dear?" He glared at me from beneath the brim of his hat, something menacing and dangerous.

"She would not. But I would," Nate remarked casually. He returned leading the last pony back to our picket line. "I have the center of the key."

"There now, see, I knew you hadn't lost it," Charlotte crowed triumphant.

Mr. Barrett gave her a warning look. "No. Nate here just stole it."

"I did, after you stole my map," Nate said evenly. "I haven't exactly worked out what game you're playing here, Barrett, but you're not going to cut me out."

I leapt to my feet. "Now just a minute, last night you handed me the ruby," I cried.

"Yes, I did," Nate said. "And then I took it back."

"When?" I demanded.

"After you went to bed." Nate said in the same emotionless tone. Who was this man who could speak to me in such a cold manor and what had he done with my fiancé? I really did not care for this side of him.

"Now ain't you just a cad?" Charlotte sauntered over, hips swaying, ready to give Nate a piece of her mind.

Nate stared back, unimpressed. Until this moment I never suspected he had stared down a whore before. What else did I not know about him?

"Don't you speak to him that way." I said rising. Now where had that come from?

"You watch your mouth." Mr. Barrett's thumbs hooked in his belt too close to his revolver.

There was a buzzing in the air.

Wait. He had hired muscle. Where was Mr. Baxter? Lying in wait to hit me again?

No. Lum was nowhere to be found. For now at least. But Nate had both hands in fists, his forearms bulging, veins rising, and flesh swollen. Could they not see the danger they were in? Did they not know what he could become and the damage he could do?

MeiLin was shouting something to Mr. Quinn in Chinese. Their voices rose and fell in that unfamiliar cadence that was more sound than language I could follow. I took a deep breath and forced myself between everyone, making a beeline to the green gardens. Mr. Barrett and Nate, if they were to fight, there was little I could do to stop it. Charlotte was an obnoxious squawking gull and just listening to her made my head pound. I needed some air.

I could hear voices, low and on the edge of my hearing. I was not sure if it was even men or women, only that it was voices, calling to me. Maybe the cards emblazoned upon my flesh had finally gained voices of their own and were demanding that they be heard because they had input on this particular puzzle. I wandered off to a set of beautiful green shrubs with waxy ovate shaped green leaves and hundreds of beautiful red-orange, egg-shaped berries about the size and shape of my last thumb joint and nail. They were beautiful. They hung heavily, bending their branches nearly to the ground in places.

"Well, I dare say, you have come a long way from the tea house," was followed by a laugh. I would recognize that voice anywhere.

I wheeled around.

Lady Catherine Thornburry, daughter of Lord Thornburry; a man of means and of a prosperous family name—she and I became acquainted last year when I was engaged to Lord Byron Goodwin. I had been doing my best to learn to be in their world. She had done her best to limit my attempts at every turn and to make sure everyone knew I was not born to a life of privilege.

"Honestly, Vivian, you have fallen quite far indeed. Surely there is a better way to get simples for your father's failing apothecary business than this. Your low-born fiancé could offer you no better life than tramping around this ill place?"

"Lady Catherine?" I tried to straighten my blouse and pat my hair back into place.

She laughed merrily, "I warned you, you didn't belong."

"I ended my engagement to Byron Goodwin," I said, still reeling in shock. How was she here?

She made a clucking, pitying noise. "Oh, of course you did."

"Vivian?"

I wheeled.

My papa knelt by a tree, carefully peeling back the bark to harvest the inner pith, "It is wondrous isn't it. All of these ingredients placed together to balance the humors to make medicine and they believe it balances the hot and cold and something called the 'Yin and Yang.' They call it harmony, but it's a wonderful way of framing the world of medicine."

I heard tittering laughter from behind me where Lady Catherine was standing. I turned back, a sharp retort on my tongue. She could talk down to me all she liked, but she would not mock my papa, a man who had saved countless lives, including those noble, learned doctors put in harm's way.

She was gone.

I turned in a slow circle. She had to be somewhere waiting to mock me and my activity. I brushed a hand down my garments while I searched, but she was gone. So was my papa.

I knelt by the tree where he had been harvesting the bark. The tree was unmarked.

Could I have gotten the wrong tree?

"Please, I'm looking after them as best as I can. I left them with Mrs. Harris. I even took this job so as I could put them in school." There was a sob, a very manly sob, but a sob nonetheless.

I crept through the vegetation to see Lum, bowler hat in hand, kneeling before a rock as though in prayer, his huge shoulders shaking. "I tried, God help me I tried."

What could he be seeing that unmanned him so? Whatever, it was not my business, but seeing him cry was more startling than seeing the visage of my own papa or the shade of the venomous Lady Thornburry in China chiding me on my appearance and my fiancé.

I needed to return to Nate.

But he was suffering from the same sort of fit, muttering something under his breath. He appeared to be ransacking a set of shrubs entirely uninterested in me calling his name. It was though he could not hear me. Not even my hand on his shoulder could shake him from his trance.

§§§

Quinn and MeiLin screamed at one another down by the water in Chinese, and Barrett and Charlotte were screaming at one another again. From what I knew of them, something was very wrong and that could only mean one thing—the demons that were attempting to keep us from reaching the points of the key were once again attacking our virtues so they could consume us at their leisure.

I did my best to not imagine wicked, horned creatures hiding in the shadows of the shrubs and trees and the beautiful pagodas to bite off our heads. I sincerely hoped something with three heads and seven eyes and large frightful bat wings were not lying in wait.

I sat down and closed my eyes forcing myself to feel with my senses. A garden is a beautiful place of birth and rebirth. But it was not something as simple as death that waited for us if we failed here. Death would merely be failure. If the Chinese demons MeiLin warned us of existed then a worse fate loomed with failure. Their demons would consume our virtues, then our souls, leaving us husks of people doomed to hunt down virtuous people unless we were slain by virtuous people.

In the tarot, *The Tower* is more than just change and chaos and upheaval. Generally, it is a picture of a lightning bolt and people either falling or leaping from a tower as their entire world crumbles around them. Change is neither inherently good or bad, but enough change is disorienting. No card is good or bad, they are merely what is. It is our reactions to them that color how we move next.

I smelled rain coming. The cool, clear, faintly sharp scent born on the wind was invigorating. It registered somewhere beneath my senses.

I forced my mind to return to *The Tower*. A sharp enough shock shattered our perceptions. Could it shatter the hold the demons would hold over our virtues? But what virtue would they be taking hold over?

The Chinese people valued temperance, they valued knowledge, they valued order and truth and willful thought and acting with intention. Surely, they valued other things as well, but I could not guess what else those would be. So what would the demons attack then?

The first temple we visited was a maze maintained by the monks as a place of contemplation, a labyrinth where one could practice mindful thought—so disorganized thought was how the demon attempted to destroy virtues. The demon had destroyed the statues and the maze. It had tried to disrupt the mindfulness of the site.

The library had obviously been a place of knowledge, so it made us ignorant.

Other virtues included temperance and order. But which was represented here? One of those or another? Which virtue had Barrett and Lum, Quinn and Charlotte encountered, or rather, which corrupted version of a virtue? The opposite of temperance was excess. A garden was neither excess nor temperance. But a garden could represent order and chaos.

My old tutor had once defined chaos as a lack of order and explanation, as turmoil and confusion. If the state of mind my companions and myself was experiencing was any indication then our mental states could be described as bedlam. Chaos could be represented here. In fact, an overgrown garden would be the very representation of chaos.

I saw a ball or an egg. And in the center, all of creation waiting to be born. All it needed was a spark.

My skin was hot and cold and my very bones ached. *The Tower*. It had something to do with *The Tower*. Or was it the lightning that was the catalyst to change? I felt it coming. It was not a meek summer storm. It was something violent and frightening, powerful and primal.

My scalp was stinging and aching. The air was hot, but more than just hot, the hot stink of metal and blood was in the air. I could not open my eyes. It would break the spell. I was close to understanding. I was so close.

The rain—cold, distracting rain. Nourishing to the garden but driving me from my thoughts. I forced it away. Nothing mattered now, not the sound of angry arguing, not the feel of cold rain dripping down my collar or soaking my trousers from the damp grass. *The Tower* and its sense of change. I just needed to understand.

I did not hear the thunder. I felt it. It was like being kicked in the chest by a horse. I tasted blood and coughed and choked. The rain was running up my nose. Somehow I had ended up on my back with my backside above me, braced against a bit of carved log by my shoulders and my neck.

"Viv!" Nate was hoarse. "My God!"

"I'm fine," I tried to right myself. "I think."

Nate stared at me as though he had just seen a ghost. "God's wounds! Vivian, I thought you were killed!"

"Of course not." I made myself laugh. "I'm fine." I sounded stronger than I felt. "What happened?"

"That pagoda got struck by—"

"By lightning?" I interrupted rudely. I couldn't help it. My mouth hung open.

"Yes." He stared over his shoulder to the smoldering wreck that had been the beautiful pagoda.

"That Tower had been struck by lightning," I whispered.

"Tower?" Nate gave a half-smile. "I guess so, it's not a very tall tower."

I let him help me up. Bits of the smoking lacquered wood had been blown all around us, but amazingly no one appeared harmed. Even the horses were placidly grazing at their picket lines as though nothing out of the ordinary had happened. But all of us stood staring at the charred remains of the tower as it crumbled and burned, marveling at the chaos that shocked us all from our earlier disordered thinking.

Had I caused this?

I stretched stiffly and stepped around a blazing bit of the charred wood. Whatever I had managed had stunned everyone out of their strange states.

Mr. Baxter stood, peering up at the pagoda held up by two huge bronze tigers. Though no expert in such matters, I believed they had to be larger than the elephants we passed when we left the DeBurghs in India.

"And just what are you staring at?" I snapped, exhausted. Then I recalled his distress earlier and immediately regretted my tone.

"The key." He pointed up to the top of the pagoda where the tiger's bronze tails touched. Balanced between their tails sat the key, gleaming in the early morning light.

Mr. Barrett turned to Lum. "You work for me and I say you shall give me a boost,"

"I have not been paid since we left England," Lum snarled back.

"I told you, you will be paid when I am," Barrett snapped.

"So far, this old boy is much closer to the prize than you will ever be and he didn't get help!" Lum thundered, gesturing to Nate.

"Help?" Exactly who had helped Barrett and his party of adventurers? And why? "Excuse me?" I demanded, starting forward only to be stopped short by a vice-like grip on my arm.

"Never you mind." Mr. Quinn took my arm to lead me away, his hand a claw on my bicep as he pulled me away.

"Take your hands off her!" Nate hollered, his voice cutting through the din. His temper was getting the better of him. His eyes were wide and dark, he looked only moments away from losing his grip on his temper and transfiguring before Barrett and his adventurers. My little show with the lightning had done nothing to settle his nerves.

I jerked my arm free. I was quite sore, stunned, and done with being a pawn.

"Why would you pull away? Unlike your fiancé, I am no thief!" Mr. Quinn said, suddenly angrier than I had ever heard him, his polished Suffolk manners lost.

"Thief?" I gasped. "Mr. Barrett stole his map long before Nate took the gem, and that was just so your employer would not cut us out of the deal with the Explorer's Society."

"The what?" Charlotte cackled. "You stupid hen—"

"Charlotte, close your hole!" Mr. Barrett said, drawing his gun. "I will not lose her favor now!"

I was too stunned to be frightened. Nate's revolver clicked into deadly readiness. I was suddenly thrown off my feet and thrust behind two men, one lean, the other massive.

"Easy, boss," Lum said, in what I supposed was what he thought was his most placating tone. "Charlotte didn't mean anything." The fact that he was standing shoulder to shoulder with Nate, protecting me against Barrett, was not lost on me.

"Whose favor?" Nate demanded, each syllable spit through clenched teeth as though it was a separate sentence.

What in the world was going on here? Everyone had gone quite mad. *Demons!* MeiLin was watching us with her mouth hanging open, her normal composure lost in the chaos of the moment. Slowly she smiled watching us descend into chaos.

"The Queen, of course," Mr. Barrett said.

The point of my left shoulder burned. I knew without looking that if I were to remove my shirt the *King of Swords* would be glaring at me, sword held in his right hand, resting cockily against his shoulder while he glared, challenging, daring anyone to speak against him. But was he upright or inverse? Was he coming from a place of authority and truth and Mr. Barrett was actually coming from our Queen, representing the interests of England just as we did, or was there something more sinister at play? Were we being manipulated? Was it just the influence of whatever was at work here in this beautiful lush, green garden?

I glanced around the garden. The stone dogs glanced at me, their stone tongues hanging out, the small tips of their teeth pressed against their lips in canine grins. How could a creature as noble as a dog be hiding something sinister? But if there wasn't a demon making everyone crazy then Mr. Barrett was lying. Could I accuse him of that? Here, with my fiancé and him standing with weapons drawn, moments away from a deadly encounter?

No one dies from wounded pride. Men often die from battle wounds. We could get to the bottom of this later. I turned to MeiLin. She was staring—white-faced in righteous fury—at us silly Westerners.

That made as much sense as anything else I guessed so I placed a restraining hand upon Nate's shoulder. This was not the time to force the issue. We would get to the bottom of this soon. My head was still reeling from the lightning striking the pagoda.

Wisely, he agreed. He gave me a small nod. We still needed them, at least to get the key.

"I'll give her a boost, she's nice and light." Lum offered, motioning to me.

I should have been offended, but Charlotte in her dress was an unpractical choice and I doubted MeiLin was willing to help with our enterprise to recover the key from such a height. Nate gave me a boost and together both men stood with one of my booted feet in each of their hands like a giant human letter A and helped get me safely to the top of the tails where the key balanced between the two tigers.

Except my hand passed straight through the key. A tiny bit of cold air, a cold wind, rested above the tiger's tails. The key was a cold, blue-white light. It wasn't anything I could touch.

I sat on the charred remains of the pagoda. Despite the beauty of this place, while it stood, the very air here felt angry, with an undercurrent of angry bees. The garden was alive with bees pollinating and moving to and fro, but while they were not physically menacing, there was a profound energy in the air humming away. In the Tarot, *The Tower* was a sudden, often drastic, change as the physical tower itself was the false premise or lie that we clung to and the lightning that shattered it was the sudden clarity shattering the illusion. As I wandered the garden my papa spoke to me despite being back in London. He was not here, he was thousands of kilometers away. So was Miss Thornburry, my rival from what seemed like a lifetime ago in London when it seemed like I was about to marry into high society. Neither of them could be here. My mind had conjured them.

Struck by the same madness, Columbus Baxter cried to nothing or everything. He had left someone dear to him with a Mrs. Harris and took this job so *they* could be put in school; children, his own or children left in his care. Nate searched frantically for something he had lost or something that was taken from him. Mr. Quinn and MeiLin argued loudly in Chinese. Mr. Barrett and Charlotte screamed and fought.

I was exhausted. I wanted to eat and sleep, have Nate take over the adventure for a time. But the piece of the key was here somewhere. There would be no rest until I found it.

My hand again passed through the key. It was there and it wasn't. Up close, it was shimmery and ethereal, like one would expect a ghost would look. The silvery sheen was similar to the rest of the silver pieces of the key.

"Well?" Mr. Barrett demanded.

"It's not here," I said.

"What!" Charlotte yelled.

"It's not here," I said again. Lum and Nate helped me down.

"What are you going on about woman? I see it, clear as day," Mr. Barrett snapped.

"See for yourself" I said, straightening my clothes.

I let them fight it out. I needed to think. There was a puzzle here, just like every other piece of the key.

As the day ticked away, everyone's mood soured.

Finally, I sat down to look at the book and the notes provided by the scholars of the Explorer's Society. Maybe there was a clue there I was missing.

Twelve signs, all represented by animals. The sketch of the circle divided into quarters was off to the side. Four sites, four trines so four sets of animals. The first set of animals was the ox, the snake and the rooster. They had been in the Temple of Yi, a temple of meditation devoted to the cyclical nature of the seasons. This set of animals all belonged together in a trine. They were associated with planning, with the slow accumulation of energy, with endurance, and with careful application of their plan. It was the cycle of planting and harvest. It was also the planning that would have to go into making a giant maze and plotting out the grand scheme of the mirrors to focus the energy to illuminate all of the maze so the visitors could contemplate the great path. The loss of the monks would create a break in this order, a loss of the plan.

The trine temple we visited without Mr. Barrett and his group was the Library of Xiaoshuo. The animal symbols we found there were the rabbit, the goat, and the pig. Those signs were calm and reasonable. They also were attracted to art and were well-mannered and detached. They were intellectual souls…animals…whatever. A library was the perfect place for them. The artistic fountain was where we found that piece of the key. When the monks were forced to leave their place of sanctuary, the demon that took up residence removed the words in the books. It attacked the very knowledge of that place, in fact, it removed the knowledge within our very minds. It was only art, in the form of music, that saved us.

I do not know how Mr. Barrett and his group recovered their piece of the key while we were in the library but since this garden was decorated with horses, dogs and tigers, it was reasonable to assume their temple had been the rat, the dragon, and the monkey. Those creatures, my book and notes said, were powerful, intense, and unpredictable. That told us nothing of importance.

But we were in a garden now, a garden decorated with tigers, dogs, and horses. Idealistic, independent, impulsive, lovers, and humanitarians all within a garden setting. Dogs and horses served men. But tigers, I was stumped. A dog and a tiger were independent, a horse was entirely dependent upon man from feed to horseshoes. Then again, a dog could be dependent, too.

By unspoken agreement, no one wished to camp right next to the skeletal remains of the shattered pagoda. No one was willing to burn the lightning scorched wood either.

I sat by the wreckage of the pagoda, the clean, white sand reflected the moonlight like a brilliant beacon framed brokenly by the broken lacquered wood shattered by lightning. The campfires behind me where the rest of our party waited were warm, with hot orange and red undertones. Just the image of them was welcoming, as the comfort of sitting in the sun with a loved one.

The moonlight on sand was cold, almost blue-white, clean light. There was nothing welcoming about it. But something was welcome in it. Something moved here. I looked up, surely clouds were moving over the moon and obscuring its light.

There wasn't a cloud in the sky.

Still something moved. Three somethings. They all moved in a slow circle dancing in and out of the cold moonlight. My eyes were playing tricks. I was tired, so tired. All I wanted to do was rest. I blinked hard. The cold, blue forms were still there. Long and lean. They moved in a circle, four legs moving just above the earth, prancing, stalking, moving along. It was not a game of chase, they were not hunting one another, nor were they running from one another. My mind adjusted to their forms, making sense of what I could call incorporeal for lack of better words. It was a tiger, a dog, and a horse. They moved around that circle of pale light. They drove one another. They made each other move.

I could see a link that united two of the three animals, but nothing that united the three of them. Tigers and dogs ate meat. A horse and a dog could eat plants. Horses and dogs served man. Tigers and horses had great size but a dog was small.

Idealistic. All were idealistic representations of a trait. Dogs were loyalty. Tigers were ferocity. Horses were strength. That was their key. They key to the key. I giggled. I must need to eat. And sleep. My shoulders ached from my sudden impact with the ground and whatever else I might have crashed into when the lightning struck.

Was the thing that united them their setting? Gardens…

"Nate, what is a garden?"

"Plants." He shrugged, "Herbs, cures I guess."

He was right, of course. But he wasn't entirely. To the layman, gardens were lovely places full of growing green things but they were also places where nature renewed itself. The apothecary and the herbalist knew the garden could heal and harm. It was a place of creation and destruction, birth and death and rot, and from the rot, new life began. It was a circle. The animals moved each other. Life could be violent but it could also move along in a humane way, in a way free of suffering. Many naturalists argued that it was only the intrusion of man that created unnecessary suffering. They served each other in a humane manner. The chase, the hunt. It was not cruelty, it was merely the circle of life: life, death, rot, rebirth.

I wondered if the word for humanitarian and the word for humane could have gotten mistaken somewhere along the way.

I suppose they all loved the other in their own way.

I had to make them move.

"Come move this statue," I called.

The tiger's noses and tails met and that was where the pieces of the key were held in the ethereal light. It was the spirits of the tiger that held the key. They would have to be persuaded to give it up. They would have to be given something of value to them in trade.

Fierce, independent, impulsive. Could we make them angry? We might be able to make a pair of spirit tigers angry but I wasn't sure that was much better than making a dragon angry. But we might be able to make them chase something. That might make them drop the key. If not, it would not harm things.

I woke with new purpose the next morning. We would have to move the statues by shifting them; I was sure the key would become corporeal then.

The tigers were the largest, the horses were the second largest, the stone dogs were the smallest. We would have to try to move those first.

The dogs were sitting on their haunches, waiting to spring into action. Each one was taller than the men and I doubted two adults could easily pass their arms fully around them. Immediately, this seemed like a bad idea. I wasn't sure even Nate could move the statues.

"We need to move these statues." I said more confident than I felt.

"How?" Columbus asked.

"Could we strong-arm it?" I asked feeling less sure of my plan.

"Unlikely, miss," Columbus said. "Even when unloading them large boats, you need block and tackle to do it right. If not and them big barrels get away from you, folk get killed. And you'd need at least two men to move any barrel weighing more than about eight stone."

"Really?" I glanced up at the stone dog quite defeated for the moment.

"If there's anything our Mr. Baxter knows, its manual labor," Mr. Barrett said absently.

Mr. Baxter was a laborer, true, but it was a skill like any other. I didn't know we needed block and tackle. I was immediately offended on his behalf by Mr. Barrett's condescending tone. It surprised me, though. I still, very much so wanted to hate the man. I decided for the moment, I merely hated Mr. Barrett more.

Mr. Baxter's arguments did not stop Nate and Mr. Barrett from at least giving an earnest attempt at moving the stone dogs themselves. Even with Nate straining at the edge of his canithrope strength, there was nothing we could do short of destroying the statue itself.

We had no chance of moving them ourselves, I had to make them move each other.

I watched Nate while he had coffee and a bit of fruit from the garden. He was as close to a dog as I could consider right now. How could I make him move if I needed to? He caught me pondering our predicament and brought me a peach and coffee. Well, that solved one problem, Nate was moved by love and devotion. I could move Nate no matter which skin he wore. I leaned against him, setting my head against his side. I gratefully sipped the coffee. I doubted the stone dog would move so easily. How would we move a dog in general?

"It was a good idea," Nate said.

Mr. Barrett glared at the top of the tigers where the key was out of his reach. How had they managed a piece of the key without us?

I wasn't defeated yet. But there had to be more to the puzzle. The figures moved one another around the moonlight in a large circle. They drove one another. They could be dependent upon one another but independent of the rest of the world. A garden would be its own little separate place, a tiny contained world. I stared at the enormous garden. Tiny was relative I suppose.

Horses would take treats but they grazed upon sweet grassy fields. Dogs ate meat, but Nate, as Ranger, preferred the cuddles and affection to the bone I had offered him on the night we met.

I glanced up at the dog's stone face. The face glimmered for a moment. It was watching us. Not the stone, something inside it, the same shining incorporeal essence that made the key that glimmered above the tigers and the same that was the three figures that moved in and out of the moonlight.

The dog spirit was watching us. Dogs did what their master bade.

I turned to Nate "Nate, would Ranger do whatever you asked of him?"

"If he understood what I wanted he'd about kill himself to do it." He smiled but then his face fell. Ranger had, in fact killed himself to protect Nate from the leywell magic beneath London. It was how they became bound; two souls into one body.

"Mr. Quinn, what is Chinese for 'dog come'?"

"As in 'come over'?" Mr. Quinn clarified, "That would be *gǒu lái.*"

I stood before the statue. *"Gǒu lái."*

The eye glimmered for a moment, but it may have been a trick of the light.

Charlotte laughed. "What did you expect, you dumb chuckie? That that damnable stone dog would come alive and follow wherever you wished?"

I didn't imagine it. We were on the right track. I needed something the dog would want.

"He does look a bit like Ranger," Nate said. "Look at the muscular body, broad chest, strong feet, low-set tail, long, narrow head. I got Ranger from a trader who had been all around the world. He was from a litter of pups. They were working dogs all designed to be farm dogs for herding sheep and cows and the like. He said Ranger'd be miserable in the city."

"He was wrong. Ranger loved you, he was far from miserable," I said.

"Do you think a dog like Ranger would herd horses?" He was staring at the nearest stone horse.

"It might," I said. Nate was brilliant; I loved that we thought the same. "What do we do with a horse if we can move it? I mean get the dog to move it," I clarified.

"A dog needs to serve," Nate said. "A horse serves, too."

I looked over to our horses and laughed, "No a dog lives to serve, a horse lives to eat, it serves because it must."

As if cued a horse looked up from grazing and nickered at me before going back to the greenery.

"Then what does it eat?"

The answer dawned on us at the same time, "Grass."

The garden was flanked off to the south by a great meadow. The dog could drive the horses there. The stone dogs could drive the stone horses into the meadow. Then what? I gave a heavy sigh. If I hadn't been there, the idea seemed quite laughable, we were trying to puzzle out moving stone animals the size of manor houses and carriages. That just left the tiger. What would move the tiger?

Tigers would kill a dog. But they would also kill horses. No, they would hunt horses.

Around the circle of moonlight, the three ghostly figures of the animals of the garden moved together, circling one another in harmony. They were idealistic and impulsive. They would serve their own aims, they were independent in that way and independent of any intervention to fulfill their cycle. This was what they were designed to do. The dog served, the horse grazed, the tiger hunted. And I believe, the dog helped man hunt the tiger. We would just need to provide a catalyst to start the cycle then it would move along as it was meant to.

The dog needed motivation, more than just being called to task. Or maybe that was the key. He needed to be told his task.

"Mr. Quinn, how would you say, 'drive horses' like a command?"

Mr. Quinn scratched his head, "I suppose it would be '*Mùfàng mǎ*.'"

I stood before the stone dog and took a deep breath. I needed this to work. Dogs needed strong leaders. They followed strong handlers. In the Tarot, *The Chariot* is driven by a man who trusts in his own spiritual power. He has turned his back upon the city and all its finery, all its distractions as he heads out aided by black and white sphinxes, creatures of mystery and knowledge. He is aided by his own force of will and his inner self. He holds no reins over his mighty steeds, it is his own force of will that guides them. I would have no chains over this mighty dog. All I would have is my own will. It would move.

"*Gǒu lái mùfàng mǎ!*"

The dog's eye blinked.

"*Gǒu lái mùfàng mǎ!*" and I pointed to the nearest stone horse, larger than our home in the countryside outside of London.

The spirit of the dog, glimmering blue-white, cold and incorporeal, stepped out of its stone form and stretched in canine delight, free from the form that had held it for so long. It bowed to me.

Our companions stared, and from somewhere behind me I heard a gasp, a curse, a sharp intake of breath.

The dog trotted off, circled the stone horse I pointed to. The horse suddenly sprang from the stone form, silvery and blue-white, and leapt out in front of the trotting dog to be driven into the meadow. The horse bent his head to crop the lush grass of the meadow, his form translucent, the ideal form of a horse in the distance. No artist could have done better.

His job finished. The dog disappeared. The horse had been driven to the meadow. The dog did as the master bid.

A low guttural growl. I turned. For a moment, I had forgotten the tigers. A single mighty stone head moved in the direction of the horse grazing in the meadow. The striped tail lashed—the cat had spotted his prey.

He ignored us. The tiger leapt from its stone form, silent ghost tiger paws made no sound as they touched the ground, stalking forward a step. Then another. The horse was oblivious of the danger.

Oh no! What had I done?

The striped tail twitched, each paw touched the ground as the tiger moved, weight shifting from one paw to the next, one shoulder to the other, beautiful and hypnotic in its movement. The tiger moved inhumanly fast for something so silent and so deadly.

The horse swished his tail, munching the grass. The tiger's belly was flat on the ground as it crept forward. I wanted to scream for the horse to run. This was not what I wanted.

The tiger pounced. The horse screamed and tried to wheel and flee. Front claws grabbed the hindquarters of the horse and dragged it to the ground. The horse tried to leap back to his feet but the tiger quickly dove away from the thrashing hooves and sunk his teeth into the horse's neck. The horse twitched twice and then was still. The mighty striped tiger tail lashed from side to side in delight.

Then they faded together. And behind us something metallic clattered to the ground. The last piece of the key. I turned. Nate was crouched picking it up. I turned back to the statues. The dog's eye glimmered. The horse's stone mane rippled with an absent wind. The tiger's mouth had the silvery-blue gleam of fresh slaver. They returned to their stone forms, but the key in Nate's hand was solid. We had what we came for.

"I'll be damned." Mr. Barrett was staring at me with what I could only guess was respect. "I cannot believe it worked."

"Who'd guess calling great stone beasties would make them come alive," Charlotte said staring at tiny stone carvings that had been on a man-sized pillar by the pagoda. "Oy, Quinn, how would I ask it for a drink?"

CHAPTER EIGHTEEN

WHEN ONE FINDS out they will be assembling a key, one assumes a key will look...well, like a key with a blade and a bow and a barrel, where the teeth fit into the lock and turn the tumblers and set the lock to open.

But all of our pieces matched in shape, angular bits of what I could only guess to be steel or maybe silver, but entirely free of scratches and tarnish; each shaped like half of a fancy letter A from an ancient illuminated monk's script. The only way they varied was the engravings on each piece. The beautiful Chinese writing continued across the pieces with no regard for the breaks, though the breaks were far from random. The reverse was some sort of a picture—an archer and a dragon, depicting the slaying of the beast with the arrow we had been sent to recover.

I arranged all the pieces and assembled the engraved picture.

The key made a beautiful silver star with a hole in the center surrounded by a ring of flames. The ruby would sit in that hole, keeping the key from falling back into four equal angular pieces. The ruby was the sun, or perhaps even the world on fire.

For once, even Charlotte was speechless. She stared at it, the light refracted from the ruby bathing her features with an eerie red glow. No not eerie, strangely beautiful. It turned her blue eyes nearly violet. I wanted the ruby more than anything else in the world. I wanted to cover it from their prying eyes and keep it secret and safe forever.

Mr. Barrett reached for the key. "Now there was no way I'm gonna let you keep that."

I shoved it behind my back, a hasty, childish gesture. The rational part of my brain screamed at me. *Stupid, Vivian, what do you think that will do?* But I had to protect it. Mr. Barrett only wished to use the key for harm.

But for the moment, we were outgunned. Nate knew it as well as I.

"Give it over." Mr. Barrett snapped his fingers impatiently.

Nate gave a small nod. We had to, we had no choice. *For now.*

But even his implied promise that we would get it back didn't make me feel better. To be parted from it for even a moment now that I had held it was a palpable pain centered somewhere within my breast. I swallowed hard and set the key into his hand. My thumb brushed the stone set in the center and for an instant I felt like I had grabbed a hot coal. My hand shot open on reflex.

Charlotte immediately made a grab for it but Barrett kept it from her and tucked it away within his waistcoat. She pouted and glared but he paid it no mind, instead he hooked his thumbs into his gun belt. The threat was clear, anyone coming close risked his wrath and his gun.

The next day we would head off on the final leg of our journey to recover the long-lost Arrow of Xihuan-Lung. Mr. Barrett and his party were the very picture of jubilation.

But the touch of the stone haunted me. It wasn't that no Chinese person could have solved the riddles, it was that no Chinese person dared. We had done something mighty, we visited trine temples that had once been guarded by monks who broke a holy relic into pieces to protect the secret it maintained. Then, just as their world readied itself to fall to foreign rule, the monks had abandoned their sacred duty, the pieces were assembled, the monks abandoned their charges and their positions were taken up by *mó*, demons that attacked the virtues of men's souls.

The book in my satchel had too much information. It was too intelligent. Whomever approached the Explorer's Society begging membership wanted access to the treasures of man the society held in trust for mankind. And that man needed to sell a tale. He did not happen upon a story of an ancient weapon. This weapon was carefully researched, the work was carefully recorded. It may have taken years to forge the path we traveled in mere weeks. Whomever wanted the arrow wanted a weapon, and the only thing he was missing was the scale he could have either gotten from the Explorer's Society or from the Royal family of China. If he had known, we never would have known of this weapon until it was too late.

The thought chilled me. I would not bet a copper penny that most men with a weapon of that caliber would just hand it over to the Explorer's Society for the good of the world.

I returned to the skeletal remains of the pagoda where I had seen the tiger, dog, and horse moving through the circle of moonlight the night before and stared at the blank, sun-warmed sand. The water that had been part of a reflecting pond before my truly impressive lightning fueled destruction had bits of charred wood still covered in bits of red lacquer floating in it. I knelt over the water to fish it out.

So much destruction we brought to China. Not just us as adventurers but all the people who didn't belong here and brought their judgements of a culture they didn't understand: British, French, Russians, Germans, Japanese; all coming to strip a land of riches and a people of their identity.

The center of the reflecting pond was a tangled bit of something twisted and turned in upon itself, like a giant knot. To my Western mind it looked a bit like a flowering artichoke. It didn't matter what it was really. It was a seed, the center of a plant, the center of life and chaos and order in all things. It was the center of all things we were not able to understand.

I knelt before the pond. "I'm sorry." I was speaking to everything and nothing at once.

The seed was shining, opening, blooming deep in the water. I leaned forward to look. There were twelve tiny circles of light. They moved faster and faster, darting like little silver minnows in the water. Their light danced in and out and around the seed until it became a circle of white-blue light, and deeper still within the circle of light, I could see the hills we had trudged along.

They were dotted with bits of stone, granite, and marble, roughhewn and chipped as though they were a part of a larger piece. Some of the pieces we passed had pieces of carvings; a leg here, an arm or a bit of a face there, and they all belonged to something greater. I tried to catch a glimpse of it as we passed but my mind could not cobble together a picture from the fragments.

At the top of the hill, a small pagoda stood, a tiny, five-sided building with no walls, just pillars of stone that held up the pointed roof and sweeping, curved eaves. The broken bits of stone had all come from here. The pagoda had an ancient air of neglect and no green moss grew, but there had been an arch within, a few of the larger blocks stood stacked still.

Mr. Barrett was the picture of grim determination. He scowled at the tumbled blocks. A fallen monument would not stop him. "Then there is a keyhole is here somewhere," Mr. Barrett said. "There has to be. Mr. Baxter, find me my keyhole."

Columbus Baxter nodded and started digging through the rubble, flipping over the blocks of stone. Nate wasted no time assisting him. Between the two of them, and the leverage created with Lum's long gun, they finally managed to unearth a block of stone with a star shaped indentation in the face. My heart beat faster when I saw the matching mark. This could be it!

Mr. Barrett pulled the key, fully assembled, from his waistcoat and set it into the depression.

The air around us shimmered and wavered like heat over a stove. It became a white-blue circle that existed where the arch would have been if the stone still stood. The absence of the stone did not seem to matter. Before us, beyond the shimmering air, lay something that was not there a moment ago: a skeleton like that of a massive snake but with huge clawed feet and a head sporting two pairs of horns, one pair that shot forward like lances, the other pair curving backward like the spirals on a ram's head. The serpentine head lay on the ground, black teeth longer than a sword, clenched in the fleshless skull larger and more menacing than anything I had ever seen before. Something so large should not exist. It was amazing. It was frightening. Dragons were saviors of mankind and possessors of great wisdom and magic. I stood in awe of a creature that could bring the rains and move the heavens. They were the keepers of this ancient world. The beauty of it touched my heart.

If such a creature fell from grace it would be a terror upon the world of man. I took a shuddering breath.

Stepping through, Mr. Barrett had the look of a man about to achieve his greatest desire. Charlotte followed him through, laughing, and threw her arms around him. He kissed her passionately.

Nate and I followed. The air just through the demon gate was cold, like I had just passed into a massive shadow. All around us lay the bones of the great behemoth. I touched one, it was cold and hard as marble. The ancient bones had long since turned to stone. I traced one leg bone, walking slowly around it. Dragons must be immense creatures indeed. Its long curving spine twined through the trees like a giant snake. Its ribs created a chamber so great both Nate and I could have easily stood within the arches they created.

"Have you ever seen something so massive?" I asked him.

Nate grinned that smile that made him a jubilant little boy, full of mischief and joy. "Never."

MeiLin was smiling, too, but the look on her face was nothing pleasant. Her pretty smile, normally close lipped, was more a grimace, displaying fine white teeth.

Stuck in the skeleton, embedded in the back side of a curved bone behind the left front shoulder that reminded me of a bird's wish bone, was a thin arrow with a narrow head, almost like a needle with several rows of wicked barbs that faced backward in all directions like the spines of an evergreen tree. The striped wooden shaft should have long since turned to dust and the dusky yellow feathers should have fallen from the wrapped sinew, but the arrow looked as though someone could fit it to a bow and fire it right this instant with deadly results. The metal head was as bright as the key itself, the same silvery bright metal. They were linked, to assume otherwise was illogical.

Mr. Barrett seized the arrow and pulled it free of the stone bones it was embedded in.

The mists had started again, rolling over our boots. It brought the smell of a bog with it. Organic and rotting, worse than merely the scent of putrid vegetation. It contained the scent of rotting flesh.

It was the scent I smelled on Molten Cay. The scent was unmistakable—it was death.

I wheeled around, snatching Nate's hand in my own shaking grasp. He sensed something was wrong as well. I shifted and spun trying to locate the source of my dread. My boots squelched in the dirt. The ground had been so hard moments ago, now it was like walking in something soft and rotting.

The mists obscured my vision. The dragon was changing. I reached out to touch the dragon's ribs only to find them warm and covered with a fine sticky film. Nate touched them, too. The film spread between the ribs like a spider's web, blocking our view of the privateers and MeiLin. Nate pushed against it, it broke with little resistance but the air around us was becoming steadily warmer.

He pushed against it again, this time it resisted his touch. He unsheathed his long seax and sliced through the webbing, now more a membrane than a lacy web.

The bones were no longer cool marble, they were wet and dark covered in a reeking red moss that spread from bone to bone, joining them together until they resembled flesh.

"Oh. My. God," Lum breathed.

For once I was in complete agreement. The bones arching around me heaved and shuddered. I heard the rumble of a long, deep breath. It was the sound a horse might make, drawing a deep breath to keep a girth from being tightened; the breath of a large animal trying to take control. It was a breath of a monster waking.

Then the tail bones, covered in red, wet lacey flesh, twitched. I turned to run.

Nate grabbed my hand. We left our packs with the horses tethered to their rope line and they were starting to panic. They whinnied and rolled their eyes. I grabbed my seax and ran for them. I slashed the guide rope they were tied to. I grabbed the lead ropes and launched myself into the saddle. I had the ropes for a second horse wound around my hand for Nate. We had to get out of there now! But the horses were in a panic. I was jerked to the side by the rope around the hand that had been gashed. My shoulder was wrenched and I gasped as I was thrown to the ground.

The one Nate had been riding reared and struck my shoulder with one flailing hoof. I hit the ground hard, the world spinning. They ran off, snapping their leads and bridles as they stepped upon them. Lum grabbed me bodily by the waist and heaved me over his shoulder opposite his humongous shoulder cannon. My head smashed into it and stars exploded across my vision. I tried not to be cross, it was kindly meant if clumsily performed.

The horses charged in their panic, scattering off into the trees, some the way we came, others surging further into the forest. Lum set me down gingerly into Nate's waiting arms. Nate wasted no time. I could feel the question in his eyes, *Could I run?*

I nodded and he grabbed me with one hand, MeiLin with the other, and dragged us stumbling after him into the mists desperate the escape the rotting, sick, sweet, scent of death.

But that scent was wherever we turned, and soon Xihuan-Lung would be fully regenerated into the monster of legend.

"What will Xihuan-Lung do?" I gasped against the stitch in my side.

"She will claim the Tianmenshan Forest as her own home and hunt the people of China as she wishes. When she becomes bored with China she will spread her foulness across the world," MeiLin said.

How was she not at all winded?

"Could she be slain again?" Barrett heaved himself against a log, gasping for breath. He held the arrow in one hand.

"Why would you take it?" MeiLin demanded.

"The Explorer's Society is charged with recovering the arrow," Nate answered for Mr. Barrett, who was panting and shoving his hand into his side.

"The West is arrogant!" MeiLin snapped. "They presume to recover an artifact without respect to its legends."

"Look, all I know is it is supposed to slay any enemy with a single shot." Barrett gasped. "Imagine what the Queen herself would pay for a weapon like that. She would knight the man who brought it to her."

"I knew it!" Nate snarled, his voice hoarse from our flight. "You vulture!" Before anyone could stop him, he pulled back and hit Barrett as hard as he could across the jaw.

I threw myself into Nate to separate the men, I knew from experience just how strong Lum was and had no desire to entice Nate into becoming a slavering man-beast intent on Barrett's blood when we had a mad and terrible dragon that would soon be chasing us.

"You used us!" Nate yelled. I felt his chest heaving under my hands. I could feel something dangerous and primal rising in him. His chest quivered, more than a mere drawing of breath, the bones themselves were quivering.

I couldn't think of anything else to do. I grabbed Nate and kissed him hard. Rough and demanding he kissed me back, his mouth opening mine, tongues meeting in a rough quick possession. I felt our teeth connect and backed off slightly. "This is hardly the time."

His eyes seemed to be glowing in the mist, their warm brown was possessive and hot. He looked over from me to where Barrett stood, Lum glowering at his side. He gave his head a little shake and wiped his mouth on the back of his hand. "Right, not here."

Charlotte stared at Nate in a new way, like he was the dish of the evening in a fancy restaurant. I didn't like it one bit. It was rather like the look MeiLin usually gave him. Thankfully he was completely oblivious to both.

We heard a groan through the mists. The sound made my knees go weak. Everyone heard that growl. Xihuan-Lung was awakened and she was on the hunt.

The forest came alive. Logs and stones shattered as the dragon stretched her mighty body, weaving herself around the landscape like a deadly river of death. There was nothing we could do but quiver like the little rabbits we were and wait for the monster to reveal herself and strike. There would be no mercy here.

Mr. Barrett waved to us, frantically trying to get our attention. He pointed to his eyes then all around. *Could we see her?*

I mouthed, *No.* My stomach was shaking so badly I could not have found my voice even if I wanted to. We had to leave. If we got back beyond the Dragon Gate and pulled out the key, maybe the gate would close behind us and seal the dragon here and we could trap her in this little place that was only accessible with this damnable key.

I took a step forward. A rock slipped under my food and broke free, banging against other rocks as it scattered scree like little gunshots. I forgot how to breathe.

Xihuan-Lung laughed. The sound turned my blood to ice. I hit the ground hard, every muscle seizing in terror. I wasn't the only one. Mr. Barrett and Mr. Quinn were cowering behind the wind-swept juniper. Not far from them, Charlotte was clasping her knees to her chest and rocking, a small whimpering sound coming from her lips.

Lum had his hand clasped hard to his side where Nate had shot him months before. He looked like he wanted to vomit.

I understood the feeling, my wound from the battle with the stone gargoyle burned. Every wound I had ever taken seemed to be throbbing as if an old fear or an old pain had been reawakened. It was an odd contrast to how cold I suddenly felt. *Nate, where is Nate?* I peeled my eyes from my forearm.

MeiLin crouched against a large white boulder. She was cursing under her breath. But whatever she muttered was not the babbling, frenzied, whispered prayers of the rest of us. She was angry, and alone unaffected by dragon fear.

It took a long moment for that to even register in my brain. Anger flooded my ravaged mind, momentarily replacing terror, *What made MeiLin so different?*

"Children of the West, I smell you." Xihuan-Lung taunted, her booming voice both beautiful and terrible like staring directly at the face of God. The dragon fear faded slightly and it felt like my heart could beat again.

"You released me from Hou Yi's arrow. For that you have my thanks. Your deaths shall be swift," Xihuan-Lung said.

Mr. Quinn was the first of us to move. He leapt up from his hiding place and tried to dart away. Like a startled deer he jerked one way then another. Xihuan-Lung lunged forward, her serpentine body weaving through trees quicker than lightning, and reared back on her hind legs. Mr. Quinn screamed. Then there was a *crunch* and Quinn was no more.

Xihuan-Lung returned to all fours, letting her massive belly rest on the forest floor. Her dark blue scales, each the size of Nate's hand, rattled like a wave of pebbles cascading down a hill. Several of them were missing, the holes healed over with what looked like the black lacquered armor I had seen in Qixiang's palace. The scales around the black patches were chipped and damaged. I wondered if perhaps these were places where her armor wasn't so thick. Perhaps they were the weakness we desperately needed.

Lum must have had the same thought. He stood and leveled the massive blunderbuss, shoulder cannon he carried. It resembled the swivel cannons found on the railings of ships. It took a man of his size to even carry one, let alone fire it.

He leveled the gun and set the flintlock mechanism to fire. The blast knocked him back a step.

He may as well have shot a stone wall. It bounced right off. Xihuan-Lung surveyed her own side and I was sure she looked amused as she regarded her undamaged scales.

Lum stood dumbfounded. He didn't have long to marvel. Xihuan-Lung whipped her head around and lunged, spearing him with one of her massive spiral horns.

He gave a startled grunt as he was hoisted into the air. She whipped him back and forth, showering the ground with his dark blood before flinging him aside where he struck the ruins of the carved pillars and lay still.

Nate worked his way to my side. I felt a clammy hand grasp my wrist. He gave me a weak smile. "Run," he whispered, "I'll give you a chance to escape."

"Absolutely not!"

"I'm not planning on fighting to the death," Nate whispered. "I'm going to get her attention, then I'm running too. I'm a fool but not that big of one."

He took a deep breath and pulled off his waistcoat and shirt. The transformation began. He fell to his arms and legs in a crawl, his spine arched painfully as the skin split and his monstrous form burst through, covered in a heavy thick brown pelt. He clenched the ground. His human skin fell to the dirt in large chunks then evaporated as the magic reclaimed it back into the hazy world of transformation.

Nate stood, his growl of pain turning to a howl.

He launched himself at the dragon's face, grasping her beard and used it to swing up onto her face. He grabbed one of her horns and kicked hard using his strong back legs to rake her face, trying to blind her.

"Charlotte, Barrett, run!" I screamed, it was uncharitable but I didn't care if MeiLin ran or was eaten by the dragon. If we were lucky, Nate could use her to cover his escape.

But I knew better. I turned to shout a warning to MeiLin. She carefully stood and walked to the clearing. She looked completely unimpressed by the scene. I stared, dumbfounded, completely forgetting we were supposed to use this time to escape.

Xihuan-Lung tossed her head and snatched Nate with one massive, clawed hand. She tore him off her face and slammed him to the ground.

Barrett turned to take Charlotte by the hand. What followed I shall see in my nightmares until I die.

Charlotte took her lover's offered hand and turned to run just as Xihuan-Lung sucked in a deep breath.

Xihuan-Lung carefully released a gout of liquid fire. It struck Charlotte in the back and splattered like hot grease. It bathed her and Barret both in liquid flames. He had been breathing in. The gout of flame rocked his head back, the burning liquid rushing from his mouth and nose like his soul itself was on fire. His short gray hair turned to ash and he crumpled into a heap, tripping Charlotte as she stumbled over her burning skirts. She screamed, a high-pitched, keening cry.

Dragon fear consumed me again. I couldn't move. I couldn't breathe. I couldn't even tremble.

Charlotte rocked back and forth trying to beat back the flames. I saw the flesh melting from her bones, coming off in chunks like slow-roasted pork falling from the bones. The smell was similar, too; a hot roasted scent beneath the scent of black powder and char. No man stood a chance against an angry dragon. Hou Yi had been right to slay the beast, it was truly beyond redemption, it was death for all mankind.

Nate dove for her face again, sinking his teeth into the flesh just behind her horns. He slashed and tore with his massive claws, sending up bits of dark blood.

She hissed and tossed her head sending him rolling to the ground. Xihuan-Lung slammed her paw down onto Nate, pinning him to the earth. She drew in a deep breath.

"No!" I screamed. It was all I could manage in the grip of Dragon fear. I could feel everything from my head to my heels to my very soul fighting to do something, anything.

Xihuan-Lung released a gout of flame into Nate's face. I could hear his keening howl. She tossed him out of her path as easily as though he had been kindling.

I sprinted forward. I didn't even think about living or dying now. Nate lay in a bed of leaves trembling and whimpering as his fur burned.

He was caught in the middle of transformation, half man and half beast, charred and battered. I reached for his hand, feeling the bones and flesh shift, stiffen and tear. He couldn't speak now, his face had mostly become human again though I wished it hadn't. The charred mass of flesh was nothing I recognized as the man I loved. It didn't resemble anything human. Dragon fire had melted his features, turning them into a single mass of twisted, burning flesh melting off his skull. He breathed out a steaming, smoking cloud punctuated with pitiful whimpering. His chest was constructing in twitching pulses, exposing charred flesh sloughing onto the ground and revealed organs flash-baked and partially melted to his white bones.

Nate gave one last shuddering sob, then was no more.

Xihuan-Lung roared, but this time the sound didn't affect me at all. I simply lay myself over Nate as though I could shield him from more damage. The heat coming off him was almost enough to force me back but I stubbornly held on, locking my frame to his. We would be together soon.

Behind me I barely registered the sound as Xihuan-Lung crushed our ponies to a mass of shattered, screaming horse flesh and bone.

"Xihuan-Lung," MeiLin shouted above the battle. Her voice was calm and clear. "You will serve me or I will return this arrow to your body and you shall remain lost in the mists for all eternity."

I turned. The arrow had been in Barrett's possession when he was killed, yet remained unblemished by the fire. MeiLin held it up in one small hand.

Xihuan-Lung dropped half of a limp pony she had been shredding and turned to face MeiLin. "What do you propose?"

I was hot. I was cold. I could not breathe. She had brought us here. She let this thing murder Nate, all so she could speak to it. She had made him trust her. She had used him and his gentle nature. He had wanted to see the best in her. Nate had defended her! He was almost too hot to touch, but I could not pull away. It was the last thing I could cling to.

"You will aid Prince Qixiang in disposing of Empress Dowager Cixi. Then I will see the arrow destroyed," she called.

"I will serve no man," Xihuan-Lung scoffed.

"After Empress Cixi is slain I care not whom you serve," MeiLin said simply. "Burn the world if that is your will."

Xihuan-Lung dropped to all four clawed feet. Faster than I could blink she wove her serpentine body through the rocks and trees until her massive head was only a dozen feet from where MeiLin stood with the arrow in her hand.

"You will destroy the arrow as soon as I burn this Empress Cixi? I have your word on that, *Huli Jing?*"

"You do." MeiLin gave a slight nod.

I only had a moment for despair. We were betrayed. And we would all pay for it with our lives.

Nate's melted flesh had managed to glue our physical bodies together. It was horribly fitting. I could not leave his side without tearing and defiling his body further.

Xihuan-Lung turned to me, I could feel her eyes boring into my back. They felt like her razor-sharp horns. I heard her take in a sharp breath and then I felt the smoke envelope me and smother me in darkness.

CHAPTER NINETEEN

AND THEN I WAS FALLING forward into the water. I had been so hot a moment ago. The seed of creation within the reflecting pond was still and closed, and the twelve little lights that danced like silver minnows were gone. I shivered at the sudden chill of the water soaking my knees and sleeves. I tried to wrap my arms around myself but I could not stop the violent bone-deep trembling rattling my teeth.

That was how Nate found me, on my knees in the reflecting pond surrounded by the remains of the pagoda I had ruined with elemental lightning as we raced to unite a key that a sacred order, much smarter than us, had separated for the good of mankind.

I felt his arms around me. He did not try to move me, just let me be as I trembled in the water in a manner that had nothing to do with the cold.

What were we doing here? In a land of ancient magic where we didn't speak the language and customs so foreign we were strangers. In a land where we were more than mere outsiders, we were considered barbarians. We could have been dumped on another planet for all I knew. But at least we were, for the moment at least, still where we had found and assembled the last piece of the key.

We stayed that way for a long time. I ached from the lightning strike, from weeks of sleeping on the ground. I was starving and filthy. But for all the misery, this was the man I needed. This was the man I loved. All the distance that had been forced between us in the last few weeks melted away. All the uncertainty I felt watching him with MeiLin was gone, evaporated into the mists. I couldn't wait to marry him and make him the master of our little manor in the English countryside. We would not leave it for a good long time.

Nate hugged me tighter for a moment before releasing me. He had been carrying a cast iron pan and some of our provisions. He must have been bringing them to me so I could start some supper. He would lose patience and char everything while somehow leaving it raw on the inside. I didn't think MeiLin even knew how to cook. If she did, she certainly wouldn't lower herself to cook for me.

I busied myself in using some of the rice flour and sweet red beans to make something that was something between a biscuit and a pancake, with bits of dried sugared pear, and, of course, tea. This way I could stretch the last of the dumplings so they would stretch into a full meal for us all as a sign of goodwill. Tonight, we would have to resort to the salt-cured fish or the dried beef in our packs unless Barrett and his privateers were willing to share their provisions.

The Chinese pigs, or *Taihu* as they called them, were a different, wilder variety than I was used to and their fat was gamier but lent a lot of flavor when used to cook flatbread on skillets. We had a small lump of it wrapped in canvas in a wooden box with our supplies. I went to fetch it now as Nate carefully untied the lines on MeiLin's tent.

My dream, if it was such, still haunted me. I stared at Nate while he worked. All I could see was his flesh melting from his bones, sightless eyes staring as he whimpered and sobbed, struggling for breath.

"Can you look after these; I need a moment," I asked MeiLin.

"I am not a cook. I am an interpreter," she said simply.

"I'm aware that you are not a cook," I said crossly. "I am not a cook either but it needs to be done and neither of us brought servants along."

She ignored me.

"MeiLin, if you wish to eat you will help!" I said, sounding harsher than I intended.

Nate casually intervened. He gently guided me out of the way and took up position by the fire to cook.

I could have screamed. Instead I gathered as much dignity as I could muster and walked to the shade of the trees to get out of the sun. I needed to think.

"She treats you poorly," I heard MeiLin observe. In the garden, sound had an eerie way of carrying.

I wanted to dash across the camp and slap her. The smell of the sizzling pork fat made my mouth water. It was also making me nauseous. In my dream, MeiLin was immune to dragon fear. She stood up to the beast, arrow in hand. Xihuan-Lung called her something…

Huli Jing.

I returned from the cool trees to the tent and pulled out the book on Chinese creatures. I had heard that word more than once and I was fairly sure where.

MeiLin gracefully accepted the flat bread Nate handed her. It was scorched in places and if Nate's past cooking was any indication, possibly quite raw in the middle. She graciously bowed to him as though he laid a feast before her and set to eat.

If I had handed it to her like that I would have gotten no end of complaints.

Nate handed me one as well but I found I had no appetite and the pork fat made it greasy in my hand. The Taihu pigs were adorable with their wrinkly fat faces. I could imagine one being butchered, its fat rendered and caught in tubs and sold as cooking lard. I wrapped it in a piece of cloth and set it into the pouch on my belt. Nate gave me a strange look but said nothing.

I flipped the book open leafing through the pages.

From this angle, the picture was more like two pictures rather than just one. I leaned in for a closer look. The sword wielding man was a king or an emperor, no in the Tarot, *The Emperor* held the staff or the Ankh and Orb, symbols of his divine right to rule. So maybe something else. The sword in his hand was something else, too, some sort of two bladed sword, a staff with a sword on each side, two blades connected at the handle? I had never seen a weapon like that before. One blade pointed upwards toward the sky, the other buried itself in the dirt by his feet, it was imbedded in the dirt. That wasn't right either.

Confusion. Chaos.

I rubbed the bridge of my nose. I was thinking too hard. I needed a break, I hated the way my mind was little mice all scurrying about for little crumbs of a clue.

The book fell from my hand. I fumbled to catch it, twice my hands struck the pages and they slipped from my grasp before it tumbled end over end and landed face up. From this angle I could tell it was not one image but two.

Two cards.

It was two cards. Two separate cards. Two separate messages. *The King of Swords*, inverse, but a king from China. A warrior king, in lacquer armor with a headdress wielding a sword, single edged and slightly curved but held high, and a single sword, curved but inverse pointed into the earth. They were overlaid giving the impression that the wielder had a double-edged blade and a sword for a spine.

The rest of the page was washed out or erased. No, not erased. It was obscured. And it was no wonder.

When swords are encountered in the Tarot, they are a great gift. They are clarity and intellect. They are tools of the mind, sometimes cool and calculating but a

The King of Swords was a man of inspiring leadership and those who lead to remain fair, to recognize the truth before them and to walk the path before them with a clear mind. The King is a reminder to use reason to get to the heart of the matter and to reserve judgement. *The Ace of Swords* was a crowned blade, the very symbol of the mind and of intellect. It is a crowned blade, hard won victory as knowledge is often hard-earned.

Both of these symbol were reversed. This was no simple charm. The knowledge in these pages was hidden, stripped, obscured. We were being manipulated by whomever placed this charm, someone or something was intentionally keeping us uninformed. With the charm in place, the information was literally lacking. Swords without training and order was chaos. We desperately needed the information these symbols obscured.

If I could summon them as I had with the lightning in the garden to the tower, maybe I could banish them as well. Release, I told them. I took a steading breath. Release, I thought. I stared at the images willing them to move with all my heart.

I closed my eyes and made my mind summon that smoky gray haze of the world at war, that place where all the world melts away except for the tunnel of light that is the battle before you. I battled men and monsters before. The world outside of that circle of light was cold and slow, the world inside hot and fast. I made myself walk that land again, this time with the knowledge that I was safe. In the distance, coming out of the haze, a pair of old swords, like a knight might wield, crossed.

I walked to them. They were the only focus I cared about. The world around me battled and came apart. The world was lost in shadow. I reached out and pushed the swords aside separating their violent clash. The bright focus and the smoky haze became one and I blinked hard.

I blinked hard at the book in my hands.

Slowly the cards cleared like fog burning off in the bright sun. Words became clear. Words in English like the rest of the book.

Huli Jing
Literally "Fox Spirits"

These creatures are neither good nor bad omens, their personalities vary with the individual and seem to date back to the Han dynasty. These fox women—for they are always women—are attracted to powerful men (and much less often, women) trading their companionship for services. They possess the power to ensnare the will of their chosen by seduction.

They are capable of taking human form and always possess great beauty, but when they use their magic their fox features become more pronounced. When they are in their fox form, they possess nine tails. They may also possess a third form possessing features of both human and fox. They also possess great magical powers, including poisoning men and bewitching or bewildering them or removing their memory. The limits of their magic are not fully understood.

A note had been added in the margin in a blue pen.

Note: Huli Jing is also used as a slang term for a homewrecking woman.

Oh, how appropriate.

My supper was ash in my mouth. Our own homewrecking Huli Jing had wandered away. That was fine. I could not even recount what we ate. My mind was too busy to wonder where she had gone. I had enough to worry about, a mystical creature wished something from Nate. As did the dethroned Emperor Qixiang. As did the Empress Dowager Cixi, only, thankfully, Nate was unaware that she wanted something from him.

Then there was the key. The key and its beautiful ruby was burned into my mind as was its touch on my hand.

When MeiLin returned she wore a pink and green silk gown with a high collar and thigh slits exposing her dark loose trousers and dainty slippers. Her straight, black hair, soft as a bird's wing, was carefully caught up in a set of jeweled combs. She was staring at us with an amused grin as she packed, that I found completely obnoxious. How could she stand there pretending to be a mortal human like us?

I sat staring into the fire letting my eyes become unfocused. The waves of heat and smoke gently spread their warmth over me. Every time I closed my eyes I could see Xihuan-Lung reforming from her bones and chasing us down before snatching us up and murdering us all—then turning her wrath upon the rest of the world. Xiezhi had warned me this could happen. The arrow had been created to slay Xihuan-Lung, that was its only purpose. It was not a weapon of war against the world. It could not be removed from the corpse of the dragon without removing the enchantment that held the dragon in death.

I shuddered. At least this was a different heat than that of dragon fire. I remembered that all too well, I feared it was forever etched into my being.

Maybe that was not what Xiezhi was trying to tell me. Maybe he was merely trying to warn us that the arrow can bring the dragon back to life if we are not careful. I understood how things worked in London. Or at least I understood how things may work; I was raised with the legends and folklore of England and the books of the fairy tales of Europe. I even had a book of Arabian Nights and the tales of Scheherazade. Now I realized my education in the folklore of the world was woefully incomplete. It was something I would have to immediately remedy when we arrived home.

A sound interrupted me. I lack the ability to adequately describe it because I'm not sure I had heard it anywhere before. I froze and straightened, glancing about to see if anyone else heard it. They were all busy setting up the camp for the evening. A *gekkering* sound, an animal cry, something foreign. I swallowed hard forcing down a sudden hotness in my throat. No, *on* my throat. *Themis*, the major arcana burned against my throat. Speak in truth and hear the truth; truth in all things—so there is truth in this. I closed my eyes to listen better.

It came again. The sound was a bit like the cry of a fox but musical, ethereal, and something beautiful and terrifying all at once. The sound was coming from our tent.

Xiezhi, strange as he was, came to reveal something I desperately needed to learn. Something I still needed to know. Perhaps he was calling to me again, drawing me away from the group so he could tell me how to stop Xihuan-Lung from rising from her grave and killing everyone. I could see Nate, trapped between forms shuddering in agony as the dragon fire melted his flesh and cooked his lungs—MeiLin standing before Xihuan-Lung unaffected by dragon fear making a deal with Xihuan-Lung before unleashing the dragon to consume all of China, perhaps all the world.

I followed the sound to the tent. MeiLin's pack lay thrown in the heap with my pack and Nate's. One of the two buckles at the top had come undone and I could see the edge of her fox fur collar with the wax dragon charm peeking out at me. I wondered why she wasn't wearing it. She said she made the charm to lead us to the grave of the dragon, but I had not seen her wear the collar since we entered the mists. Before that, I had never seen it off her neck. I ran my thumb over the shiny wax seal, careful not to blemish the gleaming wax. The ground up dragon scale glittered like tiny pieces of silver were mixed through the wax.

I turned the soft red fur in my hand and almost dropped the collar. This piece of fox fur was nothing more than a strip of skin, judging from the raw bleeding flesh on the reverse side, recently torn from the skin of some poor animal. How could MeiLin do this to some poor fox? Especially now that I knew what she was?

The campfire light was temporarily blocked as something moved in front of it. I did not wish to be caught pilfering her bags. I shoved the collar into my shirt.

We marched on the next day, nearly ten miles. I could not stop thinking of the key in Mr. Barrett's pocket and the fallen cairn we were headed to. We would reach it just before sunset. The keyhole was face down in the stone second furthest from the right, partially buried. I also knew Mr. Barrett would stop at nothing to find the dragon and, once he did, no living thing in the world was safe.

I needed time to come up with a plan, but I wasn't sure I could manage to buy us more than a few hours. Soon we would arrive at the toppled pile of stones that marked the entrance to where the dragon lay, and every step brought the world closer and closer to its doom.

The horses would need water. And I knew too well we would be stopping soon at a small stream that flowed into a quiet lake just around a copse of trees. We would water the horses there and fill our water bottles. Tiny frogs would sing from the reeds until something other than us startled them into silence. I remembered they kept singing after we already started watering the horses and filling our bottles.

And just as I predicted, there it was. I could hear the frogs singing over the horse's hooves tramping over the moist ground. I decided to water my horse a further down the stream, by the lake, where I could at least feel hopeless overlooking a beautiful view.

The frogs stopped singing. I looked down, and slithering across my boot was a serpent, pattered like a checkerboard and going along its way, oblivious to the fact that I was in its way as though I was just another log. I swallowed a scream and leapt back.

The snake turned its smooth face towards me and stuck out a forked tongue, tasting the air before turning back toward where the frogs had fallen silent, presumably on the hunt of a frog meal.

I gulped down air trying to force my heart back into a rhythm that didn't promise a coming heart attack. But it hadn't harmed me. In fact, the snake had no interest in me. My papa, more than a learned apothecary, he was also quite interested in naturalism. We have had several serpents in our gardens over the years and most snakes do man more good than harm. He taught me that the snakes with spear-shaped heads like the leaves of belladonna were venomous, the ones with smooth heads were generally harmless. Of course, there were exceptions to the rule but this snake could be a wonderful distraction and in times like this. Beggars could hardly be choosers. If fate was choosing to send me a snake to help me preserve the world from a dragon on a bloody rampage against all mankind, then a snake was a fine help-mate.

I stepped after the snake. It was not too keen on being chased and tried to wiggle away but it was no match for me. After it realized escape was impossible it resigned itself to capture and wrapped itself around my arm in a friendly manor, eyeing me with those round, beady, little eyes and stuck out its tongue, intrigued at this new development and hopefully not too annoyed that I had denied it a meal of frogs. The frogs were happy, they started singing again, rejoicing that they had gone off the menu.

But now that I had the snake, how was I to use it? I stared into its little black eyes. Suddenly it hit me. Women are terrified of snakes. Well, not me obviously. And not MeiLin, she was just too strange; but there was one woman I could rely upon to behave in a predictable, uneducated, low manner. I returned to where the rest of the party was watering the horses, the snake held carefully behind my back.

My prey was using a wide variety of pins to set her hair up on her head to protect it from the moisture. The damp was making her rogue spotty against her cheeks. And if her past behavior was any indicator of what was next, she would be refreshing her make-up after her overzealous attempts to remake her hair.

She kept her simples in one of her saddlebags, refusing to use backpacks or satchels or bags of any kind that she would have to carry on her person other than a gaudy beaded bag that clinked and caused her to curse loudly whenever it snagged on something, a near hourly occurrence. I passed by her mount and whispered an apology to both the reptile and equine about to be involved in my attempt to delay our march.

I was kneeling looking at a rather beautiful cluster of ginseng roots wondering if I had time to harvest them to add to my medicinal kit when a blood-curdling scream rang through the valley. Charlotte and the snake had found one another.

My diversion worked even better than I could have expected. One panicking horse is a danger to both horse, rider, and everyone unfortunate enough to be near. But one horse in panic tethered by a half-dozen other horses is total bedlam.

The horses screamed and rolled their eyes, bucking and rearing, tearing at their lead ropes and throwing their bits. Leather snapped and sheered as reins snapped under the force of nearly eighty stone of horse frantic to be free.

With a roll of thunderous hooves, the horses scattered. Comically, the men drew their pistols and revolvers and wheeled, trying to discern how we had suddenly come under attack. Beneath the chaos, Charlotte's gull squawk rang out like the sound of glass cutters working their trade. "There was a bloody great snake trying to sink fangs into my body and damn my very soul to hell!"

"Damnit!" Mr. Barrett wheeled around and slapped Charlotte hard enough to knock her to the ground. "What are you grating on about, woman?"

Charlotte dissolved into whimpers. I was immediately sorry. I should have found the snake in my own pack, I had been hit before and I would probably be hit again if I tried to continue this brazen path of adventuress. I should have caused the panic as well as the mischief and bore the wrath of the party.

"There is no call to strike her," Nate said, doing his best to remain calm. His eyes were dark and wild, a sure sign his righteous anger was near boiling over.

"Daft whore scattered the horses!" Mr. Barrett snarled, wheeling on Nate.

Both men still had their guns in hand.

"I'm sure she meant no harm, boss," Columbus said good-naturedly. "I'll set about gathering them up."

"I would advise on letting them just go," MeiLin said. "Horses are a crutch here, the ground is uneven."

"You shut your face!" Mr. Barrett snapped at MeiLin. "Them horses have all our gear. Unless you fancy carrying your own supplies or sleeping out in the rain you will care. And you!" He spun back to Charlotte. "I should never have brought you along!"

"Come on, boss, it's an easier job for two," Columbus offered.

"Three," Mr. Quinn said, taking off toward the horses. "I believe some went off this way. Miss Harper, would you please keep the women together while we chase after our valiant steeds? I do believe this work is more suited for the menfolk."

Nate shot me a look as he followed the men to go reclaim the horses. I half-hoped he would find some way to leave Mr. Barrett senseless and tied to a tree. It only occurred to me in that instant that he just may if I asked nicely enough.

"There was a snake in one of my bags," Charlotte muttered as I knelt by her. I fished out a small flask of gin I had squirreled away for disinfecting wounds. It seemed a pitiful peace offering considering what I had done to her.

"I don't think the snake would have harmed you," I said handing over the flask.

"You're a queer one ain't you?" she said, eyeing me. "You're not like other girls."

"We often had snakes in the garden; little ones that ate rats. I'm much more afraid of the rats," I said with a small smile.

"Rats is nothing," Charlotte said with a dismissive wave. "Back where I worked in London, we had huge rats, even the cats were scared of them. You didn't let them get near the babes." She sipped the gin. "But there ain't no tales in the Bible about rats leading Adam and Eve away from God."

"You're right there," I said.

Charlotte's face was already swelling. She would be black and blue before morning. I wet a cloth in the stream and bathed her face for her. I hoped the snake was happily back hunting down his delayed meal of frogs.

A slightly drunk Charlotte refused to head out before someone went through her possessions to insure there was no other snake hiding within her luggage. Mr. Barrett and Charlotte got louder and louder, screaming and fighting until Nate finally, in a bid of goodwill, spread out his bedroll on the ground and patiently unpacked her saddle bags one bit at a time searching for wayward serpents.

She shrieked and hollered at him, forgetting that he was one of her few allies in this venture and cuffed him for innocently finding her packet of underthings and as she put it, "Pawing through them like a wild beast."

Finally, even Nate was exhausted with her drama and it was determined that we would all set up camp for the night, only a dozen short miles from the Dragon Gate.

Everyone was silent around the fire. Charlotte was not speaking to anyone. Mr. Barrett was glaring like a dog gone mad, just waiting for someone to bite. MeiLin, Lum, and Mr. Quinn wisely kept to themselves, and the mood was so oppressive I did not feel it was right to speak to anyone. And the fox fur in my pocket was irresistible.

But I needed more than a mere delay. I needed Charlotte to give up. I was certain she was unused to the life of adventuring and if I made her miserable enough she would demand to go home. I had not expected Mr. Barrett to strike her. My attempt to make Charlotte crazy enough to give up or to scatter the horses did nothing. All I managed to do was delay our march into the dragon's maw by a few hours. I needed a better distraction.

And I needed the distraction to be outside of my own mind. I couldn't stop thinking of the key and I couldn't stop thinking of the fur. If I couldn't have one then I needed the other. There was no hope for it, I needed to touch it. I feigned exhaustion from all the excitement and went to bed early, retiring to the tent Nate erected to give us some shelter, if only from the eyes of Mr. Barrett and his privateers.

I held the scrap of fur to my nose, inhaling the scent. It should have been awful, a great bloody strip of fur, but it was wondrous. I longed to wrap myself in it, odd as it seemed. The only place I could wrap it around me was my throat.

For a moment, only a moment, it was like a thousand nettles biting into my flesh, then a warm wonderful feeling came over me, peaceful, like I was lying in the sun or a down comforter or inside a loaf of freshly baked bread.

The comforting feeling was gone, melting away and I was being crushed, flattened, and smothered, and instead of warm I was uncomfortably hot within my skin as I was being smashed from all angles at once. I tore at my throat, the fox fur had become a part of me, tiny needles digging into my flesh, turning my bones to liquid, making them flow backward in ways they were never meant to go. It was the feeling of magic taking hold and all I could do was gasp as the feeling consumed and empowered me, stripping me bare and remaking me, more and less than I was before.

Nate once told me transfiguring into his alternate form was as though his ears and nose had been gashed open with a knife letting too much sound and smell in to his head, flooding his senses. It was overwhelming and painful at the same time.

He was wrong. It was nothing so violent. The forest came alive with a thousand sounds and scents, each more wondrous than the last. I blinked for a long moment, trying to get my bearings. The leaf litter covered a fine layer of sweet rot, nothing so foul as animal rot, just the sweet scent of nature reclaiming the fallen boughs to turn them back into plant food and use them again.

A frog was singing in the background, a beautiful magical song to his mate telling her where he had found a wonderful cache of grubs and inviting her to share. She answered him, leaving the other suitor who had no meal to share.

Fish splashed in the water and my ears twitched toward the sound, the cool, clean scent of the water drawing my attention. Vivian, that clumsy human woman, so far away now, would struggle to grab a fish from its clear depths, but for a huntress such as I, it was no challenge. I crouched waiting for one to come into range. I caught one, raw and wriggling as my sharp teeth pierced its scales and spilled cold juices across my whiskers.

Ranger stood before me, pricked ears erect, tail high, inviting and challenging me. *Come play.* He bowed low on his front paws. *Chase me.*

I dove after him. He was heavier and stronger and more used to this form. He leapt to one side. I thought I would slip leaping over the log to follow him, but I was quick on his heels and I caught him easily. He was waiting at the edge of the water staring up through the holes in the canopy where the tree branches intertwined like an elegantly woven shawl letting bits of lacy moonlight spill out into the ground.

I nuzzled his ear and pressed the space between my ears against him. He smelled wonderful, like wild and grass and something undefinable that I very much wished to possess. I rubbed myself against him wishing to cover myself in his scent. Was this how he saw the world? If so, why did he ever return to his human form?

We leapt up on our hind legs, wrestling and play fighting. He easily got the better of me, spinning and whipping around and nipping one of my hind legs in a wonderful sting. I wheeled back and got a mouthful of fur. If he could laugh at me now, he would.

We chased one another through the forest until he ducked behind a tree. I lowered my nose to the ground to ground to find him again. Once he left my line of sight it just wasn't so important to watch for him. What was sight when one had scent?

Night animals chittered and made a general nuisance of themselves, an orchestra. I smelled so much—birds and rodents, and people—I could smell people. The horses the people brought, the bags of supplies, their food, the tents they pitched to shelter themselves from nature, the fires they lit to warm their hairless pelts and cook their foods. Their weapons, cold steel or hot iron after it roars and spews fire and lead, the stink of sweat and hate and fear, the scent it gave off when they would be firing blindly in the dark at us, trying to kill something they cannot even see, let alone understand.

I stared at them, two females, three males, all milling about preparing for sleep wondering where Nate and Vivian had gone. One male, dressed all in black and the female that carried his scent, his mate; giggled and made breeding jokes.

Only one of them was different. Smelled different. She sat close to the fire but did not need its protection. She smelled like woman but also of magic and of deception. She smelled like danger, sweet and hot, foreign and frightening. She was to be feared unlike the others.

I was distracted from my evaluation of these soft creatures, there was Nate's scent again. He too was watching the humans. I circled out of the firelight. There were eyes watching me. The other female. She smelled funny. Something about her was wrong. So very, very wrong, not human, not animal, not like anything I had even smelled before. Perhaps that was why the dragon didn't eat her.

I was startled from that very human thought when something much more interesting dashed through my field of vision, proceeded only seconds before by a clamoring in the brush. Strong, powerful legs, long ears, and a heart pumping hot, fragrant blood through veins as it tore through the forest trading one predator for another.

My surprise only paralyzed me for a moment, then I was after it, I could feel it. Its feet pounded the ground in time with my own; in time with my heart. My mate joined me in the glorious chase. Our paws were almost noiseless and our prey was clumsy with panic and huge, floppy feet and stiff, hot ears. Panic sweat poured off the rabbit in waves. I swallowed hard lest I drown in slaver.

My mate went wide leaving me to take the rear. Our prey turned sharply to the east only seeing him when it was too late to change course. It slid under a fallen log, popping up on the other side and trying to cut off to the west before we could correct. This might fool other dogs, other foxes but not us. We were more—so much more. And close, we were so close.

I was only peripherally aware of the startled birds that exploded out of the shrubs. They had been bedded down for the night and they thought themselves safe from predators. If we had not spied a tastier meal their night would have ended bloody and in a quick snap of flesh and feathers and light airy bones.

My tail was a wonderful ballast as I turned on quick, light paws. Our prey was no match for us. My claws dug into the soft, damp ground and Ranger and I were only a few paces behind our query.

Ranger dove for the hare. It dodged off to one side and right into my waiting jaws. My sharp, white teeth ripped into its side and it let out a screech, rolling and regaining her feet for a few steps. It bounded away splattering blood onto the leaves. One more bite was all it took, my fangs snapped her neck. Her powerful back legs kicked in a futile effort to free herself from becoming our feast raking my shoulder and then the warm trickle of urine leaked down the hare's body as it gave a final death shudder. It was the sweet scent of herbivore urine, fragrant and earthy. I couldn't wait to adorn myself in it.

But for now, the law of the jungle was too strong to ignore. We had caught our prey. We earned this meal. We each seized one half and reducing the hare to strips of flesh in moments.

I gulped and tore, never in my life had I eaten a meal as fine as this. I could not even remember any other meals I had eaten.

After I finished swallowing the hare, I licked my paws clean, savoring the richness still coating my paws and my muzzle. Ranger was still working at chewier bits, one of those ears—those flouncy, flirty ears that had so attracted my attention earlier. He chewed and chomped in obvious canine delight, rolling on his back one moment then back to his belly.

I slid close on my belly and snatched up a piece of fur. Tail flat, ears back. *Now, you come chase me!*

He did, stronger and more powerful, he rolled me easily to the forest floor but I was quicker and more agile. I got away and used part of a fallen log and then low branches to gain some distance. I took a high perch to stare at the land around us. The silly two-legged creatures with their fires and their metal stared off into the darkness looking for the sounds. Did they know we hunted, we killed, we ate so close to them, fearless?

Why did our kind fear the two-legged ones? They were soft, weak things. They all huddled close to the fire in their dull, dark shadows, smelled like man-weapons, gunpowder and steel. They needed so much to survive here. All I needed was my mate beside me.

My mate—he called to me. Inviting me to follow him. He would teach me all I needed to know. I leapt down to follow him into the moonlit night. I hoped we would hunt again. This time I wanted a bird. Silly pheasants with their long, flirty tail feathers that fanned behind them as they took wing. They must be special, delicious prey. They cheated. They flew.

The forest had grown quiet. And when I opened my eyes it had also grown unseemly bright and much too colorful. My first thought was some sort of rainbow had managed to settle upon us in the night.

Morning. It was morning. I bolted upright, realizing only then that I was naked and wrapped in my blankets. My legs were pinned by something furry and soft and comfortingly heavy. Nate. Ranger. After all, he was not bound to the cycles of night and day. The fox fur collar lay beside me, the flesh around my throat was achy and raw, as though I had spent the evening with thistles wrapped around my neck rather than soft fox fur.

I turned the fur collar in my hand. The unfinished side was still bloody and raw like it had been recently ripped from the back of a poor animal. I knew how the creature felt. I gingerly felt my neck, expecting to see blood when I pulled my fingers away.

Ranger rolled onto his back inviting me to rub his belly. His tail *thump, thump, thumped* against my blankets. My ears were stuffed with cotton, my nose clogged like I was suffering the worst sort of illness of the head. I took a deep breath in through my nose. No, I was not suffering congestion, I merely could not smell anything aside from a bit of wood smoke and something being fried on the campfires. Disappointing was not even the beginning of it. To be able to sense so much then have it smothered away; my own human senses were entirely inadequate. How I managed with them alone for so long was a mystery to me.

Ranger rose to his feet and shook his head, his ears slapping against his jaw. He yawned and stretched, first front legs then back legs in slow canine delight. He trotted over to Nate's tumble of clothes from last night, seized a pile in his mouth and slipped out the back side of the tent, wiggling his way under the loose wall.

I sat, clasping the blankets to my chest, blinking stupidly. The taste of blood, silvery-hot, was still on my tongue, more delightful than it should have been.

I never bothered to fully unlace my corset, I just unlaced it enough to slide out of it, in something I had learned from the Morgan daughters on my last adventure called camp lacing, where special, extra-long laces went through metal frames that I could easily work myself.

I put on a clean tan blouse with white pinstripes and a dark brown split riding skirt that cunningly gave the appearance of a proper skirt while I was standing still, but had more in common with the slop-trousers sailors wore. The tailor I commissioned them from nearly had a fit when I calmly explained what I wanted, but he filled my request.

I set the emerald green corset cover over my corset and braided my hair back. Out of habit I checked my reflection in the mirror before leaving the tent and was glad I did. My neck was bright and raw. It was red, blistered, and hot like a sunburn. I felt like I had seen something like this before, more than just a burn and yet I could not place it so I pushed it from my mind. I treated it with a salve and pulled the collar back up and buttoned it snuggly. It would be warm and more proper than I generally liked to appear but it would cover the mark from the fur collar.

I was dressed and looking like a lady, even more so than usual. I even tied my mother's cameo around my neck.

I stepped out to greet the day. Nate was crouched at the fire in his shirt and trousers, his braces hanging off his shoulders at his sides, and barefoot, but content as he heated water for tea. I assumed he was waiting for me to finish dressing before he returned to the tent to finish dressing and break camp.

"Is it always like that?" I whispered.

He just beamed at me.

"Why would you ever change back?"

"At first, I couldn't control it," Nate said, still grinning like a fool. "During the day, I was me. At night, I was Ranger. Then after that night on the Molten Cay in the well-spring things were different, I could be me. Or Ranger, or something between."

"Yes, but why would you ever choose to be a human if you could choose to be that."

"It's easy, Viv." He handed me a hot cup of tea. "It's what you are. Why would I be anything else?"

CHAPTER TWENTY

THE MUG IN MY HAND was nothing to the warmth blossoming in my chest. The form he kept, the control over his form was based on his own choice, and he had chosen me. Nate would choose me above all other things. He would choose me above MeiLin, he would choose me above the freedom of hunting, nose to the ground in the form of his beloved dog, and above the power of his canithrope form. The warm feelings followed me all the way back to our tent, blooming up my arms and through my core.

I placed some of those beautiful flowers we had passed last night in my hair. We paused and enjoyed their aroma last night while we hunted for the rabbit. Their sweet scent would remind him.

I picked up my brush and started working it through my hair. It would be easier to make myself beautiful in this place if I dug out my mirror as well. I pulled it out of my bag and let the reflection dance across me. I had seen this exact outfit before, not when I pulled it from my bag this morning, but before then, when my world ended.

We would have to make our move today. We were running out of time.

My throat, where the fox fur collar left its mark, burned with the desire to transfigure and run for safety. I wondered how long we could hide in the forest from Xihuan-Lung as animals. Not long enough. If Xihuan-Lung would be allowed to be raised from the dead I was sure the world would burn.

I shuddered. And dear Nate, believing I was cold, draped my leather long coat around my shoulders adding to the oppressive feel of the mists that had settled in the valley. I was cold, frighteningly so, but my coat would not soothe me, only having a plan would restore my frigid hands to warmth. I had to believe I could do something.

"Damnit."

"A true lady would never speak that way," MeiLin said softly in her singsong fashion that made me want to slap her. I flushed a bit.

I wondered what would happen if I did. Then I froze, she was the only one immune to the dragon's fear. She spoke to Xihuan-Lung as though they were equals, as though she had something to offer the ancient dragon.

My throat suddenly burned again and I desperately wanted to run my fingers through the soft, red fox fur. I could imagine it between my fingers, warm and feathery—I could use it to turn into a fox and Nate could turn into Ranger and we could run off into the mists together and leave all this behind us. We could harass and harangue the rest of the party into leaving this place. We could steal the key and bury the pieces deep in the earth where they could never be found again, then we could return to London and be married. I was never attending a dinner with Augustus Langston again.

It was gone!

I patted my pocket, then the other one. I turned to check my long coat. MeiLin was leading her horse. She stared at me, her eyes not the beautiful green I was accustomed to seeing but that odd red-brown they became when she touched Nate. She was an otherworldy creature. A creature of considerable wrath. A creature able to stand against a dragon and to give that mighty creature pause. I swallowed hard and gave her what I hoped was my usual thin morning smile.

She did not challenge me. The red-brown faded and was green again. The pinched look of her face relaxed slightly. She was beautiful again. Did she know I knew? Did she know I could see it? A dragon, a Huli Jing, twelve incorporeal animals of the lunisolar cycle, a mad dethroned emperor, and an equally desperate empress dowager. My list of unfriendly figures in China was long indeed.

There was no hope for it. When we paused to water the horses I told him everything. We could not allow the dragon to wake. Well, almost everything, I left out the part about him dying in a cloud of dragon fire. I had no desire to relive that part of the vision. I also left out the part of MeiLin being immune to the dragon. It didn't make sense. Fortunately, he didn't ask questions. Believing we were about to let loose a monster upon the world was enough to give him pause.

I could see the wheels in his head turning as he tried to come up with a plan as we marched along ever closer to the dragon's grave. We would have to steal the key. It would have to be tonight. Mr. Barrett and Charlotte would drink late into the night and, if we were careful, we could steal the key and set fire to tents, then use the chaos to cover our escape.

And fortunately, it looked as though I might just get one last night to set any last plan into motion. The sun was setting and the rocky ground was making travel dangerous for us and downright deadly for the horses. The loose rock shifted underfoot, causing Mr. Barrett to stumble in his fancy stiff boots.

"The gateway is supposed to be within the next five miles," Mr. Barrett said with a fervor in his voice I had not heard before. "If these damn horses would just move!" He gave his horse a slap on the hindquarters, trying to urge it over bits of broken rock. The horse resisted and pulled back nervously.

Nate and I exchanged a look. He heard it too and scowled, there was a lust in the man's voice that meant this could not end well. He gave a nod. We would have to take the key and make sure that lust never came to fruition.

Grudgingly, even Mr. Barrett agreed we had to stop for the night. It would be easier to undermine the rest of the party under the cover of darkness. There was nothing for it now. It was either that or we would have to try to find a way to keep the dragon from being able to rise.

We set up our own tent much as we did every night. Nate had it down to a science by now. I believe he could set it up and tear it down blindfolded. Then he helped MeiLin with her own. I did my best to swallow the coals of jealousy sitting in the back of my throat. If he changed his behavior now, it would advertise we were up to something.

Just as I expected, with the horses secured and tents erected, the two parties set to making meals from the remains of their supplies. MeiLin scowled at me. I did my best to avoid her as I generally did but I could feel her staring holes into my skull with those red-brown eyes so skillfully disguised as emeralds.

"We shall reach the dragon tomorrow, won't we?" I announced as the fires were built. I did my best to sound happy but my shirt was plastered to my skin with sweat.

Quinn laughed, "I do suppose we are entitled to a bit of celebration, eh, Barrett, my good man?"

Charlotte broke out the last of the gin I gave her after the incident with the snake. It wasn't enough to get her good and drunk. It wouldn't be enough to get Mr. Barrett drunk either. I hoped they packed more. Our own food stores were running low, I couldn't count on having another chance. As much as I hated terrorizing the horses with fire, I might have to add to the panic. I would have to get more wood.

Mr. Baxter stood staring landscape. He had left someone behind when he signed on with Mr. Barrett, a someone who was enough for the chaos demon that had taken up residence in the garden after the caretakers left, the *mó*, to use against him.

"Are you okay, Mr. Baxter?"

"Yes, thank you, Miss Harper." He said.

"This is not the adventure you planned?" I asked.

Mr. Baxter looked down at me. A sad smile graced him for a moment. He was looking out to the west where London waited, half a world away. "No, it is not."

Nate was right, I had been wrong about Mr. Baxter. There was cruelty in the world but it was not in this man. He returned to gathering wood for the fires and I returned to our plot. As much as I wanted to gather allies for what lay ahead, I also needed to secure the key.

Drastic times called for drastic measures. Nate pulled out his bottle of whiskey, something more akin to rotgut than something suitable to toasting adventure, but it would do in a pinch. "To Adventure, my good man!" Nate handed over the bottle to Mr. Quinn.

It was passed from hand to hand. MeiLin excused herself muttering something about unsuitable pursuits and went off to her tent. I was happy to see her go, free of her stare I could finally turn my entire attention to the matter at hand.

"Let's see it again," Nate said jovially. "The key that is worth all this fuss."

Mr. Barrett paused and gave him a long stare. "Don't you worry about that my light-fingered friend. It's safe, that's all you need to know."

Nate waved him off, "Oh, now, we're beyond that. I was merely protecting our stake in the booty. We separated to cover ground." Nate took a pull off the bottle, "And besides, you did take my map."

"All the same, I'm sure you will understand that I am not giving it over," Mr. Barrett said taking the bottle back.

Nate held his hands up in mock surrender.

"Oh, you two, let bygones be bygones." I forced a laugh. "Excuse me, please."

I strolled off to the bushes, then immediately turned and jogged off to the tent Mr. Barrett and Charlotte shared. It was strikingly like ours; bedding and saddlebags of belongings. There was little to go through, it wouldn't take too long.

The key wasn't there. It had to be on Br. Barrett's person. I hoped I missed it and went through his pack again. More of that obnoxious black attire. It had to be here. I went through Charlotte's bags, stabbing myself on a broach in the process. No key.

I sat back on my heels. Damn! There was movement on the far side of the tent, illuminated by the campfire. I needed to get out of there. Now!

I dove for the edge of the tent wall and searched for a place where it wasn't tacked down. Pegs were loose, placed in the soft earth at an angle. I pushed against them, rocking them in the earth. They ripped out with little resistance and I dove beneath the heavy canvas, panting.

Charlotte grabbed a bottle from her bag and pranced back out to Mr. Barrett. I lay on the earth, my heart hammering away in a frantic tempo. I could look again, but I knew the key wasn't there.

Nate could try to take it off Mr. Barrett's person, but if we just took it there would be a fight. Though anything would be better than letting the dragon escape her grave and cut a swath of destruction through China and the rest of the world.

Nate would have to be told. We could wait until they were asleep and then we could set a fire and use the confusion and darkness to steal the key. I skirted the camp to our own tent. MeiLin's tent had been placed by ours, as usual. On any other night, she would be sitting by Nate making him tea while he kept an eye on Mr. Barrett and his men. Tonight, she had disappeared to her tent before the night's entertainment, as it were, began.

I moved between the common space we were sharing. Her tent flap wasn't tied down, and from this angle I could tell her bedding was empty.

I nearly tripped over the tent's guyline. Nate saw me stumble and stood. Charlotte erupted in squawky laughter. Mr. Barrett chuckled, holding his hand out for the bottle to be passed over. I didn't know what else to do. I grabbed the rope and exaggeratedly struggled to my feet again.

"Oh, darling, tomorrow we shall look upon a dragon! Can you imagine, darling? A dragon?" I giggled loudly.

Nate rushed over to untangle me from the.

"Where is MeiLin?" I demanded in a whisper.

"Probably in her tent. She said she had a headache." he said. "What is going on?"

"I couldn't find the key. Give me your flask."

He handed it over and I took a sloppy drink, carelessly spilling some down my front. "Where is it?"

I knew where it was. MeiLin did not have a headache. She stole the key and was heading to the gateway to get to the dragon first and remove the arrow to enter into a pact with Xihuan-Lung. She didn't care about the world of men. She only had one concern, and it was only something that would concern shapeshifting fox women.

"I have to get to the gate," I said.

Nate looked at MeiLin's tent, then off to the east where we would be headed in the morning. He nodded and wrapped his arm around me, easily sweeping me off my feet. "Quite exciting, my love! Now come and sit with us."

I giggled. "Oh, I had better not, or I shall be in no shape for adventuring on the morrow."

"I shall be along shortly then," Nate said. "Miss Ratham, it appears you have bested both my Vivian and MeiLin." Nate laughed. "Give me a moment to put my Vivian to bed and I shall return presently."

"Your fine ladies may speak prettier Mr. Valentine, but men of your sort still have more fun with women of mine," she called, cackling.

"Don't bet on it," I growled under my breath as we stumbled into our tent.

Nate chuckled. "Easy, Viv. You're much more my type, I assure you."

"Keep them busy, I said, I'll be back as soon as I can." I slipped out the back of our tent.

SOS

MeiLin would not have taken a horse. They could barely tolerate her presence at the best of times, but I could. I grabbed the horse she had been riding and pulled it off the picket line. The sweet, chubby one would be perfect, she had an easy trot, even over broken ground. It was as fast as I dared move over broken ground, but it was faster than I could walk.

I untied her and climbed up on her back. It was harder than I expected without a saddle but I managed. More than the world was at stake, Nate was at stake.

I did not need much light to find my way to the crumbled and tumbled stones on the hill leading to the ancient stone pagoda. We hurried off, clearing the camp in a wide circle, my eyes adjusting to the moonlight and heading toward the place I had seen in my vision, the place where the dragon would be waiting and MeiLin would be entering into a pact with a fallen dragon for something she believed was worth watching the world burn.

I passed the spot where the pieces of the stone had been quarried out, and the river where we watered the horses when we passed this way in my vision. The hill would be too steep for the horse to pick her way up in the darkness so when I reached the foot of the hill where the greats stone blocks had tumbled down, I leapt off and went the rest of the way on foot. I did not pause to touch the carvings that I knew were there. I needed to overtake MeiLin before she moved through the gate and struck her deal with the dragon.

But the closer I got, the harder I had to fight to keep my breathing even. It was not the ride that winded me, it was the crippling gravity of my mission. I could not fail.

The Dragon Gate suddenly stood before me. The stone was incomplete, as it had been in the vision from the reflecting pool, but the air within the gateway shimmered like the air above a hot stove. The dragon's stone bones were within.

The gate was open and MeiLin was within. I reminded myself to breathe. My feet and hands were numb. Now all I needed to do was step through the Dragon Gate, not to save the world but to save myself. To save my Nate.

It was the gateway from my vision, a shimmering arch of stone; partially torn down and broken, but the key was in the lock, and with it in place, the missing portion gleamed, ethereal in its awful light. The secret it held was physical and accessible by the world of men. I should just pull the key out and trap MeiLin in the realm with the dragon.

I grabbed my seax and jammed it into the socket to pry to key out. My blade passed right through the metal, the moment the seax touched the ruby in the center it caused a deep painful throb in my arm. I jerked back shaking my hand.

It was like in the garden. The key was both there and it was not. I could not just pull it away. There would be a trick to it. I touched the ruby again. There was a frantic pulse drumming up my arm. Not so painful this time, warm, powerful, intoxicating.

Twelve symbols, broken into four trines of three animals each. Four puzzles, and I didn't know what Mr. Barrett did to solve his puzzle. I did not have time to tease the riddle out. I would have to take my chances with MeiLin and the dragon.

I took a deep breath. I needed to do this. For the world, for us. I stepped high to avoid tripping over the broken rock. If that was where MeiLin was making a deal with the dragon, then that was where I had to be.

It was like passing through water. Wet and cold, and yet I was not wet. An oppressive cold pressed upon me from all sides, it was the feel of magic. I had felt its touch before on the magical leywell on Molten Cay. It filled my sinuses, pressed against my ears, filled every hollow of my body, and slid into the cracks of my skin pressing everything else out of me as I passed through it. And just as I felt like the pressure of it was too much to bear I was suddenly though and I stepped onto the solid ground on the other side that looked identical to the land I had come from. The only difference was the awful stone monument that stood before me, a behemoth of bones, long since turned to stone by the passage of time.

The only thing I did not see before me was MeiLin.

I needed a way to stop her from taking the arrow from the dragon and bringing it back to life. The dragon loomed before me in the moonlight, daring me to desecrate this monument to evil that rose from the weeds before me. The stone bones were cold to the touch, but I knew too well that could change at any moment. There stood the arrow, exactly as I had seen it before, immune to the ravages of time, imbedded behind the left front shoulder, behind the wish bone. Though I was no expert at dragon anatomy, it had probably struck the heart.

I stared up at the monster. I had seen anatomical models in books and as bones displayed on stands carefully reassembled with fine wire. The spine, was the core of all animals be they mammal, reptile, or avian. A dragon seemed to be all spine. If MeiLin managed to take the arrow then a broken dragon would not be able to terrorize the countryside. Anyway, it was a good use of my frantic energy. I could not just wait for her to take the arrow and bring the dragon back to life. And if a Huli Jing was as powerful as I suspected, I was not sure I would be able to defeat her if it came to combat.

I carefully scrambled up the dragon's leg until I could reach the spine, and then shimmied my way up the leg until I could grab hold and pull myself up on its back. Now this would be an awful time to have the arrow dislodge and the dragon begin to come back to life.

Those were awful thoughts to have in this place, alone with only the dragon's stone bones to keep me company. The wind here was unnatural, crying mournful and high across the little pockets in the rocks and through the tall grasses. The stream I passed whispered, calling my name. I took one deep breath and held it until I felt like my lungs might burst then released it and took another.

In the darkness of my own thoughts there was a light, a lantern. A single light that gave my thoughts focus and clarity and made them find one single point. At least they were no longer a great mass of moths beating themselves silly against the lamplighter's glass. *The Hermit*. To some, he was a man seeking wisdom lost in solitude, but to those who were truly educated, he is merely casting off the trappings of civilization that blinds people to truth. He looks inside to find his own strength. I let this light guide me.

I knew what I needed to do. Moreover, I could do it. I took a deep breath and hooked my feet around the beast's ribs and started to inch forward to the neck.

Xihuan-Lung's head lay where she had fallen, spine twisted and arched in her final death-throes. I prayed when I moved, the body would not collapse and bury me in a ton of long dead stone dragon. I finished the agonizing crawl across angular dragon bones to the vertebrae I wanted and swung my foot up to a better angle, so I could kick it free.

The first blow rattled me so badly that I nearly fell from my perch.

I focused myself upon the image of the *Strength* card, the woman unafraid of her own power, unafraid of the power of others, with her hands gently but firmly holding the head and jaw of the lion. But she is so much more than the physical strength, she is the strength in women, in all people, the strength of will, the force of gentle spirit of knowing what needs to be done and the force of what is right.

I focused on the tarot card, Strength; less figurative, more literal—I needed this now. As much as I would appreciate the inner strength, I needed courage and raw physical power. I could feel it, centered upon my back, between my shoulders, spreading across them and through my being.

I could feel strength flowing through me, filling me and moving through me as though it came from the earth itself. Something in me was hot and fidgety, all at the same time. I could be strong, not for me, not even for Nate—but for man, because we all need to be saved from such a monster.

I worked my foot between the ridges of one neck bone and its neighbor and pushed with all my might. My leg was a piston driving my foot as a wedge into the small space between the bones. The hard sole of my boots refused to give and there was an audible *crack*.

There was another *crack*, like a gunshot with a light load of powder, that I was sure the entire world must have heard. I scrambled backwards, bruising my tail-bone most horribly on another spinal ridge. Two vertebrae went crashing down onto the skeleton below, then bouncing into the grass, deadly boulders of dragon bone that would have certainly murdered anyone waiting below. I scrambled down as quickly as I was able, unwilling to trust my precarious perch any longer than I needed to.

One tug revealed another folly in my thinking, these are not bones. For any animal to be able to move with a skeleton made of these the animal would have to be a monster.

Well, a dragon *is* a monster, I reminded myself crossly, taking up one of the neck bones and dragging it with both hands as I worked backwards in the tall grass. There was no chance of trying to get this as far as the quarry. That was nearly a mile. I had passed a river, silvery and swiftly moving in the moonlight, I could take one there. I gritted my teeth and dragged and huffed and rolled the stone bone as far as I could; surprised when I suddenly splashed into the river.

I dragged it to the center and let go. It tumbled over twice, then was lost into a deeper eddy of the water, hopefully lost forever.

One down.

But, it was not far enough, if someone hoped to make a slave of a dragon. This was not far enough to keep them from finding all the pieces. I was determined not to fail.

I started back, then my boots hit something slippery and I tumbled into the swift water and went sprawling, soaking my hair and my clothes, turning myself into a sodden mess of wet linen and leather.

The icy water stole my breath and I leapt to my feet and out of the water prancing around like a deranged chicken, flapping and slapping my clothes in shock.

But as I danced and stamped, something silvery caught my eye. There are times that the eyes will tell the mind that something is not quite right even when the brain cannot completely figure out exactly what is wrong.

Something was winking at me from the water.

I stopped my dance of the mad, wet adventuress and returned to the river's edge to investigate. Four arrowheads, as broad as my palm, lay in the shallows. Probably disturbed by my misadventure. I was quite fortunate I had not impaled myself upon them.

They were quite beautiful and old, but they didn't seem nearly as old as the dragon and the ancient arrow. Then I had a wonderful idea. We were after the arrow of Hou Yi. We were not told what the arrow really looked like. In fact, I doubted that an actual description of the arrow existed anywhere. And the arrow was made of wood. Surely any rational person would accept that an arrow, even a magical one, would be subject to the ravages of time. The Arrow of Hou Yi was used to kill the dragon thousands of years ago. It would be reasonable to assume that the wood and feathers had rotted away to nothing, but a beautiful arrowhead would stay forever lodged in a stone dragon skeleton.

These would make an excellent replacement to satisfy those seeking the lost arrow.

I could not ensure that no one would ever find all the pieces of the dragon's skeleton. I could not ensure that the dragon could not just regrow the pieces I was killing myself to break apart and ferret away. I could not ensure that they would not get the key just as we did and find the dragon and pull out the arrow and unleash the horror of Xihuan-Lung back into the world; but every single barrier I created made it that much harder for them to do so.

I carefully gathered up the arrowheads in my pocket. Then I returned to where the other vertebrae had bounced into the weeds and took up a tight grip, and started my hunched drag of the heavy stone. I had hours before I would be missed and I intended to make the most of it.

By the time I had the second piece buried under a small avalanche in the quarry of similar colored stones, and the third in a hole, I was nearly spent and so sore I was sure I would be crawling back to Nate and the rest of the camp. I was sure my body was one large bruise and I could barely move. I longed for strong willow bark tea and the comfort of my bed for a few hours. But I still had the false arrow to plant in the dragon skeleton.

When I returned to the exposed grave of Xihuan-Lung my blood froze in my veins. A thin dark figure crouched by Xihuan-Lung's fearsome head. The mist carried the sounds of scraping and cracking as though someone was doggedly trying to wrench something free of the corpse. MeiLin.

I had not brought my gun. I didn't think I would need to use it. I had my seax, but I carried it as a tool. Could I murder her to keep her from removing the arrow and loosing this monster on the world?

My mouth went dry, but not at the thought of murder, horrid as it is—it was the memory of Nate, fused between forms—not quite a man, not quite the canithrope, burning, melting, oozing, and bleeding, gasping in pain and agony as he twisted and writhed, waiting to die.

I drew the seax soundlessly and crept forward. Yes, I could kill her to save the world. I could kill if it meant saving just one man, if it was the right man. My blood pulsed in my ears like surf against the breakers, and for a moment I saw spots. I had to remind myself to breathe.

I would only get one chance. She was a creature of magic, ancient magic, and there was no telling what she could do, but if I struck from behind, maybe, just maybe I had a chance.

She paused and turned, looking straight at me.

"Hello, Vivian," she said softly, hands sliding past her hips, pausing only for the briefest moment at her belt before sweeping back her hood revealing her beautiful almond eyes and straight black hair.

I paused, dumbstruck. If she was concerned that I was holding a knife in my hand she didn't show it. Instead she gave me that smirking grin that said she was smarter than I was and she was laughing at me for it. I glanced over her shoulder and released a breath burning in my lungs. The arrow was where I left it. She hadn't moved it. Thank God!

I was shaking now. I sheathed my knife. I set my fingers in my pocket and absently fingered the arrowheads.

"I could not come all this way and not see the dragon for myself," she said softly.

"I feel the same way." I forced a bit of laughter. I struggled to figure out what she wanted here.

"You are all wet," she said.

"Yes." I gave another forced laugh and tried to straighten my hair. "I suppose I am. I slipped crossing the river there."

"I didn't say I cared," MeiLin said evenly.

One could get nauseous at how often I feel the urge to roll my eyes around that woman. "Well, if you are ready to head back to the camp now?" I offered as friendly as I could manage. I hated her little games.

"Yes, I suppose so," MeiLin said, staring up at the dragon. She was searching for something.

Where did one shoot a dragon with an arrow? I mean, other than the obvious place where the arrow lay hidden in the pre-dawn shadows. That must be what MeiLin was looking for. I tried not to look directly at it.

Instead, I propped my booted foot up against one massive clawed paw to tie my laces.

MeiLin turned toward the stream rushing by, I assume it was to find something else to mock me about. I fished one of the arrowheads out of my pocket and jammed it into a crack inside of one of the ribs just below eye level. If Xihuan-Lung was crouching like she was going to try to eat Hou Yi just as he was about to shoot an arrow, that might be a plausible shot that would have hit the dragon behind the shoulder in the rib cage. Hopefully, MeiLin was not an expert in ancient dragon anatomy.

By the time she turned back I was done tying my boot and I had hastily pulled a bit of gorse and bracken over the shaft of the real arrow to disguise it and was doing my best to calm my pounding heart as I stared up at the dragon, now with a hidden enchanted arrow and a broken spine missing three vertebrae. I had done all I could to ensure that if Xihuan-Lung was ever resurrected then she would not be able to wreak her terrible vengeance against the world of man.

"They will miss you," MeiLin said with a smile that was all too friendly for the demeanor I was used to. Did she know what I had done?

"Perhaps," I said. "Then I guess we should head back."

"They would miss you more if you never returned." She smiled, showing her bright white teeth. Her eyes were no longer green, they were fierce red-brown. Her face was pinched and sharp,

"Pardon me?" I inched my hand back toward my belt, where my seax rested.

"Merely an observation," she said with the same too-friendly smile. "It is very dangerous for a woman to travel here alone. You could have been washed away in the river." She paused. "And the dragon's skeleton seems to be falling apart. Several of the bones have been taken away by some thoughtless animal." She gave me a knowing look.

I did my best to keep my face blank, but despite my sodden clothing a cold sweat snaked down my spine. She knew I was up to something. I swallowed hard, how much did she know? Had she been watching me break the skeleton and take the bones away?

"Amazing, isn't it?" she continued, "That a single arrow can slay such a magnificent beast?" She reached into the chest of the dragon where the silvery arrowhead I had shoved into the crack sat.

"Well, they say the arrow was enchanted and that Hin Yan was a wonderful archer," I said offhandedly and forced a dismissive laugh.

Horribly butchering Hou Yi's name had the necessary effect. She wheeled around, her long black hair fanning out as she spun. "Hou Yi was the god of archery, more than a mere 'wonderful archer,' and his wife, *Chang'e,* was a lunar goddess they are more than your Western mind can conceive!" she spat.

She turned her attention back to the arrowhead and reverently caressed the silver surface with one graceful finger. It was the same way she looked at Nate. It made my blood boil. "This site is a holy grave and those mortals that seek to disturb it will suffer consequences most dire."

"Well, I have no desire to disturb a dragon's grave." I was proud at how smoothly I lied that time.

She glared at me. There was something different in that look. The entire walk back to the camp I did not let her walk behind me and I kept my thumbs hooked in my belt close to my seax, just in case.

As we passed back through the gate I snatched the key from the keyhole. With no living souls within the key was corporeal and easy to grab. I slipped it into my belt and followed MeiLin as we returned to the camp as though nothing had transpired. She made no move to stop me.

I must have looked quite the fright when I finally stumbled back into my tent. Nate had his back to the tent door and was busy in my bags when I pushed the flap aside and sat down with a *floop* on the pile of blankets.

"I was so worried when the horse returned without you. I thought you'd want hot tea." Nate, a true Englishman made tea when he was worried.

"Oh, you thoughtful man." I reached out to take it from him as he offered it blindly then he turned and his jaw dropped.

"Viv," he whispered furiously, "what in the—"

He didn't finish the thought but snatched up his leather long coat and hastily draped it around my shoulders. Though I appreciated the mothering, I would have appreciated the tea more.

He grabbed my feet and started pulling my laces out of their hooks and loops. "You're soaked to the skin."

"Tea," I reminded him. I handed over the key which he promptly shoved into his waistcoat.

He paused his assault on my boots for a moment to pass the tea tumbler back. He finished peeling my boots off my feet and pulled my stockings off. He threw a soft blanket over me and I slept the sleep of the dead, exhausted and lost to dreamless sleep.

The last thing I was conscious of was strong hands massaging my feet, thumbs digging into my arches soothing the sore places and knuckles rubbing just below my ankle bones easing the tension and soothing the pain from my misadventure.

§§§

The morning came way too early. I had just barely closed my eyes when I could hear the rest of the party making entirely too much noise outside my tent as they prepared for the morning. Not even the aroma of coffee and frying bread was enough to make me want to join them. I shifted to drag my blanket back over my head and was immediately humbled by the pain exploding across my hips and back. Being eaten alive by the dragon just might be a kinder fate.

My muscles burned, making it impossible to get comfortable now that I moved. I had broken whatever spell sleep had cast upon my poor battered body. I felt so awful.

I groaned and buried my face in the blankets. I loved that man; so why did all our adventures leave me feeling like death, slightly warmed over? I had always heard the adage that love hurt, but I had always passed it off as the sighing lament of lovesick poets.

I had some tincture of essence of willow in my bags. All I had to do was wash, dress, and get myself to my bags where I could find a few fortifying swigs to ease myself through my day. Though only out of reach, it may as well be back in London. Nate had not loosened my stays last night. Men had no idea how to handle a corset, even though I was wearing my corset fan-laced so it was much easier to manage, I didn't even need a maid to assist me to dress; but still he didn't even attempt it. That might have been a large part of my discomfort.

I carefully rolled and loosened my sides until I could wiggle free of my corset and out of my clothes. They were still wet. The warm blankets were bliss against my chilled, damp skin. I lay there trying not to feel sorry for myself, ignoring the bruises and wrinkles from fabric and damp. I must look how mummies feel; wrinkled and bound too tightly.

I heard Nate outside the tent trying to warn me that he was coming in without telling the others that he was trying to warn me he was coming in. A married man would not care if he disturbed his wife while she was resting or dressing or anything else women hid from their fiancés but supposedly not their husbands.

He entered with a pot wrapped in flannel. "I thought you might want to clean up."

"I smell that awful do I?" I said dryly.

Nate's eyes flew wide and he glanced at the tent flap.

I couldn't help but laugh. "Point taken, and I appreciate you stalling, I will get myself washed and dressed. Can you bring me the willow tincture from my medical bag?"

He breathed out. I could practically see his tail wag with delight. "I'll set aside breakfast, too."

"Thank you for the water," I said, but all I wanted was to sleep. Still, I set about to find my hair brush and my combs and a clean shirt so I could make myself presentable.

I assumed that a few hours of rest, a change of clothes and a bit of breakfast with willow tincture and my day would improve. As I sat in my saddle on the fat little Chinese pony bouncing across the rocky terrain, I realized how wrong I was.

I tried to take my mind off my discomfort. Mr. Quinn had studied in China for years, to hear his companions talk he had come to China as a missionary and was now practically an expatriate o China, maybe he could make sense of some of the queer things I had experienced. "Mr. Quinn? Have you ever heard of a Zizhi?" I stumbled over the unfamiliar word.

"Do you mean Xiezhi?" Mr. Quinn laughed. "Of course, my old mentor told me that tale right away. Xiezhi is a justice spirit. He has a long horn rather like a unicorn and can always tell if someone is being truthful. If Xiezhi stumbles upon liars it impales them with that horn or tramples them to death. If it likes you, Xiezhi can impart all sorts of truths, but it is good never to ask because Chinese spirits are possessive and jealous of mortals. They will do anything to possess mortals they like. Xiezhi's truth is so, well, truthful, it can destroy your mind. Only the wisest of monks can decipher the mysteries of the universe without going mad."

"I'll keep that in mind," I said.

Something in my tone made Nate turn in his saddle and give me a quizzical look.

I asked Mr. Quinn another question, to keep the conversation going. "How do the Chinese people feel about their dead? Not people of course, I'm not a ghoul, but what if one were to accidentally disturb a gravesite?"

"They revere their dead," Mr. Quinn said, the look of a zealot scholar crossing his face. "There are intricate rituals involved to appease the spirits of their deceased, and the more important the dead the more influence they have over the living. Why, disturbing the resting place could be akin to a tiger crossing your shadow."

"A what?" I said. "A tiger crossing my what?"

"Your shadow, a tiger crossing your shadow is considered a horrible thing; unlucky and painful. The tiger would hunt down everything you would hold dear and trap it deeply within the shadowlands. It is a frightful curse."

I shuddered.

Mr. Quinn directed his pony around white stone. "Forgive me, Miss Harper, would you care to explain the sudden interest in China lore?"

"Just making pleasant conversation, is all. What is a Huli Jing?" I asked, shifting in my saddle.

MeiLin hunched in the saddle but said nothing.

"Huli Jing, Huli Jing," Mr. Quinn muttered. "I'm not sure but the first part sounds something like having to do with a fox. I'm sorry the language is so subtle that it's very easy to confuse one word for another."

"Thank you kindly," I said to Mr. Quinn. There was no mistaking the word. MeiLin was something mystical, she was a Huli Jing, a fox shifter, something akin to what Nate was, and she wanted something from Nate. The fox fur collar was hers and she would not let Nate go without a fight. More so, she was bewitching him. I only hoped his desire to have someone like him in his life wasn't enough to turn him away from me.

CHAPTER TWENTY-ONE

THE FOG WAS PARTICULARLY thick that morning as we drew nearer and nearer to the gateway, more akin to the pea-soupers back home in London, when the fogs rolled in off the sea and mixed with the heavy mustard-hued smoke from all the coal fires to create a fog so oppressive you could barely see across a street. There was a thick, peaty smell was in the air.

My palms were clammy and my hair was prickling on my neck. I was sure I was about to be pounced upon by some ravenous beast.

The dragon! The same scent had been in the air when, in my vision, the arrow was removed from the stone skeleton and Xihuan-Lung was raised from the dead. My pulse hammered in my ears. Though I told Nate what I had seen, he had not seen it for himself so he would not be effected by the fog so.

But as far as I knew, no one other than MeiLin and I had left the camp, and we had returned together. Had she returned to Xihuan-Lung, doubling back to take something else from the skeleton? I suspected I had interrupted her. In my vision she held the arrow, promising its destruction, but at the skeleton she seemed to be trying to take something nowhere near where the arrow was lodged in the skeleton. And last night, if she didn't want the arrow what *did* she want? Or worse, what if she did exactly what I did, only she did it first and planted a false arrow for me to try to protect and took the real one?

Well, then, the dragon would be upon us well before now. If my vision was truthful it was likely it was truthful in all things, not only in parts or we would already be a plaything for an angry dragon.

Already, I lost sight of Mr. Barrett and Charlotte when we spread out to lead our mounts across the broken ground and the fog swallowed their voices and distorted their speech, making their conversations unintelligible. I only caught sight of them again when we stopped for a break to water the horses at a stream in one of the many small valleys, but the oppressive fog left a tension on the air that nothing could dispel.

MeiLin took a break from her mount to stretch and wash in the water, watching her pony with disdain. She hated her mount. The mare felt the same way about her. Both would soon be rid of the other and I was not sure who would be happier.

"Before long we will be back in Beijing and then with luck we will be headed home to London this week," Nate said.

"In time for our wedding." I set my arm into Nate's elbow. Soon we would be free of MeiLin; I would be the happiest at our parting, not her horse.

"We cannot let anyone else reach the dragon," I whispered to Nate.

He tightened the girth on his saddle using the cinch knot he had learned from our groom back home, or at least he was trying to, I didn't have the heart to tell him it was backwards and would slip free in no time at all.

MeiLin ruined our plan to take the key and disappear into the forest. I could not leave Nate there with Mr. Barrett and his party and trust that he would eventually be able to slip away unharmed. The further we traveled, the higher the pressure beneath my breastbone traveled into my throat.

Nate pulled me close so his voice wouldn't carry. "I still have the key. I need you to hide it or we need to break it apart or something."

"How am I supposed to break it?" I whispered.

"The ruby in the center is loose, I think if you can work it free the rest of the way the key will fall apart," Nate said evenly. "As far as Barret knows, I was the last one to rob him. Barrett won't forget that. I can keep them busy."

I nodded, he was right, but for now, I had to wait to destroy it, it was the only bargaining chip we had left. The look on his face said what he could not. If the time came, I was going to have to be daring while he bought me time. I nodded slightly and he pressed the key into my hand. I slipped it into by belt. The smooth ruby pressed comfortingly into my waist in its metal frame prison. It was a tragedy for something so beautiful to be trapped within the metal key.

There was a slight whistle in the air and Nate slapped at his neck like he had been stung by one of the biting flies that plagued us in the bogs and mires around the dragon's final resting place. A large pin was sticking out of his neck sprouting a crest of yellow and black feathers.

He collapsed face-down in the soft swampy ground. The mists swirled all around his head.

I leapt forward, only to have someone snatch my arm and a spear was thrust in front of me, narrowly missing my cheek. I wheeled around, but each of us was suddenly under heavy guard.

I had only seen spears like that in one place, the hands of the royal guards of Prince Qixiang. They must be here for the dragon. I wasn't about to let Mr. Barrett anywhere near Xihuan-Lung and I would die before I would allow Prince Qixiang to know that we were close to Xihuan-Lung's final resting place.

I took a deep breath and bashed the key on the rocks at my feet, feeling the key shatter into the four separate pieces beneath my hands like a clay plate. I threw the pieces as far as I could. For one brief moment, I was ecstatic for the distraction, we would not be blamed and the key would be lost again. It was the perfect confusion. The dragon was gone and beyond the reach of man. But in time, they might recover the pieces of the key. At the last second, I clung to the ruby. I stuffed it up my sleeve. As long as I held it, the dragon was lost forever to the realm of men and the arrow that held that awful beast in death would remain.

"Prince Qixiang order you halt!" he cried in broken English. He was wearing the livery of the deposed Emperor.

Nate lay face down in the wet leaves hidden by the mist that was rising again in the evening moonlight. I dove for him. Strong hands grasped me and hauled me back. All I could envision was that the hands wrenching me were some sort of limb crafted from metal and wire, not human flesh and bone.

"No talking!" One of our guards snapped, pulling Charlotte and Mr. Barrett apart.

"Hey!" Charlotte squeaked. "Watch it!"

"Now, now my dear," Mr. Quinn murmured soothingly. "Stiff upper lip and all."

I stared at him curiously. I wasn't sure if he was talking to me or to Charlotte. He glanced at me from under his pith helmet, his chestnut and gray hair falling into his eyes.

"Just do what they say," Lum said under his breath. He looked as though he wanted to say more, but stopped himself as they rattled a blade in his face.

They set us on our sturdy mounts heedless of the broken ground, binding my hands before me to the bow of my saddle. I twisted to see Nate. They'd tied his arms and legs tightly around his fat little pony. His head banged against the frame of the saddle as the mount hurried along in a bone jarring trot, eager not to be left behind.

I winced, he was sure to be black and blue when we reached Prince Qixiang's palace. He would be angry, what with robbing his palace of a priceless dragon scale, and destroying the tower room in our haste to find the bones of the long dead dragon. I turned in the saddle again to look back at Nate. Something hard jabbed into my ribs. The soldier riding behind me snapped an order like an angry street cur into my ear. The other guard translated.

"He tells you to stop moving around if you wish to ride to the Hidden Palace." The guard that translated at least had the manners to look embarrassed.

I elbowed the man with his arms around me hard in the gut.

"He warns you he can drag you back to the prince if that is your wish," MeiLin translated with a small smirk.

My bruised, battered body cruelly reminded me I was in no condition to run along behind the horses. And run along I would whether they tied me with a rope or not, I was as bound to them as securely as if they had bound me with a chain. They had my Nate. I would follow them to the ends of the earth if I needed to. I closed my mouth tightly and resolved to say nothing, no matter else what happened. The chill of the fog sunk into my heart, the warmth of the ruby comforted me.

The men spoke to one another in Chinese, ignoring me. MeiLin also seemed to escape their notice. Finally, she managed to get her mount right alongside mine though it rolled its eyes and snorted as she fought to keep its gait steady. "Though I admire your spirit, your fiancé is not able to help you and they will not hesitate to use us as leverage to force him to cooperate, were you to be killed before he wakes up all he will be able to do is avenge your death."

I wanted to strike her, how could she be so callous? If Nate was dead there would be no avenging him. There would be no life. He would be gone and my life would end. I stared up at the sky until my eyes watered, wishing I was better at directions. We couldn't be more than a full day away from the prince's castle.

Nate was drooling in a drunken manner. I would have given anything to be able to do a medical examination of him. Then it suddenly occurred to me, aside from tea, the chief export from China, aside from tea, was opium. It was entirely possible that he was dosed, at least in part, with opium.

"MeiLin," I called over. "Tell my captor I wish to speak to him."

She translated for me with a bowed head. I was not privy to .the exchange but it was not pleasant.

"He warns you if you speak again he will cause you pain. He is under orders to bring you alive if possible, unharmed if convenient."

I hated to be threatened this way. But I had to figure out what Nate had been drugged with and how best to help him. My captor was going to harm me. I just hoped that it wasn't anything permanent.

"Tell him I will cooperate fully if he will only tell me what Nate has been poisoned with. I worry for his safety, Nathaniel and I are to be married. My father is an apothecary and there are a great many of poisons that can be fatal if not treated properly. I just wish to treat him."

"Do not worry for him so," MeiLin said softly. "Prince Qixiang will not harm him. Nate is the weapon he needs to overthrow his mother, the Empress Dowager Cixi once and for all. It is likely opium and an *aconitum* poison that will paralyze him until Prince Qixiang's men can return him to the palace. The prince will hold you to force him to do his bidding."

I knew she was right and I felt ill. "You were going to make a deal with that dragon…what was it?" I demanded in a furious whisper.

She stared at me. I'm not sure she would have been more stunned if I turned into a dragon myself and offered her whatever deal she wanted. Clearly, I was not supposed to know about her deal with the dragon.

"What does the prince have that you want so badly that you would trade the services of a dragon for?"

MeiLin struggled for her composure then stared at me, looking through me as though I was an insect again. "She has stolen something from me."

"Who?"

"That *gǒushǐ duī*." MeiLin looked away, but not before I could see that she had tears in her eyes.

I desperately wished I spoke Chinese, even though I knew she was not referring to anyone by name and I was aware it was hardly complimentary, but what struck me was the lack of venom in her voice. There was nothing there but crushing sorrow.

I suffered the entire ride to the exiled prince's palace in the Tianmenshan Forest in silence. I was too numb to mull over my options or plan my escape. Instead, I stared at Nate, his head banging against the saddle frame in a most alarming manner. For a moment, I thought I saw him stir and my heart leapt in my chest—but it could have been a trick of the moonlight.

Prince Qixiang's men knew the land and, in no time at all, the Tianmenshan Forest began to look more and more familiar as we entered the area maintained by Prince Qixiang and his men.

Prince Qixiang's tower loomed before us. Someone had cleaned up the shards of broken glass, but the window had not yet been replaced. It was an open sore on the building, glaring accusingly down upon us as they led us through the gates. The thongs that bound Nate to the saddle were sliced free and he fell in a heap on the cobblestones.

At least he was aware enough to groan. Thank God.

The guards pulled MeiLin and myself off the horses and dragged us stiffly along. I immediately forgot my discomfort when I saw how Nate moved as he tried to massage feeling back into numb hands and feet, propelled along by guards.

I was so absorbed in our misery that it took me a moment to notice there was another feeling in the courtyard, something I could not quite put my finger upon, but it filled me with a jittery sense of unease.

It reminded me of when my papa's shop and home in London had been broken into by the Red Hoods searching for poisons last year, the same week Nate came into my life. It was the same unnamable, uncertain dread of what might lay around the corner.

I saw the magicians that were fusing magic and men. My stomach gave an unsettling lurch and I thought I might retch. I only restrained myself at the chilling thought of drawing more attention to myself.

They were loading wagons—large, upright packing crates with wisps of hay peeking out of the slats, were being loaded into one; long horizontal boxes were loaded in another. Terracotta soldiers and coffins.

Not all survive, the prince had said. I shuddered. He was moving his soldiers into position and removing those who had proven to be unfit or unable to join his unholy army.

The guard at my side mistook my shudder of revulsion as unwillingness to move so he dragged me along, causing me to trip on my own boots. If I were to return home in one piece I would not be joining the Explorer's Society, I suddenly decided. This life wasn't for me.

We were dragged into the throne room, past a token guard of the Prince's household where Prince Qixiang himself sat in his stone throne, a warlord ready to conquer the world. He leapt to his feet, unable to contain himself.

"Are you an agent of my mother, as well? Do you wish to be shipped back to the Empress Dowager in pieces?" Prince Qixiang demanded, stalking back and forth.

"I am my own man," Nate said.

"You mean the Empress Dowager?" I looked over to Nate. The blood had drained out of me, leaving me freezing cold. I was so stupid. "As well"? That meant there were more. I had an awful thought. Where were Mr. Barrett and his band of privateer treasure hunters now? They had worked for a queen. What if it wasn't *our* Queen?

Nate looked ill. For the first time on our trip he seemed at a loss for words. He had told me they smelled funny. I thought he had meant literally. Or maybe he had. He noticed something was wrong, that they wore new boots and carried all new provisions. That meant they were well funded. They had friends in high, wealthy places. And not the Explorer's Society. We had friends in the Explorer's Society; they had arranged for our transportation, but they certainly had not funded our trip, except for to arrange for a translator.

But, no that was not right, I had long suspected that the Explorer's Society had not arranged for a translator to assist us—that MeiLin was traveling with us for reasons that were all her own. And she had all but admitted it to me before when she said "She had stolen something from me." Who stole what?

If the Empress Dowager hadn't stolen something, then who had stolen from her? But the thought of the Empress Dowager stole my breath. Oh. My. God. I thought of the acting Empress of China sitting on her cushioned throne staring at us the way a cat watches mice. The world got all white and faint around the edges. When we had been arrested and MeiLin had arranged for us to plead our case we had been able to speak directly to the Empress Dowager. The man who spoke for her informed us that China was a place where a person could make a very powerful friend if they were daring. Who could be a more powerful friend than an Empress Dowager? My legs felt weak and I lowered myself to the ground beside Nate.

"You are at a loss for words?" Prince Qixiang crowed. "Did you believe my mother would not hire more than one set of agents to assassinate me? I will ask you one final time, are you an agent of the Empress Dowager, as well?"

"We are not," I said through cold lips.

Prince Qixiang was inches from us. "Then what about your man?"

I was about to swear against it, but then I realized he wasn't addressing me, he was talking to Nate. If he wasn't asking me, who was he talking about?

"Who?" But I immediately knew who. Mr. Barrett was Cixi's man, bought and paid for, as was Charlotte. Mr. Quinn was most assuredly not loyal to us. I could not yet see how he benefited, but I knew without a doubt that he was only loyal to himself, or perhaps maybe even China, certainly not us and not Mr. Barrett. That only left Columbus Baxter. What in the world had he done that made Prince Qixiang believe he was "our" man? Where was Mr. Baxter now? What was Prince Qixiang going to do with him? What would Mr. Barrett do if he believed Lum had become a turncoat?

Nate regained his feet, cautiously circling away from Qixiang. He was doing his best to stay away from him, using movement to keep the prince's attention. His eyes darted around wildly from Prince Qixiang, then around the room, searching for options for his particular mad brand of creative street fighting.

As far as I could tell his options were few, but, then again, this was a man who had caused a distraction with a sewer pipe and powdered laundry soap, and who had managed to fend off attackers with a barrel of rotten fish and a broom. Nate was a master of the creative weapon and, given half a chance, he would find a way to fend off Prince Qixiang as well.

And whatever fuels madness and desperation when one is frightened was slowly casting off Prince Qixiang's poisons, and both Nate and the Prince knew it. My Nate was becoming faster, he was moving with a grace and surety that showed us all, that he was gaining the upper hand. He was still cautious, careful to keep himself between the Mad Prince and MeiLin and myself. He had too much to watch and, for a moment, I was ashamed to be of the weaker sex. He needed every bit of himself to battle Prince Qixiang in this deadly game.

A blur stole my attention from the two. Large and imposing. For an instant, I thought it was Marcus the Bear, arrived from the Explorer's Society in London to rescue us from the Mad Prince and this beautiful, horrible place.

Instead, it was the only other man I had met of similar size, Columbus Baxter. He moved with a speed I would not have believed possible had I not seen it. Like a runaway draft horse, he bowled into Prince Qixiang and Nate, knocking them both to the ground, taking two of the guards to the floor with them in the process.

In all the confusion, a woman's voice cried out.

YaMing straightened struggling to rise. Her legs refused to hold her, and she collapsed weakly back onto her carved throne. It was a lameness more than mere surprise. Her brother, her own flesh and blood, in his own mad quest for power, was sacrificing her own wellbeing and using her to further enhance his own body, to fuse metal and muscle with unholy enchantment to make himself a monster of a man.

Prince Qixiang sprang to his feet with some marvelously athletic move that was something between a roll and arching like a cobra.

For a moment, everyone froze. Then Nate pulled a sword from one of the guards at his feet. Prince Qixiang laughed, sending an icy chill up my spine.

The prince drew a sword, straight and honed so sharp that I could tell from where I stood he could slash a man without him even knowing he had been wounded until he began to bleed.

If Nate was in his other form he might stand a chance, but Nate was no swordsman. His was more a barroom brawler.

Prince Qixiang lashed out with his sword, drawing the blade up and down. Nate's sword made the room ring with the sound of steel on steel, slowly, like the swords were singing to one another. The prince was smiling, but no humor reached his eyes. It was the look of lust, chilling and brutal, longing for another's blood.

Far from an expert in swordplay, even I could see Nate held his sword too tightly. There was no play in his grip, once the swords connected the shock of it would jar the blade from his grip. They circled one another, cat-stepping, with Nate trying to remain between those he was duty bound to protect.

Nate swung the sword, leaving himself open. The prince batted the blade away wide and drove a booted foot into Nate's chest, sending him sliding across the marble floor.

He was lucky it was only a kick that drove the air from his lungs not the sword.

Nate cursed and flung the sword over to where Lum was struggling to get me to my feet.

"Protect her with your life!" Nate shouted at Lum.

Lum nodded and pulled his revolver from his belt.

Nate tore at his clothing. For a moment, I believed Prince Qixiang had forgotten what made Nate such a valuable ally. He watched like a man transfixed. The prince was working to turn himself to a weapon of clockwork machinery, but Nate had a supernatural power all his own and they did not cost him his flesh.

Prince Qixiang used his twin sister as an anchor to bind the unholy union of clockwork machine and flesh until his body learned to work the mechanics as his own flesh and blood, but Nate's powers were a gift of love and sacrifice given to him by his beloved dog. Ranger gave up his own life to protect his master from a powerful magic as old as time itself.

Nate shook, freeing himself from the last remnants as though it were tatters of a hated suit. Then he turned to Prince Qixiang with a curled lip that spoke volumes of contempt.

Qixiang took a step back, then thought better of it and stepped forward again. I could read it on his face, no one, man or monster, would make him lose ground.

He swung the sword, it whistled as it moved through the air, advertising its deadly purpose. If he could not convince Nate to serve him willingly he would force him. If he could not force Nate then he must kill him.

YaMing, a pale porcelain doll, tried to turn away from the battle but her eyes were locked on the two men.

Did she wish for the prince to kill my fiancé? Or did she wish for her brother to perish and leave her free in this world?

Qixiang slashed high with his gleaming sword and Nate dropped to the ground, the blade passing harmlessly above his pinned back ears. Nate snarled, the sound was chilling. He lunged forward, teeth gnashing at the prince's legs, but catching open air. \ Qixiang answered with a hasty slash downward, the point of his sword skittering loudly across the marble floor.

Nate must have anticipated the move, as he dove forward again, trapping the blade against the floor with the weight of his body forcing the Prince to release it or be pinned to the ground with it. But Qixiang was faster, he released the blade, jumped back, snatched a spear from a beautiful display, and carefully circled back, daring Nate to try it again.

Nate was cunning as a man, but less so as a beast. He snapped his teeth at the spear that jabbed and danced around his face.

Before me, Lum watched warily, waiting for a clear shot at Prince Qixiang, revolver in hand.

Nate lost all fear of the spear, he was inching closer and closer, trying to get his massive claws upon the prince, throwing all caution to the wind.

To make matters worse, they circled closer and closer to the column at the far edge of the room. Soon they would be out of sight and I would not even get to watch, holding my breath for the battle to come to its bloody end.

Nate suddenly leapt to the side. I almost screamed. He was purposely putting the prince against the column, limiting how far the great spear could swing and turn. He was counting on Qixiang to forget the layout of his own throne room.

It worked, in a fashion. The spear hit the column with an almost imperceptible *tink* of metal upon stone, but it made Qixiang pause and glance at his feet.

Nate leapt forward, slamming the spear against the column and lashing out with the other fist of razer-sharp claws. The silk and leather tore and the metal beneath shrieked in distress.

Prince Qixiang knew he had been fooled. He struck back, hard and fast, and when the two men separated blood dripped down upon the marble.

Nate clasped his hand to his hip then spun, catching the Prince by one of his metal arms. Instead of trying to crush or rend him, he merely threw him bodily into the column.

Twin cries rang through the chamber.

YaMing was bound to him, bound and tied to his fate. If Qixiang had enhanced himself further since they last fought, this battle would not be as evenly matched. Nate was still drugged and unable to move as swiftly as before and he was not faring well. I knew that sound, the growl that ended in a very human groan. Nate was losing his canithrope form. The recent drugging had taken its toll. I needed to even the match, and quickly.

I closed my eyes and sought that internal calm. I needed to read them quickly; maybe there would be a clue there I could use to help give Nate an advantage before Prince Qixiang decided to stop toying with my fiancé and had us killed.

I needed a card and I needed one now. An image came to me. Fading into view as though it was both in the real world and in my own mind.

The Devil stood between Qixiang and YaMing with an iron chain, linking them like a noose around their necks. Generally, *The Devil* was more about the chains people chose to wear, and those chains were loose and easily slipped. All people had to do to escape the Devil was to choose the light. Most of the time, the chains were bound to him or his throne. But this was different, he stood between them, a leash binding them together, with the chains pulled tight, so tightly that the chains bit into their flesh.

We needed transformation, transfiguration, and more than that, YaMing needed a new beginning—one where she was unfettered by her controlling brother. I would not force transfiguration upon Nate, I know how transfiguration hurt his body, how it drained him and how it pained him but I might be able to force one change. *Death*. The death card always represented a drastic change. I brought the card to mind, a frightening image of a skeletal figure on a skeletal horse, a scythe, and a dying field; kings and peasants, young and old alike, cut down before him as he rode past, no one was immune to change—change came to all.

The chains bent and rattled, shifting between the Prince and Princess. Their twin faces grimaced and contorted. Qixiang punched Nate hard in the chest, knocking him backward a step. Nate coughed and shook his head, trying to clear it. He staggered and almost fell.

I heard the meaty sound of fists on flesh and Nate gave a strangled grunt. A very human Nate struggled to his feet. Prince Qixiang did some sort of elegant spinning kick, driving Nate into the ground. My fiancé gave a grunt and seemed to bounce on the marble floor.

Nate struggled to rise. He was shaking, and I shuddered at the damage being done to him. But no, Nate was chuckling, laughing at the prince, mocking him, taunting him. Was he daring the prince to kill him so he could not be used in the Emperor's game, or was he buying me time?

I longed to run to him, but Columbus's hand on my shoulder steadied me. No, whatever Nate's play was, he was buying us time; giving *me* time to do whatever I could.

I bit my lip. The mark on my side was suddenly so hot I gasped at the pain of it and shoved *Death* at *The Devil* with every ounce of my being. The Devil laughed and laughed at my efforts to break his chains. No one can break the Devil's hold for another one, it is a choice.

I dug deeply within myself calling upon anything I had left, *Strength*, *The Chariot*, I would take any help now. And there was a scent in the air like something was burning, a hot metal or the scent of herbs being distilled and condensed and burned. And somewhere beneath it all, the scent of blood.

I was pushing the boundaries of fate further than they were designed to go. Fate made them twins. Fate bound them. Something primal linked them, and it was that very something that man was not designed to meddle with. But it was that exact magic, that bond that anchored Prince Qixiang to this world and his clockwork limbs. It was that very magic that allowed YaMing to bear his pain and to be crippled by the mutilation he committed against his own flesh. It was that magic, old as time, that allowed him to control those limbs as easily as his own mortal flesh. And it was that bond that I had to sever.

I pushed against that bond for all I was worth. Prince Qixiang had tightened the chain around his sister's neck. *The Devil* laughed. The chains of man bound them. *Death* was transformation, *Death* would set them free. The mighty scythe cut through man, separating us from our earthy bonds

and helping us move on to our next evolution, to our next path. I forced it
along.

There was a crack like lightning, deafening and sharp. And I recoiled as
Fate itself punished me for my arrogance, like the crack of a whip across
the face. The sharp metaphysical bite of it cut deeply into my flesh, so
deeply all I could do was choke and gasp as it felt like a metal hook ripping
into my throat. I couldn't breathe in, only out. The threads of fate
connecting them finally snapped under the tension. The ends recoiled back
into me and carried all the weight of the severed ends of the web of life.
The ground came rushing up to knock the wind out of me.

I lay there, gasping and struggling for breath, knowing for all the world
as a gutted trout feels. I feared it was blood gushing out of me, but after a
moment I realized it was nothing so visceral as actual blood, it was only my
own life. I felt myself growing faint.

I forced myself up to my knees. The edges of my vision were blurry and
star-burned. I held on desperately, my hand pressed to my throat, choking
and gasping for breath. My vision was spotty, and all I could see around me
was the Tarot, the real world had faded to gray but the cards were all
around me swirling in colors I had never seen before.

Nate was wreathed in the warm gold of *Strength*, a man with the heart of
a lion ready to do anything to defend those in his care, and there, standing
before me, Columbus Baxter, a man I felt I could now trust, with the same
noble warm heart, a good and noble man, though buried within. I knew at
that moment, he would never betray us again.

CHAPTER TWENTY-TWO

SLOWLY THE REAL world returned to its usual colors and the tarot released its hold over my vision. Prince Qixiang was groaning and rocking on his back like a turned over turtle. He lay in an untidy heap on the floor. His few remaining attendants stood staring at their fallen prince and each other, unsure what to do. They looked both relieved and horrified.

Nate came to my side, concerned by my choking gasps. He had regained his trousers and his shirt. Lum turned his attention to YaMing who was being attended to by two servants.

MeiLin slowly stalked up the length of the somber room, ignoring the pain of the battle around her and the turmoil of the prince's throne room. She was burdened with terrible purpose, shaking with rage.

"Now that you are free of your brother, you will return my skin to me!" MeiLin said, her voice deadly and dangerously quiet. Her bright eyes flashed red-gold.

"I meant you no harm," YaMing said.

"You meant me no harm!" MeiLin snarled. "You had your huntsman run me to ground, cripple me with poison, and strip my skin from my bones. You trapped me here in this form," MeiLin spat. "All so you could pretend to be something you are not!"

"I had to get away!" YaMing struggled to stand only to crumble to the floor. Columbus bolted forward and gathered the exiled princess from the beautiful tiled floor, cradling her like a tiny, broken bird.

"You stole from me, mortal! You stole from an immortal creature! You and all your line shall be cursed until the end of time for shaming me so! For making me walk the lands for so long as a human!" MeiLin spat as she stalked back and forth.

YaMing burst into tears, trying to hide herself in Lum's arms. "You don't understand, my brother was hurting me!"

"Your huntsman hurt me!" MeiLin screamed at her. She tore open her shirt letting the fine silk garment fall to the ground.

Her flesh was oozing red, looking skinless, like raw meat, like the wares in a butcher's cart. I expected her shirt to be filled with blood. I rubbed my neck remembering the stinging nettle feel from one night of wearing her fox fur collar. No, I corrected myself, her own fox fur. It was her own skin, torn from her body. The pain must have been staggering.

I felt sharp tears in my eyes and blinked them away. She used us to get to YaMing. It didn't matter how she managed to find out that was where we were headed. I immediately felt both anger and pity. How could I hate her? How could I not?

"He poisoned me! Drugged me!" She repeated, her gentle melodic voice no longer pleasing, it was frantic and shrill. "Took a knife to my throat, my wrists, my ankles, he slit up my belly, my breasts—"

"Stop, please" YaMing begged clasping her hands over her ears.

But MeiLin would not allow it. She shoved Lum aside with one powerful sweep of her hands, stunning us all, and grabbed YaMing, forcing her hands to her sides. "He tore my skin from my body all so you could wear my flesh. You forced him to take what is mine. You force yourself into my very skin and every time you do, you *rape* the very essence of me for your own pleasure. Now return to me what is mine!"

The room was silent save for YaMing's sobs. She trembled and shook, but unfastened the fine red fox fur cape she wore. It slithered heavily to the floor.

With a cry of delight, MeiLin dropped the princess and clasped the cape to her. She tore off her skirt and held the soft fur to her body in ecstasy. She gave a snarl and flipped it over and in one smooth movement tore out the black silk lining YaMing had placed inside, revealing the same red raw flesh as the scrap of fox fur I had worn as a collar.

She swirled it around her like a cape. The fox fur clung to her body, becoming one with her, wrapping lovingly to her back and buttocks, settling onto her arms and legs and the little muscular clefts and valleys that made the human form. It wrapped like a lover's hands around her breasts, around her sex and settled, covering her in a fine suit of soft red fur. All except a strip around her throat. Her collar was obscenely bloody and raw.

She brought her hands to her mouth giggling like a child, dancing with joy, completely oblivious to all of us. Lum took the opportunity to draw YaMing back into his arms. She clung to him, desperate to put him between her and MeiLin. Nate slowly positioned himself between MeiLin and myself. Noble as it was, it was a futile move by both men. MeiLin was obviously not of this world. Though I appreciated the gesture, there was little they could do should she decide to vent her wrath against us.

Predictably, she turned towards us first. I grabbed my revolver in one hand and my seax in the other. I was not going to be killed by any creature, mortal or not, without a fight. But, surprisingly, she had no interest in me.

"You are far too powerful to be bound to the mortal plane," MeiLin said. "China is a land of great, powerful beings, creatures so powerful that mortals would do anything to gain their favor."

"And you are offering me yours?" Nate said slowly, in a voice like torn cloth. He cleared his throat.

"All you must do is swear yourself to me, forsaking all others, and immortality is yours. Power beyond anything you can imagine will be yours."

"All I have to do is forsake all others? I have already forsaken all others, but you're not the one I chose. I love Vivian, MeiLin. Nothing you can offer me is going to change that."

"Then, goodbye, Mr. Valentine, you will regret not accepting my offer. Your mortal life will end. For a time, I will mourn you, then I will forget you. That is the way of things." She turned to her fallen skirts. I immediately knew what she was getting, the final piece of her skin, the collar I had stolen from her and worn that she had stolen back.

"MeiLin!" I stood. My legs shook. It hurt to stand. It hurt to breathe. "You will give me what you stole from the dragon!"

It was probably unwise to gain the wrath of an immortal creature any more than I already had, even if she had tried to seduce my fiancé. *Tried and failed,* I reminded myself. But why? That little nagging thought dug like a needle in my brain, MeiLin was beautiful, exotic, and why not, she is a *Huli*

Jing, a fox woman, a fox spirit. Probably a dream lover for any man, let alone a man who is a shape-shifter, who can turn into a dog. Why wouldn't Nate want to be the immortal companion of a beautiful nine-tailed fox spirit?

I looked over at Nate. He made his choice, not only once but every time he was tested. Would we ever finish an adventure together without him being on the receiving end of a horrific beating? He shifted and flexed his shoulders, but the pained look in his eyes faded and he smiled, a worn hollow-eyed look, tired but loving. He gave me that wide grin, slightly crooked and showing the teeth just behind his eye teeth, a true, happy smile.

She pulled the strip of flesh from her skirt and held it up, readying to place it to her neck. She was ignoring me. The wax seal made with the dried fish and dragon scale shimmering in the sunlight, still sewn to the center with strong silk thread. MeiLin thrust out her hand for it.

"Now!" My voice was stronger than I felt.

MeiLin looked at me queerly. For a moment, I was sure she would pounce upon me and murder me where I stood and just take the strip of skin. Then the vicious smile turned indulgent and amused, the way one looks at a child. She reached into the air and turned her fist, producing a small angular bit of stone. I immediately recognized it as one of the dragon's teeth. So that was what she was what she was doing scraping and tearing at the dragon's skeleton. She was taking out one of its teeth.

"Is that all you took from the dragon?" I asked.

She glared at me for daring to question her.

I stared back. I would not give in. She knew it. Nate was mine. We gave her what she wanted. She had used us to her own ends, but I was done being used. I would hunt her forever if she didn't return it. She knew it.

MeiLin set the collar to her neck where the raw reverse side bound to her own skin, the red bits digging into her flesh, binding with it. The wax and dragon scale charm started to glow and melt into the skin until it was too bright to look directly at it. I raised my hand before my eyes to shield them. When I looked back MeiLin stood before us dressed in a fine silk gown of pink and green rivaling any the Empress Dowager may have worn. Yet, she stood lighter on her feet, and when she spun on her bare feet, nine fox tails peeked out from the split in the back of her gown. Bright tears shone on her cheeks. She raised her fingertips to her cheeks dimpling with delight and wiped the tears away.

"Farewell, Mr. Valentine. We will not meet again," she said, nodding. She snapped her fingers and disappeared into nothing, leaving behind a thin violet mist.

SOS

I stood at Nate's side as he purchased four tickets to Beijing, only a few miles away. This was entirely the princess's idea; we would have gladly taken her wherever she wanted to go, or at least as far as our limited funds could take her. I would have preferred India by any means possible, to meet up with the Deburghs and await the *Nomad* in their company, but she demanded that we go to see her mother.

Once there, my rapidly evolving plan was to hide out in the hotels friendly to British citizens until we returned to London on the *Nomad*. But now we were entirely on our own without a translator to assist us in our plans and it seemed that everywhere we turned there were great statues of men made of fine clay dressed in traditional armor holding weapons made of real metal clenched in clay fists. I could see Nate's eyes darting about anxiously as he too assessed them as threat or as art. I would never enjoy life sized statues again.

If they bothered YaMing, she did not show her discomfort with them. She walked with us, looking neither down or out at our surroundings. She was trying to draw as little attention to herself as possible, but she could not disguise her noble bearing even as she struggled to walk without her limp.

We made a poor, bedraggled party, Nate's ear was still healing from his first slash with Prince Qixiang's spear and Lum had to go and secure him a cane to aid him with his wounded hip. I would have confined him to a week of immediate bed rest had I not been so terrified we would be caught before reaching friendly ground. Instead, I cleaned the wound and bound it the best I could and we set off to put as much distance between us as possible.

CHAPTER TWENTY-THREE

THE FAMILIAR SIGHT of the Viridian was welcoming with its beautiful blue-green awning and flags and its white stone walls. It was a color that never would have managed to exist within London. Even being washed several times a day it would quickly turn dingy and gray, the color of a dark, soiled dove. The short rock wall surrounding it was covered in fragrant, light pink petals from flowering trees as though they had exploded into a shower of beautiful bright butterflies dancing on the breeze.

As we climbed out of the two rickshaws, I honestly could not decide what was more welcome, the little slice of Britain that stood before me with bunting in blue-green dancing in the wind, or the fact that a proper tea, a hot bath, and a soft bed awaited me just up on the third floor, four doors down the hall on the right. We had paid up through the end of the month, another two and a half weeks, give or take a day, and we had the return trip all planned aboard the *Nomad*. Now all we had to do was avoid misadventure and any bloodthirsty Chinese monsters between now and then.

The last hundred feet or so suddenly felt a thousand miles away. I struggled to put one foot ahead of another. All I wanted to do was collapse on the soft green lawn and have Nate and Lum carry me in. Nate motioned for the staff to attend to our belongings and sent word that we needed two more rooms, one for YaMing and another for Lum.

But as I listened to my fiancé make arrangements, I suddenly thought of Ranger, Nate's old dog.

I had never tried to separate Nate from Ranger. I doubted that I could. Ranger gave up his own life to protect Nate because he loved Nate so. That is why dogs are man's best friend, after all. So, if I could separate the man from the dog then maybe one, if not both, would certainly be lost forever. Moreover, would Nate want that? Ranger was his best friend. Now, wherever he went, Ranger was always a part of him.

I watched him negotiate rooms for YaMing, the princess who traveled with us now, and the hulking dockman turned bodyguard. Since Nate could provide for Lum, he considered it his duty to do so. The man had twice lost his employment due to our involvement.

No, Nate would not want that. Even if I could be sure I could protect Nate while only losing Ranger, it would be against Nate's wishes.

I loved Nate. And I loved Ranger, too. I owed them both my loyalty, my life, and my love. Ranger protected me from being attacked in the streets of London not once, but twice. I got the feeling he understood what happened to him and Nate even before Nate did; and that made sense, too. Animals just accepted, they didn't need to question the way people did.

I slipped my hand into my pocket where the dragon's fang and the ruby sat heavily, tapping against my thigh like an anchor weighing me to China. My lower back ached from being thrown to the ground and I was horribly bruised from my mission to dismember the dragon's spine. My wound from separating Qixiang and YaMing ached fiercely as though my throat had been gashed and was left feeling raw and throbbing.

Nate was watching me, staring at my throat as though he too feared the mark would open and bleed. Did he know about the ruby in my pocket? I should have left the ruby behind in the Tianmenshan forest where it would have been lost with the rest of the key, but found I could not bear to part with it for even an instant. And I could not leave the tooth where someone else might try to use it. It was the last piece of the dragon. No, both pieces were safer with me.

Besides, no one knew I had the ruby.

When Qixiang recovered, and I knew he would eventually, he would search for the key and the dragon. He would hunt for Nate all over China. The sooner we were gone from this beautiful, dangerous place, the safer we would all be.

Was the Empress Dowager Cixi so awful? She wished to bring China into the modern world. She sought alliances with powerful allies. Though we were not nobility, we had several days before we would be able to take the *Nomad* back to London and it would be wonderful to spend time together enjoying the sights that China had to offer that did not include the risk of being eaten alive by a dragon.

I felt sick, Qixiang or whatever he would call himself now would not rest until all his enemies were dead. He would not be stopped by a mere ocean between us. He would hunt Nate and me to England. He would hunt us forever, for as long as his hate would carry him.

CHAPTER TWENTY-FOUR

WE FINALLY RETURNED to London but our wedding would have to wait a bit longer. One thing about airship travel: arrivals and departures are hardly secret. The moment we had stepped off the airship I expected excited whispers and gossip along with porters ready to handle our luggage. I did not expect a messenger demanding we take a note immediately.

Nate scowled at the note. The bruises on his face, the half-healed ear that had been slashed by a spear, the swollen, pale lump from where he had been struck by the prince's dart; all these things I had grown accustomed to seeing, the rest of London stared as though he was a veteran returning from war. And it pained me to see that for now he was well equipped for it. The cane had hardly left his side these past few days, and he leaned heavily upon it. I hoped some time and rest would ease his hurts.

I hated that I had become accustomed to it.

"We are to attend Mr. Langston and Admiral Edward Seymour immediately. It explicitly states there is no time to change from travel. He requires us to bring along our precious cargo and meet him directly. His personal carriage has been left at the station for our use." Nate folded the letter once and shoved it into his waistcoat pocket. "I daresay he will not be pleased there is no precious cargo to bring."

I nodded, we had been in agreement that we could not take the arrow from Xihuan-Lung's corpse. At the time, we had no doubt that Mr. Langston would be able to listen to reason. Now I wasn't so sure. What if he tried to strip our lands and assets for returning empty handed? No, I was being silly, I had not accepted his outrageous terms. He had not sent us a translator. He had only acted like a holiday planner and had arranged for our travel to China and set a mission. He offered us no protection, no support; we owed him nothing except an explanation.

Still, I shook as I climbed into his fancy plush carriage. So much so that Nate had to offer me a strong arm to lean upon as Lum helped the porter load our meager luggage onto the back of the carriage, then climbed in opposite us. I smiled to myself as I watched him out of the corner of my eye, stroking the fine upholstery covering the cushioned seats. He was doing his best to disguise his pleasure but I had a feeling that if he had ever ridden in a carriage this fine it was attached to the back as a hired man, not as a passenger.

I could not marvel for long, however, soon we were off the rattling cobbles, bouncing toward Mr. Langston and Admiral Seymour and a declaration of our failure in China.

"Miss Harper, so good of you to meet with us." Mr. Langston and his companion, a man in rich military uniform, stood when we entered the parlor. "May I present Miss Vivian Harper of London and her fiancé, Nathaniel Valentine, Esquire. They own the former Rothechild estate west of London. More importantly, they are our agents recently returned from China."

Mr. Langston turned and gently passed my hand to a tall man with auburn hair and beard worn in a close-cropped military style. He clicked his shiny leather boots at the heel and whispered a formal kiss against my knuckles. I immediately wished I had been given time to dress for the meeting. His blue eyes had been handsome and carefree once, but now were worn sharp and cold through hard service, a military man through and through. Though his commission was probably bought as a young man he most definitely had risen above any advantage birth had bought for him.

"Admiral Edward Seymore, Knight Commander of the Order of the Bath, of her Majesty's Royal Navy, your servant, ma'am."

"Sir Edward," I murmured and curtsied.

"Sir Edward," Nate echoed. I smiled, he bowed at the waist, a fine formal acknowledgment of the man. It was well done. He worked hard to learn his courtesies and it showed. "How can we be of service to the Crown?"

"You can raise a cup with us to your success in China," Mr. Langston said with a large wide grin.

"With regret, I must inform you that we do not have the arrow," Nate said.

Sir Edward's jaw clenched tightly and a little muscle jumped. "Ahh, right to the point then." He was careful not to sound too upset, but this was not the answer he had been hoping for. "All fables and hokum then?"

"We did see a great number of strange wonders as we traveled across China," I said cautiously. "Even a great stone statue that was cunningly carved to look like a dragon. But no magical arrow, I'm afraid."

Mr. Langston cocked an eyebrow at me. I felt panic bubbling up within me. I was never a good liar.

"I was certain the arrow was more than myth." Mr. Langston turned to a serving girl standing by a small cabinet. She poured four glasses of fine sherry from a crystal decanter and passed them around us.

I folded my hands around the stem of the tulip shaped glass and took a small sip. "I am sorry, we found no evidence that it was more than a wonderful story." Tucked away, in the folds of my skirts, deep within my pocket, the dragon's tooth and the ruby were an anchor.

"We did discover something troubling." Nate set his untouched glass down on the table. He had no great love for sherry. "China is unstable, to say the least."

"What do you mean?" Sir Edward set his empty glass down, nodding for the servant girl to refill his glass. "I have accepted a post to replace Admiral Buller as Commander-In-Chief of the China Station. If you have relevant information..." he motioned for Nate to continue.

"China is unlike any place I have ever seen," Nate said slowly, searching for a place to begin. "Their prince has come up with a way to mix magic and technological advancement. He is—"

"I believe you are mistaken." Mr. Langston laughed and glanced nervously at Sir Edward. "Nathaniel, China has no prince, that is unless the Empress Dowager Cixi has named a successor."

"I am not mistaken," Nate said evenly. "Yes, the Tongzhi Emperor is deceased, but he and Prince Qixiang are one and the same. Prince Qixiang was sent into exile by his mother, the Empress Dowager Cixi. Sir Edward, Prince Qixiang is mad with grief."

"Grief?"

"He is a man obsessed," I added, relieved the conversation had shifted from the Arrow of Xihuan-Lung and the semantic dance over its existence versus its recoverability. "He grieves for his position as emperor, for his wife and child, and for his country. Grief has made him mad, and in his madness he has dabbled in magic and technological advancement that ought not be."

"As in a new weapon?" Sir Edward gave me an indulgent smile. "We have been warned; those rebels, the 'Boxers' cannot be harmed, they are invulnerable to cannon, rifle, knife, and gun attacks. They can turn invisible and their 'Red Lantern Women' are just as evil and foul tempered as their men."

I considered Prince Qixiang's clockwork soldiers. Though not invisible they hid in plain sight too well with their terracotta clay coverings. But how to explain what we had seen? Maybe if Nate were to transfigure before him that might open Sir Edward's mind to the possibility of something his disciplined military mind could not easily fit into his training. Then again, he might just reach for his pistol and saber and attempt to test himself against my fiancé. I would not risk Nate's safety for the chance of being believed if it meant protecting the interests of Britain in China. Even though that made me a bad citizen of the Crown.

"—hardly a nation that will be taken easily," Nate said trying to sound casual.

I blinked hard wishing my mind hadn't wandered back to the terracotta warriors. Mr. Langston had a beautiful statue of a Roman Venus in this parlor that I felt was staring at me. I longed to smash it with the fireplace poker until I was sure that there was nothing hiding inside.

"A nation in chaos serves the interests of the Crown better than a strong, united China," Sir Edward said casually.

I was stunned at his callousness, though I shouldn't have been. Prince Qixiang made the exact opposite observation. He argued that a strong, united China was a better ally for Britain than a slave. I wasn't so sure Sir Edward would agree. He would find a China in chaos, divided by a family battling to rule, and their followers in turn dividing the people into one faction that wished to modernize and one that wished to retain their old ways and that in turn would plunge the nation into civil war. Sir Edward would find China an easy place to defend Britain's interests and a wonderful place to advance his own career. I was sad for China's people.

I barely heard Nate. "Do not underestimate him; Prince Qixiang is mad, but he is ruthless and cunning, as well. There is war coming to China and everyone who is there when it takes place will be harmed."

"I thank you for your council," Sir Edward said, his tone not unfriendly. "It is a shame the weapon Mr. Langston spoke of was not brought into service to the Crown. But your own service will not be forgotten."

We were being unceremoniously dismissed since we had nothing else of value to offer. There was nothing to do but head home to our own manor outside of London and adjust back to the quiet country life where everyone spoke English, no one wished to steal my fiancé away from me, and the only foxes were the ones that dotted the countryside frequently pursued by baying hounds.

Sir Edward bowed to me. "Miss Harper, may I wish you a happy and fruitful marriage. When your sons come of age I would be happy to offer your family the ability to purchase a commission for them in the Navy."

Nate paled slightly, then nodded and smiled politely though too thin-lipped to be genuine. He picked up his neglected glass of sherry and drained it in a single gulp.

CHAPTER TWENTY-FIVE

WE PASSED MRS. LANGSTON in the mews as she stepped out of a hansom cab, her servant carrying two flat packages, her maid carrying a covered basket. No doubt she had just completed pleasant a day of shopping.

She removed her gloves, handed them to her maid and greeted me with a hug. "Miss Harper, it is a pleasure to see you."

"Mrs. Langston, so good to see you again."

The faint chill in the air, or the excitement of our arrival brought color to her cheeks. "Did you return with the Chinese matter resolved?"

"With regret, no. We were unable to turn up any thing substantial that proved the matter to be anything more than a myth."

"Oh, how unfortunate. Our source was absolutely sure the matter would be a potent weapon for England, once it had been thoroughly studied of course."

"Of course." Studied? I got a sudden chill. My mama would call that feeling a goose walking across one's grave. I pulled Mrs. Langston close. There was a stone bench decorated with stone lions matching the lions on the front stairs. We sat. The chill sank through my gown but I needed to make sure we were not overheard. "Who is your source?"

She waved her hand dismissing it. "Some inventor scholar. He is seeking admittance to our society based upon scholastic merit rather than traditional sponsorship. He was not aware of any member who would vouch for him. My husband promised we would evaluate his bid for membership based upon his research of the myth of this dragon and the application of the story to an artifact already within our possession. God only knows how he knew about the scale. I daresay, someone is playing a great joke upon us."

I bit my lip. I needed to talk to Nate now but he was turned away from me, scanning for the carriage and our possessions, and was questioning some poor groom as to their whereabouts. The young man glanced about nervously, finally pointing at the carriage house.

Lum was waiting for us at the Langston family carriage. "They went through your possessions, Nate." Lum informed us evenly as soon as we were seated in the carriage for the ride home. "They brought the carriage around back to care for the horses and dust the carriage or some such nonsense and they made sure to offer me beer and ham. Like any good servant, I accepted." He gave a wolfish grin.

I smiled. Even lions had to eat, I supposed.

"I was sure they would," Nate said with a sigh. "Probably looking for the arrow."

"But fear not, Miss Vivian, I made sure I kept your jewelry on my person." Columbus Baxter gave a chuckle. "It's all here, every last scrap."

A lady should be offended to hear her good jewelry referred to as scrap. A true lady, I was not. I laughed. But there was a matter at hand. I sobered quickly.

"Why did you turn against Mr. Barrett, Mr. Baxter?" I asked as formally as I could. When one was about to bring a man's loyalty into question, one ought to be as formal as possible.

"Pardon?"

"You knew he was working for Cixi? And you didn't tell us?" I pressed.

"I didn't know it," he said evenly. "I suspected. I wasn't in a position to just throw away employment before I was sure that I was on the right side."

"And, if I may ask, why were you so sure you were on the right side finally? Not that I'm complaining," I amended hastily.

"Never much liked Barrett, and Charlotte squawks like them damnable gulls that hang out on the wharf always begging for bits of scrap from the fisher boats. Bait thieving rats."

He and Nate shared a look. I knew Columbus Baxter would never betray us. I had seen his heart when we obliterated the bond between

Prince Qixiang and Princess YaMing. If he and Nate came to their own understanding then I could trust that Lum was our man now and forever.

I could not deny having an ally was a comfort since I was sure our list of enemies was just as long, if not longer than our list of allies now that the ruling family of China was unfriendly to us either due to our meddling or our lack thereof and I was uncomfortably sure Geiger was behind the clues to the murderous arrow. Nate would think I was out of my mind. After all the madness in China, I would have to take that risk. "Nate, Mrs. Langston said they were approached for membership by an individual who knew they had the scale of Xihuan-Lung within their possession. She believes he managed to apply myth to an artifact to leverage their attention."

Nate leaned forward, taking my hand. "You don't agree?"

"It's too convenient."

Nate gave me sideways look that spoke volumes, he already had an inkling what I was about to say and he didn't like it. "What do you mean?"

I was starting to fear we had been manipulated, and we were not the only ones. "If the Explorer's Society unearths treasures and then loses them, it can easily be passed off by blaming inexperienced members. It actually makes more sense if it is the rumor of a weapon uncovered by scholarly research based in myth backed by an artifact the society has in their possession. You said yourself the society is spread thin, attempting to recover artifacts and treasures of an ever-shrinking world teetering on the brink of war. We were sent because they did not expect us to find anything. If we had it would have been an amazing find. If not, it was no big loss of resources."

Nate stared at me for a long moment. "What do you think we were chasing?"

"Not what. Who." I took a deep breath. "Nate, I think we were chasing Geiger."

He paled. The bruises and marks from our misadventure stood out making him look sickly and frail. He shook his head. "No, he's dead."

I did my best to be gentle. I expected him to be angry or to think I had lost my mind. I did not expect this. "I'm not so sure. I followed the papers. No bodies were ever recovered from Sterling's factory. The fire brigade contained the fire to the warehouse and the factory, and despite a truly impressive amount of metal machinery recovered from the premises that they could not identify, the public works commission was satisfied that the investigation showed nothing else. Then there was the letter from Molly."

"Damn. I forgot about the letter." Nate stared out the window.

He may have forgotten, I hadn't. "It would have taken a brilliant man to create Sterling's factory, Nate, not to mention the machinery and the clockwork life below. That brilliant man is still out there. We managed to turn him away from the leywell, but if he has taken a berth on the *Lightning Aura* then he has set his attention to lightning. You and I both know how great and terrible that can be."

Nate took my hand. "Lightning and treasure hunting?"

"Not treasure hunting." Treasure was gold and silver and jewels, if it was Geiger, he had something else in mind. "Monsters and weapons. If he is chasing the treasures of man he is not seeking trinkets, he wants their knowledge. He wants their power. The notes were too complete. He thoroughly researched the weapon. He only needed something he could only access within the vaults, the dragon scale—at least he thought he needed the scale—or the ruby, which we should assume was in the hands of the Empress Dowager Cixi. That must be how Mr. Barrett got it."

Nate nodded. "And I doubt if he knew where to get the ruby or he would have just turned over the weapon to Crown and Country."

I was suddenly cold. "I hate to say it, but I am thankful for MeiLin. If she hadn't needed us to reclaim her skin we would not have gotten the key in the same way. We might have missed it all together, and then Xihuan-Lung would be free."

"A dragon loose on the world?" Nate shuddered.

A madman seeking power long since lost to the world of men. It was a horrible thought. There was nothing else either of us could say. I lay my head on his shoulder for the comfort the closeness he could provide.

I stared at the moon, a swelling gibbous moon spilling soft, creamy light across us both, a man and woman in love. We had come so far from when we had met. I could not imagine another grand adventure and yet the dragon tooth and the ruby in my pocket told me we were far from done.

By the time our manor loomed in the distance, expensive lights burning in the windows, welcoming us home, I had already decided that within the year we needed to be off again, this time by boat somewhere exotic and interesting, like maybe the Indies or Afrika or maybe even the Americas so Nate could invest in the railroads he loved so much.

585

"Your wedding is next Wednesday," Hiram said the next morning when I finally emerged from my quarters looking what I hoped was a bit more well rested. Jane helped dress my hair up in curls and pins and remarked that I would not need even the slightest bit of rogue I was looking so wonderfully healthy and had picked up some color from my adventure. She did remind me that should I wish she could lighten my skin with a bit of powder. Ladies do not allow themselves to become tan.

But I had lived too long without having my hair dressed regularly so I was unused to being fussed over. My fine spring dress was something much more formal than I had been wearing while we were adventuring in China.

Nate was not expected to look ornamental, he was a man, he was expected to be capable and intelligent, what he looked like didn't matter much. I suppose that worked in his favor because though he was dressed in fashionable trousers and waistcoat over a high collared shirt, he was still looking quite mangled. Our battle with Qixiang left him my throttled, mangled warrior.

"Oh Hiram, I'm not sure about that," I said with a faint laugh, in truth I wanted nothing more, but Nate looked as though he had just returned from a rousing battle in the local pub with several large burly opponents and I was not sure everything could be managed in time.

"With respect, Miss Vivian, your mother has set all the arrangements. They have been in the planning for months." Hiram gave Mother a secret look; I believe the term was the look of kittens in cream.

I quickly ticked off the weeks in my head. Had we really missed all that time? Had it really been several months since we left here in May? We had a June wedding all set, now it was the beginning of September? I would have to look at a calendar to be sure but Hiram's skill with the management of the household and my mother's management of time were flawless. If they said it was ten days before the rescheduled wedding then it was ten days before the rescheduled wedding.

Nate and I exchanged a look. Other than the obvious, we had been pretending to be a married couple for the past few months anyway. Would this change anything? We locked eyes and I blushed. Yes, this would change everything.

"I'm sure a small delay would not be amiss," I said reasonably. "This feels so rushed, doesn't it?"

"It's no matter now," Hiram said offering me a tray of tea and poached eggs and kippers over toast. "When I received word your airship was docking I took the liberty of having all of Mr. Valentine's possessions combined with yours into the suite in the east wing. The wedding cannot be delayed without scandal."

I would swear that Mama was smiling in her teacup, but Hiram kept his face entirely blank, comically so. I must have been so tired I hadn't even noticed. I wondered where Nate had slept last night if he hadn't had his own quarters to himself and who was sleeping in his bed for that matter. Mother had some explaining to do.

"I do have one other surprise, my darling," Mama said with her clever smile. "We had to clear out the west wing where Nate was formally residing. You have a guest. Though, I rather say Nathaniel may be more surprised about this development than you are.

"We sent notice of your wedding to the north of France where a good friend of his is a priest of the scholarly persuasion, even though he is Catholic, not of the Church of England."

"Father Henri Poullain?" I clapped my hands in delight like a child. "Brilliant!"

Nate was sitting with the marmalade knife held obscenely in his hand. If he were to faint he just might open a vein. As if on cue, Father Henri came into the solar for breakfast and informed Nate that gawking was unseemly.

"It is wonderful to see you again, my darling dear," Father Henri said, gently greeting me in the traditional French style of cheek kissing, first me then Nate. "You have a most beautiful home."

"Father Henri, it is wonderful to see you."

"Nathaniel, I see you have gotten yourself into trouble again," Father Henri chided gently. "Brawling with larger boys again?"

Nate laughed. "You have no idea."

"So, I am to gather you have not yet managed to make an honest woman out of Miss Harper?"

Nate went pale, even beneath the healing bruises leaving him a nasty jaundiced color. "Um, you see—"

"I jest, Nathaniel, I jest." Father Henri laughed and cuffed him on the shoulder.

Nate swallowed hard.

"I came to congratulate you on your marriage and offer my blessing only to find when I arrived that it had in fact been delayed as you two went gallivanting off to China, of all places, for another grand adventure."

"And a grand adventure it was," I said taking Nate's hand. "Though now I am thoroughly ready to become an honest woman and a wife."

"And God willing, a mother?" Father Henri asked with a quirked eyebrow.

Nate coughed something unintelligible into his napkin.

Father Henri laughed and slapped his knee. "I am a Catholic Priest Nathaniel, I am not dead. I was a man first, and as you may remember, I was a younger man when we met. It would stand to reason that I had at one time been younger still."

Mama took the marmalade knife from Nate as he still had it in a now careless grasp that threatened to make no end of things unsavory, including our newly cleaned clothing.

"I hope you do not find it presumptuous, Mrs. Harper has invited me to stay for the wedding. I eagerly accepted. Seeing you wed, Nathaniel, is more agreeable than hearing of it after the fact."

"I would not hear of you leaving before we are wed," I said quickly. "In fact, would you be able to officiate?"

Nate's face went positively alight at that. Traditionally, it was up to the bride's family to provide the officiate for the ceremony. But surely the parson wouldn't mind if Father Henri took his place, especially if we provided a substantial donation to the parish to smooth over any hurt feelings and explained that Father Henri was a friend of the family. Why, we hadn't even lived in the manor for a year yet and as I understood, though the previous owners of the manor, the Rothechild family had been the owners for the last two decades, they were only in residence for a few odd seasons. I doubted the parson even knew the Rothechild family. Surely, he would not be bothered.

I decided would send a footman over right away with a note requesting his presence for dinner to discuss the matter. Inviting him and the clerk to the wedding would also certainly smooth over any hurt feelings.

Father Henri was the closest thing Nate had to family. It only made sense he would be a part of such an important event.

"If you are both sure?" Father Henri's gray eyes twinkled at the thought.

"Absolutely," Nate said quickly. "You know Viv is smarter than I am. If I'd thought of it first I would not be taking no for an answer. You'd be tied up in a sack until you agreed!"

I shook my head. There was my husband-to-be. Threatening to tie up a Catholic priest to force him to marry us. I'm not sure, but I think forcing a priest to perform marriage rites invalidated the entire matter. I resolved to remind him of that later. For now, his enthusiasm was catching, rather like watching boys hoot and holler like gibbons at play.

But he was my gibbon, or very nearly so, which made his happiness all the more catching. Now it was the business of waiting until the Wednesday next.

S§S

I could see Columbus Baxter from my vantage point. He looked wonderful in his tan wool suit. Nate had needed someone to stand with him as his groomsman.

Out in the lawn, where Lum waited, bells and doves, carefully sculpted out of papier-mâché and painted in gold leaf and set with real feathers, hung in gazebo in the garden on the east side of the house where the wedding itself would take place. I immediately hoped Mama would have it set aside as soon as the wedding was over so I could display it in the conservatory.

Father Poullain stood at the gazebo with the parish priest, Columbus and the parish recorder stood speaking quietly, waiting for the festivities to begin promptly at ten o'clock.

I could hear a violin and a flute begin to play. It was time.

Time for my greatest adventure.

Fin

ACKNOWLEDGMENTS

SPECIAL THANKS to the friends and family who have given me their support, their love, their time, and their critiques as I ran down this path. It is all that I ever really wanted to be and thanks to you I am here. Special thank you to Rex, William, Colleen, Dani, Charlie, Aaron, Mia, Stant, and Ellie.

§§§

DISCLAIMER: Places, names, and titles are used in a fictitious manner. Much of the information presented was altered to be used in the framework of this fictional story. There was no attempt to slander any aspect of the wonderful culture or beliefs of the proud people of China nor to minimize the damage done by the foreign occupation of China done by England in the 1800s. For more information on 19th century China please enjoy the research through reputable sources, it is an amazing and enjoyable topic that cannot be covered by a work of fiction.

The Tarot is an amazing divination tool used by many cultures for hundreds of years. Though an attempt has been made not to damage the traditions of the Tarot, much of the information presented is fictitious and should not be used for actual divination. For more information on the Tarot, please contact a reputable source.

The cards represented in this story are based upon the Rider-Waite Deck.

ABOUT THE AUTHOR

Vennessa Robertson is the author of the Arcane Adventuress series. She is also active in the writing and historic reenactment communities. She taught high school with dueling degrees in Colorado and Alaska until a traumatic brain injury in 2009. Now, she lives in rural Colorado. When she is not writing or homeschooling her two small children she is managing their ever-growing large and small animal rescue ranch.

SS

www.ingramcontent.com/pod-product-compliance
Lightning Source LLC
Chambersburg PA
CBHW060856250626
47159CB00008B/2756

* 9 780999 572412 *